OVERWHELMING ACCLAIM FOR VICKI HINZE'S NOVELS

DUPLICITY

"Military romantic suspense fiction has gained a blazing new star! Vicki Hinze continues to work her special magic, with the elements of romance, danger, and intrigue." —*Romantic Times*

"[A] tautly crafted thriller . . . A roller-coaster ride of sizzling suspense, deadly betrayal, and courage . . . A great read." —MERLINE LOVELACE, Colonel, USAF (Ret), author of *Call of Duty*

"A page-turner that fuses thriller and romance." —*Publishers Weekly*

"Vicki Hinze exploded on the scene with SHADES OF GRAY and continues her meteoric rise with DUPLICITY. Finding a new niche in the romance genre takes rare courage and fortitude, but like Ms. Hinze's heroines, she displays these admirable traits with the discovery of a category one can only call military romance. Her novels, filled with tension both sexual and mystery, grip the reader from page one, and like a tenacious bulldog holds them enthralled until the last line. Ms. Hinze hones the art of character development to a razor's edge, developing them through thought, word and deed to create individuals round of form and substance." —KATHEE S. CARD, *Under the Covers*

"When it comes to the military romance sub-genre, there are no SHADES OF GRAY that Vicki Hinze is one of the top guns. Her latest novel DUPLICITY has cross-genre appeal to the legal thriller crowd as well as the military romance audience. The storyline is crisp, action-packed, and filled with insight into the world of military justice and honor. Tracey is a wonderful character whose changing conflicts bring the novel into perspective. If justice prevails, Ms. Hinze will quickly reach the top of multiple bestselling lists." —HARRIET KLAUSNER, *Painted Rock Reviews*

"A fast-paced novel with plenty of twists and turns, and a lot of great insight into the world of the military . . . You will not be disappointed with this action-packed thriller." —*Interludes*

SHADES OF GRAY

"The complications here go beyond the usual hurdles and make the romance more touching for being hard-won. And if the main action—Laura and Jake must combat terrorists amassing anthrax in the Florida Everglades—seems far-fetched, just read *The New York Times*." —*Publishers Weekly*

"SHADES is very fast-paced, filled with the kind of intrigue and plot twists that make for a great action movie . . . a great read if you're a fan of Clancy-type novels and movies. I enjoy books that combine intrigue with romance and found SHADES to be a perfect combination of the two." —*The Middlesex News* (MA)

"A great storyline that easily could sell as a romance or an action thriller. Hinze is clearly one of the leaders of military romances that emphasize action, suspense, and romance. A winner for fans of romantic suspense." —*Affaire de Coeur*

In Jake and Laura, Hinze creates two people of exceptional honor and self-control whose struggle to resist the pull of love goes down in glorious defeat." —Amazon.com Reviews

"Twists and turns abound. A crazy ex-wife, a terrorist group, and the rigid discipline of the military all come together to make this book a real page-turner."—WCRG on America Online reviewer board

"Hinze leaves the reader hanging with each word. This book is impossible to put down after the first paragraph." —LORI SOARD, Reviewer, Word Museum

"A wonderful combination of romance, family drama, and out-and-out thriller. Her characters are wonderful and vivid, the plot engrossing, and the setting is utterly fascinating. A terrific read." —ANNE STUART, bestselling author of MOONRISE

"A roller-coaster read! SHADES OF GRAY has it all— breathtaking suspense, heart-stopping romance, and fabulous characters. Hinze is a master at crafting a book you simply cannot put down! Watch for this book to hit the *NYT* Bestseller List and for Hinze to join the superstars." —DELIA PARR, author of *The Minister's Wife* and *Sunrise*

"A high-tech, romantic thriller! Suspense at its best! This book accurately delves into the world of Special Ops and the men and women who lay their lives on the line for our country anytime, anywhere. If you like Tom Clancy, Nelson DeMille, or Tami Hoag, you'll love Vicki Hinze's SHADES OF GRAY."
—LORNA TEDDER, author of *A Man Called Regret* and *Top Secret Affair*, and publisher of *Spilled Candy* newsletter

St. Martin's Paperbacks titles
by Vicki Hinze

SHADES OF GRAY
DUPLICITY
ACTS OF HONOR

ACTS
OF
HONOR

VICKI HINZE

St. Martin's Paperbacks

ACTS OF HONOR

Copyright © 1999 by Vicki Hinze.

All rights reserved. No part of this book may be used or reproduced in any manner whatsoever without written permission except in the case of brief quotations embodied in critical articles or reviews. For information address St. Martin's Press, 175 Fifth Avenue, New York, N.Y. 10010.

ISBN: 0-312-97273-3

Printed in the United States of America

St. Martin's Paperbacks edition / December 1999

St. Martin's Paperbacks are published by St. Martin's Press, 175 Fifth Avenue, New York, N.Y. 10010.

10 9 8 7 6 5 4 3 2 1

To Hubby
With love,
George

author's note

☆

As a nation, we expect much from our men and women in uniform. Often we have no idea of their trials or sacrifices, and we have no idea how much serving us costs them personally. I hope that in reading this novel, readers will have an opportunity to become aware, to understand, and to appreciate those who dedicate, and sometimes sacrifice, their lives for us.

A writer has a responsibility to weigh the costs of portraying characters and events in their natural forms against the potential impact of those portrayals. Having been a military wife for over twenty years, I consider this impact of paramount importance. For that reason, as in *Shades of Gray* and *Duplicity*, I have implemented artistic license in *Acts of Honor*. IWPT and Braxton exist only within these pages, and some of the procedures and disciplines have been altered out of respect and concern for the soldiers who perform sensitive missions and for their families. I feel strongly that their gifts to us warrant our concern and protection, and hope you'll agree.

Blessings,
Vicki Hinze

one

☆

"Oh, no." Sara West looked up from her desk and frowned. "What the hell are you doing here, Foster?"

That frank reaction earned her a rare smile. "Glad to see you, too, Dr. West." He removed his cap and sat down in her visitor's chair. "How long has it been?"

How long? How dare he do this? He ignored her inquiries into her brother-in-law Captain David Quade's death, stonewalled her investigation at every turn, and then just waltzes into her office as if they were close friends? "It's been seven months, two weeks, and four days—not nearly long enough."

Sara closed the patient file open on her desk, then slid it aside. "Now, this is a private office—mine—and not your military base, Colonel, but I'm going to be gracious and ask you once more before I kick you out on your pompous ass." She hiked her chin. "What do you want?"

His smile faded and he scanned the bookshelves spanning a long wall.

Sara grimaced. All of the titles were on post-traumatic stress disorder, and Foster definitely would notice. He never missed anything, or gave anything away. Likely a hazard of his job, though even after five years of discussions with him—mostly discussions aimed *at* him with her trying to get information *from* him about David—Sara still wasn't exactly sure what Foster's job entailed.

She knew he was military. An Air Force colonel who worked with the AID. But her discreet inquiries at the Air Force Intelligence Division had convinced Sara that even regular AID personnel weren't familiar with specifically what job

Colonel Jack Foster performed for the military. He was an enigma to them and, by extension, to her. An enigma currently standing in her Pensacola, Florida, office—which was a long way from his office at the Pentagon—staring at her in open challenge.

Being even thinner now than when they'd last met, Sara supposed she still looked fragile to him. God, how that rankled. With her blond hair snagged in a barrette at her nape, and wearing the lab coat and navy power suit she'd worn to give her PTSD lecture to two hundred psychologists and psychiatrists that morning, she felt almost prim. But she was not prim, nor fragile. She was thirty-four, stood five eight in stocking feet, and his unwelcome presence in her office had her and her temper rising to meet his challenge. "Well, are you going to answer me? Or do I get the delayed gratification of kicking you out?"

Foster grunted and tucked his cloth cap under his belt, between the loops on his slacks. "Still ticked off at me, eh?"

"Forever, plus ten years. Count on it."

"I did attempt to learn more about Captain Quade's incident, Dr. West. Unfortunately, I was denied access to his files."

Who was he trying to kid? Foster had clout. That much everyone in AID knew—even those who had needed a little friendly persuasion to admit they had ever heard of him. "Why?"

"That's classified information."

Sara grunted. He was lying to her. She'd heard whispers during her last fact-finding trip to the Pentagon that Foster's security clearance exceeded Top Secret. He could get file access. He chose not to do it.

He looked her straight in the eye. "Isn't it enough to know David is dead?"

"No, it isn't enough." Vexed that she couldn't force Foster to be honest, she stabbed the toe of her shoe deep into the teal carpet beneath her desk. "Not when David's widow—my sister—is collecting husbands the way you have a chest full of medals."

"I'm sorry to hear that. After five years . . ." His voice trailed off, and then he went on. "Well, I'd hoped Brenda, er, Mrs. Quade, would adjust."

Foster sounded sincere. But Sara had experienced his "sincerity" before. She knew better than to believe it, and let him know it by arching a skeptical brow.

A faint flush swept up his neck and flooded his face. "No progress on your research, I take it."

He'd caught the gesture. Foster was a pain, but he was swift on the uptake. "Plenty of progress on PTSD, just not on how patients' families successfully cope with it." She let her gaze slide to the window, unwilling to let him see how deeply her failure affected her. "Brenda stood on shaky ground before David committed suicide. Now, in a way, she's doing her damnedest to join him."

"Through the marriages?"

Sara nodded. "Five in four years." Guilt swam through her chest and settled like heavy stones in her stomach. Brenda was thirty-six, the older sister, and yet Sara always had been the big sister. Not by choice, but by necessity. Since grade school, Brenda had gotten herself into more scrapes than a teen with her first training bra. And Sara always had pulled her out. But on this, when it mattered most, Sara couldn't seem to find a way out.

Foster let his gaze drop to his knees. "And you feel responsible because you're an expert on PTSD and yet you still can't seem to help her."

How typical of him to lay out her feelings like bare bones and then peck at them. Bristling, Sara snapped. "Wouldn't you?"

"Yes, I would."

Surprised by that admission, Sara pursed her lips and opted to be a little more civil, though she had to work at it. She didn't like Foster any more than he liked her. The only thing that made their interactions possible was that they both knew it and were never hypocritical enough to deny it. "Thanks for holding off on the platitudes and absolutions." She meant it sincerely.

"You're welcome." His smile returned. "Does that mean all is forgiven?"

"Not by a long shot." She tugged at her lab coat cuff and slid him a glare. "I make it a practice never to forgive men I don't trust."

"Unfortunate." He feigned a sigh that held a breath of truth.

Tired of this mousing around, Sara cut to the chase. "Why are you here?"

Foster's demeanor changed dramatically, turned somber and serious, deepening the creases to grooves across his forehead. "I've got a problem, Sara. A significant one."

Worry seeped into her. In five years, Jack Foster never once had used her first name, nor had he admitted a weakness. Both unnerved her. She tried her best to bury her reaction under the sarcasm common between them. "Welcome to the human race. We've all got problems. That's why we've got shrinks, and we shrinks have shingles on our doors."

"We don't all have problems like this one." He again scanned the row of dog-eared books, clearly avoiding her eyes. "I need your help."

Surprise rippled through her. Men like Foster didn't need help, they created a need for help in others. God knew he'd given her more than her fair share of trouble—and nightmares. And his type never asked for favors. Intrigued, she paused to let her tone steady, and then quizzed him. "What? The Air Force doesn't have its own shrinks anymore?"

"This is different." He shifted uneasily on his chair. "It's . . . delicate."

Delicate? More likely, the matter was classified and he wanted it buried far from other military eyes. "Is this problem personal, or professional?"

"Professional." He sighed. This time, it was genuine, and tinged with discomfort and impatience. "I don't need military assistance. I need yours."

"This, I know. Therapy would work wonders for your disposition. But I can't treat you, Foster. A doctor should want to cure her patients, not to murder them." She rolled the end of a pencil over her lower lip, then nipped down on it. "The licensing board discourages murdering patients—though in your case, it might be willing to make an except—"

"Stop it." Foster stiffened. "We both know you're about as apt to kill someone as the tooth fairy." His gaze turned piercing, stone-cold. "This is serious, and only you can help me."

"*Me?* Help *you?* After all the times you've refused to help me?" Her temper reared and she guffawed. "Forget it."

"I can't do that." His terse tone proved he'd like nothing better.

She slid forward in her chair, laced her hands atop her desk blotter. "Look, I don't like the military and I don't work for it, aside from cleaning up the messes you guys make of some people's minds. I work with five patients at a time—no more, and no less—in a private practice. I work only with PTSD patients and/or their families, and I damn sure don't help arrogant military bastards who needlessly let others suffer—especially when those suffering others are members of my family."

"I'm well aware of what you do and do not do. I'm also aware that many of your professional peers consider your methods extremely unorthodox."

"There's a good reason for that." She lifted a hand. "By traditional standards, my methods *are* extremely unorthodox."

"Some consider you out in left field."

"And some think I'm a brick short of a full stack. So what? I don't need their approval, or care if I have it. Intensive one-on-one therapy—treating the mind, body, and spirit—works."

Foster lifted his chin, annoyingly calm and typically arrogant. "Frankly, the professional acceptance of your methods means nothing to me. You have an eighty-percent success rate on the PTSD patients you treat—far higher than the standard—and that means everything."

"Success is hard to dispute."

"Yes, it is." He stood up. His knees cracked, and he walked across the office to the bookshelf and then let his fingertip drift across the spines of the books, obviously mulling over what to tell her and what to withhold. "I can't disclose certain things without physician/patient privilege. You don't have security clearance." He stopped and looked back over his shoulder at her. "You understand?"

David. This was about David. Her heart thudded deep in her chest. Low and hard. A little breathless, she nodded. She didn't trust Foster—after five years, she had hundreds of valid reasons not to trust him—but could she afford to brush off a potential opportunity? They were *so* rare. "Okay." She conceded with as much grace as she could muster. "I'll make an exception—short-term."

Foster turned toward her. Bars of light slashed through the vertical blinds at the window, streaked across his pale-blue uniform shirt, and glinted on the metal eagle rank pinned to his collar. "So, you're my doctor now?"

"Give me twenty dollars."

He fished a bill from his wallet. She took it. "I'm your doctor." After scribbling out a receipt, she thrust it at him. "Now, what do you know about David?"

Foster leaned a shoulder against the bookshelf and crossed his chest with his arms. "I know if you do what I ask, you'll find your answers about what happened to him."

Sara's skin crawled. Foster's tone and the look in his eyes swore she'd find more. Far more. "Exactly what answers will I find?"

"The ones to all the unanswered questions that made you become an expert on PTSD so you could help others like David, Brenda, and Lisa." Foster rubbed at his chin, spoke slowly. Distinctly. "You and the Quades' daughter are very close."

He'd been monitoring them. All of them. Sara, Brenda, and Lisa.

An uneasy shiver slithered up Sara's spine, and her gaze slid to a photo of the three of them on the corner of her desk. For some reason, Foster must feel threatened. "Of course we're close. Lisa is my only niece. But what does that have to do with this?"

"It's irrelevant," Foster said. "What is relevant is that I won't tell you anything more about David's situation because I'd have to breach national security to do it. But I will put you in a position where you'll have the opportunity to discover your answers for yourself." Pacing a short path before her desk, Foster stopped and fisted a hand at his side. "I know you don't forgive and you never forget, but let me be clear about something, Sara. Playing games with me is not honorable, nor is it in your best interests."

"Now why does that remark strike me as a threat?" Tight-lipped, she glared at him. "You know, in five years, I have never—not once—given you a reason to question my honor." She cocked her head. "Can you say the same to me?"

"Our topic isn't my honor, it's your family's best interests."

Chilling her tone even more, Sara looked up at him from under her lashes. "Obviously, you don't know me as well as you think, or you'd know warning me against game-playing isn't necessary. Not when it comes to my family."

"Oh, I know you, Sara." Foster leaned forward and bracketed her desk blotter with his hands. The muscles in his forearms twitched. "I know you're weak when it comes to defending yourself, but tougher than nails at defending others. And you'd like to be even tougher on me."

She would. She didn't like this conversation, or him. Yet Foster's palms were glistening with sweat and he looked as if he wanted to heave. He clearly needed something from her— why else would he be here? But whatever it was, he didn't feel certain of getting it, which meant he had failed to stack the odds in his favor. The master manipulator felt vulnerable, and that worried her.

"I also know you avoid relationships because you feel guilty," he went on. "It wouldn't be right for you to have all your sister has lost, would it? You have to fix things for her and Lisa first—and for your brother, Steve. It really got you that his wife had him committed for psychiatric evaluation, didn't it? Isn't that incident what drove you to become a psychiatrist?"

Sara stiffened. Foster had been thorough, and he'd investigated Steve, too. "Considering my brother is one of the most well-balanced human beings walking the earth, and his wife pulled that stunt and had him committed for thirty days because they'd had a disagreement about moving out of the state of Mississippi, yes. You're damn right, it got to me. That there are laws on the books allowing that type of injustice should get to you, too."

"We all deal with injustice in our own way." He let his gaze drift to the door. "You've taken blanket responsibility for every injustice to everyone and everything in your sphere of influence since the cradle." He grunted. "If I had to guess, I'd say you're a victim of your genes. Maternal genes, or influence."

He'd be right. Sara's throat went dry. Foster made her feel invaded, as if she had no privacy, not even in her thoughts. She fought the sensation, determined not to let him get the upper hand. Once he did, she was screwed, and they both knew it. "Goodness. Amazing that I warrant all of this attention from you merely because I'm a responsible adult. I suppose I should be flattered." She rubbed at her temple with a long fingertip. "Instead, I'm asking myself why you fascinate so easily."

A tight smile threatened the corner of his lip, and he narrowed his eyes. "Actually, I bore easily. But you are your work, Sara. And that intrigues me."

Amused him, more likely, and that grated at her.

"You've pushed me hard, from all sides—as thorough as a crack operative with a dozen years' experience under your belt. At times, you've been persuasive, tenacious, and charming enough to have the devil caving in to you."

No way was she falling for this. Foster used praise just as he used people. "So the devil would cave, but you were immune. Now, what am I to make of that?"

"Perhaps the devil enjoys luxuries I can't afford." He stared at her. "Perhaps the same is true for you."

He knew her as well as she knew herself. The realization spilled over her, burned and branded into her mind. She hated it, too. And she hated even more that he was right about her work and her personal relationships. She'd never verbalized it, or dared to focus her thoughts on it, but she did want a family of her own and someone to share her life with, yet she couldn't have everything Brenda had lost. She just ... couldn't.

Gruesome thought, but maybe Foster knew Sara better than she knew herself.

Fighting not to wince, she shifted topics, heading for safer ground. "So what's your problem?" Did she dare to hope, a guilty conscience? "Why do you need my services?"

"First, some ground rules." He straightened and stepped back from her desk. "Everything I tell you falls under patient/ physician privilege. I have not, and will not, grant you authorization to release any information I share with you. None whatsoever, under any circumstances, at any time, to anyone."

"I gathered that." Sara met his gaze, and saw the tension of an emotion she'd never expected to see in Jack Foster's face. Fear. It tugged hard at the healer in her. "So what's the problem?"

"I've got an officer with scrambled brains and I have no idea why or who scrambled him." Foster stiffened, as if relieved and uneasy with revealing that. "He was on a mission—classified, of course—and went missing. Seven days later, he showed up at a secluded facility, and we have no idea how he got there."

"Could you clarify his condition? Scrambled, how? Is he a vegetable, psychotic, or what?"

"He's been diagnosed PTSD." Foster grimaced. "I need to know what happened to him, why, who did it, how, and if he's salvageable."

If he's salvageable? Flabbergasted, Sara leaned back in her chair. "And you want me to make this determination?"

"Yes, I do. Quickly." Foster didn't miss a beat. "This man has been on a lot of high-risk missions. He has Top Secret security clearance and he's having moments of lucidity. Frankly put, he's a critical security risk."

Foster's voice turned gritty, as if forced to speak, and the words burned his throat. "You have the highest success rate in the business, Sara. I need success. Until we determine the specifics I mentioned, every AID mission and operative working worldwide is vulnerable. I can't afford to lose this operative without discovering the facts of his case."

"The patient is an AID operative?"

Foster hesitated. "He is, but don't bother checking on him.
You won't find any more on him than you found on me."

Not surprised that Foster knew she'd checked him out, Sara
didn't flinch. "Why is that?"

"Because he's one of my men."

She crossed her arms over her chest. Her white lab coat
bunched at her ribs. "Your men. Who are . . . ?"

Foster paused. "I head an elite group of specialized operatives called Shadow Watchers." He gave her a chilly smile.
"You won't see that organization listed on any official documents. Actually, most military personnel don't realize our
group exists, and those who do realize it would never admit
it to other service members much less to anyone outside of
the military."

"I see." An empty hole stretched and yawned in her stomach. She'd gotten into something deeper than expected. "What
exactly do Shadow Watchers do?"

"We perform a vital service in a system that requires checks
and balances."

"Could you be a little less philosophical and more specific?"

Foster answered without embellishment. "We spy on
spies."

David had worked for Foster—as a Shadow Watcher. Suddenly, so much made sense. Except for the suicide. That would
never make sense. David had been happy with Brenda, had
adored her and Lisa. From all signs, he had been content.

Had David's death been suicide? An eerie feeling crept
through Sara. She stared into the cool, detached depths of Foster's eyes. Or had David been declared "unsalvageable"?

The question begged to be asked, but Sara resisted. Foster
wouldn't answer, and it could be advantageous not to let him
realize the question had occurred to her just yet. She pursed
her lips, tilted her head. "Serious problem." National security
implications, integrity of ongoing missions, safety of all

Shadow Watchers and regular AID operatives—those were but a few of the considerations and hazards.

No wonder Foster always seemed wired too tight. Carrying around responsibilities this weighty would do that to any man. "What you're telling me is that I cure your operative or he's deemed unsalvageable—without your finding out what happened to him."

"That's correct. Certainly not our preference, due to the potential complications I mentioned, but our resources have been exhausted."

His resources hadn't yet been tapped. Foster couldn't risk alerting non-AID personnel or his superior officers that his missions weren't secure. In his world of red tape, the man *had* to answer to someone, and his credibility would be shot. But she'd give him the lie. "So if I don't do this, or if I fail, then that means you terminate this operative, right?" What else could *unsalvageable* mean to spies?

Foster's gaze slid away.

Sara girded her loins and persisted. No way was she getting involved in this without knowing the full scale, scope, and consequences. "Am I right, Foster?"

The blinds streaked slatted shadows across his face. "We prefer *canceled*."

"Damn it, just once would you call a spade a spade? Forget your military jargon and sidestepping semantics and just tell me the truth." Sara glared at him. "I fail, and the man is murdered. Yes, or no?"

"Yes."

The breath left her lungs. She'd expected it. But expecting it and hearing him admit it were totally different things. She studied Foster's expression, his posture, his eyes. No remorse, regret, or apology. He *would* kill the operative. Reeling, she struggled to pull together a cohesive thought, settled for a mumbled, "I see," and felt damn grateful for it.

"I'm glad you grasp the gravity of the situation."

"It's hard to miss." Sara put the pencil down on her desk. Her instincts warned her to back off; she was in over her head. But if she did, then the operative would die. She had no doubts about that, nor any illusions. And then some other family would be in the position Brenda and Lisa were in, suffering the same hell they were suffering, wondering what they had done to make their loved one prefer being dead to living with them.

David hadn't committed suicide. He'd been canceled. Sara knew it as well as she knew she couldn't condemn a man to death, or a family to hell. "So who is the patient?"

Foster didn't falter. "I can't tell you that."

Typical. Just . . . typical. She squeezed her chair's arms until her palms and fingers stung. "Then how am I supposed to treat him?"

"Actually, you'll treat five patients. He'll be one of them."

"Five?" The man was arrogant and absurd. "I can't take on five new patients at once."

"Of course you can."

Sara bit down on her temper, resisted an urge to shout at him. "Look, let me explain something to you. In therapy, I operate from a base of trust, and that takes time to develop. Without it, I have no foundation—and no hope for success. That aside, I already have a full caseload and a healthy waiting list, so what you're asking me to do is utterly impossible."

"It's possible," he countered. "And your current patients won't be adversely affected. You have my word on that."

Won't be adversely affected? Was she supposed to feel grateful he wouldn't cancel them to get them out of his way? "Not to antagonize you, Foster, but your record with me on trust-inspiring issues leaves a lot to be desired. What's your word worth on this?"

He didn't so much as blink. "Finding out the truth about David Quade."

Her throat went tight. Those were the ones. The magic words. The irresistible offer.

And both she and Foster knew it.

There was no way she could take her deductions on David to Brenda and Lisa without proof. Sara straightened in her seat. "It appears you already have a plan. Why don't you just lay it out and let me see if I consider it acceptable?"

"Fine." He laced his hands behind his back, strode a brisk path between the bookcase and the door. "You'll enter a facility under the auspices of performing a short-term research project on PTSD as a psychiatrist, Major Sara West."

"Major?" Sara grunted. "Forget it. Impersonating an officer would cost me my license, and you know how I feel about your military protocol and red-tape nightmare of a system. If I do this—and I'm not saying I will—then I want civilian status, total control, and full latitude—personally, and with my patients."

"Which is exactly why you're heading the PTSD research project. The only person you'll have to answer to at the facility is the director, and, of course, to me—though, obviously I won't be inside the facility. You'll have total control over the patients and therapy, but not over the facility. I can't give you that, or civilian status. Not without exposing your cover."

"You honestly expect me to go in undercover?" She rolled her gaze heavenward, dragged her hands over her head. "For God's sake, Foster. I'm not one of your spies, I'm a doctor. What do I know about covert operations? And what about my current patients, and my license?"

"The cover is essential." He sat down, leaned forward, and then linked his fingers, bracing his forearms on his knees. "I don't know who is responsible for this, Sara. I can't take unnecessary chances with my operative, with the other Shadow Watchers and AID personnel, or with you." Foster lifted his gaze to meet hers. "Look, you wanted me to call a spade a spade. Well, here it is. There's no such thing as a free lunch. You dislike the military and you resent its dedication to discipline, rules, and order. Yet every day of your life, you enjoy the personal freedom the military provides you."

"Excuse me, but it's the Constitution that guarantees my personal freedom."

Foster's eyes blazed. "Try exercising it without us."

Valid point. She didn't like it, but historically speaking, she couldn't deny it.

"We've served you, Doctor. Now, we need your service. That military operative is one of many who provide you your freedom. If you won't assist for David or for the sake of your country or under your oath to heal, then do it for him. Make it personal. Hell, it *is* personal. Every day of his life, this operative sacrifices for you in ways you can't begin to fathom. Simply put, Sara, you owe him."

Foster orchestrated this deliberately, to make her feel responsible for the operative. Even knowing it, the tactic worked. That infuriated her. "I do not owe him, or you. I haven't asked anyone in uniform to do anything for me."

"No, but you certainly haven't objected to all we have done." He thrust out his chin. "You've benefited from our sacrifices, Doctor. That's a fact."

"Sorry, this mind-set doesn't wash with me." Her palms were damp. She pressed them flat on her desk blotter. "The draft has been abolished for a long time. Everyone in the military freely chose their career, just as I chose mine."

Foster lifted and then set back down her nameplate. It thudded against her desk. "Think, Sara. Whoever did this to him is dangerous. Human life means nothing to him. Do you think for a second a person capable of deliberately destroying a man's mind would hesitate to kill you or thousands of others like you?"

"Him." Sara picked up on the pronoun. "You said *him*. So you *do* have an idea of who is behind this."

"Him, or her, or they," Foster replied. "Likely they. And if I had any idea who was behind this, would I be here?"

He wouldn't. And her deduction proved true. This was a serious problem. For the country, the operatives, and now, for her. If overt, she'd be an assassin's target. If covert, and discovered and exposed, she would be canceled. Some choices. Either way, if she got caught, she was dead.

But what if you don't get caught? You find out about David, get Brenda and Lisa straightened out, save an operative's life, and you live.

And Foster owes you.

Sara rocked back and forth in her chair, absorbing, reading between the lines. "What you're telling me—underneath all the God-and-country-and-duty talk—is that once I'm in, I'm on my own."

"Totally. No support and, if you blow it, no knowledge."

If exposed, definitely canceled. She looked up at Foster. For the first time, she saw complete, unvarnished truth in his eyes. And she hated it most of all. It scared her in ways she'd never been scared. Her throat muscles quivered, and she swallowed hard. "I don't have a choice about this, do I?"

"No." Foster softened his voice. "I wish I could give one, but I can't. If you refuse, I'll manufacture whatever evidence it takes to have your license revoked. You'll lose everything, Sara. I know you won't believe it, but I regret having to issue this ultimatum. I oppose force and do all I can to preserve freedom."

"You stand here and say that, knowing your ultimatum will cost me everything?"

"Yes. For the greater good of a nation, I'll sacrifice you." He looked straight into her eyes. "You, or many, many others, Sara. In my position, which would you choose?"

She'd choose the lesser of the two evils. She'd choose to sacrifice herself. What else *could* she choose and still live with herself? "I'd look for another option."

"There are no other options."

True, or he wouldn't be here. She didn't want to ask, but she had to know. Her mouth dust-dry, she lashed at her lips with her tongue. "Will I be canceled?"

"The moment you become a risk. Yes, you will."

At least he was honest about it. Still, the concept was difficult to grasp. This had been just another normal day. Now, there was nothing normal about it. "And if I don't become a risk?"

"Then no good would be served by canceling you."

Sara studied him. Foster was worried; his forehead was sweat-sheened. If he'd had any other way of resolving this, he never would have come to her. She wasn't thrilled with the idea, but if there was a snowball's chance in hell she could help Brenda and Lisa, then Sara had to try it. God knew, helping them her way, she'd failed again and again. Foster's insight about David could give her what she needed to succeed. She didn't relish the idea of losing everything she had worked for, either. Especially her life or that of the unknown operative. And she had sworn an oath to heal. A damn shame they hadn't added, "when it's convenient."

Obviously, whoever had written the oath hadn't crossed paths with Foster.

Okay. Okay, she'd do it.

Something flashed in Jack Foster's eyes. Something dark and evil. "No," she said before she could change her mind. When it came to a battle between logic and instinct, she went with instinct every time. "I'm sorry. I understand your dilemma, but I can't help you. Find yourself another doctor."

"I can pull you in, Sara." Foster stood up. "I'd prefer not to have to do it, but when it regards a matter of national security, I have the authority."

Yet another threat. Enough was enough. "Look, you do what you have to do. My gut's telling me you're not playing straight with me, and until it tells me differently, I'm refusing. You want to make my life miserable? Pull my license? Fine. Go ahead. I'll deal with it. But I won't have you jeopardize my reputation and my life when you're bent on playing the very games with me that you warned me against playing with you."

"What games?" Foster elevated his voice. "I've told you everything you need to know."

"You've told me everything you *want* me to know. There's a difference. Look me in the eye and tell me you haven't held out on me."

He looked away.

"Good grief, Foster. Your body language has been screaming at me since you walked through my door. It's still screaming at me now."

He folded his arms across his chest. "What exactly is it screaming, Doctor?"

Sara stood up. Though a good six inches shorter than his six two, she glared up at him. "It's screaming that you've got a hidden agenda."

Foster stared at her for a long moment, as if torn between choking her and laughing at her. "Of course I've got a hidden agenda. I'm AID, for Christ's sake."

He had a point. Still . . . "You know what I mean. Don't you dare make this sound trivial. Not when you're talking about lives."

"There's nothing trivial about any of this." Foster picked a piece of lint from his dark blue slacks. "But my agendas are of no consequence to you."

Was he joking or suffering from delusions? "Let me get this straight. I do what you want or I lose everything—including my license, right?"

"Simplified, but, yes, that's correct."

She crossed her chest with her arms. "Well, for something that is of no consequence to me, this proposition stands to have a huge impact on my life."

He ignored that remark and dropped a business card on her desk. "You have twenty-four hours. Phone me at the hand-written number on the back."

Sara glared across the desk at him. "I won't call."

"Yes, Sara, you will." Foster spoke softly, just above a whisper, and his eyes reflected pity and regret. "Because if you don't call, Brenda is going to marry and divorce again, Lisa is going to run away from home, and an innocent man, who has devoted his life to his country and to keeping people like you safe, is going to die."

two

☆

Where am I? What happened to me?

An electric chair. He remembered being strapped into an electric chair. He hadn't been able to breathe. Why could he remember the chair and not remember who he was? What was his name? He had to have a name—everyone did—and he had to know it. John? Matthew? Kenneth?

No, no, no. None of those felt right. The chair. That felt right. He vividly remembered the chair.

Sprawled on the floor, he cranked open an eye and covertly looked for it. Nothing there. Only hospital smells, bright light, white-padded walls and floor.

White . . .

Images flashed through his mind. The chair. Straps binding him in it. A black, cone-nosed machine, emitting a pinpoint ray of red light aimed at his head. An upsurge of rage came with the images, and knowing what the rage let loose inside him, he fought to keep it leashed. He hated the rage. Hated it, and feared it.

His arms were bound to his sides. A straitjacket. He frowned down at it, rotated his shoulders, and maneuvered. With little effort, he removed the damn thing, and then tossed it to the floor. It slapped against the cushion, and he went statue-still.

Where did I learn to do that? To take off a straitjacket?

He tried and tried, but couldn't remember. The mental strain and frustration of being a stranger to himself, of not knowing what kind of man he was, what he stood for, loved, hated, believed, stirred the rage. He gripped his head, squeezing the rage out, and paced the length of the room, counting his steps. Twelve paces. Twelve. Where was the chair? It had to be here. *Why isn't it here?*

Maybe it never had been here. Maybe it never had been . . . anywhere.

Panic surged from his stomach, tightened his chest. No, it had been here. He remembered banging his ribs against the chair arm. He looked down at his bare chest, touched a hand to his left side, and flinched. Sore and slightly bruised. The chair had been real. Relieved, he sighed. "Real." The enemy must have moved it.

His bare feet sank into the cushioned floor. Hadn't it been concrete? He looked down. White. Was he walking on clouds? Maybe the chair wasn't here. Maybe he had died and this was heaven.

Rage, in heaven? No, no, no. Impossible.

Confusion. So much confusion. He was coming to hate it as much as the rage. He paced faster, gripped his head harder, squeezed tighter. The enemy had to be tricking him again. They were playing games with his mind to convince him he was crazy. Was he crazy? This place appeared to be an asylum and, straitjacketed and restricted to a padded room, he had to be a patient. He could be crazy. Why else would they isolate him?

Uncertainty swarmed him. Resentful, perplexed, he slumped back against the wall, loosened his grip on his head, rubbed at his stinging temples. Staring at the ceiling, he squinted. God, but he hated those lights. They never went off and they burned so bright his eyes ached. He looked down at the floor. White. The jacket. White.

The red pinpoint image again flashed through his mind. The rage roiled in his stomach, surged deeper, grew stronger.

Bury it. You have to bury it to figure this out. Who are you? Where are you? Why are you here?

His skin crawled. Clammy, baffled, irritated, he darted his gaze to the door, the only entrance in or out. No windows. Why were there no windows?

The chair. Strapped in. He greedily gulped in air, as he had

craved to do then. His cheek stung. He touched it, and remembered a beefy man slapping him. His lip had bled, and
he heard his own voice. *I'm a POW. I get the message . . .*

If he was a POW, then there must be a war. Was he a
soldier, then? Or a civilian the enemy had captured?

Neither felt right or familiar. Dispirited, he squeezed his
eyes shut, fisted his hands at his sides. Just more mind clutter.
Nothing real. Yet he remembered saying those words. He
could actually hear them inside his head in his own voice.
Where was that place? And how had he come to be in *this*
place? Nothing there was here. Here, there were only bright
lights. Only the enemy. Only white.

Instinctively, he recoiled, pressing deeper against the padded wall. He thrashed his head from side to side, trying to
unscramble his scattered thoughts. Blood pounded through his
veins, throbbed at his temples, and he cupped his head and
squeezed it to ease the pressure. White. He stilled. Stiffened.
Red.

The rage slammed through him.

He fell to his knees and tucked his chin, curling into a tight
ball. Maybe if he got small enough, the rage couldn't fit inside
him and it would go away.

It didn't. It coiled in his stomach, whipped through his
chest, pulsed in his fingertips, strengthening, smothering
everything inside him. It overtook him, and nothing else was
left.

Torture.

He groaned in agony. Writhed on the floor, screamed until
his throat was raw and every muscle in his body protested in
continuous spasm.

Red was bad. The enemy.

He had to kill the enemy.

The phone rang.

Sitting in her office, Sara ignored it, then realized it was
after five and her secretary already had gone home. A catch
hitched in her neck, warning her she had been bent over her

desk too long. She rubbed at it with one hand and lifted the phone's receiver with the other. "Dr. West."

"Aunt Sara?"

Sara's worry antennae shot up. Her grip on the phone tightened. "What's wrong, Lisa? You okay?"

"No. I mean, I'm safe and all that stuff." Exasperation laced her tone. "The truth is, I'm pissed. Mom forgot to pick me up after school again. Second time this week. It's not the walk, you know? It's being forgotten. She's getting to be a real pro at that."

She was, but there was more to this. Lisa saved "pissed" for heavy-duty trials; rarely used, and all the more worrisome when it was. Knowing she was waiting to see if she'd get the "go ahead and gripe, I'm all ears" or the "watch your mouth" lecture, Sara said, "I'm listening." A little dose of guilt stabbed her. Staring at her desk lamp, she shrugged it off. Lisa wasn't quite thirteen and her cursing shouldn't be condoned, but after all she had been through—and was still going through—Sara's heart just wasn't in disciplining her. Cursing was a reasonably safe stress valve, and not being compelled to object was the nice part about being "Aunt Sara" versus "Mom." Sara could choose.

"She's doing it again!"

There was no need to ask who or what. Deep down, Sara already knew. The muscles in her stomach clenched. "Your mother's getting married again?"

"Yeah. There was a note on the fridge. She's out celebrating her engagement." Lisa huffed her frustration. "Can you believe it? God, Aunt Sara, I think she's lost it—and don't you dare tell me to be grateful she's not screwing up the holidays by being a Christmas bride again. It doesn't matter when she gets married. It's how many times she's been married."

"She's searching for something." At a loss, Sara squeezed her eyes shut. How could she explain Brenda's actions when she didn't understand them herself?

"Well, whatever it is, she's not finding it. She's a wreck, and I'm sick of being the one to pay the price. She changes husbands like normal people change their underwear and my friends look at me like I'm the one who's cracked up. They say stuff about her that I know is stuff their parents are saying. Gwendolyn Pierce told me her mother won't let her come over here anymore because Mom's a bad influence." Lisa's voice was pitched high and tinny. "Gwen was my best friend."

Sara's heart wrenched. She braced her head on her hand and thumbed her temple. How had things gotten this far out of control? "I'm so sorry, honey."

"You're sorry? I'm starting to hate her for this."

"Lisa, don't. She's not herself, and we both know it."

"Well, damn it, she needs to get over it. I lost him, too, you know?"

"Yes, I do know." And her niece was hurting. From the loss of her father, and from her mother's reaction to it. "Is she marrying that dermatologist?" Brenda had been seeing him for a couple of weeks.

"No, she dumped him. It's a new guy. Mr. Williamson. H. G. or G. H. Something like that. I dunno. I only met him once."

Sara held off a sigh by the skin of her teeth. "Did you like him?"

"Not particularly. He's stuffy."

Great. Just great. "Wait a second. I thought her divorce wasn't final for another couple of weeks."

"Mr. Williamson fixed that. He's a judge."

What a day. Sara condemns a man to death by refusing to treat him, and now Brenda commits to marrying a judge she just met. Could the news get any worse?

Sara buried her chin against her palm, then rubbed at her forehead, silently cursing the jackhammers having a field day inside her head. She had a ton of work to do before morning, but Lisa needed her, and family always came first. "How about I pick up some burgers and come over so we can talk?"

"Talking about it won't stop her, Aunt Sara. We've been there and done that, you know? You're a shrink. Can't you fix her?"

"Honest to God, I'm trying, honey." When it mattered most, Sara had failed completely. Guilt shrouded her and hot tears stung her eyes. She blinked them back, refusing to give in, or to give up, and swearing she'd give all she owned if she could just end Lisa's pain. No kid should ever be dragged through any kind of hell, but especially this kind of hell. "You know it's complex."

"What I know is, I've had it. Grandma West won't even talk to us anymore. Grandpa says she's disgusted with Mom and she's taking it out on me, too, but she'll get over it. I don't think she will. And Grandma Quade just cries all the time."

"Your Grandma West was born disgusted, and your Grandma Quade has lost her husband and her son. She's hurting, Lisa. Seeing you and your mom going through this and not being able to help only hurts her more."

"It hurts me, too," Lisa shot back. "Can't we commit Mom, or something? Gwendolyn Pierce told me her mother said Mom ought to be committed, and Aunt Shelly committed Uncle Steve."

"Because she was angry and the law is asinine. Your Uncle Steve wasn't mentally ill and neither is your mother."

"Can't prove it by me. You've got to admit she's acting nuts, Aunt Sara."

"No, honey, she honestly isn't," Sara disagreed. "Your mother is reacting to trauma. She doesn't need to be committed. Gwen's mother doesn't have a clue what she's talking about."

"Whatever," Lisa interjected. "All I know is I'm about to explode. You've got to do something. *Please!*"

What was left to do that Sara hadn't already tried?

Foster's offer flickered through her mind. She stared at his card, still untouched where he'd left it on her desk. She shouldn't do it, and she knew it. He was hiding something vital from her. But he had promised she'd find her answers about David, and from the panic and desolation in Lisa's tone, Sara had better find them fast. Before she could stop the words, they tumbled out of her mouth. "I have a plan, Lisa. Just hang in there a little while longer, okay?"

"How much longer? The kids are laughing at me and calling Mom ugly names. It's humiliating. Even Taylor Baker is giving me flack."

"Who is he?"

"Only the coolest guy in the world. I've been trying to get him to notice me since fifth grade. Now he has, and it's awful."

Seeing the potential to lift Lisa's thoughts to something less depressing, Sara picked up on the Taylor Baker thread. "Is he *the* one?"

"Maybe. I'm not sure."

"If he were the one, you'd know it—first sight."

"Do you really believe that?"

Sara thumped a pen against her blotter. She prayed it. Regularly. "That's how it was with your mom and dad, and with Grandma and Grandpa West."

"Well, I guess he's not, then." Lisa let out a resigned sigh. "But he'll do until the one comes along."

Sara smiled. "So you'll give me more time to figure things out?"

"Just how much dirt am I supposed to eat on this? My gut's full, Aunt Sara."

Sara understood Lisa's belligerence and her outrage. Her own patience was about as thin as film. "You shouldn't have to eat any dirt," Sara said. "But the way things should be and the way they are—"

"Trust me, I've got a grip on reality versus fantasy. Mom's seen to that."

Sara frowned, wishing that weren't true, and snagged an orange from a basket on the credenza behind her desk. "Can you stand it for just a couple more weeks?" She dug her thumbnail in and started peeling. Pungent juice squirted out. Tugging a tissue from the box, she dabbed at the juice droplets on her desk.

No answer.

"Lisa?" Real fear gripped at Sara's stomach, and she stilled. What did she do if Lisa refused? "Please."

Lisa hesitated. "If you convince Mom not to marry H. G. or G. H. Williamson, I'll try. But I won't promise. Right now, all I want to do is to get away from here and away from her. Five years is waiting long enough—and being patient enough. She's broken, and she's breaking me, too. It's not fair." Her voice cracked. "It's not, and I'm sick of this stuff."

"No, it isn't fair. It's hard." Sara closed her eyes and offered up a silent prayer. "But you're stronger than she is right now, and I have a plan. So give me a few weeks, and I'll talk to your mom about holding off on the wedding, okay? I'll talk to your Grandma Quade, too." Sara didn't bother extending that promise to include Grandma West. They both knew Sara's mother was a lost cause.

"Okay. But that's it, Aunt Sara. If Mom marries the stuffed shirt, I'm outta here. I can't stomach another quickie marriage and divorce. I won't."

Two references to running away in one conversation. This was not good. Yet, Lisa had agreed. "Fair enough, provided you give me your word that if you do decide to leave, you'll talk with me first. I can't stand the thought of not knowing where you are and that you're okay, Lisa. Please don't put me through that." Or Brenda. She would come unglued at the seams.

"All right. If I go, I'll call you first," Lisa promised, then hung up.

Sara grabbed a fresh tissue from the box at the corner of her desk and dabbed at the sweat beaded at her temples. She understood Lisa's frustration. Oh, but did she understand it! And she was furious with her sister for dragging Lisa through this with her. Almost as furious with her as Sara was with herself for not knowing how to get Brenda beyond this self-destructive—and Lisa-destructive—behavior.

Sara did all she knew to do. She read the latest available information, scoured and studied new findings and treatments until she swore her eyeballs were going to bleed, and yet the key to Brenda's mental health—which held the key to Lisa's—still eluded Sara. What was she missing?

And what can you find out in a few weeks that you haven't been able to find out in five years of intense searching?

Dear God. What had she done? Lisa expected results, and

Sara had promised them without knowing she could provide them. She hadn't intended to promise or to lie. She'd been desperate, afraid Lisa would run away and then Brenda would lose what grip she had on her sanity—though honesty forced Sara to admit that, aside from the marriages and leaving Lisa on the sidelines while pursuing them, Brenda seemed normal. Baffling situation. Hair-pulling baffling. One not covered in any textbooks or professional journals.

A few weeks. That's all the time Sara had to produce results. Without Foster, she didn't stand a chance.

The arrogant bastard had won. He'd known he would. And which Sara resented more—his winning, or his knowing he would—she couldn't honestly say. Not that it mattered. Bottom line, only two things mattered: her family, and the life of that operative.

Ever since Foster had left, Sara had been fighting a heavy-duty dose of guilt about condemning that man to death. And she might as well admit it, if only to herself. Even without the potential for learning about David, she still would have ended up calling Foster. She couldn't not call him, knowing he would have the operative murdered. Though, for strategic advantage, she might have waited another day to make the call. Now, she couldn't afford to squander a day's time.

Sara lifted the card and then dialed the handwritten number scrawled on the back of it, hoping she wasn't making a monumental mistake. Every instinct in her body screamed this was dangerous and could get her killed. But something rating the highest priority screamed far louder than her instincts: Lisa's despair.

The phone rang in Sara's ear, then rang again.

"Foster," he answered, sounding calm and confident.

Irrationally angry that he sounded relaxed while her emotions were in riot, Sara swallowed an urge to snap at him. The knot of fear in her throat slid down and settled squarely in her chest. He needed a favor from her, and she urgently needed one from him. If successful, she would help Brenda and Lisa and save a man's life. If not . . . No. Failure was *not* an option. She *had* to succeed. "It's me," she said, certain he would know who was calling. "Meet me at Molly Maguire's pub in an hour." Her hand trembling, her stomach pitching and rolling, she braced the office phone's receiver between her hunched shoulder and ear, clipped her cell-phone to her slacks' waistband, and broke into a cold sweat. "I want to make a deal."

The pub was cramped and crowded.

The cloistering smell of so many foods and patrons' perfumes nearly knocked Sara to her knees. Why she had suggested coming here, she had no idea. All the dollar bills hanging down from the ceiling and taped to the walls made her feel claustrophobic, and she had deliberately avoided claustrophobic situations since a former PTSD patient, suffering a flashback, had locked her in a closet with his pet boa constrictor, Rudy. She had squelched forever her fear of snakes, but she'd hated closed-in places ever since. And Foster's boxing her in on this deal already had her feeling closed in enough.

A perky hostess wove through a maze of wooden tables, leading Sara to a quiet corner where Jack Foster sat waiting for her. He'd ditched the uniform for a pair of beige slacks and a yellow golf shirt, and he was smiling. At least he wasn't gloating. At this point, she'd take solace wherever she could find it.

Sara sat down and frowned at him. She wasn't happy about this situation and it was just as well she let him know it right up front. "Here's the deal, and none of it is negotiable," she said, diving in to get this over and done. "I want access to all information—regardless of its security classification—on David Quade and on other PTSD patients like him. I also want all of the undisclosed statistics and data you've compiled on successful coping strategies for PTSD family members. In return, I'll treat your five patients—provided that during my absence you have a doctor I consider acceptable work with my current patients using my methods."

Foster glanced at her as if he hadn't heard a word she'd spoken. "Would you like something to drink?"

Glimpsing their waitress's approach, Sara nodded. "A beer.

Anything on tap." If she intended to become a covert operative of sorts and to survive, then she had better start honing her observation skills and being more discreet. "No, make that a Southpaw."

"Southpaw?" Foster looked at her, clearly perplexed.

"It's a beer." She shrugged. "I want to give it a try."

Foster smiled at the waitress. "Make that two Southpaws."

As soon as the waitress departed, Sara rushed him. "Well?" She had to rush him, or she feared she'd listen to her instincts, back out of the proposal, and run like hell. Foster often had infuriated her. Now, he terrified her. She resented that, and him. Her life was chaotic enough without him dragging her into AID intelligence matters that she knew nothing about, and then dropping "no knowledge" bombs on her head if she fell short of accomplishing the required mission. Not to mention his threatening to ruin her and making her responsible for the life of his operative.

Foster waited until the waitress stepped out of hearing range to respond. "Regarding your patients, consider it done. Dr. Christopher Kale is the best we've got, and he's familiar with—and approves of—your unorthodox methods. He'll fill in for you and follow your procedures to the letter."

A simple thrill shimmied up Sara's backbone. She'd been meeting informally and corresponding with Dr. Kale for months. He was pushing seventy, an excellent psychiatrist, and devoted to her methods of therapy. But their contact also explained how Foster knew so much about her private life and her family. Dr. Kale was one of Foster's men. That betrayal stung.

"Do you approve of Dr. Kale?"

"You know I do." Forcing herself, she smiled. "He's head and shoulders above anyone else in the field."

"And he agrees with you and doesn't think you're a nut."

"That, too." Sara shrugged, not at all defensive. "Pioneers often aren't appreciated until long after they're dead, Foster. I could care less what my peers think, so long as they don't interfere. The majority of my patients recover. That's what matters most to me."

"I didn't realize you were so altruistic, Sara." Foster's eyes twinkled.

He realized exactly how altruistic she was or he wouldn't have tagged her to help him. Still, she regretted speaking freely. "We all have our moments."

Foster smiled, causing an amazing transformation in his sharp, angled features. "Kale will meet you at your office in an hour to go over your current patients' charts. I'll do all I can to get you access to the information you requested." He glanced at the two men seated at the next table and dropped his voice. "I wish I could guarantee success, but the truth is, I can't. I will do everything humanly possible."

"Provided this isn't lip service and you really do intend to follow through, your best is all I can ask or expect."

"So am I forgiven now?"

"Hardly. And don't push it." On top of everything else, he had questioned her honor. That rankled. Deep.

She thumbed the rim of her water glass, wishing the waitress would hurry with their beers. She needed serious fortification. "I don't like the risk factors in this situation."

"Neither do I," he frankly admitted. "My men being in jeopardy without me having any idea why makes me damned uncomfortable."

"If it didn't, you'd be a lousy excuse for a commander." The two men took a trip to the salad bar. Foster watched them unreasonably closely.

Unreasonable for a civilian. But maybe not for a Shadow Watcher.

She wasn't sure she could get used to being suspicious of everyone. She was sure she didn't want to have to, and she was equally sure she had no choice but to do it if she wanted to succeed and stay alive.

Damn him for pulling her into this.

Foster unfolded a napkin and pressed it across his lap. "You're very astute, Sara. How did you know you wouldn't be performing this mission from your office?"

Still uneasy with the intimacy of him using her first name, Sara shrugged. "All of these patients are security risks. When men—" She paused, frowned, and tilted her head. "Are all five of them men?"

"As it happens, they are."

Something in his tone warned her that an all-male rule didn't apply to his group, which also warned her that the needs of the military held priority over the needs of the individuals serving in it. She wished she could deny the wisdom and value in that but, unfortunately, she couldn't. "When men with top secret clearances suffer mental challenges with moments of lucidity, the military sequestering them seems prudent."

The waitress put two frosty mugs of beer on the table. "Care for menus?"

"None for me," Sara said, certain if she put anything solid down her throat, it'd come right back up. She hadn't had this serious a case of jitters since prom night in high school when her date, Rick Grayson, had spilled half a jug of Mogen David wine down the front of her white dress and she'd spent most of the night alone in a Laundromat wrapped in a stolen towel, laundering her dress to avoid having to convince her mother she hadn't been drinking.

"No, thank you," Foster said to the waitress. When she walked out of earshot, he turned his attention back to Sara. "Braxton."

A sliver of ice slid down the mug to the table. "Excuse me?"

"That's where you'll be going. Braxton Facility."

"Never heard of it." Sara lifted the mug and took a sip. The cold felt good sliding down her throat. Numbing.

"Few have," Foster admitted. "It's a private mental facility owned by the government, about thirty miles north of here."

Getting a grip on how Foster's mind worked, Sara set her mug back down on the table. "Only no one knows the government owns it."

"Correct. Just as you suspected, all military members who pose security risks are sequestered there for treatment. As I said at your office earlier, you'll have your usual list of five patients. One of them will be my operative."

He wouldn't tell her, but she felt obligated to ask. "Which one?"

Foster stared at his mug. "None of your patients' identities will be disclosed."

"So much for the honor system and building trust."

"Honor and trust have nothing to do with it. This isn't my decision. It's standard operating procedure at Braxton. On admittance, patients are assigned a number and, thereafter, they're addressed only by it. Even the staff doesn't know the patients' identities."

Sara stared at him, her jaw agape. "Unbelievable."

"Totally logical," Foster countered. "All of these patients occupy extremely sensitive positions. To reveal their identities is to expose them and their families to unnecessary—and potentially lethal—risks. It also renders them unsalvageable in their respective career fields."

She'd like to argue, but the policy held logic. *Unsalvageable.* God, but she hated that word. And she had the distinct feeling there was a lot more to this military than the reams of red tape she had experienced in her dealings with Foster about David. "What was your operative doing when he went missing?"

"Investigating an incident with suspected international repercussions. But we've conducted a full-scale investigation and nothing that occurred there accounts for subsequent events."

Sara thumbed her mug handle, wondering exactly what that investigation had entailed and who had conducted it. Asking Foster would be an exercise in futility. "How did he get to Braxton?"

"We have no idea. Security found him wandering around on the grounds. No ID on him, of course. Braxton ran a routine fingerprint search and picked up a specific coding on his computer file that referred them to AID, and finally to me."

Sara tasted the beer again. What had been cold and refreshing now tasted bitter. But it wasn't the beer. Southpaw tasted pretty good. The context of the conversation had turned her bitter. "Was he counseled immediately?"

"Why?" Foster seated his mug atop a paper coaster, squaring it over the four-leaf clover imprinted in its center.

"Patients who receive CISD—critical incident stress debriefing—immediately after the inciting incident stand the best odds of recovering."

"I'm not sure how much time elapsed between the inciting incident and when he was found on Braxton grounds. He was missing seven days. We don't know when or where the incident occurred. We don't even know what occurred. But he was seen by Dr. Fontaine, the facility director, immediately thereafter. Everything we know is in the chart. Same is true for the other four patients. When you arrive at Braxton, you'll have full access to them. I do know he's experiencing all of the classic symptoms and criteria necessary for a PTSD diagnosis."

Expecting that, as he couldn't be diagnosed if any one of the criteria had been absent, she still suffered a twinge of disappointment. The odds that he had received the CISD briefing were slim to none. Receiving it on arrival at Braxton could have helped, but to be at all effective, they needed to know the nature of the incident and they didn't. "When do I leave?"

Foster slid the salt shaker down the table, near the pepper. "Tomorrow morning, eight o'clock." He reached into his briefcase and then slid a sealed envelope across the tabletop. "Report to Dr. Fontaine. The rest of your instructions, your ID card, and some military background information are in there."

Red lettering was emblazoned across the front of the envelope. "For Your Eyes Only. Read and Destroy." Suppressing a shiver, Sara tucked the envelope into her purse. She had a lot to do between now and eight A.M. To talk to Brenda, Lisa, and Lisa's Grandma Quade. Close up her house, meet with Dr. Kale, talk with her current patients, and—

"Don't be late," Foster said. "Keep me updated by phone. Call at twenty-one hundred hours whatever nights you have something to report." He waved a fingertip toward her cell phone. "And don't use that. There's a convenience store about five miles from the facility. Use the phone there."

Twenty-one hundred. Sara snapped the flap on her purse

shut and counted off the hours. Twelve, thirteen, fourteen . . . nine P.M.

Having to count to translate time proved a nagging point. Sara wasn't ready for this. She didn't know enough about the inner workings of the military. In her five years of confrontations with it about David, she thought she had gained a gutful of knowledge. Now, she knew better. She was in serious trouble. How could she carry off posing as an officer? "Do these special instructions mean you think the phones at Braxton are tapped?"

"It's a distinct possibility." A pleased gleam lit in his eye. "And cell phones aren't secure. Anyone could be listening in, ally or enemy."

The beer in her stomach soured on the spot. "I see." And, God, but she wished she didn't.

"Not yet." Foster stood up, dropped a ten on the table, and then scooted his chair back into place. Its legs scraped over the wooden floor. "But you will soon."

Finishing her beer, Sara watched him leave. Dread dragged at her belly, warning her he was right. And that she would hate it, too.

three

☆

No sign marked the turnoff, which had to make it difficult for families first visiting to find the place, but Sara spotted the dirt road leading to Braxton. Dodging one of a million mud puddles, she hooked a left and cranked up the heater—last night's rain had turned the October air surprisingly chilly—and conceded that her conversation with Brenda had been chilly, too.

Only after Sara had confided that this was her best lead yet for information on David had Brenda agreed to hold off marrying H. G. or G. H., or whatever-the-hell-his-name-was, Williamson. God alone knew if she'd keep her word. For everyone's sake, Sara hoped Brenda did wait.

Dragging a hand over her winter-white wool slacks, Sara came to a guarded iron gate and braked to a stop. On both sides of the guard shack, tall chain-link fencing stretched across the road and disappeared into the pine woods. Razor wire topped it. Red and white signs posted every three feet warned that the fence was electric. Beyond the shack, as far as she could see, lay only more dirt road and woods. Nothing identified this as the facility, but instinctively she knew it was Braxton.

A burly guard in his mid-thirties stepped out of the guard shack and approached the window. A badge attached to his shirt pocket read BUSH, and from the stripes on his sleeve, he was a sergeant. A shiny pistol hung holstered at his waist, and he looked too comfortable wearing it not to know how to use it.

The dread dragging at her stomach increased tenfold. She

rolled down the window of her car and a gust of wind swept in, carrying the cloying smell of pine.

He stopped a safe distance from the car. "You lost, ma'am?"

"No, Sergeant Bush, I'm expected. Dr. Sara West."

He scanned a clipboard and then looked back at her. "Yes, ma'am. You're staying on the premises, I see. FYI, the gate locks up for the night at twenty-one hundred sharp. We don't open it again until seven hundred. Security reasons, ma'am. No exceptions."

She converted the times and resisted the urge to spit nails. She wasn't even in Braxton yet and already the first problem had arisen. How was she supposed to call Foster at nine P.M. from the convenience store when Braxton's security force locked down the facility at nine P.M.?

Bush thrust a clip-on name badge through the open window. "Wear this at all times—attached to your left collar point. If you're caught inside the facility or on the premises without it, you'll be detained and fined. No exceptions."

"Thanks for the warning." Sara didn't have a collar on her winter-white sweater, so she clipped it to the neckline where a collar would be if she'd had one.

Avoiding her eyes, Bush saluted. "Welcome to Braxton, Major." He waved her through the gate.

Sara drove on, and when the road curved sharply to the right, she saw the facility. Lush islands of evergreen foliage and four stories of gray stone with white-shuttered windows obscured by bars. To the distant north of the building lay a hedge maze, a pond, and what appeared to be a grass airstrip; closer in, a concrete helicopter pad. She understood the pad. It was necessary for emergency life-flights. But a grass airstrip?

A bitter taste filled her mouth and a shiver slithered up her spine. A stately building in a serene setting. Yet looking at it gave her the creeps. Braxton seemed more like a fortress than a mental facility. But, she reminded herself, it was a special facility where high-risk, mentally diminished patients harboring classified information were sequestered. And the fortress

aspects kept others out just as it kept patients inside. There
was solace in knowing that.

She pulled into a parking slot near—of all things—an airplane, and stared up at the building. That sense of unease crept
through her chest, and certainty filled her. Braxton *was* a fortress. Getting into it and functioning while here might be difficult, but her instincts shouted that those difficulties would
seem minuscule when compared to the challenges of her getting out of Braxton.

Had Foster known that before bringing her in?

Unsure, Sara left the car.

Security was as tight inside the building as it had been
outside it. Beyond the information desk, she stopped at three
mandatory checkpoints where everyone entering the facility
reported to have their passes, thumbprint, and eyes matched
to those in the computer files. Going through the identification
process made her feel like a crook.

After she passed the third security-system check, an armed
guard named Reaston who was the size of a small giant personally escorted her through a maze of barren corridors to the
office of the facility director, Dr. Fontaine. She tried twice to
engage Reaston in conversation, but he refused to utter a single
word or even to look her straight in the eye. Odd, but even
those they passed in the halls avoided meeting her gaze and
refused to return simple, courteous greetings. Getting the cold
shoulder set her teeth on edge. Were people shunning her, or
Reaston?

Uncertain, Sara followed the guard into an office where a
meek-looking woman of about forty—Dr. Fontaine's secretary, Sara presumed—sat at a desk covered with orderly stacks
of files. "Dr. Sara West," Reaston said.

The secretary nodded, dismissing him, and then ushered
Sara through the sparsely furnished outer office into the director's inner sanctum.

It looked as tired as the rest of Braxton's interior. Two
deep-green visitor's chairs with worn leather seats, a well-used
executive desk that had water rings and dull spots in its
cherry-wood surface—which was amazingly empty of anything work-related—a credenza with a photograph of a

woman, probably Fontaine's wife, and a photo of a sailboat on the wall. Not a file, a computer terminal, or even a calendar was in sight. Even the obligatory green plant was absent. There was, however, a lot of professional wallpaper. Every degree—the most impressive from Harvard—and award the man ever had won was prominently displayed in a thick gold frame. At least a dozen of them. This was not good. Fontaine was an egomaniac. Sara had trouble relating to egomaniacs.

Fontaine had his back to the door and the phone cradled between his shoulder and ear. He wasn't wearing the traditional uniform of dark-blue slacks and light-blue shirt or medical whites, but he still reeked of being military: precise, exact, and detached—just like Foster. Fifty and graying, Fontaine wore a brown suit and absently rubbed a nauseating yellow tie. She didn't need to see his face to know the man was angry; his tone spoke volumes.

"Yes," he said to the unfortunate person on the other end of the line. "I do understand the severity of your situation, but this shoestring budget is killing me." He paused, listened, and then went on. "I know that, Carl. But I'm telling you I can't perform miracles. I need money—now. We both want results, so give me what I need to get them."

"He will only be a moment," the secretary whispered and then left, softly closing the office door behind her.

Not invited to sit, Sara stood and waited, her duffel bag's strap slung over her shoulder. So far, her bags and purse had been searched twice. That wasn't uncommon in certain mental facilities, but the stringent checkpoints, advanced security systems, and wary expressions around here were very uncommon. Everyone inside Braxton looked as if they worked under a cloud of doom and gloom, which reinforced her uneasy feelings about the place. And considering Dr. Fontaine's raging on the phone at the poor soul Carl, the mood around here appeared destined to grow more grim.

First, lock-down conflicts with her Foster-appointed phone-conference time, and now this. *Well, Sara, you're definitely batting a thousand.*

"All I want to know is how much longer before we're ready

to go on this?" Fontaine held up a hand. "That's all I want to know, Carl." Fontaine swiveled around, saw her, and his face blanched white.

Clearly he hadn't realized he was no longer alone. Trying to diffuse the tension, and his temper, Sara smiled.

He didn't smile back. "I'll, um, call back later." Glaring at her, he slammed down the receiver. "Who are you, and just how did you get in here?"

"Dr. Sara West," she said, knowing his secretary was in for one major ass-chewing as soon as Sara left. "I was escorted." That was about as abstract as she dared to get.

"Dr. West." He extended a hand over his desk. "You're to do a little PTSD research, I understand."

Sara nodded. "Yes, that's right."

"Sir," he corrected her with a tight smile. "You're a doctor, but you're also a major in the United States Air Force and I'm a colonel—your superior officer. Don't let the lack of uniforms here deceive you. This is first and foremost a military facility." He blinked and softened his tone. "I realize your presence at this facility is merely a Department of Defense convenience, but Braxton and its patients will always be my responsibility. During your stay, I would appreciate your acting as a positive role model for others. Discipline is vital to performance, and performance is vital to our patients."

Perfect. Another Foster-like, hard-core military man with an attitude. But Fontaine was right. Technically, she worked directly for the DoD and Fontaine had no say about her coming here. If he had, would he have admitted her? "Yes, sir."

"My orders are to give you a free hand with the PTSD patients and their therapies. I've agreed to that, but with reluctance." He dropped his gaze. "You might as well know that I opposed this project and your research here."

Now why didn't that surprise her? His attitude certainly explained her frosty reception. Obviously, the man carried rank and influence inside Braxton that spilled over to its employees. "Any particular reason, Doctor?"

"It's my job to protect Braxton and its patients. Frankly,

your unorthodox methods create serious reservations about your techniques."

Hard-core military and closed-minded. Realistically speaking, insurmountable obstacles. As a pioneer, she'd sadly encountered closed minds often. If not for her family and that operative, Sara would march right out of here and risk Foster pulling his worst. "If you were reluctant and opposed, then why am I here, sir?"

His tapping fingers stilled and he flattened them on the desk. "Because you have enjoyed some success and the DoD members involved in the decision-making process felt differently."

Her eighty-percent success rate beat the socks off any other doctor's, and they both knew it. But Sara didn't need an enemy here, especially not the facility director, so she kept her comments to herself, and again silently cursed Foster. If she didn't know how desperately he needed for her to succeed, she would swear he had deliberately caused her complications. "The patients' interests are my utmost concern, I assure you."

"Thank you." Another tight smile that didn't quite touch his eyes. "I expect to be consulted and updated on all matters pertaining to this facility and/or its patients." Fontaine tucked his chin to his chest. "You're a short-term guest here. Please remember that and conduct yourself accordingly."

"Yes, sir." Sara glanced at the awards on the wall. Bronze star. Meritorious service. Purple heart. Now, that one she recognized. Many of her patients had earned that award. So Fontaine had risked it all for someone else? Surprising act for an egomaniac. Obviously, she'd misjudged him. Could she really blame the man for resenting her being shoved down his throat and for wanting to protect the patients? If unprotective, he'd be a sorry director.

"The head nurse, Shank—Captain Maude Shepshank—has your charts." He rubbed at his jaw. "I understand you only work with five patients at a time."

"That's correct."

"Why so few?"

Sara bristled against the implication that she was incompetent to take on a typical workload. *Give him resentment and you give him power. Do you want to give him power?* Deciding she definitely did not, and that he could have inadvertently, not intentionally, stumbled onto one of her hot buttons, she smiled. "Intense therapy is more effective."

"Very well, Dr. West." He nodded toward the door. "My secretary will take you to Shank."

"Thank you, sir." Bitterness laced her words. She buried it beneath a forced smile and asked an inane question to prove she hadn't been intimidated by his tactics. "May I ask whose airplane is in the employees' parking lot?"

"Shank's. She lives on the premises. Piloting the plane is her hobby."

Sara let her gaze sweep along the wall back to him. "Must be difficult, taking off and landing without an airstrip. The road is full of potholes." Hopefully, he would be honest and tell her there was one. It was a small test, but a telling one.

Fontaine's expression hardened. "Please focus your interest on your patients and not on members of my staff, Dr. West. They sincerely need it."

Sara wanted to blister his ears, but his expression and body language warned her that he felt threatened. To reassure him, she smiled, though it took more effort than the last one. His skepticism was typical, if irksome. Instinctively, she didn't like the man, but then she didn't have to like him. Every human being was a work-in-progress, and Fontaine just needed more work and progress than most. Yet she did need to keep him out of her way and off her back long enough to find out the truth about David and to rescue Fontaine's operative. And under the bluster, she sensed his fear that she would harm the patients. That went a long way to redeem him in her book. "It was only curiosity, sir. Seeing an airplane in a parking lot full of cars is unusual. I found it amusing. That's all."

"As I said, please focus on your patients." He stretched to buzz his secretary on the intercom. "Martha?"

"Yes, sir, Dr. Fontaine?"

Wary, he stared up at Sara. "Major West is ready to depart."

"Yes, sir."

Seconds later, the door popped open, and the secretary who had ushered Sara in, ushered her out, wearing an expression as stony as Fontaine's. "This way, Major."

Her stomach fluttering, Sara saluted Fontaine and then followed Martha, feeling more like an unwelcome prisoner at Braxton than a physician recruited to heal and rescue.

Martha escorted Sara to the second-floor nurse's station. It carried the pungent, sickly smell common to hospital wards, but rather than bothering Sara, as it typically did, it comforted her. Yet the deserted ward was different, too. Eerily quiet.

Behind a curved white desk sat a short, solidly built woman of about fifty-four, wearing a blue-flowered lab coat. Her name badge dangling from the tip of her left collar, she dragged a hand through her short-cropped red hair, snagged a clipboard, and muttered something inaudible under her breath. Captain's bars rested near the points of her collar, and laugh and worry lines creased her face.

With a curt nod, Martha turned back toward the elevator. Sara walked on to the nurse's station. "Shank?"

She looked up and smiled. The skin under her eyes crinkled. "Dr. West?"

"Yes." Finally, a friendly face. Sara extended an enthusiastic hand over the tall desk, her sleeve brushing against a short stack of files.

Shank stood up, firmly shook Sara's hand. "Welcome to the facility."

"Thank you." The simple words were heartfelt. Until now, her reception at Braxton had been frigid.

Shank motioned to a young woman sitting at the computer terminal whose expression was as sour as her lime-green slacks and sweater. "This is our ward clerk, Beth."

Expression aside, the twentyish woman had beautiful amber eyes. Cat eyes, Sara's mother would have called them. Deceptive eyes. "Hello, Beth."

"Hello." Beth nodded, as cool as everyone else Sara had met so far, except for Shank, then returned to work—without looking Sara in the eye.

Picking up on the icy reception, Shank grunted and grabbed the stack of files from the desk's ledge. "Let me give you the nickel tour."

Relieved to get away from the tension, Sara followed Shank away from the desk. "We've got four floors," Shank said. "You'll only need to go to three of them. This one is where all the PTSD patients are housed. The lab, X ray, and the like are in the basement, and of course, the last floor you'll need is the first floor. Administration's down there and it's the only way in or out of the facility."

They passed two men in the hall. Both were dressed in white slacks and shirts with rank sewn to their sleeves. One glanced at Sara. She smiled and he looked away. This avoidance wasn't her imagination, and it hadn't been directed against Reaston. For whatever reason, she was its target.

"Getting the cold shoulder, I see." Shank hitched the files on her hip.

Sara liked her, and grinned. "I could ask if it was something I said, but the chill set in before I opened my mouth."

"Yeah, I suppose it did." Shank dropped her voice, looked around to make sure the only person currently in the hallway—a vacant-eyed man dressed in a plaid robe and shower slippers—was out of hearing range. "It's envy. Flat out. Dr. Fontaine is revered and he's been wanting research money badly. They cut his budget to the bone and then hacked at it some more. When he heard you were coming in for a DoD-funded, short-term research project, he went through the roof."

"Ouch." Sara winced. No wonder he was ticked. In his eyes, she'd gotten his money. Considering that, he'd been reasonably civil.

A physical therapist rounded the corner, assisting a man in a walker. Shank dipped into her professional role. "We have two hundred twenty-seven patients in the facility. At any given time, four hundred employees are on duty or on call and accessible with a five-minute response time. Dr. Fontaine insists on efficiency."

During the fifteen-minute tour, Sara noted oddities. Well, oddities when compared to what she was accustomed to seeing

in an in-patient setting. There were no bulletin boards, no no-
tices of social activities. And in the family-housing block,
viewed from the west windows, no signs of a playground or
any children. Tempted to ask why, she restrained herself. The
reason could be something she was supposed to know.

On the walk to Sara's office, Shank glanced pointedly up
at the cameras, then down the hall. Evidently being overheard
could create challenges here.

She straightened Sara's name badge and spoke softly.
"Would you like a word of advice?"

"Anything that would help would be appreciated. I'm not
into tension and stress, and both seem a little on the abundant
side around here."

Shank grunted her agreement, and again straightened Sara's
name badge. "Fabulous Fontaine isn't reasonable. His fury is
legend. Don't antagonize him. He's got all the clout at Braxton, and it doesn't stop at the front gate."

"Powerful friends in powerful places?"

"You could say that." Shank walked around the corner and
then stopped beside Sara, looked at her name badge, frowned,
and then straightened it yet again. "I say he's a bastard when
ticked. You've got one strike against you already, getting his
research money. I wouldn't push him."

Checking to see what was snagging the darn thing, Sara
looked down. The badge seemed fine to her and, though not
sure what to make of the warning, Sara appreciated it.
"Thanks."

"No problem. It helps to have someone lay out the land. I
didn't get that when I took the job here. Learning the ropes
without a guide, you take some hits. I didn't care for the feeling, so I'm here if you need me."

"I'm grateful."

"Sure." Shank passed the stack of five files. "These are your
patient charts. Come on. Last stop on the tour. Your office."
She took off down the hallway at a good clip, stopping outside
the third door on the right from the nurse's station.

"Here it is." She unlocked the door and then passed Sara
the key. "Personally, I'd have given you the office across the

hall. It's empty and you can turn around in it without knocking your knees against the furniture. But I didn't get to choose."

"Dr. Fontaine?" Sara speculated.

Shank nodded. " 'Fraid so."

Sara withheld a sigh. He was going to make life difficult for her.

Only as difficult as you let him, she coached herself. *You choose.*

"Clever and intuitive, too." Shank smiled and stepped aside. "I like that combination in my docs." She nodded at the office. "After you've done your chart reviews, give me a yell at the station and I'll take you to meet your patients."

"Thanks." Sara stepped into the cubbyhole. Prisoners got bigger cells. An old metal desk cramped the space. She'd play hell being able to squeeze in a trash can much less a file cabinet. Not that she'd risk using one here anyway. It didn't take a rocket scientist or a shrink to grasp that the people running this place were control freaks. The office did have a window that overlooked the parking lot, though the metal bars covering it blocked a lot of the view and most of the natural light. Oh, yes. Fontaine definitely was going to be a major pain—unless she could turn him around.

"Oh," Shank added. "I forgot. Refreshments are in the kitchen, just behind the station. We keep sodas, coffee, and popcorn. There's a fridge and a microwave. Meals are at seven hundred, noon, and seventeen hundred. There's no dining room in the facility. The brass discourages interaction between the patients."

Before catching herself, Sara reacted. "You're kidding."

"Sorry. Serious as a code blue."

"Typical military," Sara muttered. Isolation at Braxton wasn't bad enough? They had to isolate the patients from each other, too?

"It's necessary." Shank lifted her brows. "For security reasons."

Sara thought about that. The men all had secrets, but they didn't necessarily know each other's secrets. Isolating them protected them from being vulnerable to those wanting to know what each of them knew. The rule had been implemented to minimize national security risks, but also for the men's personal safety. "I should have considered that before mouthing off." Shame stung her. "I'm sorry."

Letting her off the hook, Shank shifted topics. "I can arrange for your tray to be brought to your office or to your quarters."

Still thinking about the isolation, Sara blurted out her confusion. "My quarters?"

A strange look crossed Shank's face. She glanced around, saw no one, and then motioned Sara deeper into her office. "I think we'd better have a little talk."

Sara swallowed hard. The affable Shank suddenly seemed threatening. Her expression chilled and her eyes turned as frigid as Foster's. "About what?"

"Get inside."

Sara stepped back until her thighs pressed against the desk. Shank shut the door behind her and snagged Sara's badge, cupping it in her hand.

"Why did you do that?" She nodded toward the badge.

"It's crooked. I'm going to bend the clip just as soon as we get something settled."

"What?"

"Your quarters are your apartment." Shank folded her arms akimbo. "I want a straight answer, and I want it now. Why doesn't a major in the Air Force, who gets an allowance for quarters on her paycheck twice each and every month, know what the hell quarters are?"

The chair wasn't here.

It never had been here. It had been at the other place.

Images flashed through his mind, clicking off like a camera's shutter. Images of exposed wires, a metal roof, and blinding white light. Images of the chair, and of the rage.

Lying on the padded floor, he squeezed his eyes shut, rocked his head from side to side, trying to slot his scattered thoughts. The images were coming so fast. *Slow down. Slow down, but don't stop.* He'd never before gotten such strong glimpses of that place. *I can't lose you.* The images were his only clues to his past.

Except for the rage.

He always remembered the rage. Vividly. The enemy had done something to him there. His fingers had been numb. They'd strapped his arms down—and his throat. He'd gagged, and he hadn't been able to breathe. They'd led him to the chair—he'd tripped over his shoestrings, and . . . and . . . and— *What?*

He concentrated, focused intently, but couldn't remember. *Don't push too hard. The rage will come.*

He forced himself to relax. He hated the rage. Hated and feared it because he couldn't control it. But if he was patient and pushed just a little, then his answers would come. He could do that. He could be patient. He clenched his jaw, determined. He had to be patient.

Wheels clacked against the tile out in the hallway, and he smelled chicken. It was time to eat again. Was it lunch or dinner? Day or night?

He looked to the stark-white wall and imagined a window there. God, but what he would give to see the sun. Just once more, to see the sun.

Had there been sun at the other place? Why had he gone there? There had to have been a reason. Just as there had to be a reason why he couldn't remember his name or what had happened there.

They made you forget. The enemy made you forget.

He rubbed at his temple, set his jaw. He was patient. He would remember. And when he did . . .

Don't push! Don't push. The rage will come.

He rolled over onto his side and stared at the little Plexiglas window in the door. He couldn't look up at the corner. They watched him from the camera there. They were always watching him. Always waiting for him to rest so they could attack him again. He wouldn't rest. Wouldn't look. A Shadow Watcher would never look.

Shadow Watcher?

*   *   *

Shank leaned back against Sara's office door and folded her arms over her ample chest. "Well, aren't you going to answer me?"

Sara's insides churned. "I can't."

"Why not?"

What did she say? What did she keep to herself? She'd known she wasn't ready for this, damn it. But she couldn't afford to fail. "I just . . . can't."

Shank pursed her lips, stuffed a hand in her lab coat pocket. "I've been warned that you don't like the military much."

"I haven't been here long enough for you to be warned about anything."

"Braxton isn't your typical facility, Doc. You'll see what I mean soon enough." Shank straightened, pulling away from the wall. "So if you don't like the military much, then why are you in it?"

Sara didn't answer. She couldn't answer. Not in a way Shank would consider acceptable, and she was Sara's one ally. She didn't want to alienate her.

"My guess is you're not at liberty to discuss that. So I'm going to make this easy on you, Doc. I can help you here, or I can break you. I know you're legit because I checked you out myself. You've got a good reputation and, they say, a good heart. So what I want to know is, are you against the system, or against the men in the system?"

"Excuse me?"

"If you're against the system itself, that's fine. Hell, everyone thinks it needs serious work." Shank's eyes glittered. "But if you're here to do anything but help the men in the system, then that's not fine, and I'll have to stop you."

Jammed, Sara couldn't defend or redeem herself. Her credibility was shot. Still, she couldn't admit the truth. She didn't dare to admit the truth; too many others would pay the price for her honesty. "Shank, listen." Sara borrowed a phrase from Foster, hoping to make her point. "This is a . . . delicate situation."

"I figured out that much on my own." Her eyes glinted. "Now, answer my damn question."

"I'm not in a position to answer questions without hurting others. I can't do that." She forced conviction and strength into her voice. "I won't do that." She clenched her hands and her nails dug into her palms. "It's true, I'm not enamored with the system but, I swear, I would never do anything to harm these men."

Worrying her lower lip with her teeth, Shank stared at Sara for a lifelong moment. "Okay, then. I figure you've got your reasons, and I'll trust them and you—for now. But you'd better get sharp on military details or you're going to trip up and be found out. Fabulous Fontaine won't be nearly as trusting, and neither will the unfriendlies. Only God knows what they'd do to you. But you can bet flat out it'd make Leavenworth look like a cake walk at a Sunday social."

The mention of the infamous federal prison had Sara's legs wobbling. She leaned back against the desk. "Who are the unfriendlies?"

"Fontaine's allies."

Terrific. Factions within Braxton to contend with, too. "I'd appreciate your help with the military details."

"No problem. Just don't make me sorry I trusted you, Sara. And, yes, that is a warning *and* a threat." Shank clasped the doorknob. Her knuckles went white. "For the record, whatever idiot tossed you to the lions unprepared deserves a swift kick in the backside."

"I couldn't agree more. But I don't think there was a lot of choice in the matter." The strap to her duffel slid off her shoulder. She hiked it back up. "And as much as I'd enjoy delivering that swift kick, I've got a lot more important things to do right now."

Clearly still gauging her, Shank tilted her head. "Such as?"

"Trying to get these men healthy." Sara let the truth burn in her eyes. "And to keep them alive."

A satisfied gleam lit in Shank's eyes. She was protective of her patients, but her reaction proved their well-being rated as more than just professional concern. Her caring rested closer to the bone. Closer to the heart.

"So Martha didn't take you by your quarters before bringing you to the floor?"

Relieved by the topic shift, Sara breathed easier. For now, Shank was on her side. "No, we came straight up here from Fontaine's office."

"Her nose is out of joint." Shank twisted her lips to cover a sigh. "Can't blame her, though. When Fontaine gets on the warpath, she has to put up with more from him than anyone else."

"I'll keep that in mind and think kindlier thoughts about her."

"Don't bother." Shank grunted. "She'll worm her own way into your heart and irritate you to death."

Sara expected Martha would. Blunt and frank, Shank restored Sara's equilibrium, which had been off-kilter since arriving here. So much was different at Braxton, and slipping up so quickly and getting caught by Shank hadn't done Sara's self-confidence any good. She was a fish out of water, and floundering. "Is anyone around here normal?"

"Yeah." Shank grinned, the devil dancing in her eyes. "Me."

"Thank God." Sara laughed. "So where are my quarters?"

"On the first floor. Martha will be up with the keys, I suppose. She guards all keys around here like they're pure gold." Shank finger-swiped the desktop, running a dust-check, and set Sara's badge on its edge. "So, do you want your meals here or in your quarters?"

"Here's fine." Sara dumped her duffel bag on the chair. Too little floor space to put it anywhere else without tripping over it. "Thanks for everything." Sara looked up, but Shank was gone.

Shrugging out of her jacket, Sara draped it over the back of the brown swivel chair, slid the duffel bag to the floor, and then sat down with a sigh. The chair squeaked and a seat spring poked through the worn nylon and stuck her in the backside.

"Great. Just great." She should have just murdered Foster, called this done, and spared herself and her esteem a lot of anxiety. Grumbling, she flipped open the first file—Patient ADR-17.

Two hours later, after reading and making notes on her five patients' case histories and a brief, chilly visit from Martha, Sara headed toward the nurse's station. Shank was returning a metal cart to the medication room. Not wanting to bother her, Sara dropped a stack of orders on the desk, which included a list of patient names, and then walked on down the hall toward the patients' rooms. Maybe anonymity was in the best interests of national security, but it wasn't in the best interests of the patients, so she'd studied their files and assigned them fictitious names. As solutions went, this compromise wasn't great, but it beat the socks off calling these men by numbers—and she'd insist that they be called by those names. Unfortunately, she innately knew she would have to insist.

She straightened the white lab coat Martha had brought up along with the keys. Like with the pass, Sara had been instructed to wear the lab coat at all times when on the premises. Why, she had no idea. "Dr. Fontaine's rules," Martha had said. Sara supposed the coat could help people differentiate between staff and patients, and she also supposed she would encounter plenty more of Fontaine's rules and she'd like them about as much as she liked Fontaine's fabled fury.

She checked to make sure her pass was clipped to her collar, and then scanned her patient list. Four of the five assigned to her were on the second floor in regular rooms. She checked for the first patient's room number. ADR-17, now Michael, was in 229.

Michael, she recalled from his chart, had been exposed to an orphanage bombing overseas. The experience severely challenged him, as he had just returned from a mission wherein two of his buddies had stepped on abandoned but live land mines. According to the notes in his chart, Michael was "not coping well" with the graphic deaths. Exactly how that "not coping well" had manifested in him had not been noted.

Never in her career as a psychiatrist had Sara seen such

sorry charting. If not for Shank's notes, Sara would be clueless on the condition of all of her patients.

She paused outside Michael's door, and then looked inside. Empty.

The next patient was ADR-22, the bedridden and vegetative man she'd named Fred. No inciting incident or criteria for the PTSD diagnosis had been noted in his chart. She tapped lightly and then opened the door to Room 222. Also empty.

The third patient, ADR-36, an athletic blond she called Ray, suffered episodes of extreme confusion. For the most part, it appeared Dr. Fontaine had done little more than keep Ray sedated—often with the maximum dosage possible without causing a drug-induced coma. Ray, not surprisingly, was asleep. Sara tried, but even shaking his shoulder didn't rouse him.

That worried her. He was a noninsulin-dependent diabetic. Just to make sure this was sedative and not a diabetic coma, she did a finger stick and ran an Accu-check on his sugar. She stuck the testing strip into the machine's slot and waited for the readout.

Forty-nine. *Forty-nine?* Sara reached over him and pushed the nurse's call button. "Shank, it's me, Dr. West."

"Yeah, Doc?"

"Get some grape juice. Two packets of sugar in it. Ray's room. STAT."

Sara clasped Ray's shoulders, stroked his face, clammy. So clammy. He roused slightly. Grateful for it, she heard a noise and looked toward the door.

Shank hustled in, thrusting the sugared grape juice at Sara. "I brought D-50, too—just in case."

An intense dose of sugar to be injected through an IV. Sara hoped it didn't come to that. She cradled Ray's head in her arms and poured the grape juice down his throat. "Drink it, Ray. It's really important."

He gurgled and nodded. Most importantly, he swallowed.

Minutes passed. She monitored and saw him coming around. "Shank, get him a turkey sandwich up here, okay?"

The juice would get his blood sugar up, but it wouldn't keep it up. He needed protein to get stable.

"Right away." Shank hit the call button. When a man answered, she clipped off the order. "Turkey sandwich. Room 226. Yesterday."

"Yes, ma'am, Captain."

Sara looked over Ray at Shank. The patient seemed worried. To convince him that she wasn't, she asked Shank, "Are you up for promotion soon?"

"In about a year." Shank picked up on Sara's intention and ran with it. "I got my nursing degree and filled all the squares, so I should make it, but with all the cutbacks and base closures, who knows? These days, it's pretty much a crapshoot." She frowned down at Ray, who was definitely cognizant. "I'll be out in the hall."

She had something to tell Sara. From the look in Shank's eye, something important. "Fine." Sara nodded, turned her attention to Ray, talked with him for a few minutes, and then rechecked his sugar level. One-twenty. Fine.

When the orderly returned with the sandwich, Sara smiled at Ray. "I'll be back a little later on. Eat every bite of that, okay?" She nodded at the orderly. "Will you see to it?"

He nodded, bobbing his glasses. "Yes, ma'am."

Sara walked out of the room, closed the door behind her, and saw Shank, leaning back against the wall.

Anger glittered in her eyes, and she ground her teeth. "Fontaine has him on 70/30."

"I figured that out." And being a noninsulin-dependent diabetic, being on the time-released insulin had made Ray crash. He could have died. "The question is, why would Fontaine prescribe 70/30, when Ray's diabetes has been well-controlled with just Diabeta?"

Worry joined the anger in Shank's expression and both carried over in her voice. "I don't know."

"Has Ray been on a feeding tube?" Often, diabetics were given tube feedings containing sugar and the 70/30 medication was necessary to control the patient's sugar level.

"No, he hasn't," Shank said. "There's no reason for this.

But Fontaine wrote the order and William gave Ray the shot."

"William?"

"My night-shift counterpart. Strong, strong Fontaine ally."

"Cancel the damn thing." Sara couldn't figure it. Fontaine had to know what giving Ray the 70/30 would do to him. If she hadn't recalled he was a diabetic and treated him, he could have died. "Monitor him closely, Shank. I want him stable as soon as possible. If his sugar falls either side of a 70–140 range, I want to know it immediately."

"You've got it, Doc."

"And no one gives orders on my patients but me." Sara would be damned if she'd accept responsibility for the welfare of her patients with the director doing his best to kill one of them. "See to it that the rest of the staff gets the message." She borrowed the expression from Sergeant Bush that had filled her with the dread of authority. "No exceptions."

"Yes, ma'am." Shank rubbed at her temple. "Would that include Dr. Fontaine?"

"Everyone short of God," Sara insisted, her voice hinting at a yell.

"You've got it." A relieved smile twitched Shank's lips. "Flat out."

Sara stood shaking with fury, barking at the woman, and Shank smiles at her? What was wrong with this picture?

Sara blinked, then blinked again, and the reason hit her. Shank was relieved. By intimating Sara would go toe-to-toe with anyone "short of God," including Fabulous Fontaine, she had proven her intention to protect the men.

Shank went back into the room to check on Ray. Sara continued on her rounds, feeling a little more confident now that Ray's crisis had been successfully handled and she'd proven herself to her sole ally.

Her fourth patient, ADR-39, now Lou, sat in a chair beside his bed. Sara entered his room and spoke to him, but gained no response. She checked his reflexes. Lou didn't so much as blink. Heart fine, lungs clear. Pupils normal and reactive. Yet nothing. Everything she observed coincided with Fontaine's diagnosis of total withdrawal.

Lou's inciting incident had been wicked. He'd needed critical counseling immediately, but he hadn't gotten it. Under cover, he had infiltrated a hostile terrorist group and had been exposed and tortured. His release, Sara gathered from subsequent nurse's notes, had been part of a diplomatic-exchange solution that wasn't termed as such, as the government of the United States takes the official stance of not negotiating with terrorists. She supposed some latitude on that policy was warranted when the hostage had Top Secret information running around in his head.

On leaving Lou's room, she checked her list. Her fifth patient, ADR-30, whom she'd tagged Joe, was housed in the Isolation wing. For what reason, only he and Dr. Fontaine knew. Not a word as to why Joe required isolation had been charted.

Remembering those "moments of lucidity" Foster had mentioned, and combining them with the isolation, Sara guessed that Joe could be Foster's operative. She made her way over to the Isolation wing, paused at the heavy steel door separating it from the rest of the second floor, and then tapped the wall buzzer.

An intercom on the wall activated, and a man answered. "Isolation."

"This is Dr. West. I'd like to see my patient."

"Yes, ma'am, Major."

Major. The facility's gossip grapevine had been buzzing. She would never remember to use ranks or any of the other military jargon. Why did it matter in here, anyway? It was just more unnecessary red tape, like the million and one acronyms she'd noted over the years. The military absolutely loved acronyms.

The door alarm buzzed, and she walked through. The walls were white. No paintings, or even wallpaper, relieved the starkness. Fluorescent lamps recessed in the ceiling glared harsh and unforgiving light down on the spotless white-tile floor. Doors lined both sides of the hall. Not seeing anyone, she walked on down the corridor. When it made a bend, she saw a replica of the other second-floor nurses' station, though this one was protected by ceiling-to-floor Plexiglas barriers. Why, Sara couldn't imagine. A second set of alarmed doors separated nurses from patients.

A man about thirty with a blond crewcut and three stripes sewn to his sleeve sat at the desk before a row of room monitors, reading a novel. "Hi, Major."

"Hi." She glanced at his name tag above his shirt pocket. KOLOSKI. Sara nodded, letting her gaze drift over the monitors. Apparently each room was a camera room. "I'd like to see ADR-30, please."

"Second door on your left." He nodded. "I'll buzz you through."

"Thanks." Sara turned, then paused, and looked back at him. "From now on, I'd appreciate it if you'd call him Joe."

Koloski dropped his book. "Whatever for?"

She'd suffered one too many indignities today, and the urge to blister Koloski's ears hit Sara hard. Yet she had enough problems, she really didn't need another enemy, and he hadn't caused her any trouble. He'd actually, by God, looked her in the eye—a rare treat around here. And it wasn't his fault that her patience was shot. Biting back the reprimand, she opted to explain. "We'll call him *Joe* because he's a human being. Because he's lost too much already, and he shouldn't lose even more. And because anonymity isn't conducive to forming attachments, and attachments are essential for healing."

Koloski looked at her as if she'd lost her mind. Explaining, it appeared, had been a wrong move. Using her clout. That would have been the military way. Its members were huge on clout. Responding innately to it had been drilled into them since induction. Koloski was discomfited because she'd acted out of character—for a major. Maybe she could still pull her fanny out of the flames. "And because I'm a major, and I said so."

"Yes sir, ma'am." He looked relieved.

Well, she'd gotten lucky. Finally. "Thank you, Koloski." She nodded, then walked to the door outside Joe's room and waited for the buzzer. When it sounded, she stepped through.

Joe was on his feet but stooped and curled into a ball in

the corner of a padded room as white as everything else in the Isolation wing. No window. One door. He was a large man; thirty-three, according to his records. His black hair sheened glossy in the glaring light, and he had his face buried against his chest. Mumbling incoherently, he was clearly disoriented and in emotional distress.

He was also straitjacketed.

The door slammed closed behind her.

Hyperalert, Joe jerked up, glared at her. She looked into his angry eyes and swallowed a gasp. He was *the* one. Her other half. She recognized him just as her mother had recognized her father, and Brenda, David.

Rebelling against her certainty, she stared at him speechless, stunned, and unable to move. He was her patient, for God's sake. He *couldn't* be the one. She had to be mistaken.

He maneuvered and the straitjacket came off. He slung it to the floor and sprang to his feet, his face a mask of outrage. "No!" He ran toward her. *"Noooo!"*

Before Sara knew what happened, she lay flat on her back on the padded floor and Joe straddled her stomach, choking the life out of her and screaming in agony, "I wept! I . . . wept!"

Her head swam. Spots formed before her eyes. She tried to get him to loosen his grip, but even all she'd learned in self-defense training couldn't knock him off-balance. The man's physical strength was overpowering. He seemed two steps ahead of her every move to defend and disarm him. *Oh, God.*

Sara was losing consciousness. The life was draining out of her body. Her heart thrumming, her temples pounding, his image began fading into white light.

She was dying. Jesus, God. She was . . . dying!

four

☆

The door buzzed.

Shoes thudded against the floor pads, and Shank, Koloski, and two other male orderlies rushed into the Isolation Room. Surrounding Sara, they pried Joe's fingers from her neck, loosening his chokehold. The orderlies lifted Joe off her and carried him to the far side of the room.

When the first gasp brought in oxygen, Sara felt a horrible blend of gratitude and fury, of shock and relief and fear. Limp on the floor, she clasped her neck, rolled to her side, and gulped huge gasps of air into her starving lungs. *You're not going to die. You're not going to die.* The words raced through her mind over and over again. A little more time, a little more air, and she'd be able to believe them.

Shank dropped to her knees on the floor beside Sara. "Are you all right?"

"Yes," Sara answered by rote in a rasped whisper. Her throat ached and burned and her heart was about to rocket right out of her chest. "I'm fine now." Weak and winded, she held on to Shank and struggled to her feet, then smoothed down her lab coat with shaky hands.

"Come with me." Shank walked out into the hall.

The orderlies put Joe's straitjacket back on him. He appeared amazingly docile now, not fighting them at all. When the orderlies finished, they exited his room, glancing at Sara as if she'd lost her mind. Glimpsing Joe huddled in the far corner of the room, she pulled the door closed.

When it clicked shut, she rested her shoulder against the wall and then collapsed back against it, ordering her breathing to steady. What had triggered the attack? He could have killed her. He could have snapped her neck like a twig. So why hadn't he? Why had he only dominated her and threatened to kill her? Let her know he was in control?

The obvious answer was that he wasn't a killer and he intensely needed to feel he was in control. That in itself wasn't uncommon. But—

"What the hell did you think you were doing?" Shank frowned at her.

Sara frowned back, clammy, her nerves still shattered, her mind reeling with questions and damn few answers. "I was checking on my patient."

Rolling her eyes back in her head, Shank perched a hand on her generous hip. "Wearing a white lab coat?"

"Yes, wearing a white lab coat." Every word uttered brought pain. Sara's frown turned to confusion. She stuffed a hand into her pocket. "When on the premises, aren't we supposed to wear them at all times?"

"What idiot told you that?" Shank's face went red and her freckles grew more pronounced. "Where did you even get the damn thing?"

The idea that she'd been suckered crept into Sara's mind and took root. But reluctant to falsely accuse anyone, she held off believing it. "Martha brought it to my office when she dropped by the keys to my quarters."

Shank clicked her tongue against the roof of her mouth. "And she said you had to wear it all the time?"

"Yes, she did." Sara rubbed at her throat. It was so tender. Scraped and raw. "I figured it was just one more of Fontaine's rules."

"Damn him." Shank fisted her hand at her side and stared off down the hallway, as if battling with her conscience and seeing far more in this than Sara could see. "I guess this is his sorry-ass idea of humor."

Finally getting a grip on her shaking, Sara straightened and shoved away from the wall. Her thoughts whirled and she had to struggle to keep up. She lifted a staying hand. God, but it hurt to talk. Her entire neck throbbed and her throat felt scalded. "Wait," she said, knowing innately what was coming but wanting it verified. "What are you talking about?"

Shank slid her a disgusted look. "You *never* wear white around the PTSD patients. *Never.* Their condition disintegrates into episodic rage every time."

None of her patients had disintegrated into episodic rage, and wearing white lab coats was her norm. "Shank, I deal exclusively with PTSD patients and I routinely wear white lab coats. I've never had a patient react violently as a result. So if it's a known fact that *these* PTSD patients react violently to white lab coats, then why did Martha—" Sara stopped dead in her tracks.

Shank pursed her lips and looked up at Sara over the frames of her glasses. "Do I really need to answer that?"

Dr. Fontaine. Well, hell. Why deny it? The man deliberately and willfully had set her up. Sara gave Shank a negative nod. Nothing more needed to be said. Fabulous Fontaine hadn't forgotten that tidbit of trivia. He resented his shoestring budget, her getting his research money, and her being in his facility.

The sick part of all this was that Sara understood his position. But deliberately putting her life in danger? He'd gone too far. The question was, what did she do about it? Did she take exception directly with him? Or did she take exception with Foster and let him have the pleasure of coming down on Fontaine like the wrath of God?

No, Foster wouldn't get directly involved. He'd dumped her here on her own. No support, and if she blew it, no knowledge.

Her first instinct was to march down to Fontaine's office and show him the real meaning of fury. But even through her anger, she couldn't deny that that would be gratifying but shortsighted. Letting her temper think for her was stupid. She had to tread easy. Lives were at stake. "You know, Shank," Sara said, "I'm developing a real attitude about that man."

"I'd say that makes you normal. But blow it off for now. Your time will come. Dirty deeds always come back to people who pull them, and they bite them on the ass at the worst possible time. It's universal law. Flat out, inescapable."

Shank patted Sara on the shoulder and led her down the hallway. "I'll get you fitted out with some flowered lab coats. Then, when you're ready, we'll take another run at"—she hesitated, scanning her memory—"Michael? Or was it Joe?"

"Joe." Sara sidestepped a scale resting against the wall. *The one.* She *had* to be mistaken. "It was Joe."

Nodding, Shank stepped around the station desk to a small room. A coded alarm was affixed to its door just below the doorknob. She pressed in four digits. Four distinct beeps sounded, and then the door opened.

Inside, shelves of supplies lined the wall. She snagged a couple of lab coats, came out and shut the door behind her, then twisted the knob to double-check the lock.

"These should make your next visit with Joe less confrontational. Though, to tell you the truth, he's never overly friendly. Actually, I'm surprised he spoke to you. He doesn't talk much to anyone." She passed the items over, including Sara's name badge. "Need something to drink to soothe that throat?"

A double shot of Grand Marnier sounded tempting. It would numb the pain. But considering how seldom she drank alcohol, it'd knock her on her butt, and she had the distinct feeling that she'd better stay firmly on her toes to avoid any more of Fontaine's land mines. "No, thanks." She clipped the badge back to her collar. It must have come off during the scuffle.

Shank examined Sara's neck. "It's gonna bruise."

"Yeah, it is. From the way it feels, I'm lucky not to be spitting up shards of cartilage." Sara frowned thoughtfully down at the lab coats. "Shank, when Joe was choking me, he kept screaming 'I wept.' Do you know what he meant by that?"

Shank deliberately avoided Sara's eyes. "Sorry, I don't."

She was lying to Sara. Not willingly; her body language proved she felt bad doing it. But she had lied. The question was, why?

Knowing she wouldn't get an answer, Sara didn't ask the

question. It just hung there between them as thick as fog. "Too bad," she said, breaking the silence. "I appreciate the save."

Regret burned in her eyes. "Any time, Doc."

Clutching the flowered lab coats, Sara went back to her office to take another look at her patients' charts. Maybe she had missed the warning about wearing white. Either way, she wanted to know for fact. If she had missed it, fine. But if it wasn't there, then she could resent Fontaine's antics guilt-free and with conviction, and she could report them to Foster with a clean conscience and a generous helping of indignant outrage.

By four o'clock, she had reviewed all of the charts a second time. Nothing in any of them warned her about the color white being an episodic-rage trigger. But, scanning Joe's file, something niggled at her. She stopped fanning the pages, went through them one by one, and figured out what. A block of Fontaine's notes had been written in peacock-blue ink. Odd. He generally used only black ink.

She skimmed through the other files. All of them had a similar block of peacock-blue notes, though the dates and times written on them varied, and the content seemed deliberately ambiguous.

They weren't authentic. Couldn't be. So what did they mean?

Unable to answer that, she pulled the pages from each of the files, walked down to the nurse's station, and copied each of the pages.

Beth spared her a sidelong glance from her seat at the computer terminal. Well, she spared Sara's waist a glance. No one except Shank, Joe, Koloski, and Fontaine looked her in the eye.

"I can copy those for you," Beth said, obviously curious.

"No problem. You're busy and I've got the time." Sara finished quickly and then returned to her office. She substituted the copies in the charts, stuffed the folded originals into an envelope, and then addressed it to Lisa. Sara didn't dare mail it from here; the envelope would never leave the facility. When she went to call Foster, then she'd mail it. Unless she missed her guess, when the time came, these notes could be her ticket out of Braxton. Her patients' tickets, too. The notes proved the facility existed, Fontaine directed it, and patients were present and treated here.

She left the office and made a sweep by her patients' rooms. Room 222 was empty, but the sheets on the bed were rumpled, and the head of the bed had been elevated whereas before it'd been flat. Odd, as ADR-22—Fred—was supposedly a vegetable. If true, not much question of salvageability there.

She spoke briefly with Michael—totally unproductive— and then with Ray, who was exhausted and mildly confused. Normal, considering the wild swing in his sugar levels. Keep him stable, and in a few days, they'd know what they were dealing with there. But she wouldn't wait to file the incident report on him being given the 70/30 insulin medication. Fontaine might be the director, and filing it might antagonize him, but regardless of consequences, it was the right thing to do. Legally, ethically, and morally.

Lou didn't acknowledge her existence. She left his room fighting a knee-buckling sense of defeat, and wondering why Foster hadn't just tagged his operative. She could answer that question, of course. *Unsalvageable.* Yet his Shadow Watcher's identity seemed obvious to her already. She might be making a hasty, premature judgment; it certainly wouldn't be the first time, or the first time she'd been wrong. But it didn't feel wrong. It felt inevitable. Which meant she had to go back to see Joe.

The prospect terrified her, professionally and personally. And it intrigued her. Maybe she was fretting over nothing. Maybe she'd been wrong and misinterpreted her instinctive reaction to him. With everything happening, her intuition could be on overload hiatus. Joe couldn't be *the* one. Mentally diminished, her patient, a man who had attempted to choke her to death—she *had* to be wrong. Yet she was wary of putting herself to the test and finding out.

Face it, Sara West. You're more afraid of that than another attack. But you've put it off as long as you can. It's time to face it.

Wishing she could ignore her conscience, and knowing she couldn't, Sara turned down the wide corridor leading to the Isolation wing. Her stomach lurched, her throat constricted. The tender skin on her neck had bruised from him choking her and the idea of subjecting herself to that violent behavior again made her queasy. She'd do it, of course, because she had to and because, after the way he'd countered her defensive and offensive tactics, she instinctively knew Joe was Foster's operative. Sure, there was a chance Foster's operative could be Michael, or maybe Ray. But the as-yet-unseen Fred and Lou were too damaged to be serious contenders. Foster knew that as well as she did. . . .

A light bulb went on inside Sara's head. Foster *did* know that as well as she did. Which meant Foster intended for her to easily and quickly detect his operative.

She couldn't confirm it, but the tactic made sense. Foster could rest assured she would be working with Joe without having to compromise security by pointedly identifying him as a Shadow Watcher. Joe was the most likely candidate. The one Foster could most rationally question whether or not he was salvageable.

Maybe she suspected Joe was the operative because he had reacted automatically to her self-defense maneuvers. Maybe because he was the only PTSD patient in Isolation. Or maybe the need she felt to pay special attention to him had nothing to do with Foster and everything to do with that damned *the one* feeling and the anguish she'd seen in the man's eyes when he'd screamed, "I wept."

She glanced over at Koloski. Talking still set her throat on fire, but she forced her words past her lips. "Keep a close eye on the monitor for me, okay?"

His brows shot up on his forehead. "You're going back in?"

Sara nodded. "I can't help the man from out here."

Frowning, Koloski looked torn between admiring her and requesting an immediate sanity evaluation. Cocky by nature, he clipped a nod, but in his eyes she noted his worry. "Yes, ma'am, Major."

She glanced at the monitor. "What's that in Joe's room?" A white cylinder of some sort.

"A trash drum. William put it in there last night as a barrier between him and ADR—er, Joe."

Brilliant move. Joe would use it as a weapon against William—successfully, judging by his attack on her. "Thanks," she said, then walked on to the main door.

The buzzer sounded. She went through, entering the wing, walked down the corridor, and then stopped in the hallway outside Joe's room. Her hands shook, her heart beat hard and fast, threatening to rupture through her chest wall, and tiny beads of sweat broke out on her skin and trickled down between her breasts. She was scared, and smart enough to admit it. Who in their right mind wouldn't be? But she was determined that this second attempt to get to know her patient would end far differently from her first. She glanced down at her lab coat. Blue flowers, black slacks and top. Not a speck of white anywhere.

The room's door buzzer sounded.

A shiver slithered up her backbone. Shaking it off, she sent up a quick prayer. *Please, please let me be wrong about him. Please!*

She took in a deep breath and then opened the door and paused at its threshold. Joe sat on the floor, leaning back against the far wall, his head lolled back and his chin thrust upward, dark with a stubbly five o'clock shadow. He was an attractive man. Strong face, fit, with broad shoulders capable of carrying a lot of weight. He didn't look at her or give any signal that he had heard her enter, but he knew she was there. She sensed it down to her bones. Just as she sensed that, regardless of challenges and ethics, she was not wrong. God help her, he was the one. "Joe?" Shutting out her personal feelings, she gripped the edge of the door and waited for him to acknowledge her.

No reaction.

Emotional numbing? Maybe. Maybe avoidance. Sara set the trash drum out in the hall, then stepped back inside. The door shut behind her, and her mouth went dry. He was straitjacketed, but he had removed one before and could again. He could lunge at her at any moment, and she feared him. After the attack, what woman or doctor in her right mind wouldn't fear him? She mentally prepared for defense and focused intently, watching for early warning signs. "Joe?"

He swiveled his gaze to her. His eyes narrowed, gleamed like steel shards caught in the sun. "Is Joe my name?"

He didn't know? There'd been nothing about amnesia in his chart. Had to be suppression, not amnesia. Maybe the white lab coat had brought back a memory that triggered the attack. Or the attack could have triggered a memory. It could have happened either way.

"I asked you a question." He stared up at her. "Is Joe my name?"

"No. No, it's not." A lucid moment! Excited, Sara swallowed hard. "I don't know your name, but I didn't want to call you by your patient number, so I named you Joe. Is that all right?"

"Would it matter?" He leaned his head back against the wall and stared at the ceiling. "Does what I want ever matter?"

"All the time, to me." Sara wanted to walk over to him, to sit down beside him, and get the lines of communication open. But she didn't dare to move. Not yet. The bond between them was too fragile and new. Joe needed time to adjust and to accept her being here, and she needed time to gauge him and to work past her fear. His chart was pitifully absent of notes. So far, she hadn't seen signs of shock or disbelief, or fear or grief—all of which were essential elements to a PTSD diagnosis. But she had noticed disorientation and the episodic rage earlier, and she was picking up on a sense of betrayal now. Betrayal trauma was prevalent in war veterans and sexually abused children, and both often experienced psychogenic amnesia to maintain attachment, which greatly enhanced their chances for survival and return to mental health. So some of the classic symptoms of PTSD were present, including maybe emotional numbing and psychogenic amnesia.

"I don't care what you call me." Bracing against the wall, Joe stood up.

Mesmerized, she stared at him. "I'm Dr. Sara West," she said, wishing her voice sounded stronger and held more authority. With the rasp, it sounded as husky as a bourbon baritone. "Do you know where you are right now?"

He looked around the stark room. "The white place." His pupils intensified to points and his face paled. "Get me out of here."

"I will as soon as I can." Sara licked her lips. He was at least six two, powerful shoulders, lean and in good condition. More evidence that he was Foster's operative—and that he could snap her neck in two seconds, if he chose to do so. Her knees went weak. "Do you remember attacking me earlier?"

He looked at her as if she should be locked up. "I don't attack women."

No recollection whatsoever, and he clearly and genuinely deemed the attack totally out of character for himself. That was good news in her book.

"I'm tired of people messing with my mind."

"I'm not messing with your mind."

He slid her a skeptical look. "If I attacked you, then why did you come back?"

Valid question. "I'm your doctor." She shrugged. "I can't help you if I don't see you."

He stared at her so hard she felt sure he was seeing just how afraid she was of him. "You don't attack women?" she asked, letting him hear her need for reassurance. In her experience, exposing her vulnerabilities often aroused an inherent desire in the patient to protect and defend her.

"No, I do not."

Even straitjacketed he maintained the military posture. That too was telling. "What do you do?"

Opening his mouth, he started to speak but stopped, clamped his jaw shut, and said nothing. Tense moments passed, and then he stiffened his shoulders and looked her straight in the eye. "I want out of here."

"Why?"

"I don't like it here. I want out." He dragged an impatient hand through his dark hair. "I want out—now."

Sara considered the risks. Some innate instinct was telling her to get him out of this room, but if she did and he turned on her again, she'd be out of luck and he could hurt himself—or someone else. She couldn't risk it. Not yet. The other patients too would be vulnerable. "I understand, Joe. As soon as it's safe, I'll get you moved."

He rolled his eyes back in his head. "That's what they all say."

She had to prove herself different. Fast. She was losing him already. "I'm not one of them. I'm a private doctor who agreed to come here short-term to work with five patients who are suffering from post-traumatic stress disorder. You're one of them. I don't like the military much, and I don't give a damn what the others did, I do things my way."

"Then why come here?"

"Because here is where the research grant is, and here is where you are." She gave him an imp's smile. "And the other four patients."

No response. But he studied her intently, gauging her.

She stepped closer, leaving about eight feet between them. Showing a growing trust, yet still close enough to make it to the door, if necessary. One thing she knew was that she couldn't go toe-to-toe with Joe in a physical altercation and win. Unusual, considering her training, but a fact. And she had the bruised neck and raw throat to prove it. "Earlier, you told me, 'I wept.' What did you mean by that?"

His expression hardened, turned as unflinching as his eyes. He let his gaze drift wall to wall, ceiling to floor. When he looked back at her, he had totally detached. "Get out."

"I need to talk with you." She stared at his back, determined not to show fear by moving toward the door. "I want to help you, Joe. I can't do that if every time I come in here, you attack me or force me to leave."

He glared at her over the slope of his shoulder, his face a contorted mask of rage. "Damn it, I told you to get out. Do it—now!"

He began shaking, head to toe, as if it were all he could do to hold himself in place. He was fighting against an urge to attack her, she realized. Fighting it, hard. "I'll be back." She motioned at the monitor for the attendant to open the door. "Koloski."

"Get me out soon." Anguish again flooded Joe's face. "Please."

It ripped at her heart. "Just as soon as I can."

He stiffened, his eyes wild. "Go!"

The door buzzed. Sara rushed through it, yanked it closed behind her. Joe stormed across the room, slammed his body against the door. Pressing his face against the cool Plexiglas window so he could see out, he pounded on the door with his fists.

Sara watched him work through his rage in awe. Stunned. Overwhelmed. And so happy she feared she might cry.

Joe had protected her. From himself.

He was attaching.

five

☆

For the next three days, Sara watched him.

Sometimes from the window leading into his room. Sometimes on the monitor. Joe pulled at her, intrigued and fascinated her, professionally and personally. That cost her sleepless nights, where her emotions and ethics collided with no resolution in sight.

While she battled her demons, so did he. On occasion, Joe won. On others, he lost ground. But always he fought an admirable fight. At times, he knew she was there. He'd watch her as closely as she watched him. At other times, he seemed unaware, and yet there was something in the tilt of his head, in the shift of his shoulder, that warned her he was aware after all and he too was observing.

It was a challenging means of building trust and forming bonds. Progress came slowly. But it was coming. Little by little, his hesitations were growing longer before shutting her out.

She leaned against the door outside his room, lectured herself to bury her personal feelings and to summon her professional and common sense, and then rolled her shoulder against the wall to look through the window. Sitting on the floor against the far wall, he slung his arms over his bent knees. His feet were bare, his pajama bottoms stretched tight across his thighs. When he lifted his head and looked right at her, her heart rate kicked up, beating faster and harder, and she sent him silent messages. *Trust me, Joe. Let me into your world so I can help you.* Her breath blew against the Plexiglas window and fanned back over her face. *You matter to me.*

Won't you trust me enough to let me help you?

He stared at her for a long moment, his gaze searching and then skeptical. He teetered there on the edge for a full minute, torn between refusing her and taking that leap of faith.

She fisted her hands against the door, either side of the window. *Come on, Joe. Do it. Take the chance and do it!*

His resolve wavered. Skepticism faded to doubt, and he frowned; a hard, grim frown that tugged down the sides of his mouth and hardened his eyes to that same flinty gray as when he'd attacked her.

Refusing to buckle, Sara stood firm, continued to hope and pray he would let her into his world.

Confusion creased his brow. He stood up, walked closer to the door, and then stopped. Sara pressed her hand against the glass, palm flat. *Please, Joe. Please!*

He hesitated, stared at her palm for a long moment, and then lifted his hand to touch the glass. *Yes, Joe. Yes. Come on. Come on.*

Mere inches away, he suddenly stopped.

No, Joe. No, don't shut me out. Panic surged through her. *Please don't shut me out. I want so much to help you.*

He blinked hard, stepped back and shrugged, shunning her. Then, he turned away.

Damn it! Disappointment rammed through her. The back of her nose tingled and her eyes burned, then blurred. *I won't give up on you. I'll never give up on you.* Sara sucked in a sharp breath and backed away from the glass.

Tomorrow, she'd try again. There was solace in knowing she would, in knowing that despite his superior physical strength, she was emotionally stronger. Her will had always been her greatest asset, and she would use every ounce of it to get through to Joe. Every single ounce.

This is becoming personal, Sara. You're failing at compartmentalizing.

The accuracy of her conscience's warning warranted a sigh. Joe was gorgeous, fascinating, and intriguing, but none of that lured her as much as knowing he was hurting and he needed her. That mattered, maybe more than it should. But what was wrong with wanting to stop someone's pain, with feeling needed?

Nothing. But not like this. Not by a patient. There's nothing clinical about this. Or professional.

Sara's stomach rumbled and roiled. Rebellion fell to virtue. This kind of involvement *was* personal *and* wrong. He might be the one, and like it or not, accept it or not, he had snagged a corner of her heart, but she couldn't stay on as his doctor. Not feeling this way. And yet she couldn't walk away or he would die.

What choices were left? She couldn't go or stay.

What *could* she do?

He lay on his side on the cloud, his knees drawn to his chest.

Doctors. He hated them all. But what had made him hate them? Why couldn't he recall? What had the enemy done to him?

Seeking clues, he summoned the images, but they refused to come. Anger and frustration churned in his stomach, tightened his chest, stirred the rage. He stood, paced, and fought the anger, silently repeating his mantra. *I'm patient. I'm not pushing too hard. I'm patient . . .*

A snapshot image of Sara flitted through his mind. It calmed him, though he didn't know why. She was a scrap of a woman with wheat-blond hair that hung straight to her chin. Maybe it was her eyes. She had remarkable green eyes that saw straight through to a man's soul and made him damn glad they did. He still couldn't figure that one out. Eyes that made a man see too much were dangerous. So why did they tempt him? Why did she?

She's a doctor and you don't hate her.

No white. No red. She wasn't like them. No, he didn't hate her.

So why make her afraid of you?

She had been afraid of him, yet she hadn't cowered or run, she'd trusted him. Didn't that prove she wasn't the enemy? The pinpoint red beam of light ricocheted off the walls of his mind. Maybe the enemy was deliberately confusing him again.

No. He clamped his jaw and gritted his teeth, shutting out doubt. Her eyes had been clear, not clouded by deceit. She couldn't be one of them. She really wanted to help him. When he had shut her out, hadn't she been about to cry?

She had been, and that made him feel like hell. He didn't let people get that close; he sensed it strongly. So why her? There must be a good reason.

She nearly cried out of gratitude because you didn't hurt her again. You bruised her throat.

Memories of him brutally attacking her flashed through his mind. He *had* choked her. Appalled, he stilled, not trusting the images. He *couldn't* have done that. He didn't attack women!

You attacked Sara.

He denied it. But the images were too sharp, too clear, too vivid. He stared at his hands in disbelief, saw his fingers clenched around her throat, and his hands began to shake. He shook all over, and a sick feeling welled up in his stomach. Guilt and shame suffused him. God forgive him, he had nearly choked her to death.

He recoiled, rebelling. Never before in his life—not even when he'd walked in and caught his ex-wife and best friend having sex—had he struck a woman, much less nearly murdered one.

Whoa, wait. Wait. He'd had a wife? A best friend who'd betrayed him?

He had. But why did he remember that and so little else? Shank had said that his memory could return in snatches.

You nearly murdered Sara with your bare hands.

Shocked to his soul, he felt his stomach muscles clamp down. Cold fear fused with the guilt and shame. What kind of man had he become? What had the enemy done to change him into this—this bastard monster?

He slammed back against the padded wall and slid down into a crouch. All of his life, he had lived by his own code of honor. He must have. What man didn't? Now, it was crumbling, disappearing—he was crumbling and disappearing— and he didn't know why. He didn't know . . . why.

You hurt her. Damn near killed her.

He had. And somewhere deep inside, he knew he'd killed before.

He stared at the little window in the door, terrified for her, of himself. Who—why—had he killed? Why had he nearly killed Sara?

She was sick with fear of you. But she's strong. She came back, and she will come again.

She *had* come back. After what he had done, that had taken guts. And she had watched him. Often. Openly from the door. He'd felt her gaze at times he hadn't been able to see her, too. God, how he'd felt it. Good and warm and strong, it stretched down, straight into his soul, and helped him fight the rage.

The enemy doesn't help, it invades. Of course she wants to help. She's not the enemy, Major. She's safe.

Major? Excitement shimmered through his limbs, down his arms to his fingertips. Was he a major, then?

He strained to recall. Pressure tore at his temples. *Okay. Okay, I'm patient. I'm not pushing too hard.* He rubbed at his left temple, pulled up the warmth he felt from Sara. No red. No white. Sara could be safe.

She is safe. You know the drill. Trust your instincts.

The drill. The drill?

Duty first. Accomplish the mission. Whatever, wherever, whenever.

Shadow Watchers. The creed! He rubbed at his jaw, his nape. Yes. Yes, he remembered it. He remembered the creed.

He rolled onto his back on the padded floor, and squeezed his eyes shut to block out the bright light that made his eyes ache, the white walls, ceiling, and floor. The creed. He was a Shadow Watcher.

But who are they? What do they do? And why does Sara want to help you?

No idea. Yet instinctively Sara seemed somehow familiar. Distantly familiar. Did she know him? Or maybe he knew her.

No. No. You never met. You knew of her.

How? Did she know why he was here? How he'd gotten here?

More importantly, where is here*? And who are you?*

Again, he didn't know. And his inability to remember terrified him as much as his attacking her. If she hadn't brought up the attack, he still wouldn't know he had done it.

He lifted his lids to half-mast and focused on a machine in the corner, near the ceiling. Dull black. An evil shudder rippled through him, and seeing a red pinpoint of light, he blinked, then blinked again. No. His mind was playing tricks on him. Not a cone-nosed machine. No red light. A camera. They were watching him. Always watching him.

The same way you watched others.

That instinctive revelation settled on his shoulders like a heavy boulder, and his stomach sank. Had he done to others what had been done to him?

No. Please, no. The possibility repulsed him. He couldn't have done this to someone else. He couldn't have—not and lived with himself.

Was that why he was here? Was he in an asylum because he couldn't live with what he'd done? People block out horrific things. Had he done things so horrific he couldn't stand to remember them and blocked them out?

No, no, no. The enemy did this to you. The enemy.

The pressure in his head erupted. Images flashed. The chair. Exposed wires. Metal roofing. Straps, cutting into his chest and throat. Him fighting for every sniff of air, unable to breathe. The bright light. White. Red.

Rage.

Betrayed.

Oh, God. Betrayed.

"I wept." He twisted and fell to the padded floor. Clammy with sweat, he curled into a tight ball and whimpered. "I . . . wept."

And then he began to scream.

Sara watched Joe on the Isolation observation monitor.

He pounded on the door. "Sara. Sara, get me out of here. Sara!"

Seeing him trudging through hell had her eyes stinging and

a lump lodged in her throat. She knew she was getting too emotional, but she couldn't distance herself. She lacked the will to even look away.

"Oh, God, Sara. Get me out." He backed away from the door, dragging his hands through his hair, then paced the floor, counting his steps.

Little by little, he regained control. When the episode ended, he dropped to his knees, exhausted, and then rolled onto his back for a moment before curling into a fetal position and beginning to whimper.

Those whimpers tore her heart right out of her chest. He was a huge man, strong and obviously dedicated and disciplined or he never would have been trusted with Top Secret information or sensitive missions with international repercussions. And he wouldn't have been sequestered at Braxton. This man had known he could hurt her, and he'd chosen not to do it. He'd chosen to protect her. He'd touched a part of her heart no other man had or could touch, and he was suffering. Knowing that, how could she distance herself from him?

Staring at his image in the monitor, she silently promised, *I can't let you out, Joe. Not yet. But I will help you, and protect you. I swear, I will.*

Her conscience tugged at her. *Stop it, Sara. This isn't healthy. You can't help him if you're too involved. It's unprofessional. What about doing the right thing? This is wrong and you know it. You've got to stop this.*

It was wrong. Human, but wrong. She gave herself a two-second lecture on the value of not becoming emotionally attached—a lecture she rendered and ignored with monotonous regularity in less offensive, less guilt-inducing situations—and followed it with another lecture to squelch her physical attraction to him. In her practice, she never before had encountered this complication. Why now, when so many had so much to lose? Why him?

A metallic noise sounded behind her. She glanced back. Shank barreled up the corridor, pushing a wheeled cart filled with medications and charts. Her heavy footsteps sounded dull on the drab gray carpet. For the first time, Sara slowed down long enough to notice it was growing threadbare. How many of the patients were feeling that way, too? Worn and frayed, threadbare and hopeless? How many of the staff?

Shank stopped beside her, just outside the station desk. "How did it go with Joe this time?"

"I'm not sure." Sara answered honestly, beginning the walk back to her office to get out of Koloski's earshot. "I'm still on distant observation."

"A good deal of it in the past few days, I hear."

"A fair amount. Building trust takes time and effort." Outside her office, Sara paused and leaned a shoulder against the door frame, smelling hot buttered popcorn. Someone at the nurse's station had put the microwave to use. "You know, when he told me to leave his room the other day, I'm certain he was fighting the urge to keep from attacking me again."

"If he protected you, then that's a first." Shank stopped the rolling cart, leaned against it, and locked the med tray closed. Looking troubled, she dropped the key into her pocket. Its long and curly red cord dangled against her hip.

"What's wrong?" Sara asked.

"Well, it doesn't make sense to me, Doc." Shank shrugged. " 'Course, I'm a nurse and not a doctor, so a lot doesn't make sense to me."

A good RN often knows a patient better than the doctor. Shank was a damn good RN, and they both knew it. "What are you talking about?"

Assuring herself she wouldn't be overheard, Shank glanced up and then down the hallway. Not another soul was in sight, but she dropped her voice to a whisper, anyway. "Joe goes berserk when he sees white. So why lock him up in Isolation where everything is white? Other patients get violent and we restrain them. We don't straitjacket and isolate them. So why isolate Joe?"

Sara thought about it a long moment. But her instinctive reaction remained the same as it had been before hearing Shank's comment. The isolation was just one more shovelful in the heap of mounting evidence that Joe belonged to Foster.

Sara crossed her arms over her chest. "Who was Joe's primary doctor before me?"

"Dr. Fontaine treated all of the PTSD patients." Shank hesitated, clearly on the verge of saying something and silently testing the wisdom of it before mentioning it. "He's good. I'm the first to admit it. But I don't understand why he's got Joe isolated in a white room."

"After Joe attacked me, you mentioned that all of the PTSD patients react to white with rage. Is that so, or were you just upset?"

Clearly thinking about it, Shank frowned. "I was upset. Him choking you scared the hell out of me. Not all of them react violently, but some, like ADR-22—"

"Fred," Sara corrected, identifying the one patient of hers she'd yet to run down and evaluate.

"Fred," Shank repeated, "doesn't. The poor man doesn't know what planet he's on, much less the color of things in his room."

"What about Michael?" Sara asked.

"Of the five, I'd say he's the least damaged. I can't say flat out how he'd react to white. So far as I know, he's never been isolated or exposed to it. He's pretty good-natured, but that's easy when you're in denial, and he's in major denial."

Sara nodded her agreement. "And Ray?"

"He has reacted like Joe at times, though not consistently. But white sheets drive him right over the edge. Only made that mistake once before I figured it out."

"Did you note it in the chart?"

"Of course."

So Shank's warnings had been removed. Fontaine's peacock-blue notes swam through Sara's mind. Obviously, he'd elected not to include the warnings in his edited version. What else had he left out?

Shank chewed on her lower lip. "You know, Doc, I'm wondering if a lot of Ray's problems aren't actually with his medications."

"That's a distinct possibility." Shank's comment niggled at something in Sara, and she let her mind drift from patient to patient, mentally reviewing their charts and comparing them with what she'd actually seen and observed.

The truth hit her like a sledge. In both the charts and the patients—with the possible exception of Joe—what she'd seen and observed were huge inconsistencies between the symptoms and behavioral patterns of PTSD patients and Braxton's PTSD patients. Huge inconsistencies.

Shank reclaimed Sara's attention. "And Lou, bless his soul, is gone. Well, his mind is gone," Shank amended. "Sad to see a thing like that happen."

It was sad. Sara hated to agree with Shank's evaluations, but she couldn't disagree, and she was more convinced than ever that Joe *had* to be Foster's operative. He could be isolated due to the outbursts of rage. But it could also be due to those worrisome-to-Foster "lucid moments." Time would tell.

"I wrote some new orders in Joe's chart," Sara said. "Will you implement them as soon as possible?"

"Sure." Shank leaned a hip against the med cart. "What are they?"

"Nothing major. I want to avoid sedation." All of her patients were too heavily sedated. She couldn't treat them if they were kept in drug-induced stupors. Had that been deliberate to keep them quiet? Or was it just easier on Fabulous Fontaine? "I'm including relaxation exercises, meditation, and hot baths in Joe's physical therapy," she told Shank. "I want music in his isolation room—Celtic music." Soft and soothing. "And I'd like his diet loaded with foods like warm turkey, cream-based soups, and baked potatoes."

Shank looked surprised, but not opposed. "Are these foods significant?"

"Indirectly. They're significant to producing the lethargy I want him to feel."

"I don't get it." Shank scratched her head. "Is this some new ideology?"

"Actually, it stems from an old tradition." Sara hiked her brows. "Think back to last Thanksgiving. How did you feel after you ate your feast?"

"Lethargic." A slow smile spread over Shank's stern face.

"You know, Doc. I think you might just be good for the PTSD patients. Especially Joe."

She'd better be. If he proved to be Foster's operative and she failed, he was dead. More accurately, he was dead, Lisa and Brenda were in deep trouble, and Sara's private-practice patients were screwed because she'd be out of a license and in deep trouble, too.

Will I be canceled?

The moment you become a risk. Yes, you will.

Sara bristled. Why hadn't she asked Foster what specifically would have him classifying her as a risk?

Maybe she hadn't asked because that was the one question she feared he would answer.

Unsalvageable.

Deep trouble? She grimaced. Steeled herself. She'd better follow the advice she had given Foster, and call a spade a spade. She'd be dead.

Shank waited.

When the elevator door closed with Sara inside it, Shank reached for the phone, depressed the secure-line button, and then dialed a number she had long since committed to memory.

A man answered on the first ring. "Foster."

Popping the top on a canned cola, she paused to tuck her pencil behind her ear, and waited until the drink stopped fizzing to take a sip. "I'm not sure this was a good idea, Colonel. Three days ago, she damn near got killed." Shank's mouth went stone-dry. Maybe Foster wanted Sara dead.

"How?"

"Patient attack. ADR-30—Joe, she calls him—choked her."

"Is she all right?"

Shank frowned into the receiver at his clinical tone. She should be used to Foster's detaching to assess damages by now, but she wasn't, and she resented it. Couldn't he bend his professional code of conduct enough to even pretend a mild concern? She straightened a stack of orders Beth needed to key into the computer when she returned from lunch. "She hasn't complained, but her throat is bruised and it has to be sore because she sounds as raspy as a smoke-inhalation victim."

"And Fontaine's reaction?"

"As expected. He's riding her hard, but she's handling him, too. She's tough. I'll give her that. But she doesn't know spit about the military. Lucky for us, she blew it with me and not one of the unfriendlies."

"She was briefed." Resenting her unspoken reprimand, Foster's tone turned crisp. "What did Fontaine do to her?"

"He caused the incident, so naturally he's been mum about acknowledging one occurred. I meant, he's riding her hard overall."

"How did he cause the attack?"

"He sent her into Isolation wearing a white lab coat. With Joe, that's a known trigger for episodes of rage." Shank had to work at it to keep her disdain from her voice. It was a luxury she couldn't afford. Traditionally, as soon as Foster detected the first trace of emotion, he quit listening.

"Interesting." Foster paused, then asked, "Does she realize the act was intentional?"

"Oh, yes, sir. She realized it right away and pegged Fontaine as the source."

"Has she confronted him, then?"

"Not yet." Shank thought about it, took a swig from the can of cola, then set it down on her desk. "She wanted to, but she held back." The can formed a wet ring on the desktop. Shank swiped at it with her hand. "I'm not sure why."

"No problem. I know why."

How could he know? "Dr. West has been a little busy, sir. Her focus has been . . . splintered."

"In what way?"

Shank dropped her gaze to the desktop, stared blindly at a chip in its white Formica, and grimaced. "Dr. Fontaine tried to kill Ray—er, ADR-36—with 70/30 insulin. If Dr. West hadn't intervened, he would have succeeded."

"Very interesting."

"I thought so, sir." Interesting and scary. Shank's hand

grew sweat-slick against the receiver. It always did, when talking to Foster. He wanted that star on his shoulder, and nothing standing between him and it would remain standing. With his power, that would scare the sandals off the Apostles, much less her.

"She's got him on the run." Foster sounded as thrilled as a deer in rut picking up on a doe's scent. "Is she playing it by the book?"

"It's too soon to say, sir." Shank grimaced at the pencil holder, tapped it with her fingertip, and withheld a threatening sigh. "So far she is, but she hasn't yet filed the incident report."

"When she does, E-mail me a copy."

What made him so certain she would file it? "Yes, sir." Shank hated to ask, but she had to know. After all, she'd warned Sara not to do anything to antagonize Fontaine. "And if she elects not to file the report?"

"She'll file the report. It's mandatory."

"But—"

"She will, Captain," Foster said sharply. "Sara West might delay and agonize over it, but eventually she'll file the incident report."

Shank licked at her dry lips. "Sir, I don't mean any disrespect, but Dr. Fontaine is already making her miserable. She's got to know if she files that report he'll only get worse."

"She knows," Foster said. "But she can't not file the report."

He sounded so certain. Shank couldn't see the reason. "May I ask why?"

"Sara West does what in her mind is the right thing."

"Always?"

"For the past five years, yes. I'd say that makes her behavior predictable."

So would Shank. "Yes, sir." She shouldn't be surprised. Actually, she should have expected he'd know precisely what Sara West would or wouldn't do. Foster left as little as possible to chance in every situation that affected his career. He always had. For that tunnel vision and single-mindedness, Shank both respected and hated him.

Foster shifted topics. "Any signs of attachment surfacing in our patient?"

Shank hesitated. "Maybe."

"Maybe is not an acceptable answer, Captain."

"Maybe," Shank insisted, not at all intimidated by Foster's icy tone. She was stuck at Braxton forever. What else could he do to her? "A few days ago, Koloski was on duty in Isolation, monitoring. He said Joe was on the verge of episodic rage and he warned Dr. West to get out of his room."

"He protected her?"

"That's the report, sir, and she's confirmed it." Shank stretched to drop an EEG report on Ray into Beth's stack. Sara West was thorough, checking to see if there was any oxygen-deprivation damage to Ray's brain due to the sugar crash. "I didn't witness this myself. But I'd say it's encouraging."

"Was this before or after ADR-30 choked her?"

"After."

"So she went back to see him again, after the attack?"

"Yes, she did." Shank grunted, thinking Foster sounded pleased with himself. As if someone he'd expected to behave or react in a particular manner hadn't disappointed him. "Colonel, may I speak freely, sir?"

"Yes, Captain."

"Sara West was damn brave, going back in there." If Foster intended to kill Sara, Shank couldn't stop him, but she could let him know he'd be wasting a valuable resource. "It took two orderlies, Koloski, and me to pull Joe off her. To tell you the truth, sir, I doubt I would have gone back—at least, not so soon."

"It's not just bravery, Captain." His tone turned crisp. "I warned you that she was sharp."

What did he mean? Shank stilled, stiffened behind the desk, and stared at the fire alarm across from her on the far wall. "Sir?"

"She's made him."

Foster thought that Sara West had identified the Shadow

Watcher? Shock streaked up Shank's backbone. "Already?"

"Already."

Remembering Sara's questions, her intense observation of Joe, and her new orders, a sinking feeling swept through Shank's chest and hollowed her stomach. She pressed a trembling hand over it. "Good grief, sir. I believe you're right."

"Now." He sighed as if satisfied. "We only have to wait to see whether or not she admits it."

And that, Shank realized, would determine if, when Joe was healed, Dr. Sara West lived or died.

six

☆

The smell of rubbing alcohol burned Sara's nostrils.

Twitching her nose, she sat down in the cubicle near the nurses' station to dictate the mandatory incident report on Ray and Fontaine and the 70/30 insulin medication.

Except for Beth, the station was deserted. Glancing at her watch, Sara grasped why. Quarter of three—shift change. Like most everyone else around here, Beth still refused to look Sara in the eye. But rather than grating at her nerves, for once, Sara appreciated the reprieve. Still, she opted to silently key in the report rather than to orally dictate it.

She adjusted the computer terminal's keyboard. As soon as her fingertips touched the keys, a sinking feeling hit her stomach and she started trembling. She stared at the blinking cursor.

You have no choice. Just do it.

And she did. But for every key stroke she typed, it seemed she had to backspace two to delete errors. Fontaine wouldn't take to the report kindly, and it didn't take a genius or a shrink to know it. The way her luck was running, she'd probably set a new standard for his legendary fury. That worried her. He would retaliate. But, how?

Whatever he did, it would be bad. She swept her damp palms down her thighs, agonizing. The friction of brushing her nubby slacks fabric felt good. Bottom line was it didn't matter what he did. She'd have to deal with it. Filing the report was mandatory, and the right thing to do.

Finally finishing it, she hit the Save key, and then forwarded a copy to Risk Management and—what the hell—a copy to Fontaine. He'd know about it momentarily, anyway. No sense giving him the illusion that she was ducking him.

After signing off the system, she noted that she had filed the report in Ray's chart, and then gathered her things. Before she could leave the desk, the phone rang.

"Second floor." Beth answered it. "One moment, please." She called out to Sara. "Dr. West, you have a call."

Dreading what was coming, Sara lifted the receiver. "Dr. West."

"Report to Dr. Fontaine's office, Major. STAT."

Martha. And her stiff tone warned that she and her boss had read the incident report, and he was not happy. That, of course, meant Martha was miserable.

"Be right there." Sara cradled the phone and headed down to the director's office, reminding herself not to antagonize him further by forgetting the "sir" stuff. Fabulous Fontaine was big on the "sir" stuff. Huge on the "sir" stuff.

When Martha ushered Sara into Fontaine's office, he glared at her until Martha retreated and shut the door. Sara imagined the woman scurrying like a rat back to her desk to tap the intercom and eavesdrop.

As if on cue, the light on the phone lit up. Fontaine was too intent on gearing up for an explosion to notice.

"Delete it, Major," he said without preamble. "Delete it, and forget it ever happened."

He had to be kidding. Sara stiffened, narrowed her eyes. He didn't appear to be kidding, but he had to be. That, or he'd lost his grip. "That's illegal, sir."

A muscle in his jaw twitched. "Not at Braxton."

Sara stared at him a long moment, giving him time to cool down and think about that remark—which they both knew was a blatant lie. But when the twitch in his jaw muscle showed no evidence of slowing down, she accepted that the man was indeed an egomaniac and he wasn't going to calm down, so she went on. "Dr. Fontaine, there is nothing personal against you in the report. If you'll notice, your name doesn't even appear. I only related the facts of the incident."

"Everyone in this facility is aware that I handled all of the

PTSD patients, Major." He fisted a hand on his desk. His knuckles knobbed. "Delete the report. That's a direct order."

Sara clamped her jaw shut to keep from snapping back a sharp retort. He deserved it, but the costs of giving it to him were too high to pay. "If I delete that report, then this could happen again. The man could have died. Someone else could die. Do you want to be responsible for that? I certainly don't."

Fontaine jumped to his feet, sending his chair spinning into the credenza behind him. It crashed with a loud thud. "I issued you a direct order, Major. I strongly advise you to follow it—immediately."

Sara stared at the man. His face was blood-red, twisted by rage, and the veins in his neck bulged. This was indeed Fontaine's legendary fury, and he'd levied every outraged morsel directly on her head. She softened her expression and her voice. "With all due respect, I can't do that, sir."

Closing the gap between them, he leaned over the desk and grated out from between his teeth, "You have no choice."

Every instinct in her body urged her to back down. But backing down was wrong. Sara locked her knees and stood firm. "Yes, sir, I do have a choice. I have an agreement with the Department of Defense on this project that gives me full authority over my patients. Ray is my patient, and I find it hard to believe that a man capable of attaining all of this"—she swept a hand toward his display of gold-framed, professional wallpaper—"would ask, or expect, me to jeopardize a patient's health or my professional integrity."

"I'm fully aware of the terms of your agreement with the DoD, Major." He lifted a hand, snagging the end of his purple tie. "And I repeat my warning that this is a direct order. Delete the son of a bitch."

Flustered, she dragged a hand over her head, shoving her hair back from her face. "For God's sake, Doctor, doesn't it bother you at all that you nearly killed a man?"

Fontaine's voice exploded, and he jabbed at the air with his index finger. "You will *not* undermine my authority at this facility."

"No, sir. I will not," she agreed. "If you'll read the report—

without your defenses engaged—you'll see that there's nothing in it that even remotely undermines your authority or your competence." And that had been damned difficult to manage. You'd think the man would be grateful. She could have crucified him.

"Lower your voice, Major, or I'll charge you with insubordination." Fontaine glared at her, openly hostile. "This isn't a debate. There will be no negotiations. You delete the report, or I deem your work unsafe to the patients. The DoD will cancel your contract."

He had screamed and pushed, and now he had threatened her. And she'd maxed. A little pushing back was not only warranted, it was long overdue. "Look, let's get down to brass tacks, Doctor." The "sir" stuff wasn't working. Maybe reminding him of his Hippocratic oath would get him to see reason. "I am not deleting that report. I'm required to file it, and we both know it. It's filed. If you want to deem my work unsafe to the DoD, fine. Feel free. But when you do, I'll be required to give a full accounting, and that accounting will require you to explain your own inefficiency in dealing with these patients."

"*My* inefficiency?" His jaw gaped and incredulity flickered through his eyes. "*What* inefficiency?"

She stared deeply into his eyes for a long moment, clenched her jaw, and then dropped her voice even lower. "You'll get to explain why you misdiagnosed these five men."

The blood drained from his face. "Excuse me?"

Having seen more colorful cadavers, Sara stiffened her back, preparing for the fallout. "Only one of these men could possibly be PTSD." She'd said it. Out loud. Oh, God, she hoped that wasn't a mistake. "I haven't yet diagnosed the others but odds are you have, even though your diagnoses aren't in the charts."

"You're wrong, Dr. West." Fontaine veiled his expression to a mask. "Each of those five men is suffering from PTSD, and that's all I have to say on the matter."

He was lying to her, and they both knew it. And he would make her pay for crossing him. Dearly. The question wasn't

if he would retaliate, but in what form. She lifted her chin.
"My report stands, sir."

"You're going to regret this, Major." His eyes glittered pure
hatred. "For a long time to come."

"I already do, sir." She let him see her sorrow and her
disgust. "If a conversation such as this one isn't worthy of
regret, then I don't know what is." She turned toward the door,
leaving Fontaine glaring at her, his anger boiling and about to
erupt.

Her hand on the doorknob, she paused and looked back
over the slope of her shoulder at him. "For the record, sir,
whatever consequences I suffer for filing a mandatory report
had better not be as blatantly overt as another incident I've
encountered at Braxton and not yet report—"

"Another incident?" he interrupted. "*What* other incident?"

"I was instructed to wear a white lab coat at all times when
on the premises, including into Isolation, and it's a known fact
to the staff that the color white stimulates episodic rage in
Braxton's PTSD patients. That information was deliberately
withheld from me, which makes it a criminal act."

"I know nothing about this."

Lying again. He really was lousy at it. His gaze darted like
Ping-Pong balls being whacked during a masters' tournament,
and he looked through her, not at her. "Of course not, sir. But
your secretary did, and she specifically informed me that wearing the coat was your rule. That act deliberately endangered
the life of one of your staff members and, as I understand it,
the facility director carries direct responsibility for the actions
of everyone under his command—including his secretary and
the physicians on his staff—even if the physician is a temporary staff member employed by a limited DoD contract. Is
my understanding accurate, sir?"

"Theoretically, yes."

"Deliberately endangering the life of a staff member carries
steep penalties. It'd be a shame to see anyone at Braxton
brought up on charges. Courts-martial are so . . . public."

He gave her a blank look. As if he'd underestimated her
and couldn't quite absorb the fact that he had.

"According to the Uniform Code of Military Justice," she added, "the persons responsible could do time in Leavenworth and lose their pensions. That would be extremely unfortunate."

His jaw went slack. Before he could bellow at her, Sara left his office and, feeling plenty angry herself, slammed the door. "Chew on that, you sorry bastard."

Martha sat at her desk, looking stunned and more than a little frightened. Her finger slid off the intercom button. In the dead-silent office, it clicked loudly.

Sara spared her a glare, then marched out of the office and down the hallway. She'd probably said too much and gone too far. The penalties for what he'd done were severe, but for what she'd done, they could be catastrophic. Fontaine couldn't kick her out of Braxton, but he could slap her with conduct unbecoming, insubordination, disrespect to a superior officer, refusing to obey a direct order, and only God knew what else he could find in the Uniform Code of Military Justice. She hadn't yet read the whole thing. But he had deserved everything he'd gotten, and then some.

Turning down a deserted corridor, she thought of Ray and muttered. How could Fontaine sleep at night? How could he meet his own eyes in the mirror? He hadn't shown so much as a speck of remorse, regret, or shame. Only pride. Ray's life or Fontaine's pride—that's what he'd been asking her to choose between protecting. And he had seemed honestly surprised that she had chosen Ray's life. In choosing between pride and a life, where was the challenge?

There wasn't any challenge, or any dilemma.

She stopped and leaned back against the wall, hoping her heart rate slowed down before her whole chest exploded. Fontaine beat all she'd ever seen. God, but she despised egomaniacs. How could he show no remorse? He'd made a life-threatening error. Didn't he place any value on Ray's life, or on anyone else's? Could he really only be concerned with his own reputation? And what fool would put such a self-centered jerk in charge of anything—much less Braxton? The whole place was one huge security risk.

That truth smacked her like an unexpected blow to the

stomach. All of Braxton *was* a security risk. With the military, exactly what did that mean?

Sequestered.

Will I be canceled?

The moment you become a risk. Yes, you will.

She stared down the empty hall, at the white walls and worn tracks in the gray carpet, and the truth settled over her like a shroud. She was in a place that didn't exist, treating patients that had been sequestered. All of Braxton *was* a risk.

And that worrisome niggle, warning that her leaving Braxton was going to be a challenge, sharpened to full-fledged fear.

Michael, Keith, Kevin, Adam.

He tested each of the names, but none struck a chord. Rolling over on the floor, he switched from crunches to push-ups. He needed to exercise more. He was getting soft, being locked up in here.

After a couple of sets, he stood up, then began running in place. He closed his eyes, visualized the sun, the fresh smell of the air after a summer shower, the tickle of the wind breezing over his heated skin. As he ran, he let his mind wander, and it wandered to Sara. He might be a damn fool, but he trusted her. She kept coming back, watching him. But she wasn't like the enemy with its camera. The enemy watched him. Sara watched over him.

A vision flitted through his mind. Him talking with a man in uniform who seemed familiar, like a friend or a well-known associate. "Sara West called again," he heard himself say. "Third time this morning."

The familiar man clicked his tongue to the roof of his mouth. "Three times?"

The paddles of a ceiling fan clopped overhead. He could see them, but not his own clothes. Was he wearing a uniform, too? "She's definitely persistent."

"She is that," the familiar man said. "I'll tell you one thing. If I ever get into a serious jam, I want her on my side, bailing me out."

He felt himself smile. "So she's finally wearing down the opposition."

"Hell, no." The familiar man denied it. "But she never forgets, and she never gives up. Sara West just keeps on coming."

The vision disappeared.

Having worked up a respectable sweat, Jarrod switched from running in place to cool-down exercises. If he could trust the vision, he hadn't known Sara West before coming here, but he had known of her. His instincts on that had been right. And whoever the familiar man was, he'd been right, too. Even threatened and nearly choked to death, Sara West didn't give up and she did just keep on coming.

The elevator door slid open.

Shank stood waiting and, gauging by her expression, the news wasn't good. "What's wrong?" Sara stepped out. "Is it Ray?"

"Ray's fine." Shank straightened Sara's name badge. "William, on the other hand, is pissed to the gills. Give him a wide berth tonight."

Sara had encountered William fairly often. The second-floor, night-shift RN was a strapping man in his late twenties with rough-hewn features, a booming voice, and a disposition as frosty as everyone else's around here. The difference with William rested in his eyes. He'd hated Sara on sight. According to Shank, he and Fontaine were staunch allies, so of course William would. At least the man wasn't a hypocrite. He made no effort to conceal his feelings, and Sara respected that, even if it made a tense environment even more intense. "What's wrong with him?"

"Fontaine deleted the order for the 70/30 insulin in Ray's chart."

"What?" Surprise streaked up Sara's spine. "He can't do that."

"He can, and did. Hold still." Shank unclipped Sara's name badge, bent something on it, and then cupped it in her hand. "I told you. Fontaine has all the clout at Braxton."

"But that makes it look as if William injected Ray with the

70/30 without a scrip." No prescription, no order. No order, and no Fontaine involvement in the incident. Sara thought she might just be sick.

"Yeah, it does." Shank nodded. "Which is why William has just been demoted to lieutenant and fined a month's pay."

"This is absurd." Sara swiped at her head with her hand. "It's outrageous."

"It's typical." Shank shrugged, snapping the clip of Sara's badge with her thumbnail. "Someone had to take the fall and it damn sure wasn't going to be Fontaine. It never is." She leaned closer, her gaze burning into Sara's. "Understand? It *never* is."

Fontaine had screwed up before. From the intensity in Shank's eyes, often. And he'd never accepted responsibility.

Maybe Foster could fix this. *Somebody* had to fix it. Even if Fontaine stopped short and required surgery to get William's nose out of his backside, William shouldn't be penalized for Fontaine's mistake.

Shank rubbed at her forehead and dropped her keys into her pocket. They jangled. "I warned you not to antagonize him, Doc."

Sara walked past two men in the hallway, tripped over the edge of the scale against the wall, and stumbled to her knees. Pain streaked up her thigh.

"You okay?"

"I'm fine." Sara slapped her hand against the rough wall for balance and hauled herself to her feet. "No, damn it, I'm not fine. I'm ticked." She rubbed at her stinging kneecap. "Right is right, and this is wrong, Shank. Another mistake like that one and we're talking about a dead patient and us notifying next of kin."

Shank's face paled.

"What? Did I say something wrong?" Sara frowned. "Don't we notify next of kin?" In a military installation, who knew how many layers of red tape had been inserted into the process?

Regret and remorse burned in the depths of Shank's eyes.

She fidgeted with her keys. Her hand wasn't steady. "No. Actually, we don't."

"Well, why not?" Sara couldn't figure it. Of all her medical duties, she found losing a patient most difficult. But notifying the family ranked a close second. She hated both with passion and conviction.

No answer.

Sara held off a sigh by the skin of her teeth. "Shank, there are two hundred twenty-seven patients in this facility. Are you trying to tell me that none of them—not one of them—has a next of kin? Because if so, I don't believe it."

Shank slid Sara a "sooner or later you'll figure it out" look that had the little hairs on her neck standing on edge. She kept forgetting that this was Braxton. Military. High-risk security. "Some of these men must have families. So if we lose one, why don't we notify them?"

Orderlies wheeled two men down the hallway on gurneys. When they passed, Shank still didn't look Sara's way, but she did answer. "I couldn't say."

The elevator bell chimed and the clanking of the gurney wheels soon faded. "I know their identities are secret," Sara whispered, "but you're telling me something special about this, aren't you? It isn't just that some cleric notifies them."

"No." The thumbnail clicking of the name-badge clip grew more rapid. "No chaplain calls on them."

"Well?"

Shank sighed and stared at the wall.

"Whatever your message is, I'm not getting it." Frustration etched Sara's tone and she clasped Shank's upper arm. "Just tell me."

Shank stared at Sara's fingers, avoiding her gaze. "Nothing to tell, Doc."

There was something to tell. There was plenty to tell. "Nothing?"

"Nothing."

That was the biggest something of a nothing Sara had ever heard in her life.

David. Shadow Watchers. Top Secret information at risk.

Butterflies swarmed in Sara's stomach. "Shank, do the families of these people know the patients are here?"

Shank looked at her then, her eyes shiny and wet and overly bright. A muscle twitched at the corner of her mouth. "Braxton doesn't receive visitors."

"Ever?" Surprise sent Sara's pulses racing.

"Ever." Shank dropped her keys back into her pocket and fingered them. They clinked together. "Considering everything, I'd say that makes the possibility of their families knowing anything highly unlikely, wouldn't you?"

Sara answered that question with one of her own. "Well, where *do* the families believe these men are?"

"Think about it." Shank swallowed hard and shoved Sara's badge into her hand. "Just . . . think about it."

Unsalvageable.

The word popped into Sara's mind and stayed. They report the men dead and then sequester them at Braxton? She shuddered, rebelling against going to the dark place her thoughts were taking her. No. No, not even the red-tape-loving military would do something that god-awful. Would it? "Shank, are you telling me—"

"I'm not telling you anything." Shank lifted her chin, defiant. "I'm just saying you might want to check it out."

Shank walked away, and Sara stared at her retreating back. *Check it out?* How did she do that?

First Foster and now Shank. They thought Sara could just snap her fingers and find a way to do any—She rolled her gaze, and it lit on the computer.

It's standard operating procedure at Braxton. On admittance, patients are assigned a number and, thereafter, they're addressed only by it.

Foster had told her about this. The patients had permanent admission records. The military definitely kept tabs on who was where—secret assignments, or not. Sara worried her lip with her teeth. Accessing those records would be a violation of the Privacy Act and probably a fistful of military regulations. She'd be fined, demoted, and whatever else Fontaine could manage to destroy her reputation and career. Yet this patient information could be a key to what happened to them and to David, and Sara needed that key to help Brenda and Lisa, Joe, and her other patients. And, damn it, their families deserved the truth, too.

She thought it over, weighed the pros and cons, the risks and potential rewards, and decided. The scales tipped heavily toward the cons, but she still had to take the risks. She couldn't *not* take the risks. Outside of Braxton, the families of 227 patients had no idea what was happening to people they loved. Inside Braxton, 227 patients were surviving without the comfort of their families.

Loving her family, craving one of her own, and imagining them in this situation stomped her Achilles' heel. Hard.

Tapping into the computer held a firm bottom line. Sara would be doing the wrong thing, but for the right reason. The families and her patients needed each other. She had to turn every stone to help them. Not because of Foster. Well, indirectly due to Foster. He'd wanted her to know this—about the records. He'd anticipated she would need the information and he'd given her the means to get it—without being overt, of course. Foster never did anything overt. But about one thing, he had been right.

At home, living her own life, she had been blissfully ignorant. She hadn't known, or even thought about, what the men in Braxton and their nonsequestered counterparts did day in and day out. But in her time here, she'd learned the realities of their sacrifices and the personal costs they paid to provide others with personal freedom. She owed them. It was that simple.

That simple, and that complex. Now, not only was she responsible for her own life and Foster's operatives, in a very real sense she was also responsible for Brenda's and Lisa's, and for the lives of these men. They'd all acted to protect her. Now, she had to protect them.

And, God help her, she wasn't sure she was up to the task.

seven

☆

Sara checked the nurse's station. *Empty.* Looked both ways down the hall. *All clear.*

She rounded the edge of the desk and sat down at the computer, eager to gain access to the records now that she had made the decision to do it. She keyed in her code and signed on to the system.

"What are you doing?" Beth appeared out of nowhere.

Sara jumped guiltily. *Think! Think!* "Just checking to see if the results on Ray's EEG are back yet."

Beth crossed her chest with her arms, crushing the front of her hunter-orange blouse. "They're not."

Damn it. Five more minutes and Sara would have had access. Being stymied wouldn't have irked her so much, but this was her third failed attempt. She glared at Beth.

Holding a canned soda in one hand and a package of cheese crackers in the other, she sighed. "If you're done, Dr. West, then I can get back to work."

Sara signed off the system and then left Beth's chair. "Don't you ever go home?"

"This is my home."

Sara rubbed at her forehead, worked at making her voice less confrontational. "I meant, to your quarters."

"Of course." Beth slid down onto her seat. "Are you complaining about the quality of my work, Doctor?"

"No." *Only about your constant presence.* Sara ground her teeth. "Just concerned that you're putting in too much overtime."

"My health is excellent," Beth said stiffly. "So are my performance ratings."

"Of course." Sara swallowed down a gallon of frustration and checked her watch. Ten P.M. had come and gone. She might as well call it a night. With food and drink, Beth intended to settle in for a while.

For appearances, Sara jotted a note in Joe's chart. He wasn't happy with the changes she had made in his care, and she wasn't happy with the amount of time she spent thinking about him.

That, she didn't note in his chart, but it worried her. He was the one, and knowing it drew the woman in her like a magnet. To the professional Dr. West, that magnetism was deplorable. She leaned a hip against the desk's edge. Actually, it was worse than deplorable. He was her patient. Her mentally diminished patient.

With Beth covertly watching her every move, Sara closed his chart and slotted it in the metal file holder with the others. Her first four days at Braxton had been long and eventful. Her throat still hurt, and so did her feet. She'd been on them more here than during her residency at Tulane. But neither came close to the emotional workout she had been suffering with Braxton's rigid protocol and restrictive conditions. Her patience was shot, and she was fed up with the staff giving her the cold shoulder about William. At least, she thought the reason was about William. At Braxton, it was damn hard to tell. But the people here hadn't thawed toward her at all. They ignored her, refused to answer friendly greetings in the hallway, and still avoided her gaze.

Privacy proving as nonexistent as free speech inside Braxton's walls only added to her frustration. It didn't matter where she went or when, someone else was always around. For all her attempts, she still hadn't managed to see Fred or to get any damn time alone at the computer. If she was going to commit a felony—and she was—she'd just as soon do it without an audience of witnesses.

Beth punched away at the computer keys, irritating Sara even more. Trying to melt the throbbing knots of tension in her muscles, she rubbed at her neck. More than anything, she wanted to put a serious dent in some junk food, take a long, hot bath, and see if she couldn't get herself a better attitude.

She made her way down the hallway, intending to drop in on her patients once more before heading to her first-floor quarters for the night. Maybe, just maybe, she'd get lucky and finally corner Fred. So far, she'd heard nothing but lame excuses for why she couldn't see him. But at this time of night, where would he be except in bed?

Lou's room was closest. Holding out little hope for him, she ducked inside. Accepting his condition as permanent carved a hollow in her heart and a gaping hole in her confidence. She'd work with him. She'd do everything she could think of to do, but in the end, she feared Lou was in Braxton for the long haul.

Ray wasn't much better off. Lying on his side in his bed, he babbled and drooled. Sara tried talking to him, keeping her voice low and soothing, but he didn't respond to her. Not even involuntarily, by blinking. At times, he had talked almost coherently, but about things that had to have happened eons ago. Things she could easily enough apply to a young child, though why they devastated the man remained a mystery to her. None were traumatic, or even discomfiting. And while profound, the changes in him since she'd discontinued the 70/30 insulin hadn't proven to be his only challenges. His confusion ranked far too intense for just that recovery. Yet nothing else in his chart or his behavior gave her a clue as to why he kept mumbling, "Betrayed."

Fred was again absent from his room, though he evidently had been there. Earlier, the military-stiff sheets on his bed would have withstood the bouncing-quarter test. Now, they were mussed. Weary and tired of minding her manners, she wondered if Fabulous Fontaine had a rule about that. Okay, she conceded, so some of his rules were valid. But, bluntly put, some were control-freak asinine.

Something blue flashed at the doorway. Sara glanced over and saw William. Wearing surgical gear, he headed toward the nurse's station at a good clip. She called out to him.

He stopped and looked back at her. "Yes, Major?"

"Where is Fred?" Four days and at least two dozen attempts to check on him, and she still hadn't seen her elusive patient. If she didn't know better from Shank, Sara would swear the man was a phantom.

William cast her a blank look. "Who, Major?"

"ADR-22," she informed him. "My patient. Fred."

"ADR-22 is in hydrotherapy. He's showing some breakage in the skin along his backbone. Dr. Fontaine has increased his sessions to q.i.d. to prevent bedsores."

Four times a day? Well, right before bed probably would relax Fred so he could sleep better. She'd like to take exception to Fontaine's interference on her turf, but already she'd learned the hard way, via William and his demotion and fine, that the director covered his ass. On paper, he either had issued the orders before Fred had become her patient, or Fontaine had backdated the orders to read that he had. As it happened, this time, she agreed with his orders so she'd let his interference slide. "Thank you, William."

"Major?"

William too seemed fixated on the "sir" stuff, only his took form in rank. Considering he'd just been unjustly stripped of some of his, she supposed she understood that. Compassion softening her gaze and her voice, Sara looked back at him. The stethoscope hanging around her neck gouged against a sore spot on her throat. Hissing in a sharp breath, she removed it and tucked it into her lab coat pocket. "Yes?"

A frown creased the skin between William's heavy brows. "I don't think Dr. Fontaine would approve of you giving the PTSD patients actual names."

Fontaine's staunch ally issuing her a warning? Now what was she to make of that? "Thanks for your concern." She meant it sincerely. "But the loss of identity creates a problem with their therapy, and I'm responsible for them, so I have to do what I think is in their best interests. That includes giving them fictitious but actual names." She offered him a smile. "I'd appreciate your cooperation."

His lips pinched down into a flat line. "Is that a direct order, Major?"

"Only if it must be for you to cooperate."

He shot her a cool glare, and then walked on.

Sara refused to sigh. She wanted to—adversaries crawled out of the woodwork at an alarming rate around here—but she refused to let them get to her. William had just reasons to be upset, and as soon as she found out what could be done to correct his situation, she would talk with him about them. Until then, thanks to Foster, she had far more to worry about. Still, she wondered. Why was everyone except Shank so prickly?

William's demotion and fine could be part of the reason, but not all of it. The big freeze had started as soon as she had arrived. Fontaine had power and influence here, but the staff members feared him, they didn't respect him. Tagging him "Fabulous Fontaine" proved that. The freeze couldn't be due to anything as simple as research money. So what was it? What was making people avoid her?

Maybe from the beginning the staff had pegged her as a security risk. And maybe they didn't want to appear to be her allies and get sucked down with her.

Possible, but not certain. Sara walked on to Michael's room. He was asleep. So were Lou and Ray. It'd take a while for the heavy sedatives to work out of their systems. Sara left Ray's room and headed toward Isolation to see Joe.

She paused outside his room, leaned back against the rough wall, and shut her eyes. "Okay, Sara," she whispered to herself. "Squelch everything that isn't focused on resolving his challenges. *Everything*."

She ran down the laundry list. He resented being locked in and wanted out. He mentioned that on every visit—and wanting to see the sun. Maybe a control issue spurred his bouts of episodic rage. . . .

So check it out. Give the man some control.

Ignoring the buzzer signaling her inside, Sara knocked on the door.

No answer.

Was he testing her, seeing if she would enter without being invited? She knocked again. *He is the one.* Why him? *Squelch it.* She stuffed a shaky hand into her pocket.

Still no answer.

"Joe?" She called out. "May I come in?"

"Why not? Everyone does whenever they choose."

"I won't come in if you don't want me to," she said. "Is it okay?"

"Yeah. It's okay, Sara."

Smiling at the little victory, she walked inside. *Sara.* God, but she liked the way he said her name.

He stood in the middle of the room, staring at her as if she'd committed the ultimate betrayal. "Why did you knock?"

He didn't appear even remotely fierce now, or capable of committing murder. Looking at him, she could almost convince herself the choking incident never happened, except for her raw throat and the bruises still peppering her neck. But he did look and sound extremely confused by her knocking. "You've asked me to leave here several times in the past few days. I wanted to make sure I was welcome. This is your room."

His expression softened some more, and his eyes weren't the color of steel, she realized, but a gentle dove-gray. "This isn't a room, it's a prison," he said. "And I know what you're doing. I've seen you watching me. You're playing mind games with me. Damn it, I hate mind games."

"Braxton isn't a prison," she said calmly. "It's a mental health facility, and I'm not playing games. I never play games with my patients. They deserve better, and that's what I give them. My best. Sometimes it's enough. Sometimes it's not. But it's always what they get from me."

"You've watched me." His eyes glittered. "I've seen you."

"Yes, I have. I believe in treating the whole person, Joe. Mind, body, and spirit. To do that well, I have to observe you." Sara tilted her head and looked up at him. "It's been a long day and my feet are killing me." Her day had started at an ungodly five A.M. That alone could do her in. "May I sit down?"

He backed away from her, as if the commonality of the question had surprised him. Automatically glancing down to her feet, he hesitated a long moment, and then nodded. "Floor's all yours."

The straitjacket looked extremely uncomfortable. Sara had put one on once just to see how it felt. She'd experienced her first symptoms of claustrophobia since the boa constrictor incident, and the sensation had steadily grown until now she went into cold sweats in any kind of confinement. She fought it—always fought it—but even being in the Isolation wing, much less in a windowless padded room, made her uneasy as hell.

She sat down and watched Joe lean back against the far wall and then rub, as if trying to scratch his back. "Got an itch?" She smiled up at him.

"Yeah. It's driving me crazy."

Good sign, that terminology. Patients who believed they were crazy avoided the word as if it carried plague. She could remove the jacket. It'd be a great opportunity to build trust. Of course, he could attack her again. But unlikely, as he'd insisted she leave on three occasions when he could have attacked her on any or all of them. He had chosen not to hurt her. Mmm, maybe trust needed to come from both of them. "You've removed the jacket before. Why haven't you taken it off now?"

He looked away and his voice went whisper-soft. "I remembered."

Where he was? What had happened to him? Afraid of jumping to wrong conclusions, she trod carefully. "What have you remembered?"

"Attacking you." He hung his head, sounding appalled and ashamed.

A crossroads. A step toward her. He didn't trust himself not to hurt her again, so he protected her by making attacking her more difficult. But this wasn't about punishment. It was about fear. It was about the loss of control and protecting others even if that meant hurting himself.

Sara understood that, understood all of it. But she also understood he was volatile and could change moods on a dime. Did she dare to risk it? "If I remove the straitjacket, do I have your word not to attack me?"

He glared at her. "I don't attack women."

"Earlier, you attacked me, and you've said you remember it. Do you deny it now?"

"No." He snapped his jaw shut.

She had to be truthful. He was testing her, and down deep at gut level, she knew it. "But you also sent me away to keep from attacking me again." She crossed her outstretched legs at her ankles and rubbed at her stinging arch with the toe of her other shoe. "If you're going to beat up on yourself for what you did that you feel was wrong, Joe, then you owe it to yourself to praise what you did that you feel was right. It's only fair. Wouldn't you give someone else that benefit?"

"Sometimes it's easier to be fair to others." He slid her a level look. "Sometimes you expect more from yourself because you know your standards and abilities."

"True, but double standards aren't right, either. You can't expect more from yourself than from others. Or more than you're capable of doing or giving."

"I remember the attack." He squeezed his eyes shut. His face flushed and his mouth flattened into a thin, grim line. "I don't deny it."

He didn't deny his responsibilities, either. That was certainly clear. And he looked and sounded perfectly normal. It was also clear that she knew little more now than what Foster had told her, and she'd stopped holding her breath, waiting for Foster to get the data to her that she'd requested. Her only hope for straight answers was to go to the source. "Do you know why you attacked me, Joe?"

A long moment passed, then he opened his eyes. "Joe?" His dark brows lifted to arched slashes on his wide forehead. "Who is Joe?"

She repeated what she'd told him earlier, that she'd given him the name.

He pursed his lips. "That's not my name." His tone turned

razor-edged and agitated, and he began pacing. "That is not my name."

"Fine." Sara spoke softly, just above a whisper. If he had to strain to hear her, perhaps he'd concentrate on listening and they could avoid a situation. "Then you tell me what to call you."

He opened his mouth to shout a response. His eyes went blank. He stood there, trying to remember, caught in some netherworld she hadn't yet identified. "I don't *know* my name!"

The anger and terror in his voice chilled her to the bone. She stood up. "It's okay. It happens. Right now, let's just pick a nickname you like so I know what to call you. We'll worry about your real name later."

"Didn't you hear me, woman?" He glared at her. "I don't know my own name. I did know it. Why don't I know it now?"

Trying to reassure him, Sara moved closer to him, her hands lifted, her palms upward. "I don't know why yet. But we're going to work together and find out."

"I've lost everything, Sara." Agony glistened in his eyes. "Even myself."

Her stomach flipped over and his pain streaked through her chest. "No." He was a man at war, angry and frustrated, feeling futile and betrayed by everyone, including himself. But he had protected her. Attachment was essential, and he was in pain. The timing being right at this moment was a calculated risk she had to take. Knowing she could be making a mistake that would push him over the edge, she reached out and clasped his straitjacketed shoulder. "Joe, listen to me. You haven't lost anything. You suffered a trauma. That's why you don't remember. Remembering is painful right now, so your survival instincts have blocked your memory and suppressed it to keep you safe from the pain. It's a kind of amnesia that's common, Joe, and it's temporary. When you're ready, your memory will come back."

He glared down at her hand. "Let go of my shoulder."

The venom in his voice surprised her. Burying it, she stepped back, away from him.

He softened his tone. "I don't like to be touched."

Sara breathed easier. Joe felt threatened, not violent. "Okay." To diffuse the tension, she sat back down and laced her hands on her lap. "So what nickname would you like?"

He stared at her knuckles and then met her gaze. "Joe is okay."

Her name for him. The beginnings of trust. Feeling as if she'd just topped Mount Everest, Sara smiled. "Joe it is, then."

"They betrayed me, Sara." He swallowed hard, bobbing his Adam's apple in his throat. "You're not like them. I know that."

Having no idea who "they" referred to, she kept silent, and mentally noted that both he and Ray had referred to the emotion of betrayal. It could be significant, a piece of the puzzle. Or not.

Joe stared deeply into her eyes, searching and searching, as if trying to see straight into her soul. His expression softened, changed, and he let her see his anguish. "Can you help me?"

Tears stung the backs of Sara's eyes and burned her nose. The urge to touch him nearly overwhelmed her. She stood up and tilted back her head to look straight into his eyes. "If you'll let me, yes. I think I can help you, Joe."

His dark brows knitted. "No mind games?"

"None. You have my word."

"Do you lie?"

"No." She never had, not to a patient.

He sized her up, dragging his gaze from her head to the toes of her shoes, and then nodded slowly. "Okay."

"Okay." Sara swallowed hard. "I'm going to take off your jacket so you can move around a little more. My goal is to get you out of here and into a regular room as soon as possible."

"Fontaine will veto it."

Sara's hand stilled on the clasp. So he knew and remembered Fontaine. Not unusual, really. Strong impressions often lingered. "He might veto it, but it won't do him any good."

She bent to look around Joe's side to his face and smiled. "I'm your doctor, and I have full authority on your therapy."

Joe grunted. "He'll veto it."

She loosened the last strap, then removed the jacket. It slid off his broad shoulder and into her hand. "Maybe, but I'll override him."

Joe's brows shot up on his forehead. "Can you do that?"

"On your therapy?" Sara nodded. "Not only can I, I will." She lowered her voice to a whisper and turned her back to the camera. "Just between you and me, I don't like him very much."

Why had she said that? Nerves. She'd just set free a man who could—and nearly had—killed her. A man whom, despite her desires, she considered the one.

"He's not very likable." Joe stretched. "I want out of here. I want to see the sun."

"I know. As soon as we can, we'll go outside and get you moved."

Joe's pajama top was thin and tight, hugging his muscles. "You can stop shivering, Sara."

He sounded gentle, but he looked like a small mountain, standing and flexing to loosen up. "I won't hurt you again."

"I'm not shivering." Indignance filled her tone. She tossed the jacket to the floor.

He looked down his nose at her and his tone thickened with reprimand. "You said you don't lie."

He had her there. "Okay, so I'm a little nervous. You nearly choked me to death, Joe. It's asking a lot for you to expect me not to be a little nervous."

"You're scared out of your wits."

"I am not." She wasn't. Maybe she should be, but she wasn't. "I'm just a little nervous. Trust is a fragile thing, you know? And it works both ways."

He studied the bruises on her neck. Swallowing hard, he lifted his fingertips, let them glide in the air over her skin. He didn't touch her, but she could feel the heat radiating from his fingers. Surely he wasn't going to choke her again. He didn't look as if he were about to choke her again. *Oh, God, please don't let him choke me again.*

Exercising sheer will, she forced herself to meet his gaze— and nearly wept. Never in anyone's eyes had she seen such remorse.

"Sara," he said on a ragged whisper. "I'm so sorry I hurt you."

"I know." She smiled to reassure him she meant it.

"I really do want your help." He blinked hard. "You're not like them."

Twice now, he'd said that. But who he meant by "them" would come later. Right now, she had a higher priority. Trust.

She stepped closer, praying he couldn't hear her heart thundering. She had only been this nervous once in her life. A few weeks after the boa constrictor incident, when the elevator at First National Bank had died and she'd been pinned between two floors for over an hour. *Serious* claustrophobia. Dead of winter, and she'd had to sleep with the windows open for three days. "I'll do my best, if you'll do your best. Deal?"

"Deal."

She risked lifting a hand, offering to shake. Touching was important. The sooner Joe formed a true attachment to something outside himself, the sooner they could make good progress.

He stared at her hand for a long moment, debating. Sara waited patiently, nonthreatening, making it obvious that the choice was his.

Finally, he reached across and enclosed her hand in his. It was huge, dwarfing hers, and its warmth radiated up her arm and through her chest. Caught off-guard by her strong response to a simple handshake, Sara stared into his face.

It wasn't a simple handshake. He held on, silently studying her fingers, the curve of her palm, and then swept her knuckles with the pad of his thumb. But there was no attachment in his touch. Sadly, it was strictly clinical. Frighteningly clinical.

He flipped her hand over and went rigid. The color drained from his face and he couldn't seem to tear his gaze away from her fingers. "Red." He muttered the word as if it were a curse.

Sensing the change in him, Sara stilled. *Don't panic. Just stay calm and—oh, God, don't let him hurt me again!—don't panic.* "It's just nail polish, Joe."

Their gazes locked. His grip grew hard, crushing. "Red."

Pain shot through her fingertips, her wrist, up to her elbow. What had happened inside him? "Joe, what's wrong? Why does my nail polish bother you?"

"Red is the enemy."

So white *and* red bothered him. That hadn't been in the chart, and Shank hadn't mentioned red being a trigger in their discussions about the color white. "No, Joe. It's just nail enamel. Red paint. It's supposed to be pretty."

Letting out a guttural groan, he dropped her hand. "Go away, Sara." He backed up until he collided with the wall, then flattened against it, burying his hands behind his back. "Go!" Urgency flooded his voice. "It's . . . coming!"

If only she could talk him through this. "What's coming?" Sara stepped toward him.

His face contorted in agony. "The rage."

eight

Sara watched Joe's every move on the observation monitor.

Mesmerized, agonizing with him, she watched him struggle, fighting his way through the rage. By the time the episode ended and he collapsed on the padded floor exhausted, she stood in a cold sweat—and kept watching.

He lay motionless, soundless, for a full ten minutes, and then dozed into a restful sleep. Frazzled and trying not to show it, she grabbed his chart from the nurse's station and ignored William's I-told-you-so sneer. "If Joe has another episode, let me know right away."

"Yes, Major." William fixated on the monitor.

She supposed she should say something about his demotion and fine. Though the fault was his ally Fontaine's, the injustice of it, and a tinge of guilt at her involvement, niggled at her, and she hadn't yet found a way out of the facility to go phone Foster and ask him to intercede.

Resolved to face William now, she stopped beside his chair. "I'm sorry about what happened to you with Ray and the 70/30 incident. You weren't to blame and, if it helps, well, I know the truth."

William's eyes glinted. "It took me two years to earn that rank, Major, and another year to pin it on."

"I'm sure you worked very hard for it." Sara resisted an urge to slump and shuffle her foot. "I'm not indifferent to what the incident cost you, William. I want you to know that I'm doing what I can to correct it."

"Correct it?" He guffawed. "Done is done, Major West."

"Maybe so." Sara looked him straight in the eye. "But I have to try to fix this. It's not right."

Confusion knitted his brow. He rocked back in his chair and crossed his chest with his arms. Ten reflections of him glared at her from the monitors. "You have no idea, do you?"

"Excuse me?"

He shook his head, his gaze sweeping then stilling on her name badge. "Nothing." He dropped his voice and looked back at the monitors. "I guess I've been a little hard on you." Some stiffness left his shoulders. "I'm sorry about that."

Fontaine's staunch ally apologizing to her? William seemed sincere but caution signs flashed through her mind, creating doubt.

He looked up at her, his eyes turbulent and rife with warning. "If you're smart, you'll leave this alone."

She tucked Joe's chart under her arm, trying to get a fix on how William's mind worked. "What do you mean?"

He stared at her name badge, chewed at his lip, and then snagged it.

Startled, she stepped back. "What the hell are you doing?"

He jerked open a desk drawer, stuffed the badge into it, and then slammed it shut. "Just leave what happened to me alone, okay? I can take the hit, and to tell you the truth, I'm not sure you can."

Obviously, William was trying to tell her something without speaking openly. But why had he taken her badge? He knew she had to have it on at all times. Was this another setup? No, it couldn't be. Too direct for Fontaine. Sneaky was more his style. "No, it's not okay. There's an issue of responsibility and justice involved in this that—"

"Look, Major," William interrupted. "You have no idea what you're getting into, and I'm not at liberty to explain. Just—just leave it alone."

"I can't just leave it alone." She lifted a hand. "I hear your warning, William. I don't understand it but I do hear it. Still, I can't just leave it alone."

"You're going to get hurt." His tone went flat. "Bad."

The prediction sent a cold chill racing up her spine.

"Maybe," she said. "Probably. But I've got to be able to live with me. If I do nothing, then I can't face me. That's a hundred times worse than anything anyone else could do to me." Sara reached for the desk drawer, brushing aside his hand.

He let her retrieve her badge. She clipped it back to her collar and then stared at him a long minute. From his body language, it was apparent that this conversation was over and he wouldn't explain his cryptic statements. "I do appreciate your concern."

"Bad," he repeated. Frowning, he turned his back to her, then stared blankly at the monitors.

Sara's nerves sizzled. His warning hadn't been idle, or off-hand. He'd been torn about issuing it. But was it sincere, or was he setting her up for Fontaine? She'd already felt the director's sting, and it seemed likely he would use an ally to zap her again. Yet William had to be resentful. He'd been demoted and fined, for God's sake. The question then was, how deep was William's resentment, and what had occurred privately between him and Fontaine? Had they made a side arrangement? Agreed for William to take the hit on Ray's 70/30 incident publicly and, later, Fontaine would make it worth William's while?

Debating the feasibility of that, Sara took the elevator down to the first floor to her quarters.

The numbers were painted black on the white doors. She followed them down the hall to number 111, and then went inside. The three-room suite was hot and stuffy. She reached behind the door and cranked down the thermostat. The air conditioner clicked on. Maybe by Christmas it would cool down.

The bedroom, living room/kitchen combo, and bath comprising her quarters were larger than her office, though the coloring was the same dull gray as everything else at Braxton. She'd hated the place on sight. The furniture was early garage sale, but clean and serviceable. The kitchen had a fridge, phone, and a stove, not that she'd had much use for any of them. And the mattress on the bed didn't have too many lumps, though she hadn't slept much since she had gotten here.

At first, she had blamed her insomnia on being at Braxton. But then she had met Joe and recognized him as the one, and that had let loose the demons of hell inside her. Guilt had kept her awake, pacing the floor, ever since.

She glanced around. With her things scattered here and there, the place seemed more like home. Well, like her refuge, anyway.

She dumped her purse on the sofa and skirted the maple kitchen table. At the far cabinet, she tugged open the door and grabbed a bottle of bourbon she'd seen on her first day here. The seal hadn't been broken. Shank had to have left it for her. Anyone else here would have left her cyanide.

Still shaky from seeing Joe suffer the rage, and from suffering it with him, Sara grabbed the bottle and a glass, then added some ice and poured herself a healthy shot, pretending it was Grand Marnier. These feelings for Joe were definitely different. She'd been in love before, but from her reaction to seeing him suffer, she now knew she had never before loved a man. There was a hell of a difference. One she normally would have welcomed in her life with open arms. But not here. Not now. And not him.

Sara sipped at her drink. William's snatching her name badge zipped through her mind. On its heels, she recalled something else. Something seemingly incidental. Time and again, Shank had straightened Sara's badge or bent the clip so it would hang straight.

The iced spirits burned Sara's raw throat, but she sipped again, thinking back. In fact, every time Shank had straightened the badge, she had talked about something delicate. Something she wouldn't want overheard.

A tingle shimmied through Sara, set her teeth on edge. She looked down at the badge, took it off—and between the sides of the clip, she saw it. A listening device.

Someone had bugged her—and Shank and William had both known it *and* had warned Sara. Shank, more subtly.

Monitored? Like a crook on a cuff? Baffled, infuriated, Sara glared at the device. This was America, by God. She had rights.

But evidently not at Braxton.

Furious, she grumbled, "Fontaine."

She slammed back a long drink from her glass, then slapped it down on the tile counter with a healthy *thunk* that rattled the ice cubes. Security rated more intense at Braxton than at the damn Pentagon. Who else but Fabulous Fontaine would dare to cut a trick like this?

She had taken enough. She was *not* going to tolerate this, too.

Rummaging through the drawers, she found a butter knife, pried the stick-on, button-type device from inside the metal clip, gave in to her anger, and dropped it into her glass. The device plunked down, bourbon splashed onto the counter, and the device sank, tumbling through the cubes of ice. "Enjoy that, you jerk."

She turned and marched out of the kitchen. A long, hot bath, a little meditation, and maybe—just maybe—she'd ditch some stress and get murder off her mind.

The hot water steamed up over her. She cranked back in the tub and propped her foot on the silver faucet, feeling an intense urge to talk to Joe about her troubles. Definitely a bad idea. More worries, he didn't need. Besides, she was a listener, the one others talked to about their trials. She seldom shared her own.

The urge still didn't subside. She soaped herself, rubbing hard, then rinsed and rocked back again, sliding down into the water up to her chin, hoping she'd sloughed off the urge.

She hadn't. Sighing, she grimaced at the faucet. Okay, so Joe was special—the one. And he had a good face. Not classic or perfect, but rich with character and signs of having lived in his skin a while. From the fine lines, he'd done his fair share of worrying and laughing, and that balance made him more attractive to her. She tilted her head against the tiles. Actually, a lot about him made him attractive to her. But nothing more than her instinctive certainty. Her mother, for all her faults, had been right about knowing at first sight. Brenda, too.

Was he married?

Her stomach knotted. She slapped a hand over it and

rubbed, side to side. He couldn't be. Oh, God. He couldn't be. That would be the ultimate wrong.

Stop it, Sara. Are you trying to bury the man? Your interest must be strictly professional. It has to be that way, and you know it.

She wasn't trying to bury him. Of course she wasn't. But she couldn't stick her head in the sand on this, either. Professional interest never before had put knots of panic in her stomach or filled her with a sense of incredible despair and sadness. Even with her rubbing, the knots wouldn't go away.

You'd better get a grip, Sara. His life is in your hands. You get too involved and you'll screw up. Screw up and he's dead. You'll be to blame.

Her instincts were right. Totally and completely. She reached for the soap again, determined to wash these personal feelings off her skin and out of her system. She'd never gotten personally involved with a patient and God knew this was no time to start.

The warm, wet washcloth slid over her breasts. Yet, there was something special about Joe. When she had taken off his straitjacket, she had seen small scars peppering his arms from his wrists to the sleeves of his pajama top, above his elbows. Odd-looking scars. Almost like some kind of bites.

He had to be Foster's operative. Had to be. None of the others looked as if they had trudged through the dark side with monotonous regularity—except maybe Fred.

Since he had continued to elude her, she couldn't say squat about him with authority. But Fred wasn't a viable candidate for a Shadow Watcher. Not if he was the vegetable he'd been reported to be. As a vegetable, he couldn't be salvageable.

If. An operative word.

Tomorrow, she swore to herself, she'd know Fred's status firsthand and for fact. She dunked the washcloth in the hot water and then draped it over her breasts. The warmth felt good, and she wondered. Did Fred react with violence to white and red, too? And what really triggered Joe's rage? Could it be as simple as the colors red and white? Just colors?

The key to helping him—and, her instincts said, to helping

all of them—lay in learning exactly what trauma Joe had suffered. Someone had to know, or he couldn't have been diagnosed PTSD. But who?

According to his chart, Joe had been diagnosed prior to being admitted to Braxton. She'd already grasped that patient charts couldn't be trusted around here—at least not on Fontaine's patients. But alluding to a previous diagnosis left a paper trail. Someone had to be able to follow it or Fontaine would be leaving himself wide open. Fabulous Fontaine didn't leave himself wide open. William and Sara could attest to that. Yet a previous diagnosis didn't fit in with what Foster had told her about his operative. According to him, Fontaine had made the PTSD diagnosis, and the operative had shown up here scrambled, wandering around the grounds. If so, how had he gotten past the guards? The electric fence? If he had managed both, and that postarrival diagnosis by Fontaine was indeed true, then Joe couldn't be Foster's operative.

If, it seemed, was the question of the day.

She sank lower in the tub, tapped the faucet with her foot to add more hot water. And then there was her futile search for information on David. So far, she'd found nothing. Not a snippet. Had Foster lied to her about that? Had he set her up to come here, using David, too? And if Joe wasn't Foster's Shadow Watcher, then who was he? Who had diagnosed him, and what had happened to him? Had he received immediate critical counseling? What had been—

The phone rang.

Irked by the interruption, and as stressed now as when she'd gotten into the tub to de-stress, Sara grabbed a towel, wrapped it around herself, and then rushed to the kitchen phone, leaving wet footprints on the carpet.

On the third ring, she snatched up the receiver, hoping this wasn't bad news about Ray. His sugar had been fairly stable, but his eating patterns were totally out of whack, which meant he required micromanaging to avoid wild sugar-level swings. "Dr. West."

"My office, tomorrow morning at eight hundred," Fontaine said. "This is a direct order, Major."

More military clout-and-clutter troubles. Oh joy, oh rapture. She had to bite her tongue to keep from telling Fontaine to stuff his direct order and his bugging device up his orifice of choice. "Yes, sir."

Crackling tension, she slammed down the phone. What Fontaine wanted, only God knew. It could be he had decided on his means of torturing her for filing Ray's incident report, or it could be he had been informed that she'd found the bug and ditched the damn thing.

Sara toweled herself dry, not certain which would bring her more trouble.

At eight o'clock sharp, Martha ushered Sara into Fontaine's office.

The smell of pine cleaner made her nauseous. Almost as nauseous as Martha's pitying look. The woman was about as sincere as a campaigning politician. She'd known what she had been doing, giving Sara the white lab coat, and nothing in this world would convince Sara otherwise. Martha might fear Fontaine, but Sara damn well didn't. His vindictive manipulations were bad enough, but electronically bugging her? That, and this summons were outrageous. The electronic surveillance was downright illegal.

In a civilian community.

Surely tapping someone was illegal at Braxton, too.

Careful. Get caught and you're on your own. Totally. No support and, if you blow it, no knowledge. Other people are depending on you.

Hearing Foster's voice inside her mind, Sara clenched her jaw and silently murmured, "Oh, shut up."

Fontaine fingered his tie. It was a god-awful shade of orange. She'd heard in the rounds that Mrs. Fontaine always matched his clothes, and she had gone on a European vacation. All of Braxton should rejoice on her return.

Fontaine checked his watch. The blatant intimidation attempt irked Sara. She slung him a halfhearted salute for appearance's sake and then sat down in his visitor's chair, not waiting for an invitation. If she was going to be challenged here—and she was—then she would face it from equal ground and on her own terms.

He frowned at her and stood up. "I understand that you've altered the therapy on the PTSD patients, Major."

She nearly smiled. He wasn't conceding his perceived superiority in his position-jockeying game just yet. If he had known her better, he'd have kept his seat and spared them both the ritual. "Yes, I have."

"Why?"

She arched a brow, letting him know she owed him no answers. Her patients were her domain. "I've implemented methods proven effective."

"They're unorthodox, not proven."

He was irritated. "They're proven to me." She smiled up at him, knowing it would only irritate him more. "That is why I was chosen for this project, Doctor. Because I'm unorthodox *and* effective." She rubbed a fingertip over her temple. "Didn't we cover this already?"

He grunted and a muscle under his right eye ticked. "I strongly suggest you reconsider your choice of treatment. The changes in ADR-30's treatment are radical."

"ADR-30 is *Joe.* And in my practice, these changes are not radical, they're standard operating procedure." How many times had Foster thrown that maddening term her way? "But if you're looking for reassurance, you've got it. Under the provisions of my research agreement with the Department of Defense, I have full authority over the therapies I choose to incorporate and full responsibility. I'm within the defined parameters."

He grasped the back of his chair and squeezed, denting the leather. "I'm well acquainted with your agreement, Major," he said sharply. "My point is, we have reasons for not using these patients' names."

"Security risks. Yes, I know. But there's nothing to worry about, sir. The assigned names are fictitious. Of course they have to be. I don't know my patients' real names." Not yet. But she would. By God, she would.

"We prefer numbers." He moved behind the chair, putting it and the desk between them as barriers.

Interesting. Sara tilted her head, looked sideways at him. "Why?"

His eyes widened at being questioned. "Because it's my policy, Major, and I'm the director of this facility."

"I see." She leaned forward, spread her slack-clad thighs, and braced her hands on her knees. "Well, I'm sorry to have to breach your policy, sir, but stripping PTSD patients of their identity is in direct conflict with my mission."

He folded his arms over his chest. His jacket gaped open. "What *exactly* is your mission, Major?"

She answered simply, free of guile. "To heal my patients, sir."

Incredulous, his jaw dropped open. "You expect to heal these people?"

"I expect to give it my best shot."

"But you've evaluated them. How can you reasonably expect to cure them?" He let out a rushed breath. "Dr. West, are you delusional?"

Now, he'd gone too far. "No, Dr. Fontaine, I am not delusional." Sara chilled her voice to cool the outrage piping through her veins. "I'm doing my job."

"Incredible." He shook his head, lifted and dropped a hand, slapping the leather chair. "This, they funded."

"Yes, they did." Sara stood up. "If you have a problem with that, I suggest you contact your superiors, sir, because until they stop funding, I'm going to continue to do my job. I'll make every effort not to conflict with your policies, and I'm certain you wouldn't expect it, ask it, or even suggest it, but for the record, I will not compromise the potential for recovering a patient due to your rules."

His brows flattened to a slash. "What I expect, Major, is for you to do everything humanly possible not to disrupt the normal operations of this facility. Because while you have full authority over your patients and their therapy, you do *not* have any authority over my facility."

He was going to continue running roughshod over her at

every turn. Sara folded her arms over her chest. "If you feel
my presence here is a disruption, sir, I have a solution."

"What?"

"Sign the papers to transfer my patients to a facility in
Pensacola. That would be more than acceptable to me."

"I will not." He spat the words at her.

"Fine." She stood up. "So long as we understand each
other, I won't requisition such a transfer." She moved toward
the door and paused, cupping the doorknob in a death grip. "I
respect your authority here, Dr. Fontaine. But my first concern
is the same as any doctor's: my patients. I hope you understand that."

"Oh, I understand you, Dr. West." Hatred brimmed in his
eyes. "Completely."

"I'm glad to hear it, sir." Though tempted, she didn't get
in a dig by mentioning the bug. He knew that she knew about
it, and that he had planted it on her. That was enough. "I
answer directly to the DoD, and I don't think the people there
would appreciate spending their money only to have someone
deliberately sabotage their efforts. As I hear it, bad attitudes
really piss them off." She gave him a false smile and a sassy
salute. "Have a good day, sir."

Sara left the office and returned to the second floor still
fuming.

Not that it would do her any good, but tonight she'd be
calling Foster. If he wanted results, then he had better find a
way to get Fontaine off her back. At least now she had a valid
excuse to yell at Foster, provided her damn throat got well
and she had voice enough to yell at him.

With the conditions of these five patients and all that was
at stake, she didn't need the added stress of an anal-retentive
facility director, but she certainly had one. She didn't need the
added stress of a cold-shouldered staff, or the worries of
whether or not Fontaine's forged peacock-blue notes were going to be enough to get her and her patients out of Braxton
alive, either. But she had those things to contend with, too.

She turned the corner into the main hallway. She'd also
better call Brenda and talk to her and Lisa tonight. Brenda had

agreed not to marry H. G. or G. H., whatever-the-hell-his-
name-was, Williamson—for now. But Sara had been forced
to stoop to blackmail to get her to agree, and God, but she
hoped Lisa never found it out. She was the closest thing to a
daughter in Sara's foreseeable future, and already Lisa thought
Sara was a worthless failure of a shrink. She didn't want her
niece's opinion of her sinking any lower—provided it could.
Her professional instincts were screaming that she was running
out of time with Lisa.

Panic stabbed at Sara's stomach. She pressed a hand over
it, warning herself to calm down. The last thing she needed
was *more* stress.

She paused at a water cooler and got a drink. The icy cold
felt good in her throat. Foster had promised she would find
her answers about David here. So far, she hadn't caught Foster
in any lies, so she would give him the benefit of doubt—and
leave no stone unturned in checking for information. Maybe
this would be her lucky day, and she'd find out something
about David, see Fred, and get access to the computer.

Her mood lightened at the prospect, and she swung by the
nurse's station.

Shank was on the phone, taking lab results. She pointed to
Sara's patients' charts, tapping them with her pen.

Sara reviewed them, starting at the top of the stack, though
everything in her urged her to look at Joe's first. She really
had to get a grip on her personal feelings. All five men were
her patients, and no one man deserved more attention than the
others. An imbalance would be extremely unprofessional—
and unacceptable.

*So sayeth Sara, model of propriety, caught in the throes of
a serious crush on a patient—a mentally diminished patient
she instinctively knows is the one.*

Biting a frown from her lips, she scanned the new notes in
Michael's file. No significant changes. Fred had enjoyed a
comfortable night. Maybe the late-night hydrotherapy was
helping him to sleep better. Ray hadn't been so lucky. Episodic paranoia, flashbacks of the trauma, hypervigilant. She
checked his medication listing, allergies noted, and then pre-

scribed a lighter sedative. The man was still loaded on down-ers. Until she got him off the drugs, she couldn't do much for him. But his sugar had stabilized. That was good news. The EEG results still weren't back from the lab. The guys there were either slow or swamped.

She closed his file, opened the next, and then scanned the notes. Lou had isolated himself in the bathroom inside his room, and no matter how often William had returned Lou to his bed, on every check, he was back in the bath. Attempts to remove him had been met with "extreme resistance." For his own protection, he had been restrained in his bed. In a sense, this too was good news. In four days, she hadn't seen Lou so much as blink. That he'd gotten to the bath to isolate himself was reason to celebrate. It seemed certain that the sedatives were working their way out of his system. That sparked a little hope for his recovery.

She skimmed the rest of William's notes—they were as worthless as Fontaine's—and then saw one Shank had added. On seven-thirty A.M. nurses' rounds, Lou appeared semicog-nizant. Asked why he had isolated himself, he said, "Every-one's turned against me. They lied to me." Asked what he meant, he replied, "The enemy. Betrayed."

A cold chill swept through Sara. *The enemy. Betrayed.* Just like Joe and Ray.

Betrayal had to be a key in all of this. But what kind of betrayal? She closed Lou's file and set it on the "reviewed" stack. What did all five cases have in common?

On seeing Joe's file, an expectant tingle swam through Sara's chest. She flipped the binder open and then read the notes. Shortly after she had left him yesterday, he had ripped out a section of the padding from the wall in his Isolation room. He'd refused the cream-based soup brought to him at dinner. Complained about the irritating music. And attempted to stuff the therapist working with him on relaxation exercises into the trash drum William had brought back into Joe's room as a safety barrier. Orderlies removed the shaken but uninjured therapist and the drum, and then straitjacketed ADR-30— William, damn him, refused to use the name Joe—and Joe had huddled in the corner for the next five hours. He had not slept.

Subsequently, the therapist had notified William she would not be working with ADR-30 again.

Several things were exceedingly clear. Joe had protected Sara on multiple occasions. When he had felt the rage coming, he had ordered her to leave the room. Yet, he was not reacting similarly—or well—to anyone else's presence. The attachment was solely to her, which meant that her only hope of helping him was to work with him personally on every phase of his therapy—and to keep the resistant William away from him.

Fontaine was going to love this.

Why had William taken the drum back into Joe's room? Why did he refuse to call Joe by name? Why had he warned Sara? That had to have been a sham to seduce her into taking him into her confidence. He had to still be Fontaine's ally.

Sara dropped in on Michael, Ray, and Lou. Fred was again absent from his room, and Sara had the sneaking suspicion that her missing him time after time wasn't accidental. More of Fontaine's pranks she did not need. She walked back to the nurse's station.

Shank hung up the phone. "Busy night last night."

"Evidently." Sara drummed her fingers against the files. "Why is Fred never in his room?"

"Most of the time, he is there." Shank avoided Sara's eyes. "He's having extra hydrotherapy sessions, but otherwise, he's there."

He wasn't, and he hadn't been. Shank flushed at the lie, appeared reluctant and bitter. She was being forced to be dishonest with Sara; that Sara sensed down to her toenails. But by whom? Certainly not by Fontaine. "I want Fred in his room at four o'clock today, Shank. No excuses."

"Sixteen hundred, Major," Shank corrected, and tilted her chin up at Sara. "Am I hearing an accusation behind that order?"

"What you're hearing is a frustrated doctor wondering how the hell she can treat or help a patient she's never seen. He's my responsibility, Shank. Four o'clock, or I'll be ending my day like I started it."

"How's that?"

"Going toe-to-toe with Fabulous Fontaine."

Worry flickered through Shank's eyes. "I'll see to it Fred is there."

"Thank you." Realizing she had spoken sharply, Sara paused and turned back to Shank. "I don't mean to take anything out on you, okay? You're the only one who's treated me decently. I'm just frustrated, that's all."

"It's okay, Doc. Really." Shank smiled. "Hey, did you notice that I got Joe to eat this morning? He usually refuses breakfast."

"How did you manage it?"

"I told him if he didn't at least eat part of his breakfast, you'd be worried."

"And that worked?"

Shank nodded, her eyes sparkling with warm light. "I think you're starting to get that attachment factor going."

"I hope you're right." Boy, did Sara hope it. For Joe and everyone else who was depending on her to handle this well. "Have you noted any one thing common to all of the PTSD patients?"

"Only the typical, clinical reactions."

Those were one-eighty degrees out the realm of normal in all of the patients, and Shank was too sharp an RN not to know it. Which meant she was being subtle again, forcing Sara to take a close look to make sure she had noted it, too. "And their reactions to the color white."

"Except for Fred and Lou. Bless his heart, Lou's too far gone to react to much of anything."

He had reacted to something last night. "What about the color red?" Sara asked. Joe certainly had reacted strongly to her red nail polish. Polish she had removed with acetone immediately after watching him suffer the rage.

"Can't say I've noticed anything on red." Shank pursed her lips. "Why do you ask?"

"Just a thought." Sara gave the files a final tap. "Thanks," she said, then headed toward the Isolation wing.

Shank watched her go.

When Sara rounded the corner and stepped out of sight, Shank lifted the phone, punched down the secure-line button, and then dialed.

He answered on the first ring. "Foster."

"She's demanding to see ADR-22—Fred, sir. Today at sixteen hundred."

"It's too soon," he said. "Stall her."

"Stall her?" Easy for him to say. "Have you ever tried to stall a Mack truck barreling up your butt, sir?"

"Yes, I have, Captain, and I suggest you remember that this Mack truck is sharp. Play it safe and keep it low-key."

"But, sir. She's not going to brush this off or just let it ride. He's her patient and she has demanded to see him. Either he's in his room at sixteen hundred, or she's going to raise the roof with Fontaine. Martha said he raged for an hour after their confrontation this morning." Shank grabbed a breath, then continued. "Aside from that, things are moving fast. Dr. West has asked me about her patients' reacting to white *and* red."

"Red, too?" He sounded mildly surprised. "Already?"

God, but Shank hated him. Especially when he was right, and she'd never known him to be wrong. "Already, sir."

"Damn, she's good." He sounded pleased with himself.

"Yes, she is." And they were doing her dirty. Shank let out an exasperated breath. Oh, but she hated being put in this position. She actually liked Sara. The woman not only had stood up to Fontaine, she had intimidated him into backing down. And it was about time someone did. "You might have to run a little interference between her and Fontaine. He's on the warpath, big-time."

"Sara West can handle Fontaine."

Shank suspected Foster was right about that. Sara was a capable woman. But even capable women needed a little support now and then. "She's what's got him on the warpath. She found the bug and got rid of it. And she bucked him on naming the PTSD patients."

"She'll handle him," Foster repeated.

Subject closed. Shank fought to keep her frustration out of her voice. "With all due respect, sir, I think Dr. West could also handle the truth."

"You know my policy, Captain. Never trust outsiders."

"I know, sir, but—"

"She's not military."

"We can't control her." Shank bluntly restated the crux of the matter.

"Exactly," Foster agreed. "I can't risk her taking this situation outside. The last thing we need to do is alert the enemy."

Especially those enemies who were supposed to be allies. Hard-nosed, but once again, Foster was right. "So what about Fred?"

"Damn it, Captain, use your training. Create a diversion. Do whatever you have to do but you keep her away from ADR-22 until I give the word."

"Yes, sir." Shank grimaced and tossed a wadded-up piece of trash from the floor into the wastepaper basket. "My guess is, she'll be heading to the store tonight."

"What for?"

"To make a couple of calls. Mainly to chew ass, sir. Unless I'm mistaken, yours."

"It's time." He paused for a brief moment. "Do what you can to help her get past Security."

"May I ask why you didn't tell her there's a secure phone line on the premises?"

"I want to see how resourceful she is, Shank."

How could he be amused? It was beyond her, but the lilt in his voice was unmistakable. Shank grimaced. "Know your enemy."

"And your allies," Foster amended. "Even those who don't know they're your allies."

Another senseless test. *Accomplish the mission. Whatever, whenever, wherever.* "Yes, sir." To keep from bellowing, Shank bit her lip until she tasted blood. Why couldn't he just play straight with Sara? She was tough and fair. She could handle the truth, and she could be trusted not to go outside.

Create a diversion. Do whatever you have to do but you

keep her away from ADR-22 until I give the word.

Shank hung up the phone, and just stared at it. Keep Sara away from her own patient. Now just how in hell was Shank supposed to pull that off?

nine

☆

Koloski was minding the monitors and reading Nelson DeMille's novel *The Charm School*. Hearing her approach, he marked his spot on the page with a fingertip and looked up. "Hey, Doc. What's in the box?"

Not once had he bothered to glance at the monitors. Still, aside from Shank, he was more friendly than anyone else. Sara dredged up a smile. "Some therapy aids." White and red might have triggered Joe's episodic rage, but Sara doubted that the violent attacks could be in response to anything that simple. So she wanted to check it out.

The box shifted and slid against her hipbone. She clutched at it, and nodded at Koloski. "Will you buzz me through?"

"Yes, ma'am. Joe's been asking for you all morning."

Joe. Koloski was trying to be accommodating, putting in a lot more effort than William. "Thanks." She smiled again, and heard the buzzer.

"No problem. He ripped a little padding off the wall in his room. Dr. Fontaine wasn't happy."

"Why did Joe do it?"

"I can't say, and he wouldn't." Koloski shrugged. "It's good to hear your voice sounding better." He returned to reading his book. "If you need me, I'll be right here."

Her voice was better. Not normal, but better. "Appreciate it."

In the hallway outside Joe's room, she jammed the box between her stomach and the door frame and knocked. "Joe? It's me, Dr. West. Can I come in?"

"Okay, Sara."

So much for professional distance. He'd remembered her name and used it. Well, this attraction was her problem, not his, and anything that helped him attach was going to have to be okay. She'd just have to deal with it.

She turned the knob and stepped inside. The door closed behind her and the buzzer shut off. Joe was wearing pale blue pajamas, a size too tight. Long sleeves. No robe or slippers, and no straitjacket. "Hey, you shaved." She offered him a genuine smile.

"I did?" He rubbed at his smooth chin. "I guess they did it." Worry clouded his eyes. "I don't remember it."

"No big deal. That'll come." She set the box down on the floor. "Aren't you going to ask me what's in the box?"

"Okay." He smiled. "What's in the box?"

God, but he had a terrific smile. It lit up his eyes from the bottom. "Stuff." She glanced over to the gouged padding. "We're going to decorate your room."

"I don't want to decorate." He frowned and crossed his chest with his arms. "I told you, I want out of here."

Sara had expected this, and she was ready for it. "I know. And I want you out of here. But first, I have to know in my heart that you don't pose a threat to the other patients or to yourself." She braced a hand on her hip. "Your safety and theirs is my responsibility, Joe."

"I'm responsible for myself." He glared down at her. "I always have been."

Sara's heart shifted, tripped a beat. She stilled opening the box, the smells of cardboard and paint tickling her nose. "Have you?"

"Yes. And I want out of here."

"What about your parents? Weren't they with you?"

"They were there, but it was like . . ." He stumbled and stopped; took in a deep breath, as if hoping he'd inhale the answer with it. "I don't know what they were like." He dragged a frustrated hand through his hair. "Damn it, I hate this."

"I know. PTSD patients always hate it. It's hard, but it gets easier when you just relax. Then, you work past it."

Skepticism twisted his mouth. "I want out. I want to see the sun."

"I understand. And as soon as I can, I'll move you. That's the best I can do." She pulled some things from the box. "I'll tell you what. Let's work on decorating your room, dabble in a few other things I've got in mind that could help you relax, and if all is well tomorrow, then I'll take you outside for a while. We've got to do this by steps, Joe. So we're both comfortable with what we're doing. Does that sound like a fair deal?"

He studied her a long moment, and then walked over. "Provided you turn off that damn music. I'm sick of it."

"Really?" Surprised, she straightened up, a paintbrush in her right hand. "Celtic music is very soothing. I thought you'd enjoy it."

"It's driving me nuts."

Sara smiled. Clearly Joe didn't consider himself nuts or he would never use the term. That was always a good sign. "Ah, but since you've been listening to it, you haven't had to fight the rage."

He set his jaw, showing her a potential stubborn streak. "I've come close."

She lifted a fingertip. "But you haven't done it."

"No." He stuffed his fists into his pants pockets. "I haven't done it."

"So, that's progress." Worried that she was gaining too many points without conceding any and he would see the scales as unbalanced on give-and-take, she asked, "Can the music stay until we get some other relaxation techniques going?"

"For now. If you think it's keeping the rage away." He nodded toward the box. "What's in there, besides that paintbrush?"

"Paint." She laughed. "Big surprise, eh?"

"A real shocker." He cocked his head, clearly amused and determined to hide it.

"You said white made you uneasy, so I thought you would like some color. We're going to paint tons of color in here."

"And die from fumes."

"Nontoxic." She crossed her chest with the paintbrush. "Scout's honor."

He grunted, doing his best to look irritated, but the hint of a smile tugged at the corner of his mouth. As if afraid she'd notice it, he turned away.

Sara's heart swelled in her chest. God, but she loved making Joe smile. She passed him a brush and a small can of paint.

He hesitated at taking them. "No red?"

"No." Her heart felt squeezed. "No red."

He took the can and began painting on the far wall, next to the gouged wallpad. Sara painted a sun, sky, and a green meadow, then dotted the grass with small blue flowers.

When it occurred to her that Joe had been quiet for a long time, she covertly glanced over to see what he had drawn. A black box. A coffin? Maybe.

He put the finishing touches on another item, and then stepped aside. Sara stared at it, her heart stuck in her throat. "Joe," she rasped in an unsteady whisper. "Why did you draw an electric chair?"

"It's not electric. It doesn't have headgear."

Odd answer. But it didn't have headgear. Still, she'd known immediately what it was. "Why did you draw it?"

He frowned at it, and then at her. "I don't know. I just see it in my head all the time." He moved on down the wall, painted trees, a rock-strewn brook, and in the water, a body.

Sara wanted to interrupt, to ask whose body it was, but she had the feeling she would learn more about what had happened to Joe by watching from a distance and keeping her mouth shut. She painted a fish, a bird, a street lamp, and a row of buildings.

Before long, she and Joe had come full-circle, painting scenes on all four walls within the room. The ripped-out padding was now a creative cave. A pretty good one, too. Just looking at it had her feeling stirrings of claustrophobia.

Sara put the brush back in the box, braced a hand at the aching small of her back, and surveyed his work. Nothing else questionable after the coffin and chair. "You're quite the art-ist."

He put his paintbrush down by hers. "I used to like color."

She smiled. "Glad to hear it." She reached into the box, found a sketch pad, and tacked it to the wall. On the floor beneath it, she set down a box of twenty-four crayons.

Joe grunted and nodded toward the crayon box. "I'm a little old for that."

"How old are you, exactly?"

"Thirty-three." A devilish twinkle lit in his eye. "And you?"

"Thirty-four," she answered without missing a beat. So he knew his age. Encouraging. "Coloring is good relaxation ther-apy. I highly recommend it. Draw whatever the mood tells you. Whenever."

A furrow knit between his brows and he stared down at his pajamas as if surprised to see himself wearing them. "Where are my clothes?"

"I'm not sure." She wasn't. "I'll check for you." She walked around the room, closely studying all he had painted. Everything centered on a theme. So subtle a theme that ini-tially she'd missed it. A dog in the middle of a country road, a car coming around a blind curve toward it. A huge oak, but a tiny tombstone beneath it. A crashed plane near the body in the brook. Definitely a theme. Death and dying.

Joe came up behind her. "I like the flowers."

His breath warmed her neck and her senses went on alert. *God, please not another attack. Please.* "Thank you." She stepped away, cursing herself as forty kinds of fool, because even as she feared him, she was attracted to him. "Well." She swiped her paint-smeared hands on her lab coat. "I've got other patients to check up on."

As if sensing he had frightened her, he laced his hands behind his back.

The thoughtfulness in the gesture tugged at her heart. She lifted the box, then looked up at him. His expression was un-readable, and she hated the sudden tension between them. "I hope you'll color, Joe." She'd learned more from his paintings than from their talks.

"Maybe I will." He spared the sketch pad and box of crayons a glance. "I used to like color," he said again.

Now, he hated red and white. "Tomorrow we'll focus on some meditation exercises and, if the rage has still stayed away, we'll go outside and see the sun."

He blew off that remark, clearly doubting her.

"I don't lie, Joe." She willed him to believe her.

He rewarded her with a smile. It was magnetic, and she smiled back, feeling drawn to him in ways she shouldn't, in ways she had promised herself she wouldn't.

He's your patient, for God's sake.

Guilt rammed through her, bore down on her, unrelenting. "I've got to go."

"It's okay to think someone is special, Sara. You shouldn't feel bad about that."

She snapped back to look at him. "What do you mean?"

"I mean, I know what you feel. I feel it too, and it's okay."

No, it wasn't okay. It was *not* okay. "Joe, you're my patient. You're special to me as a patient is special to me."

The warmth in his eyes shuttered, closing her out. "You think I'm less of a man because I'm—"

"No." She elevated her voice. "No, of course not. You've suffered a trauma, Joe. Soon you'll be your old self again, only different because experience teaches. But you'll be fine."

"Yes, I will." He searched her face, her eyes. "So will you, Sara."

Rattled. Not uncomfortable that he'd seen her feelings. Not uneasy. Nothing that simple. No, this was complicated. Definitely rattled. "I've, um, got to go now."

Joe nodded.

She hit the buzzer. The door opened, and she walked out.

Just as the door closed, she remembered something. Propping the box on her hip, she knocked on the door. "Joe?"

"Yes?"

"Don't open the box of crayons." Oh, damn. Damn, damn, damn. How could she be so stupid? So thoughtless and stupid? "All of the colors are in the box. I forgot to take two of them out. Can I come back in and do that?"

No answer.

"Joe?" She knocked harder.

Still no answer.

She dropped the box. Hit the alarm. "Koloski, open the damn door!"

The buzzer sounded and she shoved the door open.

Joe stood staring at the crayon box, his shoulders slumped. "Joe," she said, shaking head to toe, feeling lower than a slug. If she hadn't been preoccupied with this attraction, she might not have forgotten the damn things. And never had she been more at risk for an attack than now. "Can I come in?"

He didn't respond.

"Please, Joe." She licked at her lips. They were desert-dry. "I'm sorry. I really am. I was thinking about . . . about something else, and I forgot." She stepped inside, held the door open with her foot. "It was a terrible mistake for me to make, but I did it. Can I please come in and take those colors out of the box?"

His shoulders heaved. He bent down, picked up the box, and then thrust it at her as if touching it had scalded his hand.

Damn it, why had she messed up? He had been doing so well. She took the box. "I'm going to turn around so you don't have to see them, okay?" And she was going to pray he didn't grab her from behind in a stranglehold.

He stared at the box. Mesmerized. Terrified.

"Joe, is that okay?" Her mouth dry, her palms damp, she clutched at the box.

He jerked a nod.

Sara swallowed hard, then slowly turned around, praying he could contain the haze of rage simmering in his eyes. She opened the crayon box, pulled out the red and white colors, stuffed them into her lab coat pocket, and then turned back to face Joe. His eyes shone bright and he blinked hard and fast.

He was fighting tears. And she had done this to him. He'd been so fierce and noble, fighting the rage. Why tears . . . ?

Fool, your emotional involvement is blinding you. Can't you see, Sara? He never trusted the rage. He could always fight it without feeling conflict. You, he trusted. You betrayed him.

Oh, God. No. Why hadn't she thought? She passed the colors back to him, fighting down a lump in her throat. Whatever he had been through, he'd suffered enough. Why in the name of all that is good did she have to add to his pain? A tear slid down her face. "I am—" Her voice cracked. She swallowed hard, and then tried again. "I am so sorry."

He looked up at her, saw the tear, and frowned. But the rage slowly faded from his eyes. He reached out, touched a fingertip to her tear, and then clasped her hand in his and gently squeezed her fingers. "It's all right, Sara."

He'd won. He'd battled the demon and won! A second tear followed Sara's first. Being thoughtless, she had caused him more trauma, and from the paintings, she knew now what had happened to him, if not why it had happened.

He had been tortured.

Looking torn, seeing her anguish, he pulled her closer, into a hug. "It's really okay, Sara. Don't cry." His chin at the curve of her neck and shoulder, he whispered, "Your music's on. The rage won't come while your damn music is on."

Cry? She could fly. Shout from the rooftops and fly. Joe, her darling Joe, had attached.

Her joy bubbled outward. She wrapped her arms around his sides, rested her face against his chest, and smiled. "Thank you, Joe."

He stiffened, pulled back, and looked down into her upturned face. "My name isn't Joe."

"I know, but we agreed to call you that. Remember?"

"No, I don't." A muscle ticked in his jaw. "My name isn't Joe. Don't call me that."

"Okay." Her smile faltered. "What do you want me to call you, then?"

"Jarrod." A wrinkle furrowed his brow. "My name is Major Jarrod . . ." His voice trailed off and his gaze went blank. "Major Jarrod . . . *Something*."

ten

☆

Sara left Isolation on such an emotional high over Jarrod's progress and his being attracted to her, she swore she could float. And she left on such an emotional low, over crossing the professional line, that she would have to climb up to be down.

Talk about a walking contradiction!

Flushed, she walked past the heavy metal doors. Koloski was gone. William sat at the monitors, glaring at her. No need to ask. He'd seen what had taken place. She stiffened her shoulders. "Hi, William."

"You hugged him, Major. I saw it."

Great. Just great.

Shank was coming up the hall, definitely within earshot. She pulled her cart to a halt beside the desk. "What's the problem, William?"

He turned his glare from Sara to Shank. "She hugged ADR-30. I saw it on the monitor. And she painted the pads in his room. Color is banned in the Isolation wing. Everyone knows it."

"William—" Shank started.

"I'm aware of the rules, William," Sara interrupted. "And I can see that you're genuinely distressed, so I'm going to explain this to you—once." She forced her voice stern, hoping it didn't waver. "But after this, if you question me again, I'm going to take disciplinary action against you. I outrank you, and I'm a doctor. You're not. Do you understand what I'm saying to you?"

A muscle in his lean face twitched. He jerked a nod in her general direction.

Sara clenched her jaw and borrowed from Fontaine. Him, William respected—enough to accept a demotion and a fine and still spy for him. "Yes, ma'am, if you please. Or, yes, Major. Either is fine with me."

"Yes, Major." Anger glittered in William's brown eyes.

"Fine." Sara leaned against the Plexiglas barrier. "Rules are made to help, not hinder. If they hinder, you break them. They were hindering, so I broke them."

She pulled back, softened her voice but kept the lecture tone that had served her so well in the past. "Joe has an adverse reaction to white. Being in a room that is absent of any color but white isn't conducive to his healing. It's stagnating him. Because of his recent attack on me, and not wanting to endanger the other patients, I couldn't move Joe to a regular room with color, so I compromised and painted some color in his room."

Sara felt her face heat. If only with herself, she had to admit she had felt far more during the hug than she could classify as professional. "As for hugging, it holds specific therapeutic value, especially to PTSD patients. They tend to detach from everyone and everything around them. The key to helping them begins with getting them to attach. To do that, you have to understand their pain and do what you can to relieve it. Hugs release endogenous opioids. Do you know the term?"

"I've forgotten." William's gaze turned speculative. He was listening. Whether or not he was hearing was anyone's guess.

"Endogenous opioids are the body's natural pain killer," Sara said. "Now do you understand why I hugged him?"

"Yes, Major." William looked away.

"Good." Sara walked back to the second-floor station with Shank.

Rolling the cart beside her, Shank checked to make sure they were out of William's earshot, and then slid Sara a sidelong look. "Nice save, Dr. West."

"Yeah, right." Sara bent down and picked up a scrap of paper on the hallway carpet. "Every word was true, but Fontaine will know each detail before I can walk to Fred's room."

"Flat out." Shank paused by the second-floor station desk. "Tell me something." Her eyes twinkled. "Did that hug feel as good as I'm imagining it did?"

Sara grunted. "It felt a hell of a lot better than him choking me half to death."

"Uh-huh. I'll just bet it did." Shank emptied some files from her cart onto the lid of the desk.

Sara withheld a retort. Beth was sitting at the computer listening avidly and pretending to be stone-deaf.

Stretching toward Beth, Shank passed over two files. "Orders in these two need to be entered right away."

"Yes, Captain," Beth said, retrieving the files without glancing at Shank.

Sara jotted a couple more notes in Jarrod's file. She started to write down that he had revealed his name, but afraid Foster would go paranoid and deem Joe unsalvageable, she kept that information to herself. And it hit her that maybe Fontaine's notes had been ambiguous for the same reason. Maybe he had substituted the peacock-blue ones for the original notes because he too had been protecting the patients.

The man had won a Purple Heart, the Bronze Star, and a medal for meritorious service. Congress was stingy with those things, so there had to be some good in the man. It could be possible . . .

Oh, hell, if that was the case, then she'd misjudged him. The protective scenario fit. It was possible. And, if true, then he would resent her being here and changing orders. He would be terrified of her doing anything that could upset the status quo and have Foster terminating the patients.

She'd have to weigh this carefully. As impossible as it seemed on the surface, Fabulous Fontaine could be one of the good guys.

She checked her watch. Three-fifty. She'd have to sift through it all later. She had a date with her phantom patient at four. "Fred's in his room, right?"

"Not anymore." Shank rolled the cart behind the desk.

"Damn it, Shank. I specifically ordered—"

"Hold on a second, Doc." Shank left the cart near the medicine room and returned to the desk. "During the night, Fred kept thumping at his chest, so this morning while you were with Joe, I had them run an EKG on him." Shank dipped her chin. "You ordered it, by the way."

"*I* ordered it?" Sara fought not to shout. "I'd prefer you not do that."

Shank shrugged. "You were busy. It needed doing. I did it. I wouldn't give meds or anything like that, but this seemed harmless enough."

Sara supposed the woman was right. She didn't like it, wouldn't tolerate a steady diet of it, but under the circumstances . . . "So what did the EKG show?"

"Tape's in the file. Bad stuff. Flat out." Shank left the cart and walked back to the desk. "Fontaine happened by, saw the report, and shipped Fred out."

Surprised, Sara frowned. "To a regular hospital?"

Shank dropped her voice so Beth wouldn't hear. "To one of ours."

From the corner of her eye, Sara saw Beth watching their every move. "When will he be back?"

"No idea." Shank cut her eyes toward Beth. "I'll keep you posted."

Someone didn't want Sara to see Fred. Why, Sara didn't know. She looked at the computer terminal. But she damn well knew how to find out—if she could ever get just a few minutes of privacy.

Sara walked away from the station. Passing Fred's room, she saw a yellow piece of paper taped to his door. Staph infection. She couldn't enter. No one could enter without proper gear, and no cart holding that anti-infection gear had been stationed outside his door.

She turned and walked back to the desk. "Shank?"

She looked up from the paperwork she was charting. "Yeah, Dr. West?"

"Why is there a staph warning on Fred's door?"

"The room's been reassigned to another patient. He has a staph infection."

"There's no cart," Sara said, tension coiling in her stomach. Shank had been her only ally. She'd lied, albeit reluctantly, but now she was stonewalling Sara.

"We're waiting for it to come up from downstairs. Should be here in a matter of minutes."

"Who's the patient?" Sara persisted.

"ADR-40."

Sara stuffed her hands into her lab coat pocket. "Is he PTSD?"

"No. Bless his heart, he's too far gone for anyone but God to help. I thought poor Lou was about as bad as a body can get, but ADR-40 is even worse."

There was a message in that remark. Sara saw it in Shank's eyes. What it was niggled at the corner of her mind. She tugged, but it remained just out of reach.

Turning back down the hallway, she slowed her steps at Fred's door. Inside, Dr. Fontaine talked softly. The patient, ADR-40, mewled. At first, Sara couldn't make out what he was saying. But when she did, it stopped her dead in her tracks.

"I wept."

eleven

☆

Sara pored through her patient files.

It was hot in her office. Since it had warmed up again, the air conditioner was needed. Instead, the heater was on and under the influence of a master control that maintenance couldn't seem to alter. But she was determined to sweat it out, literally, and find the common denominator between her patients and Fontaine's new one, ADR-40. He hadn't been admitted under the guise of PTSD, but his mewling "I wept" warned her that there was a connection.

She began a list, working backward by their patient numbers.

ADR-40: more damaged than ADR-39, Lou
ADR-39: more damaged than ADR-36, Ray
ADR-36: more damaged than ADR-30, Joe
ADR-30: more damaged than ADR-17, Michael
ADR-22: Fred. According to Shank, a vegetable damaged somewhere between Lou and ADR-40.
ADR-17: Michael. Least damaged of all.

Three of them cited betrayal. Two, "I wept." And—

Sara blinked, stared at the listing, and then blinked again. Her heart beat hard and fast. Except for Fred, the higher the patient number, the more damaged the patient.

If these cases were connected—and her gut instincts and her intuition screamed that they were—then whatever had been done to the men had started out mild with Michael, had gotten severe with Fred, had eased up with Joe, and then had progressively gone downhill from severe to catastrophic.

One thing was clear. These incidents hadn't been accidents or coincidences any more than they were cases of PTSD. Someone, somewhere, was causing this. And due to the pattern of damage, she had a sick feeling in her stomach that it had been intentional.

But who would do this? Why would *anyone* do this? And why didn't Foster know who and why? He spied on spies, for God's sake.

Or did he know?

Is that why he had brought her here? To prove or disprove his suspicions?

Sara leaned back in her chair, dabbed the sweat from above her upper lip, from her forehead. In recruiting her, Foster had gone outside proper channels. So if his intention had been to prove or disprove suspicions, then it stood to reason that once those suspicions had been proved or disproved he intended to bury them and the proof. That meant he also intended to bury her.

Will I be canceled?

The moment you become a risk. Yes, you will.

Sweat trickled down between her breasts. She'd become a risk the moment he had mentioned Braxton.

Her stomach muscles clenched. The taste in her mouth turned bitter. Could he really do that? Bury her?

She sifted back, through five years of memories and confrontations with him. Panic surged up from deeper and deeper inside her. Not only could Foster bury her, he would.

Unless you stop him, Sara. You choose. Fight to stop him, or let him do it.

Shaking, she stacked the files and grabbed her purse. Her every instinct was to run to Joe, to wrap herself in one of his hugs and shut out the world. But she couldn't do that. This problem wasn't going to go away. She had to face it. And to solve it.

She had to face Foster. To talk to him, anyway. The sooner, the better.

*   *   *

His name was Jarrod.

He lay flat on his back on the padded floor and tucked his folded arms behind his head. Jarrod. Amazing how much pressure it relieved just to know his name.

The Celtic music beat a soothing tattoo inside his mind. He hated to admit it, but Sara had been right about it. About the music, and the rage. About a lot of things.

Now that there was color, his whole room felt . . . calmer. Having experienced the rage, he appreciated calm.

He knew his name. That he'd been a major. That he'd been a Shadow Watcher. That he was halfway in love with his doctor—a woman he had known of before coming here. A woman he nearly had murdered, who had cried for him. For . . . him.

Images came to mind. Images of the familiar man. Images of, he suspected, his mother. And images of a woman he sensed belonged to him. She was beautiful, with long black hair and brilliant blue eyes. But they were cold. She was cold.

Feeling her chill, he rubbed at his arms. No, not cold. Betrayed. She had betrayed him. How, he didn't know. He had known, but he'd forgotten again. That was okay. When he was ready, the memory would come back.

He closed his eyes, watched the spots from the bright lights overhead dance on his eyelids, and thought of Sara. He didn't want to care about her any more than she wanted to care about him. But he did.

God help him, he did.

Sara monitored the grounds.

No dogs, but guards patrolled the facility's perimeter every half hour, and one person remained in the guard shack at the entrance gate at all times. The entire perimeter fence was electric, topped with razor wire, and enclosed even the grass airstrip. One exit in and out, blocked by an armed guard. That damned fence. How was she supposed to get out of here?

There had to be a way, and she had to find it. She had to

talk to Foster. And to Lisa. Sara checked her watch. Eight-forty. To hell with subterfuge.

She pulled out her car keys, slung her purse over her shoulder, and hustled to her car. Okay, so she'd get out fine. The problem would be getting back in. If worse came to worst, she could sit in her car parked outside the gate until morning.

She braked to a stop on the road near the shack, and a guard stepped out. In his late twenties, he had three stripes on his sleeve and a grim expression on his face. She hit the window button, and with a little squeak, the glass lowered.

"Dr. West?" He tilted his head to keep from blocking the light.

She didn't remember having seen him before, but evidently she had at some time. She scanned his name tag, sewn just above the pocket on his uniform shirt. Ah, the uncommunicative guard who had escorted her to Fontaine's office when she'd first arrived here. "Hi, Reaston."

He checked his watch. "It's not long until lock-down."

"I have to risk it." She pretended an embarrassment she didn't feel. "I have to run to the store."

"You can get everything you need here, ma'am."

"No I can't. The facility exchange store is out of, er, what I need." *Think fast, Sara. He's young and brash. He's going to ask what you need.*

"Maybe I can rustle it up for you." Reaston checked his watch again. "You'll be hard-pressed to make it to the store and back before lock-down."

"I'm going to have to risk it."

"If you're late getting back, I can't open the gate for you."

"I know."

"What is it you need? We can put out a call. Somebody around here's bound to have it."

"I'd rather not do that," Sara insisted, scrambling for an answer.

"Don't worry about it, Dr. West. We help each other out all the time."

Sara hit on her answer. "Not with feminine hygiene products. I'd rather not announce to all of Braxton that I'm having a period."

Reaston stammered, and his face turned red. "Try to hurry." He opened the gate and waved her through.

Smiling to herself, Sara hit the gas, and drove down the dirt road. When the lights from the guard shack faded behind her, she shrugged out of her lab coat. The corner of the ID badge dangling from her collar stabbed her in the thigh. She shoved it over on the passenger's seat.

Five miles down the road, out in the middle of no-man's-land, she spotted the convenience store. It stood alone, a white cinder-block building with a flat roof and a sandy, weed-infested parking lot. The store was pitch-dark, but Foster's recommended phone was bolted to the cinder-block wall beside the front door. The shelf meant to hold the phone book was empty. The directory dangled from a silver cord, its pages fluttering in the crisp breeze.

She pulled into the empty parking lot and stopped in front of the rusted-out Coke machine. Its red paint looked dull and weather-worn, and it reminded her of Jarrod. *Joe.* She had to think of him as *Joe* or she'd slip up in front of someone else, and word would get back to Fontaine. Protective or rotten to the core, Fontaine had more ears than employees inside Braxton, and if he was rotten and not patient-protective, then a slip could cost Joe his life.

She fished two quarters out of her purse and looked around. Through the store window, she saw lights from a drink cooler, and debated. Should she leave the headlights on, or turn them off?

Safer not to be spotted. She cut her headlights and the engine, and then got out of the car and stumbled on a beer can. It splattered beer on her shoe and smelled potent. The wind raised goose bumps on her skin. Since the sun had set, it had gotten nippy. And no moon. The sky looked desolate with no moon illuminating it.

Stepping over the concrete curb marker, she felt her way to the phone, lifted the receiver, and dropped a coin into the slot.

No dial tone.

She pushed the coin-release button. Nothing happened. She tried another coin. Still nothing. "Great. Just great."

She hung up and then made her way back to her car, certain Foster had planned this additional little complication to torment her. He had specified this store and this phone.

Back in the car, she checked her watch. Nine o'clock, straight up and down.

No phone. And she couldn't get back into Braxton. Not tonight.

She drove to the nearest phone, which proved to be at another store nearly fifteen miles farther down the road. Foster didn't answer. No surprise there, as it was nine-thirty. But Brenda did.

Sara couldn't admit even to herself how good it felt to hear her sister's voice. "It's me."

"What's wrong with your voice?"

She touched the skin at her neck. Still tender and bruised. "I picked up a little sore throat. That's all." No sense in telling Brenda that Joe had nearly killed her. She'd been after Sara for years to change careers, and she would make Lisa call their parents—since their mother wasn't speaking to Brenda—and then their folks would start harping on Sara again, too. No, thanks. She'd gotten a bellyful of "why do you want to work with crazy people?" from them already. "No news on David yet, but it shouldn't be much longer. I don't want to say much on the phone," she said, knowing Brenda was holding her breath, hoping. "How are things there?"

"Lisa's being totally unreasonable. Will you talk to her?"

Totally unreasonable in Brenda's eyes could mean Lisa had left her room a wreck—perfectly normal for a twelve-year-old—or she'd run away. Sara wasn't in the mood for guessing games, or a twenty-questions session. "Put her on."

A few minutes elapsed. Then Sara heard, "Aunt Sara?"

Lisa. She hadn't run away. Saying a silent thank-you, Sara looked up at the stars, then down at the dirt. "Hi, honey." She stepped on a wood roach crawling near her foot. God, but it was huge. "How are you?"

"Maxed out."

"Your mom didn't marry—"

"No, she said she'd wait a couple of weeks. God, Aunt Sara. It's so embarrassing. Gwendolyn Pierce says even if Mom doesn't marry H. G. or G. H. Williamson, she can never come over here again. They're Catholics. They stomach stuff. They don't get divorced."

The cold breeze ruffled over Sara's skin. Wishing she had kept on her lab coat, she rubbed at her arms. "You okay with that?"

"No," she flatly stated. "But I don't get to choose, do I?"

Sara stared at the dirt. "Apparently, you don't. But who your mom marries is definitely her decision." And in this case, God, but Sara resented that. "How are things otherwise?"

"Okay. Taylor Baker invited me to the Autumn Festival. Mom says I'm too young to date, so I'm meeting him there."

"I see."

"Don't snitch, Aunt Sara. He's the only good thing in my life right now."

"Just be careful. Don't fall too hard too fast, okay?"

"I won't. He's not the one, but he is fun. He makes me laugh." Lisa's voice dropped a notch. "Mom said she wouldn't get married, but I saw her looking at bridal books today, and we both know what that means. She's got the itch. Bad. And I heard her tell Mary Kitchens, the lady next door, she was considering a Christmas wedding. I didn't want to tell you before because I was scared she was listening in. But now I know she isn't."

"How do you know?" Sara watched two men walk out of the store, chugging beers. They crawled into a rusted-out pickup truck and pulled out, their spinning tires churning gravel, their tailpipe spitting smoke.

"She's on the sofa in a lip-lock with the judge. I'm in the kitchen."

"Lisa, are you spying on them?"

"No way. It's gross. They're *sooo* old!"

Biting back a smile at the "sooo old" remark, and glad to hear Lisa considered lip-locks gross, Sara watched a woman drop a letter into the mailbox slot right beside the phone, and then enter the store. Her sandals flapped against her heels.

Staring at the mailbox, Sara remembered something important. "Lisa, I need a favor. I'm mailing you an envelope." Sara pulled the envelope holding Fontaine's peacock-blue notes from her purse. "Do *not* open it. I want you to take it to my office and give it to Dr. Kale. Put it in his hands. That's vital, okay?"

"Sure, Aunt Sara. What's up? You sound nervous."

"I'm fine. Tell Dr. Kale I urgently need verification of the dates the documents were written and to know if they were all written by the same person." With luck, the only page that would be dated differently would be the sample of Fontaine's writing she'd lifted.

"No problem."

"Lisa, this is critical." The wind whipped at Sara's hair. She smoothed it back from her face. "I'm counting on you."

"I'll get it done."

"Thanks." Sara dropped the envelope into the mailbox's slot. Her heart lurched and she swallowed hard. "You need anything from me?"

"Yeah, I really do."

"You name it, kid." Sara smiled.

The line went silent. In a tiny voice, Lisa whispered, "A miracle."

Sara's smile faltered. Staring at a star, she spoke past a lump in her throat. "I'll see what I can do."

The dial tone droned. Sara hooked the receiver and then walked into the store. Heat blasted her in the face and the Coke machine stood nearly empty.

"We're having problems with the cooling system," a male clerk about forty with thick glasses and a crooked nose warned her. "It won't hold a charge. A guy's supposed to be out first thing in the morning to fix it."

That wouldn't be a lot of help to her at getting a cold drink now. "Do you have anything cold?"

"Just beer." He nodded to an ice chest on the floor at the far wall. Cans peeked out from crushed bits of ice.

Sara pulled out a frosty can, snagged a box of tampons from the shelf, and paid for her purchases at the cash register.

Outside, someone was using the phone. A guy wearing a dirty white T-shirt and cutoff jeans. Barefoot. A blue bandana held his hair tied back in a ponytail that was longer than Lisa's. It rubbed against his shoulder blades.

Sara waited near her car, and looked around. Isolated area. Dormant fields, ditches, and tons of bugs, but few people. In fact, she scanned up then down the road; except for the Ford parked on the side of the building, hers was the only car around. She suspected the Ford belonged to the store clerk, so where had the guy on the phone come from? He must have walked for miles.

"Yeah, I'm at Tim's out at the crossroads." He slurred, as if he'd had one beer too many. "Move your ass getting here, Callie. I ain't waitin' all night."

Jerk. Sara bit her tongue to keep her mouth shut. She needed to save all of her outrage for Foster.

The guy hung up, gave her the once-over, which she ignored, and then walked back inside. His T-shirt was hiked up in back and the top of his underwear stuck out above his jeans. About as sexy as a mudpack, that. What did Callie see in him?

Sara considered going over the phone receiver with an antiseptic wipe, but figured, why bother? The beer would kill the germs. She dialed Foster's number. It rang three times. Finally, he answered.

"Hello."

"It's me." She automatically looked around, and then chided herself for it. Absurd. Out in the middle of nowhere, who cared who she talked with on the phone? She wasn't a spy, she was a doctor. "I tried calling earlier. The phone you chose was out of order."

"Yes, I know," Foster said. "So, Dr. West, where are you calling from, and what do you have to report?"

"Another store," Sara said, resisting the urge to shout at him. "And not a lot to report aside from a ton of interference, which I said I wouldn't tolerate."

"From who?"

"Fontaine. He's having conniption fits because I got his research money—at least, I think he is. To tell you the truth, Foster, I'm not sure about Fontaine. He's either a very good man doing his best to protect his patients, or he's a cold, calculating bastard."

Foster chuckled. It sounded strange. Sara didn't think she'd ever before heard the man chuckle. "You should know which by now," he said. "You've been there five days."

"I've known you for five years and I still can't decide about you."

"Maybe I'm a bit of both." He changed the subject. "So what have you learned?"

Maybe they all were a bit of both. "Well, I've damn near been killed."

"Oh?"

He wasn't surprised. He tried to sound it, but Sara sensed Foster knew all about Joe and the choking incident. Now who would have told him? *How* would anyone have told him? She was here at the store because the phones inside Braxton weren't secure. "I want hazardous-duty pay."

"I'll arrange it."

"A lot of it."

"Very well."

Hell, she was on a roll. Might as well go for the moon. "And I want you to get Fontaine off my back."

"You'll have to handle him, Sara."

"You don't understand. He's interfering at every turn, issuing orders on my patients, countermanding my decisions, and making me miserable. He even bugged my name badge."

"I understand Dr. Fontaine is a challenge. But you need to understand that if I interfere on any front at this point, then your cover is shot and so is my operative."

Unsalvageable. "Your covert stuff sucks dead canaries."

"Very often, yes, it does." Foster paused, as if sipping from a drink. "So, tell me why you've been at Braxton for five days and you still don't know anything about it."

"I've been a little busy, nearly getting murdered by one of your patients and trying to get a handle on my patients." She debated mentioning Fontaine's peacock-blue notes and quickly decided against it. "About my patients," she started, figuring she might as well begin at the beginning. "The primary criteria for a PTSD diagnosis is that the patient experienced a traumatic event which threatened death or injury and felt fear, helplessness, or horror. If the symptoms persist for longer than a month and they've caused significant distress or impairment, then we typically see evidence from three other symptom clusters."

"Like what?"

"Intrusions, such as flashbacks or nightmares, avoidance, and hyperarousal—where the patient exhibits physiological signs of hyperviligence or elevated startle response."

"So what are you telling me?"

"I'm telling you that none of these patients should have been diagnosed as PTSD patients."

"I suspected that." He let out a little grunt. "What happened to them?"

He suspected that? Then why not mention it? Why recruit her? Until now, she had been under the impression, and Foster baldly had stated, that he needed her help. PTSD patients need a PTSD expert. Logical. But not the case. So if he didn't need her skills as a PTSD expert, then what did he need? Why her?

"I don't know what happened to them—yet."

"Suspicions?"

"Tons of them. But at the moment, none firm enough to discuss." Especially since most of them involved him. "Fontaine's notes in the charts are sketchy at best—essentially worthless—and he shipped out one of my patients—Fred. ADR-22. I never even got to see him."

"Why was he shipped out?"

Again, she sensed Foster's lack of surprise. "An arrhythmic heartbeat found on an electrocardiogram." Unease threaded her voice. "You wouldn't know anything about him being moved, now would you?"

"How could I?"

She twisted the silver phone cord, letting it slide between her fingertips. "You're resourceful."

"I don't know anything about it."

Foster was lying. Sara stabbed the toe of her sneaker into the sandy dirt. It lifted a little cloud of dust. Did it take an act of Congress to get anyone to tell the truth anymore? "Fontaine nearly put one of my patients into a diabetic coma. He lied about his involvement and blamed the nurse. William is his name. He got demoted and fined. You need to fix that, Foster. It's not just. The fault was Fontaine's." She explained how Fontaine had written and then deleted the 70/30 prescription order.

"Did you file an incident report?"

"Of course. And Fontaine has given me hell for that, too. I think he's planning to bring me up on charges. Probably a court-martial."

"For filing a mandatory report?"

"For refusing to obey a direct order to delete a mandatory report that I filed." She hiked up the mouthpiece and blew out a sigh. "I suppose you're disappointed because I didn't spend a lot of time boning up on Braxton right away. But honestly, Foster, a doctor wouldn't do that. It'd be out of character."

"Not for a major."

"Oh." Well, hell. He had her there. "I guess I'm having a little orientation problem with the military aspects. There's a lot to it all—most of it unnecessary."

"If you still believe that, then you do have a lot of adjusting to do, and a lot to learn."

The breeze whipped her hair over her face. She shoved it back from her eyes. "You're disappointed in me, but I'm not as naïve as you think."

"Oh?" He didn't sound convinced.

"Did you really think I'd come here, not trusting you, without knowing anything about what I was walking into?"

"There is no unclassified data on Braxton, Sara."

"But there is information available."

"What kind of information?"

"Oh, the usual. Built right after World War Two as a training facility, though it's doubtful it was ever used for that. It was in all the papers. Then, in the sixties, some senator from

California started asking questions about the place, and suddenly it dropped off the map. Official word, I hear, is that it's been closed down since the early seventies. Of course, that's when it became the Braxton Facility we know it as today."

Foster didn't say a word.

"What I don't understand is why there are still remnants of a grass airstrip near the pond to the southwest of the main facility. Easy to spot that from the air, I expect. And I don't understand why there's a helicopter pad, though you'll say it's to transport patients too ill for ground transport. Of course, if access in and out is restricted, then not many patients get transported, do they?"

"Transports do occur. Mostly by air."

"What, Peter Pan drops 'em in?"

"No, we use people with appropriate clearances."

"In other words, Shadow Watchers."

No answer.

Sara didn't need one. His silence spoke volumes. She stared at the guy who had been on the phone earlier. Pacing alongside the road and clearly agitated, he lit a cigarette. Its red tip glowed in the dark. "Not that you'll care, but I'm also disappointed in you."

"Why?" Foster sounded stunned.

Sara supposed he was stunned. He probably hadn't had those words directed at him very often in his life. Having second thoughts about disclosing her true reason for that remark—telling Foster she had pegged his operative could get Joe and her killed—she opted for an alternate reason. "You sent me in here unprepared."

"For what? You're a doctor, acting in that capacity."

"Have you spent any time here?"

"No."

"Well, let me clue you in." Sara toed the wall below the phone with the tip of her shoe. "This place is weird. Aside from the two hundred twenty-seven patients, four hundred employees live here. At least, that's my understanding, and yet none of them seem to have any family. There's not a single kid in the housing block, or in the facility's quarters. Come to think of it, there's not a sign of anyone who's even married."

"There are no married people there, with the exception of Dr. Fontaine. But I believe his wife already had left for vacation when you arrived."

Confirmation. Some people *were* allowed to leave Braxton. Fontaine's wife had. That news was a relief.

"Braxton isn't a healthy environment for children," Foster added.

"What about spouses? Out of four hundred people, why is only Fontaine married?"

"Fontaine is a lifer. The others aren't allowed to leave the facility."

Not allowed to leave? That disclosure had shivers sliding up her spine. Well, what about Mrs. Fontaine? She'd left. "How long do they stay there?"

"However long their tour of duty happens to be."

Sara was on to something. She sensed it. "Some people are here for a year, maybe two."

"Some are there far longer," Foster countered. "Is there a point to this?"

"Yes, there is. You people are crazy, Foster. You can't lock people up like this and call it part of the job. It's not natural."

"Not only can we, we do." He paused. "Now before you take my head off, listen. They don't know where they are. We have to keep it that way because if we don't, then Braxton and the men in it are vulnerable to attack, and so are their relatives. All of the staff volunteered, and each of them receives additional pay for the hardship tour there. It's an equitable solution, Major. Everyone wins."

Afraid she could answer the question already, Sara forced herself to ask it anyway. "What do you do if someone finds out where they are?"

"Cancel them."

Sara knew he was going to say that god-awful word. She hated it as much as she hated *unsalvageable*. Her grip on the phone tightened and she worked at keeping her voice level. "And when their tour of duty here is up, do you cancel them then, too?"

"It isn't necessary. They have no idea where they are."

Did he think she was stupid? "Shank flew her damn plane here," Sara reminded him. "How can you say she has no idea where she is? Are you going to kill her, Foster?"

The sound of him swallowing carried through the phone. "Employees only become a threat on learning of, or on leaving, their location, Sara. Keep that in mind during your interactions with the men and women serving there."

So Shank never could leave Braxton. Ever.

When she didn't say anything, Foster went on. "Look, we're not ogres. Don't make this worse than it is. It is an equitable system."

But they *were* ogres, and the system *wasn't* equitable. Shank was a lifer, too. Not by choice, like Fontaine, but because she had flown her plane to her new assignment. Now, she either stayed there for the rest of her life, or she died.

"What about Mrs. Fontaine? She knows where she's been." And policy was to cancel all who knew.

"She's an exception."

And Sara wasn't.

That truth reached up from the depths of her soul and bit her hard. Foster was going to let her do this assignment and then kill her for knowing about Braxton. And she had no one to blame but herself.

She'd known from the beginning he couldn't be trusted and that he was keeping something crucial from her. She'd known it. But she wasn't going to just accept this edict of his. No way.

So how did she prove what he was doing? How could she gather enough evidence to stop him?

"Is there anything else to report?"

Sara snapped out of her thoughts. "A couple of questions."

"Go ahead."

"Do you have any idea why my patients would react adversely to the colors red and white?"

"I'm not sure."

Too smooth. And evasive. Very telling for Jack Foster. He knew exactly. Sara clenched her jaw. Just once, she wished

.the man would play straight with her. "But you do have suspicions about it."

"When I know the facts, I'll pass them along."

"You'll pass along the information on all of the PTSD patients you promised, too, right?"

"I'm working on it."

Sure he was. Of course he was. Fat chance. He was interested in *these* patients, not ones suffering from PTSD or their families. It'd be a cold day in hell before she got the statistics and data she'd requested. She bit back her frustration on that and at him for not sharing his suspicions. If he would share, then at least she would have some clue about what she was working with here. "What about the phrase 'I wept'? Does it mean anything to you?"

Foster didn't answer, and Sara had the strangest feeling he couldn't answer. She waited him out. Damn it, sooner or later he'd get tired of listening to line static and say something.

Finally, he did. "I'll check into it."

"And will you correct the injustice about William? He was a victim, Foster."

"At the appropriate time, I'll see to it that William is compensated and his rank is reinstated."

"Why not now?"

"Because then Fontaine will know I've got an operative working inside Braxton. Aside from the complications that will cause, he'll be even harder on William."

That made sense. "Okay, but when you do fix this, William gets back pay."

"Agreed."

Foster had been firm but sharp and fair, and Sara couldn't fault his logic. At least, not regarding William. She twisted to see what was moving around her, but everything was still and quiet, except for the crickets. You'd think that after all this time, she'd be able to get a fix on Foster. But even now she floundered, uncertain if he was honorable or an ass. Either way, she had to know the answer to a question she had avoided. "Foster?"

"Yes?"

Her hand went slick on the receiver. The guy who had been on the phone walked out of the store and climbed into a white pickup with red clay dirt splattering its sides. "When exactly do you view me as becoming a threat?"

No answer.

Sara's skin prickled. "Not that I'll believe you anyway, but I want your word that when this is over, I'm going to walk out of here."

"Good night, Sara." Foster hung up the phone.

She stared at the receiver a long time. Before asking, she had felt reasonably certain that he would give her his word. But he hadn't. This turn of events she hadn't expected, and she had no idea how to change them. The bottom line, it appeared, was that once you knew about Braxton, you were a risk. And once you were positioned inside it, there was only one way to get out.

To die.

twelve

☆

Shank waited impatiently for Beth to leave the nurse's station.

She'd been off-duty for a couple of hours, but lingered, which wasn't uncommon. The facility's theater didn't start this week's new movie for two more days, one could only bowl so many games, and the facility's exchange provided limited shopping. There was nothing else to do. Bored and restless, Beth often put in hours of overtime to just stay busy. Normally, it was appreciated.

Tonight, it was not.

Ten more minutes passed. Shank watched the red second hand sweep around the clock, growing more and more agitated. It was 2110. Already ten minutes into lock-down. She had to do something. If she didn't get the call in soon, it would be too late.

"Beth." Shank swiveled her creaky chair. "Would you do me a favor and run a visual check on ADR-40?" She'd have to suit up in protective gear because of the staph infection. That would give Shank a little more time. "His call light flickered," Shank lied, and nodded toward the panel. "I don't know if he needs something, or if there's a short in the system and I need to call Maintenance."

"Sure. No problem." Beth left the station and walked down the hall toward ADR-40's room.

Stretching over the desk, Shank watched Beth pull the yellow gown, face mask, cap, and gloves from the cart in the hallway outside ADR-40's room, and then begin putting them on. Considering it safe, she punched the secure-phone-line button and dialed the guard shack at the front gate.

On the first ring, a man answered. "Sergeant Reaston."

Relieved it was him, Shank spoke softly. "It's me. Let Dr. West back into the facility. Keep it quiet, and make her think she's pulled off getting you to do it. Use the taking-pity factor."

"Is Fontaine aware of this?"

"No," Shank said, not at all surprised by the question. Around here, the staff had to keep straight where, and from whom, orders originated.

"Higher up?"

"You've got it."

"Will do."

Shank dropped the receiver into its cradle and looked up.

Beth stood behind her, her expression grim and accusing. "You want to explain that?"

Caught redhanded. No evasive tactics were going to work. Shank arched a brow. "Not really."

"Fine." Folding her arms across her thin chest, Beth twisted her lips. "Then you can explain it to Dr. Fontaine."

"I'd rather not." Shank stood up. "And if it looks as if I'm going to be forced to, one of us is going to commit suicide." She turned an uncompromising gaze on Beth, and watched the color drain from her face. "It's not going to be me."

Sara drove back to Braxton and stopped outside the gate.

She turned off the ignition, cut the lights, and then stared at the iron bars, hoping Reaston was still on duty. His blushing earlier about her reason for going to the store gave her an advantage.

Tired, worried sick, she unsnapped her seat belt and slumped in her seat, letting her head loll back against the headrest.

A few minutes later, someone tapped at her window.

She opened her eyes and looked over. Reaston. She cranked the engine and lowered the glass. "Hi."

"Are you planning on spending the night out here?"

She shrugged. "I don't have a lot of choice. The store was closed, and I had to find another one. I tried to get back in time, but I couldn't do it. I figure I'm safer here with you on guard duty than I would be sitting in the store's parking lot."

"I'm sorry, I can't open the gate, Dr. West." Reaston looked torn. "You want some coffee or something?"

"No, thanks. I've been on the run since five this morning. I just want some sleep. It's hard to give your patients your best when you're dragging, you know?"

"Yes, ma'am. I've pulled double duty plenty of times. You get so tired you can't think."

"Exactly. I'm pushing that envelope now." Sara yawned.

"I hate the idea of you being dog-tired and having to sleep in your car." Reaston looked up then down the road, chewing on his inner cheek. "Look, Doc. I'm gonna let you through, but don't you dare tell anyone." He hardened his voice. "I mean, no one. What happened to William will look like nothing compared to what Dr. Fontaine will do to me if he finds out about this."

Another William-type incident on her conscience she did *not* need. "Thanks, but I can't risk getting you into trouble. It's not worth it."

"It'll be okay," Reaston assured her. "The cruiser passes through the employee parking lot on the half hour and the hour." He cut a quick glance at his watch. "If you go now, you've got time to make it. When you get to the parking lot, kill your lights—just in case. Mick Bush is on duty, and he's a fanatic about keeping the rules."

Bush. She knew the name. Yes. He had been on gate duty when she had arrived at Braxton. "Are you sure?" Sara straightened up. "Sleeping out here appeals about as much as a swarm of mosquitoes, but I don't want to cause you trouble."

"Yeah, I'm sure." He shrugged. "If we don't take care of you, then you can't take care of them. Give me a second and I'll get the gate."

"Thanks, Reaston. I owe you one."

"No sweat, Doc." He smiled. "Just be sure to kill those lights."

"Will do." Sara palmed the gearshift.

Straining to see the shadow of the road, she moved slowly

and waited until after she was inside the gate and away from
the guard shack to turn on her headlights. She drove the rest
of the way at high speed. When the parking lot came into
view, she turned her headlights off. Seeing was no problem.
The parking lot was nearly empty. If people can't leave the
premises, then they don't have much use for cars.

She pulled into a slot across the lot from Shank's plane.
Parking near an aircraft would draw more notice when she
moved the car.

Proud of herself for thinking to consider that, Sara grabbed
the bag, her purse, and her lab coat, and then left the car.

"Halt!" a man yelled out.

The shout startled Sara, and she dropped her keys. They hit
the asphalt with a dull *thunk. Oh, God.* Shoving the bag under
her lab coat, she snatched up her keys, searching for a plausible reason to be out here. If she got Reaston in trouble, she
would never forgive herself.

A flashlight beam swept to her face, blinding her. From the
darkness behind it, the man asked, "Dr. West, what are you
doing out here?"

Had to be Mick Bush. *Think. Think!* Her heart lodged
somewhere near her throat. "Just starting my car so the battery
doesn't fizzle."

"You've been here less than a week."

It seemed far, far longer. "How long does it take a battery
to run down?" She let out a little laugh. "My days have always
started early and ended late—especially during my residency.
I never learned much about cars."

"You just finishing up your rounds?"

"Yes, I am. I started at five A.M., hoping to get a little down
time, but my patients require a lot of attention right now."
Lame, but patient concern was honest and it had worked with
Reaston. "May I ask who you are?" She tilted her head, squint-
ing away from the bright light. "I can't see you with that thing
shining in my face."

"Security, ma'am. Sergeant Bush. But everyone calls me
Mick."

The fanatic Reaston had warned her to avoid. Great. Just

great. Sara reminded herself she was a major, she outranked him, then stiffened her shoulders. "Well, thanks for keeping such a close watch on my car, Mick." She began walking toward the building. "I'll see you."

Hearing his feet shuffle against the asphalt behind her, she angled her path, cutting through the cars to see what he was doing. Staring at her, he stood next to her front bumper, his palm splayed flat on the hood of her car.

Damn it. No doubt the man wondered how the engine had heated up so quickly. She tensed. Waiting for him to order her to stop, she had to concentrate on her steps, to force herself to keep her pace slow and steady.

When it became apparent he was wasn't going to stop her, she let out a held breath. No doubt about it. She *had* to find another way out of here at night. Mick Bush might not have stopped her, but being a fanatic, he would be watching her every move now.

That could be a pain and a perk. Being under a fanatic's close surveillance could definitely be an asset when Foster or Fontaine—depending on who proved to be dedicated and who proved to be scum—decided to kill her.

Sara slept like the dead and awakened dreaming of thunderstorms.

Dragging herself past the haze of sleep, she realized it wasn't storming. The phone was ringing. She glanced at the clock—four A.M. Finger-tapping her way across the nightstand to the phone, she hoisted the receiver to her ear and bumped her chin. Grunting, she mumbled, "Sara West." Her dry throat scraped. Still sore and raw.

"Major, this is William over in Isolation. Dr. Fontaine said that if ADR-30 started damaging property again to let you know right away. I'm letting you know."

"Who?" she asked, forcing the issue of the name.

"Joe." William's voice seethed resentment. "He's ripping more padding off the walls."

Disappointment shafted through her. The rage had come back. "I'll be right over." She hung up the phone and slung back the covers. *Thank you so much, Fabulous Fontaine.*

Ten minutes later, she arrived in the Isolation wing and paused near William's shoulder to study the monitor. Joe was still ripping at the wall pads.

"He's been raising hell for about half an hour. I tried calming him down. He refused a sedative and threatened to shove it up my—" Watching the monitor, William stopped talking, then shifted subjects, pointing. "Look. He keeps going to those same two spots and tearing deeper. What does he think he's pulling out of there?"

Sara bent forward, studied the monitor closely, and picked up on what Joe was destroying. The cave. And the coffin and the electric chair. "Let me in, will you?"

William's tone went stiff. "I don't think Dr. Fontaine would approve, Major. The patient is clearly violent and out of control."

"Which is why I'm depending on you to keep a close eye on the monitor." Sara worked at sounding calm and confident, reminding herself that Joe had protected her from himself several times now.

"I object, Major. The regulations clearly state that you're not to put yourself in personal jeopardy."

"William?"

He swung his questioning gaze to her. "Yes, Major?"

Again, she borrowed from his ally, Fontaine. "This is not a debate, and there are no negotiations. Open the damn door." She glared at him, conceding that at times rank came in handy. "That's a direct order, Lieutenant."

William snapped his jaw shut and flipped the switch.

The buzzer sounded.

Sara walked down the white hallway, doing breathing exercises to lower her pulse rate. She stopped outside Joe's room, and rapped on the door.

No answer.

"Joe?" She knocked again. Louder. He probably couldn't hear her over the sounds of ripping padding and his own shouting.

Still no answer.

"Joe, I'm not going to leave you like this, so you might as well answer me."

Silence. That was progress. At least he had stopped shouting and tearing at the pads. "They called me. You're having a rough night. Can I come in and help?"

"Okay." He sounded uncertain.

She opened the door so he could see her. "You're sure it's okay?" She deliberately looked at the torn padding strewn on the floor, the messy walls, and at the bits of padding he held wadded in his fists, then let him see that she felt vulnerable and unsure of him. "Is it safe?" she asked, proving his word held worth to her and he had her trust.

"It's safe." He emptied his hands and slapped them together, dusting off lingering bits of padding. "I won't hurt you again, Sara."

She watched his body language, his eyes. No rage. Weariness, but no rage. He was in control and, from appearances, lucid, though that certainly contrasted with his actions—unless he'd had a breakthrough and he was working out resentment.

Daring to hope, she stepped inside. The door closed behind her. "I thought maybe we could do some relaxation exercises. When I'm . . . restless, they help me a lot."

He nodded, definitely not of a mind to talk.

Sara sat on the floor, motioned to him, and Joe sat down across from her. Their knees brushed. "Okay, first we're going to breathe."

"I'm already breathing."

"I know, Joe. But you're not breathing like this."

His back to the camera, he dropped his voice to a whisper William wouldn't be able to detect. "My name isn't Joe."

Knowing their every move and word was under scrutiny— and William would break his neck getting to Fontaine with anything overheard or done—Sara leaned toward Joe, putting his broad back between her and the camera, and then whispered at his chest. "I know, Jarrod. But it's important to both of us that no one else knows."

His clear eyes glittered. "How important?"

"Vital."

He nodded.

She lifted his chin and her voice. "Now, position your head like-this. A little tilt upward." She dropped her voice again, her hands cupping his chin and nape. His five o'clock shadow grated against her palm. She loved the feel of it, and hated loving the feel of it. "They can't find out that I know who you are." She let her gaze meet his, felt his warm breath on her face. "If they do, then we both become threats to them."

Understanding flickered in his eyes, and he blinked slow and hard to let her know he understood.

Sara smiled. "Now, straighten your back and put your hands like this"—she laced her fingers, demonstrating—"in your lap."

Joe mimicked her and gave her hands a reassuring squeeze. Her heart thudded, and guilt swamped her. She tamped both, hoping to keep both tamped, and began teaching him the breathing techniques.

Either he was a record-breaking fast learner, or he already knew them. She couldn't tell which, and his Foster-like expression didn't give anything away. She hated it, but she had a hard time seeing past Joe's looks. He was more than attractive. Black hair, dove-gray eyes, a strong chin, and broad forehead. The tiny lines in his face told her he had worried more than he had laughed, though he had done some of that, too. Accepting it as another thing they had in common, she experienced a desire to change that ratio so he laughed more. From their therapy sessions, she had compiled quite a list of things they had in common. They liked the same music, the same TV programs, the same books. They both hated strawberries with a passion and loved banana-nut bread. He didn't like putting food in his mouth that was laced with preservatives he couldn't pronounce, and Sara had a serious penchant for junk food, but aside from that, they shared a lot of common ground.

She reached for his neck.

His hand snaked out and clamped down on her wrist.

Startled, Sara stopped, darted her gaze to his steely eyes. "I—I was just going to check your pulse rate."

The look in his eyes softened and his mouth relaxed. "Okay," he said, letting go of her stinging wrist.

"I'm sorry, I forgot." She flattened her fingertips at his carotid. "Next time, before I touch you, I'll tell you first."

"Thank you." He stared at her without a trace of wariness, then blinked, telling her he was performing for William.

She blinked back, thinking this little signal between them could be helpful. "That's much better." She lifted her fingertips from his throbbing pulse. "Do you feel calmer?"

"Yes." He stared at the strewn mess of padding, as if he wasn't sure how it had gotten there, and then at the wall.

"Joe, why did you destroy the coffin and the chair?"

He didn't look back at her, but his voice lowered to a wisp of sound. "Red haze."

"What is that?" She waited but he didn't answer, so she asked again. "Joe, what is the red haze?"

He frowned and swiveled his gaze to hers. She saw his frustration in his eyes, in the tight drawn line of his mouth, in the rigidity of his shoulders; his frustration, and his fear. "I don't know."

"It'll come," she whispered. "Don't worry about it now, and don't rush it."

"I don't push. I'm patient. I don't like the rage."

"Neither do I." She studied him. The ripping of the wall pad hadn't been the rage. "Joe," she whispered, knowing he had been working through resentment. "What did you remember?"

"Not now, Sara."

Either he wasn't ready to tell her, or felt he couldn't tell her here. "Let's do some more relaxation exercises." She changed her position, lying flat on the floor, nose and toes up, and then waited for him to mimic her. When she felt his body heat along her side, she ordered her hormones to go dormant. They ignored her.

"Okay," she said. "Pick one word that makes you feel calm and tranquil. Then focus on your breathing like before and whisper the word inside your mind over and over. Only one word. If your mind drifts, bring it back, focusing just on your one word."

He began, silent but moving his lips.

He'd chosen her name.

Sheer pleasure seeped through her. Guilt absorbed it, but it persisted, and a satisfied warmth spread deep, arousing a heat that wasn't satisfied. Realizing she was staring at his mouth and feeling an intense urge to kiss him, she virtually kicked herself, and closed her eyes. She couldn't do this. She'd made herself a promise. One that was important to both of them. Focusing on her breathing, she chose her word—Jarrod—hoping for an exorcism. Repeating it, she felt her mind drift and the tension ebb from her body. She grew calmer, quieter, more and more relaxed. More and more drowsy . . .

"Sara?"

Feeling someone's touch on her shoulder, she dragged her eyes open. They were dry and gritty. She blinked to focus and saw Joe, staring into her face. Befuddled, she frowned.

"You fell asleep." He gently brushed her hair back from her face.

Heat swam up her neck and Sara sat up. "Sorry."

"No. You demonstrated relaxing very well." A smile tugged at the corner of Joe's mouth. "But do you always snore?"

Her face went hot, but Sara chuckled. "Only when I'm really tired." She shoved her hair back and looked at him, still sprawled on his side beside her. "How did you do?"

"Well enough for you to go back to bed now."

"No more upset?"

"No." He blinked. "I'm fine. I promise."

"Why did you do it?" She glanced at the wall-pad bits scattered around.

"Later." He tugged at his ear and helped her to her feet. "Go now and get some rest."

He didn't want what he had to tell her overheard. She smiled from the door. "I'll see you tomorrow, Joe."

He didn't answer.

She looked back over her shoulder at him. He lay staring at the white wall exposed by the ripped padding and, as she watched, his expression went from clear and calm to baffled, and then blank. "Joe?"

He didn't look her way. "Where are my crayons? I need my crayons."

He needed color. She got the box from the floor, near the sketch pad. He'd been lucid a lot longer this time. That was good progress. Still, she fought the depression of seeing him slip away from her.

"Here they are, Joe." She passed the crayons over.

Joe didn't blink. This wasn't a performance for William.

Disappointed, Sara requested to be let out and then walked to the door, trying to figure out why Joe had slipped back into the netherland.

Something had to trigger the regression. But what?

Out at the station, Sara circled the Plexiglas barrier and paused at the monitors. Joe lay curled in a ball on the floor. He didn't look distressed. Actually, he appeared calm and at ease.

Yet he clutched at the box of crayons.

If she could figure out the trigger, then she could help him. It wasn't just that the ripped-out wall pad exposed the white wall. If that section of the wall bothered him, he would just look away from it, too. Joe looked away from the camera because it made him uncomfortable. But was it being watched that bothered him, or the camera itself? Which was the trigger?

She had no idea. All she really knew for certain is that none of her PTSD-diagnosed patients suffered from PTSD. Not even Joe. But they were somehow connected. Perhaps through some kind of betrayal and maybe, whatever it was about, this "I wept."

What had happened to them?

Look for more common bonds. Things all of them share.

She gritted her teeth, swearing she would, if only she could get some privacy and access to a computer.

She detoured by the second-floor station. Beth wasn't there, but Koloski was. Sara wouldn't gain access on this attempt, either.

Bitter, she took the elevator down to her quarters and then

crawled into bed. Tomorrow, she thought, punching her pillow, she would gain access to those files—even if she had to lock Beth in the med room to get it.

Sara fell back on the pillow and stared at the ceiling. Damn it, all she wanted was the truth. It wasn't as if she were begging for a fistful of miracles—though she certainly wouldn't snub her nose at them. She just wanted . . . the truth.

thirteen

☆

The truth.

Sara awakened shortly after seven, starved for it. And with two goals plaguing her mind. One, to get a grip on her un-professional feelings for Joe, so she could start sleeping and stop choking on guilt; and two, to get privacy and access to a computer. She *would* get a look at her patients' admission records. *Today.*

She stretched and tossed back the covers. The chill air raised goose bumps on her bare legs and she tugged at the tail of her T-shirt. First order of business, the truth. It was time she deciphered who was giving it to her, and who was putting it to her. She made a pit stop in the bath and craned her neck at the mirror. Her bruises were fading from deep purple to green and yellow. While chugging down a cup of piping hot coffee, she dragged on jeans, a creamy top, and her flowered lab coat. And since Jack Foster had pulled her into this night-mare, she'd start with him.

Fifteen minutes later, she stood at the nurse's station, watching Shank restock the med room with bandages, sy-ringes, and bottles of sterile saline. She shut and locked the med room door, and then dropped the keys into her pocket. Sara smiled. "Good morning."

"If what I read in William's notes was right, it's more like an extension of yesterday for you." Shank gave her the once-over, looking worried. "Up really late with Joe?"

"A little early." Sara pulled her patients' charts and tracked their progress.

"Sara, be careful, okay? They didn't get in this shape in a

day, and they can't get out of it in one. Don't burn yourself
out, trying to make the impossible happen."

"I won't," Sara promised. Long hours, hellish schedules,
and interrupted sleep had been ordinary for her. She had gone
where she was needed, when she was needed. Private practice
had spoiled her to working regular hours. Outside of Braxton,
that couldn't be the case for Shank, though. Not with what
Foster had said.

Remembering his warning, Sara knew she shouldn't probe
that topic with Shank, but she had to do it. His credibility had
been breached before, and now again. He had instructed her
to call him from a store where he knew the phone was out of
order, at 9 P.M. when he knew Braxton would be locked down
at 9 P.M., and he had refused to promise her when all this was
over, she would walk out of Braxton alive. After thinking on
it, she understood. He was testing her. He'd *always* tested her
about David. He knew she was impatient and he deliberately
pushed her hot buttons. She thought she just might hate him
for that.

Sara leaned against the desk and trod easy. "How long have
you been here, Shank?"

Shuffling some reports from her desk to Beth's, Shank
shrugged. "A couple of years."

"How long do you plan to stay?" Sara kept her voice light,
but the look in Shank's eyes and the tremble in her hand
proved she knew the questions weren't idle.

"I'm not sure. Probably until I retire." She frowned at Sara.
"Why?"

"Just curious." Sara poured herself a cup of hot coffee, then
returned to the desk. Studying the steam lifting from her cup,
she probed deeper. "Life here is so isolated and restrictive.
How do you cope?"

"It's a military thing."

What did that mean? "Protocol?"

"Not exactly." Shank set a plastic bottle of saline down on
the desk ledge. "Way back, people served in the military because they considered it their duty. Then we went through a
time where people saw joining as a career. But now those days

are over, too." She cocked her head, gazing off into space, seemingly talking more to herself than to Sara. "In a way, we've come full circle, back to duty. Yet, now it's even more complex. Serving is about duty, but it's also about having a desire to preserve ideals that most people don't even think about anymore. And it's about honor." She nodded, adding weight to her claim. "Mostly, it's about honor."

Sara leaned against the desk, propped her chin on her hand. "You'll stay isolated here until you retire as a matter of honor?"

"Not exactly." Shank grabbed a soda from the fridge, rejoined Sara at the desk, and then popped the top. The soda fizzed. "It's hard to explain."

"I appreciate your trying." Sara chewed on her lower lip. "Is it a need to serve mankind to feel validated?"

"It's not my honor, Doc." Shank grunted. "It's theirs."

Totally baffled, Sara lifted a questioning brow. "Whose?"

"The patients'," Shank explained. "Yeah, I'm isolated here. There isn't much of a social life, or much to do outside of work. I used to work pediatrics, and at times, I still miss the kids. But what I'm doing here matters. I make a difference to these patients every single day, and nothing I do is wasted."

"So you volunteered to come here?"

"Yes and no. I didn't know where 'here' was, but I volunteered for an indefinite, remote tour. And I'm not sorry, Sara. None of us are sorry."

Amazing. Seldom had Sara seen such an intense focus on purpose. And so far, nothing contradicted anything Foster had told her. She brushed her hair back from her face and noticed the phone. It had five lines. Four had numbers. The fifth was coded red and had no numbers on it. "I'm still feeling a little like a fish out of water."

"Fontaine's riding you hard, but he'll back off sooner or later. Just maintain discipline."

"It's not that." Beth was away from her computer, but Sara still lowered her voice. "It's just that things are strange here. Have you ever worked in a facility where there weren't blood drives, fund-raisers, or social events like picnics and ball games? I haven't. All you see on these boards are employee directives."

"Well, Braxton is a little different from other facilities."

"I know about the security factor. But those type events are emotionally healthy and necessary for morale. Why doesn't management have them here?"

"I don't know." Shank set down her pen. "Never thought about it."

Dead end. Shank had shut down. "So what's the word on Fred?"

"A cardiologist did an initial workup on him yesterday. He's still having irregular rhythms. They start treatment to-day."

"Good." Sara turned. "I'm taking Joe outside. I want to see how he reacts to stimuli."

"The patients aren't allowed outside."

"Joe is today." Sara gave Shank a grin, but there was steel behind it. She'd maxed out on interference. "He wants to see the sun."

"Whatever you say, Doc." Admiration gleamed in Shank's eyes. "Stick pretty close to the building, and notify Security. We don't want another incident."

"Will do," Sara said, knowing she was lying and that Shank knew it, too. "Shank, why is that phone line coded red?"

Shank's face flushed, but there was an appreciative twinkle in her eye. "It's a secure line."

"A secure internal line?"

"It's external, too." Shank looked away.

No, he couldn't have. "Is a secure line in here the same as everywhere else?"

"What do you mean, Major?"

Beth was back, and listening. "I mean, is it private?"

"Yes, ma'am," Shank said, shifting on her feet. "No one taps in, flat out."

Anger boiled in Sara's stomach. That sorry bastard. Foster could have told her there was a secure line here. There was no reason for her to go through the guard and lockdown bit. Tests. Him and his damn tests.

She grabbed a wheelchair and then a straitjacket from the supply cabinet. She should have kicked him out of her office on his ass when she had the chance.

In the hall, she passed Mick Bush on her way toward Isolation. "Morning."

"Doctor." He watched her pass.

Feeling the heat of his gaze, Sara resisted the urge to shrug and walked on to the nurse's station.

Behind the Plexiglas, someone new sat at the desk, watching the monitors. A blond woman; painfully thin, early thirties, with a stiff chin and cool eyes. Sara nodded. "Morning. I'm Dr. West. Would you open Joe's room, please?"

"Joe?" The young woman looked confused.

Since William had briefed her, and he refused to use Joe's name unless forced, no doubt the woman was confused. Sara resisted a sigh. "ADR-30. His name is Joe."

"Yes, ma'am." The woman buzzed Sara through.

Outside his door, Sara parked the wheelchair. The wing smelled stagnant, stifling. Claustrophobic feelings reared their ugly heads, and Sara drew in a long breath. *There's plenty of air. It's just warm, but there's plenty of air.*

Calmer, but still eager to get outside, she knocked on the door. "Joe, it's me. Dr. West. May I come in?"

This time his answer was immediate. "Okay, Sara."

He had shaved and put on fresh pajamas. They were blue, too, and snug. The long sleeves ended far above his wrists. "Are you ready to go outside?"

"I'm not sure." He looked toward the wall, down at the bits of padding still littering the floor. "Am I?"

"If you're aware enough to ask, then I'd say odds are good." She wanted to help him. He wanted her help, and that was great. But she didn't want him to go ballistic on her again, and he stood between her and the door. "We need to talk about a couple of things first, okay?"

He swerved his gaze to her.

"This is your first outing since the incident."

"Which incident?" A muscle in his jaw twitched. "There have been several."

His memory was improving. That was good news. "The incident where you choked me." She could barely force herself to meet his eyes. "Because of that, I'm going to put you in a wheelchair and in a jacket to take you outside."

"No." His eyes glittered anger.

"Joe, I have to do it." She pleaded with him to understand. "I can't put the other patients at risk. You know that as well as I do. If all goes well, we'll get rid of them, but until I know everyone is safe, I can't do this any other way."

He turned his back on her. Yet what she sensed wasn't his anger, it was humiliation. As if he resented lacking control over his own temper. Compassion jerked at her. Hard. "I don't like this any more than you do, but I have no choice. Haven't you been in situations where you've had no choice?"

"Yes, I have. Plenty of them." He rubbed his hands together. "Okay. But get reassured that I'm safe quickly. I said I wouldn't hurt you again, and I won't. I won't hurt anyone else, either. You have my word on it."

"I appreciate it, Joe." Lucid, he would keep his word, but would he remain lucid? That was the question. Still, she appreciated the reassurance.

"I want this part over, Sara." His serious expression turned grave, grooving the lines alongside his mouth from his nose to his chin. "I'm not crazy."

"Of course you're not crazy. Good grief, why would you even think that?"

"I'm locked in the Isolation wing in what is obviously a mental facility, straitjacketed more often than not, and I'm out of line to consider it?" He had a lot more opinions and observations on this, but from the set of his squared jaw, he wasn't interested in sharing them. At least not with her, and not now. Staring at the wall, he seemed suddenly irritated. "Where are my colors?"

Was he losing lucidity? Color. The trigger hit her. He'd been staring at the white wall when he had become irritated. He sensed the change in himself and wanted his crayons to add color—to get rid of the irritation.

She stepped between him and the wall, blocking his view

of the white. "Joe, may I explain something to you?"

"I'm listening."

"Please look at me. Not at the wall."

He turned a forceful gaze on her, and she continued, hoping her voice didn't shake. "I can't help someone who is genuinely crazy. I can help you, if you'll cooperate with me."

"Got it." He nodded. "Ready?"

"As soon as we get the gear on."

She helped him get into the straitjacket and then into the wheelchair, parked just outside his door in the hall. When she snapped the seat belt across him, he sucked in a huge gasp and his face went white. "What's wrong?" Sara asked. "Joe?"

"I—I don't like straps. I *hate* straps. Take it off, Sara. I—I can't breathe."

She unsnapped the belt, and coached him in his breathing. A white line circled his mouth and sweat beaded on his forehead and rolled down his temples. She dabbed at it with the tail of her lab coat. "You okay?"

"Better." He spoke from between his teeth, his grip tight on the arms of the chair. "Get me out of here."

"We're going." She rolled him down the hallway, heading toward the heavy metal doors. "You doing okay?"

He looked back at her. "I hate straps."

"I know. But they're not connected, they're just resting on your knees." And, boy would she catch hell if anyone noticed. "I don't like being confined, either." Talk about an understatement. "But we have to prove that you're no threat to the others."

"I have to prove it to you, too."

"Yes." She refused to feel guilty about that, though it pricked at her.

"I can't breathe when I'm strapped down." His eyes glittered. "My chest can't expand and I can't get enough air."

Sara had to head this off. He was moving toward the rage, she could see it in his eyes, in his tense posture. She stopped the chair, walked around to its front, and stooped down in front of him. "Joe." She rested a hand on his knee. "Please don't be upset. Please. You are not confined to this chair. The straps are not connected. They don't cross your chest."

"They did."

"But they don't now."

"I can't move my arms."

"The jacket and chair are steps we have to take along the way. They're important, but just a speck on the big picture. Please don't let them upset you."

He didn't answer. But the glaze faded from his eyes, and they turned that soft dove-gray. He was lucid again.

She glanced up, and the trigger for his agitation hit her. The hallways, floors, and ceilings in this wing were all white. Damn it, she shouldn't have missed that. "I know the white bothers you, Joe. That's what has you upset. But it'll only take a couple of minutes and we'll be outside, so try to ignore it, okay? If you can't do that, then just shut your eyes."

"I can do that." Strain edged his voice. "I'm patient."

Calling upon his inner strength again. A good sign—and one that made her wonder. How often had he been forced to do that? Under normal circumstances, in his life as a Shadow Watcher? "We're going to go now, okay?"

He gave her a curt, crisp nod.

Grateful, Sara got behind the chair and grasped the handles. Moving down the hallway, she chatted to keep his mind too busy to worry. Joe listened, but said nothing.

The big metal door opened, and she wheeled Joe through the opening. The woman behind the desk gasped, and before Sara even had passed the nurse's station, she had the phone in her hand. No doubt informing Fontaine.

Sara kept going. She followed the hallway to the elevator and pressed the button. It lit up.

"I don't like boxes. There aren't any sounds or smells."

Odd way of putting it, but she knew what he meant. Probably the elevator reminded him of the coffin. "I don't like them, either. I got stuck in one once." Another common bond. "But we have to go down in the elevator. Can't take the chair on the stairs."

"I don't like boxes," he said more emphatically. "No sounds or smells."

"Neither do I, Joe," she repeated. "I've hated anything that closes me in since a patient locked me in a closet with his pet boa constrictor."

"Why did he do that?"

"He was suffering a flashback," Sara explained. "Anyway, the snake was hungry and I was in sheer terror that I'd be lunch. But I survived the closet—though, I admit, I no longer hang up my coat on emergency house calls—and you'll survive the elevator ride down to the first floor. We will get outside and see the sun." She pressed the button again, wishing to hell it would hurry and get here before he could work himself into a panic—or worse, a rage. "Just do your breathing exercises. And close your eyes."

"Did the snake bite you?"

"No. It didn't choke me, either. I have no idea why. I sat statue-still, expecting the attack any second for hours. But it never happened. Finally, my patient's wife returned home and let me out of the closet. I was lucky, I guess."

"Very lucky, and you got over your fear of snakes."

"I did." Surprise streaked up her back, tingled the roof of her mouth. "How did you know that?"

No answer.

"Joe, how did you know that? I didn't tell you I used to fear snakes."

Still no answer.

She let her hand slide from his shoulder to his nape. His skin was cold, clammy. "Joe?"

He looked up at her, his eyes glazing. "I want to see the sun."

The bell chimed and the elevator door opened. "I'm taking you outside. Right now. See? We're on our way."

Sara rolled Joe inside, and pressed the first-floor button. Her hand wasn't quite steady. Neither, she noticed, was his.

One floor. He just had to stay calm for one floor. She covertly glanced at him and figured the odds at fifty-fifty.

The door slid shut and the elevator began its downward descent. Sara stayed quiet, monitoring Joe's breathing. When it began accelerating, she placed a hand on his shoulder and gave him a reassuring squeeze. "Almost there. Hang tight, now."

He didn't respond, but his breathing did slow down.

The door opened and Sara gave a quick prayer of thanksgiving. She rolled Joe out into a gray hallway. Along the walls hung photos of former directors. Amazing that the Foster-types allowed the display—until Sara remembered the facility directors were lifers. They came, they ruled. But they never left, or went home.

Something about that niggled at her.

Then she remembered. Mrs. Fontaine and her European vacation. That didn't make sense. But if Sara started ruling out the nonsensible, she'd rip the heart right out of Braxton.

The doors leading outside opened automatically.

Sara wheeled Joe out into the full sunlight, and then stepped to the side of the chair to observe his reaction. He leaned his head back, breathed in deeply, and lifted his face to the sun. A serenity unlike any Sara ever had seen settled over him.

Her instincts had told her to get him outside. They'd been right. Taking a leap of faith, she shoved the straps off his lap. The metal ends pinged against the chair's frame.

Joe smiled, straight from the heart. "The sun feels good, Sara."

"Yes." Her heart melted, and she smiled back. "It does."

He let his gaze sweep over the lawn, the garden, the islands of blossoming flowers, and down the hedge maze toward the pond. "Look, Sara," he whispered. "Look at all the colors."

The wonder in his voice rivaled a child's on seeing his first snowflake. And seeing this through Joe's eyes—an infusion of color after deprivation—Sara shared the feelings. Dear God, that was how he'd been tortured. The box, the coffin, the confinement—no smells or sounds. Logical. And highly probable.

Fontaine didn't want him to remember. That's why he'd isolated Joe. Or Fontaine was trying to protect Joe, and Foster wanted Joe isolated to protect his security clearance. One of them didn't want Joe to remember. So they had kept him sensory-deprived. But how had that worked? How had keeping him away from color kept him from remembering?

Unable not to touch him, she rested a hand on his shoulder. "The color is beautiful, Joe."

He dipped his head, capturing her hand between his shoulder and his face. His warmth felt good, and the sense of isolation and fear she had fought and suppressed since arriving at Braxton faded.

"Can we go to the pond to see the water? I like water." Joe let out a little self-deprecating laugh. "When I was a kid and I'd get upset, I always went to the shore. I'd look out over the horizon and nothing seemed too big for me to handle."

He was remembering! Sara nearly stumbled from shock. Not wanting to break the spell, she kept quiet and judged the distance between the door and the pond. Two minutes; maybe, three. Deeming that safe, she pushed the wheelchair, rolling it down the stone path toward the pond.

"I like it out here," Joe said. "No boxes. Lots of sounds and smells." His voice went whisper soft. "No white. No red."

"Good." Joe's torture had definitely included sensory deprivation. No doubt about it.

Sara stopped near the water's edge and stepped to the side of Joe's chair. He smiled up at her. "I like the way the sun shines on your hair."

A rush of pure pleasure swept through her. The guilt chased and buried it. *Don't think or feel it. It's not right.*

It's honest.

It's still wrong.

"Sara." He looked up at her, clearly worried. "Are you all right?"

"I'm fine." She forced herself to smile. This was her problem. Not his. And she couldn't make it his problem.

"I want to walk on the grass. I like feeling the grass under my feet." He grinned. "My dad used to say, 'Man wasn't meant to walk on concrete.' "

With that banal comment, the truth hit her. Some time ago, Joe had snagged a corner of her heart. But at some obscure point since then, he'd claimed it all. She loved him. Right or wrong, professional or not. "Are you married?" Her heart went on hold.

"Not anymore. Once. But not anymore."

Relief washed through her. "Maybe next time you can walk in the grass, Jarrod."

He frowned up at her. "Don't call me that."

"Why? We're alone out here, and they can't—"

"Because you could get confused and say it at the wrong time." He turned his gaze from the rippling water to her. "If they know, then I'm a threat. And if I'm a threat, I die." He sucked in a sharp breath. "God forgive me, so do you."

She agreed. She knew why she agreed, but what made him so certain? "Why do you think this?"

"Because you'll know the truth."

"What truth?"

"Who I am. What I do."

So her fears weren't paranoia or unfounded. Lucid, Joe understood how things worked, too. "I won't do it again."

I won't do it again.

Jarrod stilled. Another woman's voice sounded inside his head. A woman with long black hair and tear-filled eyes, pleading with him. *I won't do it again.*

And the memory returned. His wife, Miranda, having an affair with his best friend, Royce. A long-standing affair. And Jarrod had caught them having sex. He'd demanded a divorce, and she'd sworn, *I won't do it again. . . .*

"Joe, are you okay?" Sara clasped his shoulder.

He stared at her. It took a moment to remember where he was, who she was. Sara. She was Sara. He knew her. No. No, he didn't. But he had known *of* her for years. His boss, Colonel Foster, had related a lot of their clashes to Jarrod, and he'd come to half-love her—though he'd resented it—long before he had seen her.

Had he really gotten the divorce?

He thought back, glimpsed himself standing in a courtroom before a judge. Yes, he had. And he'd thrown himself into his work, volunteering for any and every mission. Foster and the other Shadow Watchers had ribbed Jarrod, saying he had steel balls. He didn't. He just had nothing left to lose.

"Joe, may I ask you a question?" Sara stepped around to

the front of his chair. "You might not be able to answer it, and if so, then that's okay."

"All right." She had no idea he knew of her. And finally he knew why.

She shifted her weight to one foot, tilted her head. "Do you know a man named David Quade?"

A photograph flashed through Jarrod's mind. A professional, military photograph. A captain with black hair and brown eyes. It was Quade. "Why?"

"He was my brother-in-law," Sara began, and then went on to tell him about Brenda and Lisa, and how David's death had affected them and her.

Jarrod needed time to think. Time to let the memories come without pushing too hard and arousing the rage. He needed to put all of the puzzle pieces together before he opened himself up to anyone, including Sara. "I don't remember him."

Disappointment flashed in Sara's eyes. "It's okay. I—I just needed to ask."

Guilt stabbed him hard, and Jarrod dipped his head, capturing her hand between his shoulder and face. "I'm sorry, Sara."

"Me, too." She cupped his chin, squeezed, and then backed away. "Are you ready to go back inside?"

"I wish I could help you." Resenting the straitjacket that kept him from taking her into his arms, he let her hear his sincerity. "I care about you, Sara."

She sucked in a sharp breath, stared into his eyes, and let her breath out slowly. "Don't. Please don't."

He cared, but he didn't want to care. About her, about anyone. Caring brought memories. Memories, pain. Pain, the rage. He hated the rage. Yet Sara was different. He knew her inside. Deep. He knew the risks, and he cared anyway. "Why not?"

"Because it isn't right." She looked down at her feet.

"It isn't wrong," he countered. "I know what I feel, whether I want to feel it or not. I'm not crazy."

"I know." She studied the grass. "It's not that."

"Then what is it?"

She glared at him. "I'm your doctor, for God's sake."

"That's not pertinent. Fontaine was my doctor, but I don't care about him."

"It *is* pertinent." Licking at her lips, she began pacing before him. "You're supposed to be able to trust me implicitly. There are boundaries I'm not supposed to cross. I'm not supposed to—"

"To hell with the boundaries." Jarrod stood up, shrugged out of the jacket, then tossed it to the seat of the wheelchair.

"You're, um, supposed to keep that on." Sara stared up at him, wide-eyed.

"To hell with boundaries." He circled her with his arms, pulled her to him, and kissed her hard. He tasted her surprise, her fear, and her longing. He hadn't been mistaken. She cared. Of course she cared.

His heart thudding hard, he pulled back to look into her eyes. "Tell me, Sara," he whispered. "I feel it, but I want to hear you say it. Tell me you care about me, too."

She did. She shouldn't. It wasn't right, but she did. She backed away and smoothed down her lab coat with a shaky hand. "You weren't supposed to take off the jacket, Joe."

"Damn it, Sara. I just kissed you, and you kissed me back. Forget the jacket and all the supposed-tos and just damn tell me you care about me."

Oh, but she wished she could. How she wished it. But she couldn't do it. Not without it costing her and him. She would deny him because she had to, but she damn well couldn't look him in the eye while she did it. "We've, um, got to go back now."

"No." He gripped the chair, stopped it from moving. "Tell me, Sara. Don't deny the truth. Don't you lie to me, too."

"I'm not lying to you, Joe." Near tears, she looked up at him. "This is . . . difficult for me. All of my life, I've lived by *my* standards. I've lived by *my* code of ethics. I believed in them, and now they're being challenged." And they were losing. "It's . . . hard."

"This is about honor." He dragged a hand through his hair. "I understand honor." His voice went soft, somber.

"I need time to come to terms with this. To sort through

and make sure I can live with my actions." She wrung her hands. "What I do—I have to be able to live with what I do, Joe."

"You're not debating on launching an initiative attack against a foreign power, honey." He clasped her hands in his. "You're just being honest about your feelings."

"Yes. And I can't afford to be wrong, can I?" She frowned up at him. "Isn't something like this too important to be wrong?"

"It is to me." His steely gaze softened. "You're important to me."

"Then give me the time I need to work through this. This is my integrity and self-respect, Joe. It's my life."

"Time." Joe's thoughts swirled, twisted and tumbled. His shoulders went stiff, and his hands went lax.

"Joe?" Sara swallowed hard. "Joe?"

His eyes went blank.

Lucidity had gone. What had triggered—*time*. The word *time*. So specific words *and* colors triggered his detachment.

Definitely sensory deprivation.

Sara wheeled Joe to his room in Isolation, settled him in, and then walked down to the second-floor nurse's station. Her emotions were in turmoil. Regret, resentment, guilt, anger—mostly self-directed—gnawed at her, and under it all, that sense of what was between her and Joe feeling so right. How could anything wrong feel so right?

Shank frowned at Sara from across the desk. "Fontaine's been looking for you. Word is, he's heard about the hug. Before you can get to his office, I expect he'll also have heard about the kiss."

"How could he know about that?" Sara's face burned hot. "How can you?"

"Half the facility knows. Mick Bush observed it."

Oh, hell. Terrific. Just . . . terrific.

"Word is, you're pretty torn up about falling in love with a patient. Is that true, Sara?" Shank asked. "Are you okay?"

"I'm great. Don't I look great? Why wouldn't I be great?" Her professional reputation was shattered, her character was in question, and her integrity—something she had fought hard all her life to protect—was shot. She was just damn thrilled.

Sara grabbed the phone and called down to Fontaine's office. Martha issued her summons, sounding snobbier than usual. Sara cut her off mid-sentence. "I'll be down in ten minutes."

"Make it five. Dr. Fontaine—"

"Don't damn push me, Martha. I'm sick of it," Sara erupted. "I'll be there in ten, and that's final." She slammed down the phone.

Shank grabbed Sara by the sleeve and led her into the med room, then shut the door behind them, leaving a gape-jawed Beth openly watching.

Turning her back to the glass, Shank shook Sara. "Are you crazy?"

"Maybe. It's possible. Hell, it's highly probable." Grunting, she shoved back her hair. "But not for what I said to Martha. She deserved what she got."

"Maybe." Shank frowned. "But giving it to her like that still wasn't a brilliant move."

"Probably not. But I'm sick of being pushed around, and I'm damn tired of Fontaine's interference."

"Then pop his ass. Pop Martha's, too. But do it the smart way. The right way, Sara. Not in a way that's going to get you hurt." Shank glanced back through the glass. Beth stood watching their every move. "Fontaine will have Mick Bush following you so closely now he'll be between you and your shadow."

"Okay. Okay, I blew it." Sara paced a short path between the metal rack holding supplies and the far end of the small room.

"Yeah, you did. But that's okay. Under the doc, you're a woman, and even women who don't want to, have feelings." Shank softened her tone. "All of this upset isn't about Fontaine. It's about your feelings for Joe."

"Oh, I'm plenty upset with Fontaine," Sara assured her.

"You're more upset with yourself about Joe." Shank's expression softened. "Look, you can tell me to mind my own business. You can tell me to go to hell. But don't lie to me, okay? There's enough of that here, away from me and you."

"Of course I'm upset about my feelings for him." Sara stiffened her hands into fists. "I feel guilty as hell. This wasn't supposed to happen. I'm still not sure how it happened."

"It happened the first time you saw him," Shank said. "If you didn't notice, it's because you were blinded by it. Love's like that, Sara."

"Not for me."

"Oh, above it all, eh? Not subject to the same emotions as the rest of the human race?" Shank grunted. "Listen to you. A great shrink, and you're spouting garbage. Quit being stupid about this. So you fell in love. So what? You think in the history of mankind you're the only person this has happened to?"

"It's not supposed to happen to me." Sara clenched her jaw. "But it did."

Sara shunned it. "It's not right. It's a matter of integrity."

"Oh, I see." Shank nodded. "So you've lied to him."

"I have not."

"Then you took advantage of him and plan to exploit him?"

"Of course not. But you're splitting hairs, Shank. You know damn well crossing professional lines is wrong."

"What I know is that love is a rare and fragile thing, and if you don't recognize it for the gift it is, then you're an ungrateful fool, because few of us ever get to experience it." Shank blinked hard. "If ever men needed pure love, it's the men in here, Sara. Count your blessings and let Joe count his. Flat out."

"I can't do that." Sara's voice cracked. "Don't you see? I can't do that."

Shank expelled an exasperated breath. "You're the only one who can. But first you've got to forgive yourself for being human. Celebrate life, Sara. Give yourself permission to love. God knows you want it, and he needs it. Love can heal him in ways you can't imagine."

"It's *not* right." Why couldn't Sara get the woman to understand?

"Love that's pure is never wrong." Shank gave Sara's arm a reassuring squeeze. "Never. You think about that."

Sara didn't know what to say. Her heart and mind couldn't agree.

"Now, you'd better get down to Fontaine's office and grovel a little to calm him down. Don't antagonize him, Sara. He's not a fool and he will get his pound of flesh, no matter who he has to hurt to do it."

With Shank's warning echoing in her mind, Sara took the elevator to the first floor. Fontaine would get his pound of flesh. From her, or Jarrod.

The elevator door opened—and Mick Bush stood waiting, his eyes glinting anger. "Dr. Fontaine thought you might need an escort to find your way to his office." Mick's hand was on his gun.

The full impact of Shank's warning hit Sara. "I know the way, Mick. I was with a patient who couldn't wait."

"I noticed." Mick lifted a hand. "This way, Major."

Embarrassed, her face went hot and her temper rose. But she had no defense. None. So she stiffened her spine and did her best to cool both.

Fontaine raged.

Sara stared at his empty desktop, at the photo of his wife, wondering when she'd get back from her European vacation and divert some of his attention.

"Since the moment you arrived," Fontaine said, "you have disrupted the normal functioning of this facility. You've deliberately and willfully committed acts that you knew were in direct violation of policy and acceptable procedure. Now, not only are you developing an intimate relationship with a mentally diminished patient, you're taking him outside. Patients who require isolation are *not* permitted outside, Doctor."

Of all her transgressions, Fontaine took greatest exception to her taking Joe outside? Maybe it *was* Fontaine and not Foster who wanted Joe isolated and sensory-deprived.

Fontaine crossed his chest with his arms. "You embraced ADR-30."

William, the backstabbing cutthroat, had ratted on her. "I hugged him, yes. It's not uncommon, sir."

"Oh." Fontaine tapped his fingers against his forearm. "And is kissing your patients common, too?"

Sara saw red. Chewing her backside was fine—she'd earned it—but being condescending was *not* fine. "Let me explain this to you one more time, Doctor. I have full authority over my patients. The DoD agreement supersedes your opinion of my actions. Continue with this judgmental interference and I'll have no choice but to report that you're hindering my research and request an immediate transfer."

"Your research? *What* research?" He guffawed. "Cease and desist violating facility rules, regulations, and policies. Now, Major. Or get the hell out of my facility."

"If I go, my patients go with me." Counting her blessings that he couldn't just kick her out, she stared across his desk at him. "Is that what you want, sir?"

Fontaine hesitated. The veins in his neck bulged. "I'll take that under advisement and notify you. There is an alternative you're forgetting. I could contact the OSI or the IG and request a full investigation of your conduct."

More military acronyms. Fortunately, both of these Sara had encountered on numerous occasions in her search for information on David. The Office of Special Investigations checked into all manner of suspected improprieties, from contract inconsistencies to unacceptable personal conduct allegations all the way to murder investigations. The Inspector General could be called in to investigate any incident in which violations of military law, rules, and/or regulations were suspected. In her experience, the men and women in both organizations had been fair and thorough. "I'd welcome either one, sir," she told Fontaine. "Any time."

Anger contorted his face. Obviously, that hadn't been his hoped-for response. "I'll apprise you of my decision. For now, get the hell out of my office."

"Yes, sir." Sara saluted, then turned and left, choking on curses clogging her throat.

fourteen

☆

Jarrod walked barefoot in the grass.

Shading her eyes from the sun with a hand cupped to her brow, Sara stepped back from the edge of the pond and watched him. Obviously, he loved it. He was usually calmer outside, but today she sensed he felt restless and on-edge. "Joe, where did you get the clothes?" He was dressed in jeans and a green T-shirt.

Bending down, he scooped up a rock. "Martha said you sent them."

Martha. This was not good news. Martha brought specific things to mind, like summonses and electronic listening devices.

He tossed the rock into the pond and watched the water splash and ripple. When it had calmed, he brushed the grit from his hands and turned to her. "I want to say something."

"This might not be the best time." Sara deliberately blinked.

He frowned, and nodded.

She motioned to the hedge maze, then walked toward it. When they stepped inside it, she tugged at her ear then patted her pockets, signaling Joe to check himself out.

Understanding flickered in his eyes. He turned his jeans pockets inside out, pulled the tail of his T-shirt from his pants, then ran his fingers around its hem. When he began ripping, Sara knew he'd found something.

He examined the bug, showed it to Sara, and then tossed it toward the pond. "Damn you, Martha."

"Not Martha," Sara corrected him. "Fontaine."

Joe strode deeper into the maze, burning off some anger.

Sara followed him. "You okay?"

"Yes." Jarrod stopped and faced her. "No. No, I'm not okay. I swore I wouldn't care about one person again. That's why I do what I do. But I was wrong, Sara. Like it or not, I do care. I care about you."

Understanding that restlessness and turmoil now, she stopped at a little alcove among the sweet-smelling hedge. It was time for the truth. "I promised myself I wouldn't, and I know I shouldn't, but I care about you, too."

"Good." A taut muscle in his face relaxed and he reached out, clasped her hand in his.

She wanted to kiss him, but didn't. The moment seemed too special for that, and she had the feeling that they both needed time to accept this. Shuffling deeper into the maze, she laced their fingers, and again saw the scars peppering his arms. "Joe, where did you get these?" She touched her free hand to his forearm.

He looked down at the scars. "I was taken hostage by hostile forces on a classified mission a few years ago. When I wouldn't tell them what they wanted to know, they put me in a rat trap." He stopped walking, went statue-still. Staring at her, he blinked, and then blinked again. "Sara." His voice sounded soft, uncertain, tinged with fear. "I know who I am."

Surprise rippled up her spine and butterflies swarmed in her stomach. Sara pressed her fingertips over his lips. "You don't have to tell me."

He kissed them, then lowered her hand. "You can't help me unless you know the truth." He gave her a wary look. "I have a problem with trust. It happens when you've been stabbed in the back one time too many. But I know in my gut I can trust you."

"How can you know that?" Guilt hit her hard, slammed through her. He didn't know about Foster. He didn't know she had come to Braxton with a hidden agenda. And he didn't know Foster would kill her before letting her leave.

"I just know," Joe insisted. "It's not all clear to me, but I've had glimpses, and I know you won't betray me."

"But someone did." Foster, maybe? Fontaine? The wind

caught her hair, and she swept it back from her face. "Do you know who?"

"Not now, but it'll come." He let a fingertip drift down her face. "Will you help me, Sara?"

She nodded, caressing his hand on her face. "Of course."

Joe gave her a gentle smile. "You need to know what I know." He took in a deep breath, then slowly let it out. "My name is Major Jarrod Brandt. I'm an Intel investigator."

Determined to be totally honest with him, Sara swallowed hard and hoped he'd listen to her. "You're a Shadow Watcher."

Surprise flickered through Jarrod's eyes. Surprise, and suspicion.

She had to squelch it, and she borrowed from Foster to do it. "The creed. 'Accomplish the mission. Whatever, whenever, wherever.' "

"Colonel Foster sent you." Jarrod stepped away, digesting.

She nodded. "To help you." She wanted to reach out to him, but couldn't. He had to decide where they went from here. "I think Foster knows that I've learned you're one of his operatives, but I haven't admitted it to him."

"Identified, I become unsalvageable."

She nodded again.

"Thank you, Sara."

Taking the risk, she clasped his hand and he let her. "How did you get here?"

"I'm not sure." He plucked a dead leaf off a bush of fragrant jasmine. "I was sedated."

Sara stopped beside him. Watched him finger the leaves. "What do you remember?"

"I was on a mission," he said. "Orders came down to evacuate and report elsewhere immediately. I wept." He looked from the leaves to her. "There's a gap I don't remember, but I know two guards strapped me into a chair."

"The electric chair?"

He nodded. "But it wasn't electric. No headgear." Still, he shuddered. "My instincts warned me that this chair and what would happen in it weren't part of the program, but I didn't listen. Then, it was too late."

Joe was growing too agitated. Sara had to give him some breathing space. "How did you come to join the military?"

"They recruited me into Air Force Intelligence right out of UCLA. I was a technological advancements expert. Hard to believe that was eleven years ago."

And not at all hard for Sara to believe that since then he'd honed his skills and become expert in more areas—most of which, she'd bet the bank, had military applications and were classified Top Secret, which left him free neither to discuss them, nor to admit them.

Strolling by, Sara plucked a leaf off a bush. "Are you ambitious?"

"Depends on your standard. I decided early on I wanted to act honorably in my own eyes. That never changed."

Simple ambition, simple man. Sara glanced his way. "I like that."

"It's challenging, especially when you're saddled with a commander in chief who spends the lion's share of his time evading the truth."

"He embarrasses you," Sara speculated.

Jarrod nodded. "I've often considered putting in my papers and getting out of the military, but to do that I'd have to leave the country vulnerable." He spared her a sidelong look. "In my job, one person *does* make a difference."

"And leaving the country vulnerable violates your personal ethics."

"Yes, it does."

She liked his attitude, and his style. "Comparatively speaking, embarrassment seems like a minor burden to carry."

"I've thought so enough to stay on. I admit I'm cynical and I trust few people now, but I hang on to the hope that tolerance for conduct unbecoming will become unacceptable again and the spirit of the law will win out over people seeking loopholes in the law." He stared straight ahead, as if he weren't totally comfortable with letting her see parts of himself he typically didn't expose. "It's probably idealistic, but in a world where

the absence of punishment constitutes praise and too little
proves noble, all a man has is hope."

She also loved his philosophy. He seemed calmer now,
more surefooted. "So why did the guards strap you to the
chair?"

"I don't know—yet. It's fuzzy, but I know I was betrayed.
I feel it down to my bones."

"You were tortured. I feel that down to my bones," Sara
said, eager to ask him about "I wept."

Swift footsteps sounded on the stone path, and William
suddenly appeared at a bend in the maze. "Dr. West." He
sounded winded. "Dr. Fontaine wants to see you immediately."

"Thank you, William." Sara grimaced. The RN was dressed
totally in white, shirt to shoes, intentionally trying to affect
Joe.

Jarrod sucked in a sharp breath. Sara spun around and
looked back at him. His eyes were blank. *Damn it.* "Joe?"

"Where are my crayons?" He patted at his pockets. "I need
my crayons."

William's whites had triggered Joe's detachment. She
pulled the box from her lab coat pocket and then passed the
crayons to Joe. "Here they are."

Joe clutched at the box, crushed it in his fisted grip.

She could pulverize William for this. Instead, she had to
pretend she had no idea what had happened. That was safest
for Joe. Sara clasped his arm. "Come on. We have to go back
inside now."

Sara walked him back to his room. William followed, and
when she'd gotten Joe settled in and left his room, she wasn't
at all surprised to see Mick Bush in the hall, waiting to escort
her to Fontaine's office.

At least now she understood. Joe hadn't meant "I wept" as
in "I cried." To him, "I wept" was a place he'd been sent on
a mission. A place. It was one of the military's acronyms.

But an acronym for what? It could be anything, or anywhere. The military had millions of acronyms. And Joe was
a Shadow Watcher, subject to go anywhere to do anything.

How did she find out—without arousing suspicion or revealing that she was looking?

The answer popped into her mind and rooted.

Shank.

Sara listened to Fontaine raise the roof for the second time that day, repeated her offer to move her patients to another facility, and then made her way back to the second floor.

The thrust of Fontaine's remarks, she blew off. But one of them, she couldn't get out of her mind. *Major, only the DoD can remove you from Braxton, but I can make your worst nightmare seem like a sweet dream. Stop pushing me. . . .*

He could do it. She believed it. If he had shouted that remark, she would have blown it off, too. But he hadn't. His delivery had been cold, quiet, and calm—a thousand times more terrifying than his blustering.

Shank was coming up the hall. Sara stopped at the station, turned her back to Beth, and motioned Shank into the med room. "I need some saline."

"Sure, Doc." She pulled the red coiled cord from her pocket, keyed the lock, and then opened the door and stepped inside.

Sara followed her. The door swung shut behind her. Keeping her back to the window, she asked Shank a question she doubted she would answer. "What does 'I wept' mean?"

"I don't know."

Expected, but still disappointing. Sara resisted a sigh. "When I asked before and you denied knowing, I knew you weren't being honest. I didn't push because I'm not in a position to be totally honest with you. Others could get hurt." God, but Sara hoped she wasn't going too far. "But I need this information, Shank, and it's vital that I get it quickly."

Shank grabbed a plastic bottle of saline off the shelf and shoved it at Sara. "I know it doesn't mean that Joe wept literally, but I don't know what it does mean. Flat out."

"I think it's an acronym for something. Actually, for some place. But I have no idea where to find out for what."

"Could be any of a thousand things." Shank worried her lip and grunted. "I really don't know."

"Okay." Sara propped the saline in the crook of her arm. "I'm going to talk straight, and pray I don't regret it. A lot of people are at risk, Shank."

"I'm listening."

"I've needed privacy and access to a computer for days, and I haven't been able to get it. Beth works twenty hours a day, and the computer is right next to the monitors in Isolation. Someone is always at that desk."

"Try the lab—down in the basement. It's the most deserted place around, and"—she paused to check her watch—"in fifteen minutes, it'll be empty. I'll be calling down for someone to come up and draw blood."

"Thanks." Sara nearly wept with relief. The fear coiled in her stomach loosened. Shank was helping her.

"Sara." Worry shone in Shank's eyes. "Be careful. You're treading on dangerous ground. The minute you access those files in the computer, Fontaine will know it. He won't let it slide."

"I know." Sara shrugged, plenty worried herself. "I'm violating the Privacy Act, probably a dozen military regulations, and definitely breaking facility policy. It'll cost me some rank and maybe my license. Only God knows what else. But it's the only shot I've got. If I can find the common link between these patients, then I can help them. There *is* a link, Shank. I know it."

"I agree, but you're missing my point." Shank turned her back to an avidly watching Beth and lowered her voice. Her reflection shone in the glass separating them. "You're risking your life, Sara. And the lives of your patients."

So cool, so calm. Shank wasn't exaggerating or embellishing. She believed exactly what she was saying. "No," Sara said. "Maybe mine. But Fontaine won a Purple Heart, a Meritorious Service medal. He's a jerk, but he won't kill the men."

Shank cocked a brow. "Whatever his personal agenda is, you're screwing it up. He's an egomaniac facing exposure. Don't tell me he won't kill the men. He'd murder his mother.

And so would his wife. She's as bad as he is. Flat out."

A sinking feeling bottomed out in Sara's stomach. "What can I do? I don't have another option."

Shank looked her straight in the eye. "You take the risk."

"Yes." Sara's chest went tight. "Yes."

"I'll get the word out."

Sara frowned at her. "To whom?"

"The friendlies." Shank lifted a hand. "Don't ask, just be grateful."

"I am." Sara squeezed Shank's hand. "Truly."

The hallway was dark and deserted.

Sara made a maze of her path down to the lab to be sure Mick Bush wasn't following her. The basement felt damp, smelled musty. Recessed into the ceiling, every fourth light was on, making long shadows on the white tile floor. Her footsteps sounded hollow. She stopped, listened, but heard nothing indicating anyone coming up behind her, so she walked on.

Turning at a corner, she slowed down. Light spilled out of an open doorway just ahead and streaked across the hallway floor. On the wall beside the door, she read a blue sign with white lettering—Lab—and then looked inside.

Not a soul in sight. Murmuring a silent thank-you to Shank, Sara paused at a long lab table. Considering the size of the facility, the lab was large and well equipped. The lights were all on, specimens stood lined up like soldiers on a second table, and tubes of blood had been racked in oscillators that soundlessly rocked.

It wouldn't take long for the lab attendant to draw blood and get back. She spotted the computer terminal on a small desk in the back of the lab. At least being distant from the door, she would have a little warning if the attendant returned.

Fingers of guilt clenched down on her stomach. This wasn't right. Her feelings for Joe weren't right. And Shank had called it on the nose. As soon as Sara gained access to those files, Fontaine would be notified. He would be antagonized. And he would retaliate.

You're risking your life, Sara. And the lives of your patients.

True, damn it, but what choice did she have? Either she found the common bond between the patients, found out what the acronym "I wept" meant, or helping the men was impossible, and whatever was happening to them would continue to happen to others.

This was her only chance at helping them, her only prayer of protecting them.

She keyed in patient number ADR-17, and then watched the screen.

RECORDS SEALED. CLASSIFICATION: TOP SECRET.

One after the other, she keyed in all five patient numbers and then ADR-40's. The message on the screen remained the same.

Think, Sara. Think. Where's the back door?

Minutes ticked by. Frustrated minutes of failed attempts. With each of them, Sara felt more upset and urgent and hopeless. At the end of her rope with nothing left to try, she glared at the screen. *Help me help them, damn it. Please!*

Nothing. No luck. More failures. Ten minutes. Fifteen. Twenty. Still stymied, she began to sweat, to see Foster's face in the reflection on the screen, chiding her for failing the people who had sacrificed for her. She squeezed her eyes shut, forked her hands through her hair, swallowing a lump of bitter frustration and defeat from her throat. What in the name of God did she do now?

She sat staring at the clock, agonizing. She had failed them.

Make it personal. Hell, it is personal. Every day of his life, this operative sacrifices for you in ways you can't begin to fathom.

Foster. Yes. Yes. The thought struck and held and an idea formed. It was extremely risky, but the only thing left she knew to try. Her fingers trembling, hovering above the keys, she took in a deep breath and keyed in the phrase that gave her shivers. "Shadow Watchers."

A box appeared on the screen, and Sara broke into a cold

sweat. *Now what?* Obviously, if she were a Shadow Watcher, she would know what to do. She wasn't and she didn't.

Wait. What had Foster said? The creed. Yes, the creed. What was it?

She knew it. She'd repeated it to Joe. But she was so nervous, she couldn't remember it. She darted her gaze to the clock. Twenty-five minutes. Panic struck her stomach. She pressed a hand over it. *Calm down. Just calm down and think.*

She swiped her hands down her slacks, concentrated hard. Finally, the memory came, and she typed it in, suffering a volatile mixture of elation and dread. "Accomplish the mission. Whatever, whenever, wherever."

The box disappeared. The screen flickered, went blank, and then a message appeared. ACCESS APPROVED.

Certain she was pressing it on time, she quickly keyed in the patient numbers. The files appeared, except for Fred's. It was blocked. ACCESS DENIED. But the others gave her access, and Sara examined each of them quickly. No printer was attached to the terminal, damn it. She pulled up Joe's file. "Major Jarrod Brandt." He *had* been lucid.

She scanned down the page, and her gaze grabbed "Date of Death: Fifteen June—" *Date of Death?*

Oh, no. No. She browsed back to the other files. Michael, Ray, Lou, ADR-40, and then again looked at Jarrod's. Her stomach soured, spots formed before her eyes, and she feared she might be sick.

They all had been declared legally dead.

Appalled, outraged, stunned, Sara shoved the emotions down. She couldn't afford them now. Any moment, she would be caught in the lab. Fontaine couldn't kick her out of Braxton, but he definitely could make her miserable and her efforts futile. And, over this, he would.

God, but it was hard to not feel. Their poor families had no idea. They had no idea. . . . Why couldn't she find any reference to David? And why was Fred's file blocked and not the others? That made no sense. None at—Scanning Joe's admission form, she felt her gaze grab and jerk to a dead halt.

"Patient transferred from Intelligence Warfare Psychological Training Center."

Sara ran a quick check on the other patient files. All read the same. Chills sweeping up her backbone, she gasped. "IWPT."

fifteen

☆

"What are you doing here?" a man Sara didn't know demanded from the doorway.

She signed off the system and shut down the computer. He wasn't Mick Bush, and he was carrying a tray for drawing blood. She pressed her hand to her chest and drew in an exaggerated breath. "You scared me."

"Who are you?" His solemn expression didn't waver.

"Dr. Sara West," she said with a smile. "I was running a check on ADR-36. He's a diabetic. I'm watching him pretty closely."

His expression cleared. "It's normal," he said. "Ran it myself earlier this morning. Didn't you check with Shank?"

"She was busy with a patient. I checked the file. Must have missed it." Sara made her way to the door. "Thanks." Before he could stop her, she left the lab.

Midway down the hallway, she heard footsteps and ducked into a darkened room. Adrenaline pumping through her veins, she watched through a crack in the door. Mick Bush strode down the hall, his boots thundering on the tile.

She held her breath and waited for him to pass. When he did, and she estimated he'd had enough time to get into the lab, she ran for the stairs. She should have thought of it before going to the lab, but she hadn't. She desperately needed an alibi.

Joe. She'd go to—No, no. The monitors.

Where, then?

She charged up the stairs, scraping her knuckles against the rough wall. Not to the second floor. Shank would cover for her, but Beth wouldn't. Isolation. She had nowhere else to go but to Joe. And she would pray hard that William wasn't pulling a double shift.

Koloski, bless him, sat at the desk. On the run, Sara ordered, "Buzz me through."

"Yes, ma'am, Major. Glad to hear your voice is back—"

"Thanks." Sara shoved through the door, and then knocked on Joe's. Her chest was heaving. As soon as the buzzer sounded, she opened the door. "Can I come in?"

"Sure." He was lucid. Alert and coloring. Green. "Sara, what's wrong with you?"

"I need your help." She whispered to keep Koloski from hearing her. "I need to know that you trust me. I realize with betrayal being one of your issues—"

"You're digressing." He squeezed her hand. "What's wrong?"

She turned her back to the camera. "It involves helping David, Brenda, and Lisa. It involves all of my patients, Joe, including you."

He frowned, stared hard into her eyes. "Sara, what have you done?"

"I—" Mick Bush's face appeared at the Plexiglas window. In a cold sweat, she stiffened and her voice faded to a wisp of sound. "Oh, God."

Mick looked inside. Sara glimpsed him in her peripheral vision, and started shaking. "Show me what you've been doing."

"Tell me what you've done." Joe noticed Mick, but gave no sign of it other than to let Sara know with a slow blink.

The door opened. Mick stepped inside. "Dr. West, were you just on the computer in the lab?"

Joe stepped between them. "Dr. West has been in here with me for over an hour." He looked up at the camera. "Ask Koloski."

Mick Bush didn't look convinced. He looked angry, and doubtful. Still, he left the room and went out to the desk.

Sara's heart thudded hard, threatening to rocket through her chest wall. "Joe, a man saw me down there."

"I know. His name is Hal." Joe clasped her arm, showed her the bend in his elbow, covered with gauze and tape. "It's okay, Sara. You're covered."

Joe had been the blood donor. "But the computer."

"You're covered," he repeated, cutting his gaze toward the camera. "Outside."

Sara looked at the camera. "Koloski, get the door. I'm taking Joe outside."

The door alarm sounded. Sara moved toward it. Joe didn't. "What?"

"No jacket or chair?"

"No." If he was well enough to cover for her, he was thinking more clearly than she was and didn't need them. She opened the door. "Come on."

Mick stood at the end of the desk. "So she was here for an hour?"

"Right here," Koloski said. "Been watching her on the monitor."

Sara couldn't believe it. Koloski was helping her, too. Shank had galvanized the friendlies—the Braxton underground. That startled her. Braxton had factions *and* an underground.

"Mick, did you need me for something?" Sara paused beside him.

Joe stopped at her side.

"Someone tapped into the computer in the lab using your code," Mick said, scrawling a note on his clipboard.

Sara frowned. "How could anyone get my code?"

"I'll let you know when I've concluded my investigation." Mick looked up from his clipboard. "Security will issue you a new password within fifteen minutes. Don't attempt to use your old one."

"Okay." Sara feigned concern. "Is there anything I can do?"

"No, ma'am. Koloski's verified your whereabouts. That'll do it."

Sara sent Koloski a warm look of appreciation, which he wisely ignored. She turned her gaze to Joe. "Are you ready to go outside?"

"Yes. I like it outside. Where are my crayons?"

Sara had forgotten them, but absently patted her pocket. They were there. Joe had covered her on that, too. "They're right here."

They took the elevator to the first floor and then walked down to the pond.

"Stay away from trees," Joe said. "Some have cameras in them. And the hedge maze is sixty percent wired."

"What?" Sara stilled, looked out on the sun-spangled water. "How can you know all of this?"

"I told you," he said softly. "I remember who I am. Which also means I remember what I do, and how to do it."

"Then you know you're a victim of psychological warfare."

"I deduced it, but didn't know it for fact."

"Did you go to IWPT for training?"

"I think so. There are gaps, Sara. I remember a lot, but some things are hazy. Others, well, they're just blank. That's one of the blanks."

"Joe." She stepped closer. "I'm certain you were tortured. Almost certain you suffered sensory deprivation. I know specific things trigger the rage. Colors, like white and red, and certain words."

"Don't mention them. Not now."

"Okay." She smoothed back her hair and squinted up against the sun at him. "I'm convinced that whatever happened to you and the others happened at IWPT." God, how she hated to have to tell him this. "I don't think it was accidental, Joe. I'm not sure it was deliberate, but I think the results were expected."

"Betrayed." He'd known it, had felt it down to the marrow of his bones. And he felt the same sense of outrage and disbelief now that he had felt the first time he had been betrayed by his wife and best friend, Miranda and Royce.

"It all fits, Joe." Sara watched him closely, terrified she would say too much too soon and he would regress.

"Now, they're trying to cover it up." He laced his hands behind his back, lifted his face to the wind.

"I suspect that's what's happening. I know that they've declared all of you legally dead."

Joe clenched his jaw, stared out onto the water. Tiny lines creased the skin beneath his eyes, and his voice sounded strained. "Does that include Colonel Foster? Is he on the right or wrong side of this?"

"I don't know," she answered honestly. "He brought me here to help you, but he could be on either side." She grimaced. "One thing is certain. Fontaine is up to his crooked neck on the wrong side of this. For a long time, I thought he might be protecting the patients, but he's not. He can't be. You were all damaged at IWPT, declared legally dead, and then transferred to Braxton."

Joe interceded. "Where we've been sequestered and, for all intents and purposes, forever forgotten."

Fred had been here over five years. Jarrod, since June. Sara stared at the murky water. "Not by me."

"No." Joe swerved his gaze to her. "Not by you." Joe chewed at his inner cheek, thinking. "This couldn't work without Fontaine's full knowledge."

"I agree." Sara stepped back, away from the water's edge. "But he is in the military. What if he's been acting under direct orders? Wouldn't he have to do what he was told to do?"

"If he disagreed with the orders, he had recourse. He could have gone up the chain of command, or to the OSI or the IG. If he filed a formal report, the OSI or the IG would investigate. With an informal phone call, the OSI would have monitored the situation." Joe shoved at a rock with the toe of his sneaker. "No, Fontaine's involved. And this is definitely a high-stakes conspiracy."

"But who is in it with Fontaine? What exactly have they done to you and the others, and why?" She didn't want to upset Joe, but more questions nagged at her. Could whatever they'd done be undone? How? Could Fontaine and his allies be stopped before they damaged more men?

"I don't know."

"Neither do I. But there are so many questions. I need help to answer them."

"You need expertise."

"I agree. But the only one I know with expertise is Foster, and he could be involved with Fontaine."

"He could." Joe frowned. "I've known the man a long time, and I've put my life in his hands more times than you can imagine. I can't see it, Sara. I really can't. But I don't know for fact he's not involved. He would be the first to tell me that until I know, don't trust. I hate it, but I'll do my job here."

"So who else has expertise? Where do I go for help?"

"The obvious person is the one who's been helping you all along."

"Shank?"

Joe nodded. "Shank."

The next morning, Sara checked on her patients and then waited in the women's rest room on the second floor. Sooner or later, Shank had to come in there. Things were getting too hot to risk signaling her near Beth, who probably had reported the med-room conversations to Fontaine. No doubt, now it was wired, too.

Sara leaned against a stall, stared at the row of three sinks, then at the mirrors above them. Twenty minutes passed. Then ten more. She racked her brain, trying to think of another way to contact Shank, but the phone was out, as was calling her into any patient's room. Inside and out, most of Braxton was wired. And more than ever before, Sara empathized with Orwell's characters from the novel *1984*.

The door opened. "You okay?" Shank barreled inside. "Beth told me she'd seen you come in here a good half hour ago, but she couldn't leave the desk to check on you."

"My stomach's just a little upset."

Before Sara could say any more, Shank pressed a shushing fingertip over her lips, warning Sara that the rest room was wired for sound. Sara ran hot water in the sink until the mirror above it steamed up and then wrote on the glass with her fingertip. *Outside. Need help.*

Shank nodded, then wiped down the glass with a hand towel from the dispenser. Crumpling it, she tossed it into the trash. "Well, if you're sure you're okay, I'll get back to work."

"Thanks. And tell Beth I appreciate her concern." Sara held up five fingers, signaling to meet her in five minutes. When Shank nodded, Sara left the rest room and headed outside, praying she wasn't about to make a mistake that would put nails in her and her patients' coffins.

They met at the pond.

Sara stopped beside a palmetto. "It's okay to talk freely here. Joe says it's a safe zone."

"It is." Shank pulled a pair of sunglasses out of her pocket and then adjusted them on her nose. "I take it Joe is doing some remembering."

"Some, but it's more haze than certainty. Coming outside has helped him enormously."

"Do you know what happened to him?"

"Not yet. But I've deduced that he was tortured, and I'm positive sensory deprivation was involved."

"So that's why he's so sensitive to colors."

"To red and white. It's all connected. I'm not yet sure how." Sara shifted away from the sun. "Thanks for your help with the lab." Sara's face went hot. As an operative, she had failed on a grand scale—and developed a new respect for people who function in that capacity. "I didn't think about an alibi until Mick Bush was crawling on my back."

"You don't think 'covert.' "

"No, I don't," Sara admitted, then diplomatically let Shank know she had realized the truth. "But I'm grateful that you and Joe do."

"I don't think 'covert,' Sara. I think 'survive.' " Shank stuffed her hands into her pockets. "So did you find anything of use?"

Here it was. The ultimate moment of truth. Did Sara admit her findings, bring Shank totally into her circle of trust, or did she lie?

She weighed the risks, and took them. "I examined the records—except for Fred's. His were blocked. But the other patients were all transferred here from the Intelligence Warfare Psychological Training Center."

Shank's jaw dropped and she whipped off the sunglasses. "I wept."

Sara nodded. "And they've all been declared dead."

The wheels turned in Shank's mind, the facts clicked into place. "Holy cow."

"I don't know who to trust, or who to blame." Sara lifted a hand. "Is Fontaine protecting the patients, or is he covering up IWPT's screwups? And if he is covering up, is he doing it for personal reasons, or is he acting under orders? He could be working under the direction of the OSI." Sara didn't add, though she could have, that those same questions, including those regarding the Office of Special Investigations, applied to Foster. Shank had said she was helping Sara to survive, not that she was expert or involved in covert operations. And Foster's warning about enlightening people here on his existence or on anything to do with Braxton had burned into Sara's mind. She couldn't carry the added risk of causing Shank to be canceled. "What do they do at IWPT?"

"I can't say exactly." Shank stuffed her sunglasses back into her pocket. "I know everyone in the military has to have psych-warfare training, but mine wasn't at IWPT. I've never even heard of it."

Sara weighed Shank's remarks. No hesitation, no body language that conflicted with what she was saying. She was being honest and forthright. "Could IWPT be reserved for people in extremely sensitive positions?"

"It's possible." Shank rubbed at her lip. "Operatives get extended training on a lot of fronts that the rest of the military doesn't." A frown furrowed her auburn brow. "But judging by the cases coming to us from there—was ADR-40 a transferee from IWPT, too?"

Sara nodded.

"Then I'd definitely say more is going on there than the standard—for any military member, including operatives."

Sara sat down on the grass and watched the water lap at the bank of the pond. "What could be going on there?"

"I'd say they want to shut these men up."

"About what?"

"That, I don't know. But they've been successful. Hell, Sara, Michael's the least damaged and Joe's recovering. If they don't know what happened to them, how can anyone else?"

This was Shank's way of asking if Sara was withholding information. "The patients don't know." Sara cupped a hand at her brow to block the sun. "What happened during your training?"

Shank sat down next to Sara, tugged at a blade of grass. "It was like a survival school for your mind."

"What's survival school like?"

"You're taught strategies, and what to expect if you're ever taken POW. It's role-playing and you're a POW. They put you through the paces, so you know how to fight it."

"Fight what?"

"Torture."

Sara's chest went tight and her stomach pitched and rolled. "We need to know more about IWPT. Who runs it?" Whoever was in charge had to be Fontaine's contact, regardless of whether he was acting on a personal agenda or working with the OSI.

"Give me twenty-four hours." Shank fingered the blade of grass. It snapped between her thumbnail and finger. "I have a friend." She tossed the grass down. "Until we get a grip on this, stay out of Fontaine's path. He can't prove you hacked into the computer records, but he knows it. He'll be gunning for you."

He did, and he would. "I'll be careful." Sara stood up, swiped at the dead grass clinging to her lab coat. "I need all the research you can find on psychological warfare with military applications."

"All of it?" Shank gained her feet. "You're talking about mountains of material here."

"We know from Fred's records that this has been going on at least five years. We have to go back that far."

"You've got it, but it'll take a while."

"Thanks." Sara swatted at a bug buzzing Shank's shoulder. "I appreciate all you're doing."

"This is important to me, too."

Sara nodded, then turned and walked back toward the facility. Outwardly, she might appear in control. But inside she was rattled, and feeling incompetent to be holding the lives of so many people in her hands.

Earlier, she'd had doubts that she was up to the task. Now, she knew she lacked the needed skills. But she did have some things working in her favor. Joe, Shank, and passion. This mattered to her, these people mattered to her, and that had to help in some way.

A short distance from the building, Shank paused. "Sara, does Joe know any of this?"

A test. Shank knew he wasn't totally unaware or she wouldn't have chosen him to donate the blood to keep Hal busy and out of the lab. "Some."

"Does he know he's dead?"

Sara hesitated at answering. "If I tell you, either way, then I'm dragging you deeper into this. That's not healthy for you, Shank."

"You've got to tell him. How can you not tell him? He has the skills, Sara. No offense, but you don't."

"I'm doing the best I can."

"I didn't say you weren't." She dragged a frustrated hand through her short hair. "Damn it, this is just too complex."

Sara studied the edge of the concrete, then let her gaze slide out over the grass. No self-respecting weed would dare to mar Braxton's perfect lawn. "I agree that Joe has to know the truth. So do the others—at least, those capable of understanding." Which excluded Lou. "They've all been betrayed enough."

Shank slid Sara a level look. "We've all been betrayed enough."

"Yes, we have."

Shank cleared her throat. "Under the desktop in your office. All you ever wanted to know about psych-warfare with military applications."

Sara slid her a puzzled frown. "I just asked you for that

information. How did you get anyone to gather—"

"I didn't." Shank sniffed. "You're not the only one around here who's noted irregularities. And you're not the only one who's been trying to figure out what and who's hurting our men. For both our sakes, let's leave it at that."

That response raised a question. Was Shank working alone, or under someone else's direction? It was a question Sara couldn't ask without putting Shank on the spot. And since Sara didn't want to be on that spot herself, she let it go unasked.

"I hope it gives you what you need to stop them, Sara. I tried—read every word—but I didn't know enough to do them any good." Regret and remorse burned in Shank's eyes, turned the tip of her nose red, and put a tremble in her voice. "I've felt like a failure many times in my life, but never more so than when trying to decipher what's going on here. I couldn't protect them."

"I'm sure you've tried everything imaginable." Sara gave Shank's shoulder a reassuring pat. "Ease up on yourself. You've done a lot right."

"Knowing that I was trying worked until ADR-40 showed up." Shank swallowed hard. "Then, I knew nothing had changed. I hope you can stop this, Sara. The thought of there being an ADR-41 haunts me."

"Me, too, Shank." Sara opened the facility door, praying she wouldn't fail. "Me, too."

Shank returned to the second-floor station ready to heave.

Every instinct in her body warned her that events had taken an unexpected twist even Foster couldn't have anticipated.

She debated calling him, and checked the clock. Ten minutes more and Beth would be back from lunch. Shank really had no choice. She picked up the phone then depressed the secure-line button.

He answered sounding calm and collected. "Foster."

She sat here in turmoil, and he had the audacity to be calm? That infuriated her into dismissing courtesies and rank. "She knows they're dead."

"How?"

"I don't know." Shank lied with a clear conscience. "May I speak plainly?"

"Yes, yes. Go ahead, Captain. I want the truth."

"I've been told that the truth is relative, sir." She had. By him.

"Say what you have to say, Shank."

"This situation is critical. In my opinion, not playing straight with Sara West is a serious tactical error that's going to blow up in your face, sir. When it does, the only stars you'll be seeing won't be rank on your shoulders, but in your eyes."

"Playing straight with her is too dangerous, for us and for her."

"*For her?*" Shank guffawed. "Please, sir. Don't insult either of us. We both know you'll never let her leave Braxton alive."

"You're overreacting again, Captain."

"Overreacting?" Shank's temper flared, deeply enough that protocol flew right out of her head. "I'm the one stuck inside this hellhole forever. I'm the one who came for ADR-22, who saw all the others come after him—and they're still coming. For five years, I've watched them come and I've seen them suffer. Don't you twist the truth to me, sir. Don't do it. I know my job. I'll deal with it. Just tell me when you're going to stop this."

"Captain, I strongly advise you to control your emotions."

Shank clenched her jaw. "To hell with my emotions, sir. This is about my life and the lives of all of these patients. It's about ADR-41."

"There is no ADR-41."

"If you don't stop this, there will be," Shank shot back at him. "This is about Sara West's life, too. She's a good woman who only wants to help her family. Putting the screws to her is wrong. This is not why I serve in the military, sir. I took oaths. They mean something to me."

"Are you questioning my honor, Captain?"

"Yes, sir. I guess I am. I'm questioning my own, too. And everyone else's who's involved in this nightmare."

"There are times when we're required to act on faith, Captain. When we have to trust the character of the people who lead us, and to believe they are doing what is right. I'm aware of the costs Dr. West has paid, and of those she will pay."

Did Shank dare to keep putting her faith in him? Would she doubt her decision when ADR-41 was admitted? She stared at the fire alarm on the wall across the hall. "So this is one of those times, right, sir?"

"Yes, it is." Foster went quiet. Static crackled through the line. "Bring Sara to meet Fred."

"Really?" Shank failed to hide her shock.

"I expect a full report on her reaction. Then I'll decide what to tell her."

Encouraged, Shank felt hope flare in her heart. "Yes, sir."

"Sara West could accept this," Foster said without passion. "Or she could run straight to the press."

Shank swallowed hard. Her hand, holding the receiver, grew sweat-slick. If Sara even appeared to be leaning in the direction of going to the press, or so much as made an off comment, within an hour, Braxton would be leveled and everyone in it would be dead.

Within two hours, all evidence of the facility, employees, and patients would be eradicated. And it would appear to all the world as if none of them had ever existed.

sixteen

☆

Sara waded through the stack of research material.

Most of it she'd seen before. Dr. Kale, who was currently caring for her patients at home, had forwarded copies to her. Since he'd had a long-standing relationship with the military, in the form of twenty-odd years' service, Sara hadn't thought it unusual. Now, she realized that he'd had a specific reason for his interest in PTSD, as he too believed that had been the diagnoses on her patients here. He worked for Foster. Had Dr. Kale investigated events here, too? If so, he had failed. And if, even with his military experience, he had failed, how could she succeed?

"Sara?" Shank appeared at Sara's office doorway. "Could you come with me for a second?"

"Sure." Sara stood and smoothed down her lab coat. Checked to make sure her name tag was attached to her lapel. "What's up?"

Moving down the corridor, Shank answered, "We're going to see Fred."

"He's back?" Sara fell into step with Shank, heading toward Isolation.

"He never left," Shank confessed without looking at Sara. She nodded at Koloski to open the doors.

Sara followed Shank through them. A swoosh of air whisked over her skin as the doors swung shut behind them. "I think you'd better explain."

Shank continued moving down the hallway, passing Joe's room. "I was under orders to isolate him from you, so I did."

"Fontaine?"

Shank rolled her gaze. "No, he doesn't know about this."

"Who, then?"

No answer.

Tired of this, Sara insisted. "Who, Shank?"

Midway between room doors, Shank stopped and leaned back against the hallway wall. "Look, I'm damn tired of being between a rock and a hard place. He should play straight with you, and I've told him so myself. But I know the man, and all he's worried about is getting his promotion. His damn star. Well, I'm going to get hung out to dry anyway, so what's the difference? I believe you really are driven to help these men, and that's what matters to me, so I'm going to tell you. Colonel Jack Foster issued me the order to keep you isolated from Fred."

"You work for Foster?" Sara couldn't even pretend not to be shocked. Yes, she'd deduced that someone inside had to be working with Foster—but Shank? She was as much a prisoner here as the patients.

"Anyone in uniform that Foster chooses works for him, Sara."

"And some out of it." Like her.

"Yes." Shank shoved away from the wall. "Fred's in here."

Sara entered the room. Unlike Joe's, it had a bed, a bedside table upon which supplies had been stacked, and a nightstand that was empty. She walked around the foot of the bed to get a look at the man lying in it.

Her heart slammed into her throat. She rushed to the bedside, cupped a hand to the man's lean face. "David." Tears sprang to her eyes, rolled down her face. "Oh, my God, David."

Shank gave Sara a few minutes to accept this, and to get herself under control. Her own throat felt thick and her eyes stung. When Sara glanced back at her, Shank knew the time for explanations had come. "He's a vegetable, Sara. Legally dead, like the others."

"But *why*?" Anguished and hurting, she motioned to David. "How could anyone consider him a security risk?"

"I don't have your answers. I wish I did. And Foster doesn't have all of them, or you wouldn't be here."

"Fontaine, then? You think he's got the answers?"

The expression on Sara's face warned Shank that, at the moment, the woman would kill Fontaine to get those answers. But killing him wouldn't do her any good. "No, not Fontaine," Shank said. "My best guess is what you want to know, you'll only find out at IWPT."

Sara grabbed a tissue from the bedside table, swiped at her nose, and kept a protective hand on David's shoulder. "Then get me in there."

"I can't. I don't have the clout—"

"Then you get to Foster. You tell him I want answers and, by God, I want them now."

"Foster's not a good man to threaten, Sara."

Sara began a full examination of David. "I'm not a good woman to threaten, either." Sara gritted her teeth. Fred was David. Foster had blocked David's computer file, just as he had isolated David from her. God, but she hated that arrogant bastard. Tears blurred her eyes, rolled down her face. *Oh, God, David.* "Twenty-four hours. You tell him, Shank."

seventeen

☆

In her quarters, Sara paced.

Did she tell Brenda and Lisa about David? Would telling them put them at risk? Did she force Fontaine to show his hand?

No. No. Stupid move. Confront Fontaine and she'd never get out of Braxton—not even temporarily. And she had to get to IWPT.

IWPT brought her thoughts to Foster. She walked into the kitchen, pulled a glass and the bottle of bourbon from the cabinet, and tried to get inside Foster's mind. Why had he kept David from her?

Because if she'd seen David right away, she would have gone through the roof and all of the men here would have been exposed. Braxton would have been exposed. Foster had let her get attached to all of her patients, just as he had let her have time to fall in love with Joe.

Had he really brought her here to help Joe? Or to expose the connection between IWPT and Braxton? Did even Foster know what was happening at IWPT?

Of course he knew. She splashed bourbon over ice in the glass, chucked in an extra ice cube, and then took a quick sip. Well, maybe he knew something about it. What had he expected Sara to find here?

She tapped her glass with her fingertips. He could be working with Fontaine and IWPT, but if Foster was, then he wouldn't have brought her here to expose Braxton and IWPT—unless he wanted them exposed.

Wait a minute. Just a minute. She sat down on the sofa, set

her glass on the coffee table and stared at it. Foster was up for promotion to general. He wanted that star. Maybe he also wanted to get respectable, so to speak. Maybe he had been working with Fontaine and IWPT and he had decided to disassociate, but he couldn't expose either IWPT or Braxton directly, so he'd devised a plan to disassociate indirectly, using her *and* Joe.

That fit. She snagged her glass and belted back a long drink. It burned going down her throat. She set the glass back down. That . . . fit.

Another possibility struck her. Maybe Foster had brought her here to bury her with the rest of Braxton because she wouldn't relent and just accept David's so-called suicide. She grunted. Her instincts had been right on that one. Poor David. Poor Brenda and Lisa.

That possibility also fit. Sara had dogged Foster for over five years about David. Time during which she now knew David had been right here at Braxton. Foster knew she wouldn't give in, or give up. Ten years from now, she would still be dogging him for information on David. She'd dog him until she discovered the truth about what happened, regardless of how long it took. That tenacity made getting her out of his way both attractive and imperative to Foster.

She finger-swirled the ice in her glass. So which was it? Was Foster a good guy, using her and Joe to expose the corruption? Or was he corrupt and wanting to bury her with the rest of the evidence of his corruption?

She could just ask Foster. But experience proved she'd die of old age before getting any information from him that he didn't expressly want her to have. And it could be advantageous for him not to know she was considering the possibility that he was corrupt. What she needed was a deeper insight into his character. She rotated her wrist, listened to the ice cubes crash against the glass. And there was someone who could give it to her. A woman who'd certainly had contact with him in the last six months. Joe's mother.

The idea struck and clung. Sara checked her watch. Via Shank, Sara had given Foster twenty-four hours to give her answers. She chewed at her lip, hoping she'd left herself enough time.

"Joe?"

Sara awakened him with a hand at his shoulder and a gentle shake.

He came alert. "What?"

"I'm going away for a day. If anyone asks you about me, will you tell them I just left you and you don't know where I've gone?"

Facing the camera, Joe blinked.

"Shank will help cover my absence. If you need anything, go to her."

He leaned close, tilted his head to his chest. "Where are you going?"

She looked deeply into his eyes and let her hand drift down his jaw to his chin. She couldn't make herself tell him that she was going to Gulf Shores, Alabama, to see his mother. She didn't have the heart to tell him she was about to see a woman he might never again have the opportunity to see. "In search of truth."

"Be careful."

She blinked, whispered so the sound wouldn't carry through the devices to the nurse's station. "I want you to know something." She forced herself to look him in the eye. "You really matter to me, Joe."

"I know." He smiled softly and caressed her with his gaze. "Stay safe and come back to me."

She squeezed his hands. "I'll do my best." She would, and she prayed her best would prove good enough.

Jarrod paced the padded floor.

Sara was searching for truth. Soon, she would discover that in military intel matters the truth was relative to who was telling it and why. She'd lived in a black and white world most of her life. Now, she had stepped out of her comfort zone and into gray areas that she might, or might not, be willing to accept. Not providing herself with an alibi during her computer-access mission proved she wasn't equipped with the stealth necessary to handle gray areas. She needed help.

He let his gaze slide down the murals they had painted on the walls. On this search for truth, what wouldn't she have thought to cover? She had said she'd be gone for a day. . . .

The car. Her car in the parking lot would be missing. A mistake that neither Fontaine nor Mick Bush, both adept at maneuvering in gray areas, would overlook.

Jarrod looked up at the camera. A glimmer of rage rose up from deep in his stomach. He latched down on it. "Koloski," he said to the camera. "Get Shank. I need to talk to Shank."

Sara sat down in a beige overstuffed chair in Jarrod's mother's living room. She liked the feel of the house. Neat, simple, traditional, with a spring bouquet of fresh flowers in a squatty vase on the coffee table. A nice touch, especially on a dismal-looking fall afternoon. The family appeared upper-middle-class comfortable, and their home reflected it.

Mrs. Brandt, lean, gray, and weathered from too many years in the sun, came in from the kitchen carrying a tea tray. She wore a peach dress with a white collar and belt that complemented her coloring.

As soon as Sara had mentioned Jarrod, the sparkle in Mrs. Brandt's eyes had snuffed out. It still hadn't returned. Sara hated causing Jarrod's mother more pain, but she had to have answers.

Mrs. Brandt perched on the edge of the sofa, stretched to the antique-rose tea service, and then poured not tea, but coffee. "Jarrod died on a mission, Dr. West." She passed a cup and saucer to Sara. Her hand wasn't steady. "In his line of work, they don't tell you where or how. At first, I thought that was a blessing. Now, I know it's a curse." She tilted her head. "You imagine all kinds of atrocities."

Sara could easily see that anyone would. Hadn't she, about David? Her gaze slid to the fireplace mantel. Awards lined it, and on the wall beside it hung a framed photo of a younger Jarrod, a bright-eyed, brash lieutenant in uniform. "Who came to tell you Jarrod had died?" Sara asked, letting her gaze skim

over the awards. Purple Heart. Meritorious Service. Several
she didn't recognize. Jarrod had certainly been highly deco-
rated. After the way he had covered for her, that didn't surprise
Sara. It seemed his nature to protect and defend. In a sense,
as natural to him as drawing breath.

"Colonel Foster told us," Mrs. Brandt said. "He talked to
Miranda, too."

Jarrod's ex-wife? Sara tried to keep panic out of her voice.
"But I thought they had divorced."

"Oh, they had. But she was still the beneficiary on Jarrod's
OSGLI insurance policy."

"Odd that he overlooked that," Sara mused. "Seems he'd
have caught it during the course of the divorce."

"He didn't overlook it. It was intentional. He warned his
father and me that he was doing it."

Intrigued, Sara set down her cup. "Why?"

"Theirs was a complicated relationship, Doctor." Mrs.
Brandt's face flushed. "Miranda remarried six weeks after Jarrod's death—not that it surprised any of us. She would never
have remarried as long as he was alive."

Searching for a foothold of understanding, Sara ventured,
"She didn't want the divorce?"

"This is sordid, and I hate to air dirty family laundry, but
I know you said it's important to your patients for you to
understand—"

"Everything you say to me is confidential, Mrs. Brandt."

"Miranda had been having an affair with Royce Winters for
three years. Jarrod caught them. That's why he divorced her."

That explained his betrayal issue. "I'm sure that was difficult on everyone."

"It was. Miranda was wrong for Jarrod. We tried to tell him
she lacked focus, discipline, and ambition, and we knew she
lacked the fortitude to function as a military wife. That's essential when a man is in a job like Jarrod's. A woman has to
be flexible and self-sufficient, capable of standing on her own.
Miranda wasn't."

And that had left her feeling inferior and her self-esteem

shattered. Enter Royce Winters, substitute hero. Sara had seen this scenario many times.

"My husband and I knew the day they married that Jarrod and Miranda would eventually divorce. But what can you do? As parents you try to equip your children to make good choices, but kids are kids. You can't tell them. They make their own choices, and even if you know they're wrong, you've got to respect them."

"We learn from experience. Still, watching people we love make choices we know are going to scrape their knees is challenging."

Mrs. Brandt concurred with a ladylike grunt. "It's damn difficult."

Sara smiled.

Leaning toward the coffee table, Mrs. Brandt set her cup to her saucer. The porcelain on porcelain grated. "But Miranda added insult to injury."

Sara sipped at her coffee. Chicory. New Orleans blend. Strong enough to put hair on your chest and tongue-burning hot. "How did she do that?"

Anger flashed through Mrs. Brandt's eyes. "Miranda didn't just have an affair. She chose Jarrod's best friend since grade school as her partner. Right or wrong, that was a calculated move on her part. She'd become disillusioned with being a military wife by then. She turned bitter, and then vindictive. She wanted to hurt my son. And she did."

Double betrayal. Wife and best friend. Unfortunately, also typical. But because Sara cared so much for Joe, her emotional reaction wasn't distant or typical. She felt his pain. And his rage. "I imagine that hurt him deeply." *God, don't let my voice falter. Not now.*

"Enough to get him killed."

Sara set down her cup. "I don't understand."

Mrs. Brandt touched the petals of a sunflower in the squatty vase. "Jarrod caught them together, Dr. West. He left. Miranda had second thoughts. Within a week, she was begging Jarrod to forgive her. She realized what he had known all along. She needed him. Jarrod was her rock. Her security and safe harbor during storms. He always had been."

"But Jarrod refused to forgive her?"

"He refused to take her back. It was . . . difficult. He loved her, but he understood that refusing her was what she needed to grow as a person." Sadness tinged her tone. "Unfortunately, Jarrod didn't factor in his own growth. He volunteered for every high-risk mission that came along. Colonel Foster told us that." Mrs. Brandt sighed and her voice trembled, turned watery. "Jarrod never talked to me or my husband about any of this. After he . . . died"—she paused and pulled in a deep breath—"Colonel Foster shared it with me. Jarrod was a very private person. I guess he didn't want to cause more tension between us and Miranda and Royce, so he talked to the colonel." Pain flooded Mrs. Brandt's eyes. "Those two sat at our table for Christmas dinner for three years, knowing they were betraying our son. I can't forgive them for that. I just . . . can't."

Sara's heart went out to the mother. "I'm so sorry."

Sara waited for her to get through the hurt and anger so she could go on.

"That's why Jarrod volunteered for all those suicide missions. Because he felt he had nothing to come home to anymore."

Sara shouldn't do it. Couldn't *not* do it. "No, Mrs. Brandt," Sara softly disagreed. "Jarrod might have felt he had nothing left to lose, but that isn't the real reason he put his life on the line in those missions." On this, Sara knew she was on firm ground. "The reason he did that was because he believed in what he was doing. And because the others who would have taken on the missions he refused to take *did* have something left to lose."

"That's what Colonel Foster said." A soft smile of pride and remembrance touched her lips. "He said all Jarrod did was acts of honor."

Sara's throat went thick. "They were." This, Foster had done right. The way he had treated Mrs. Brandt and had handled this situation, giving Jarrod's mother some comforting words, had been exactly right.

"The colonel really respected Jarrod. It was mutual. Jarrod thought the world of him." Mrs. Brandt scooted back on the sofa cushion and crossed her legs. "He helped us a great deal, after Jarrod died—still checks on us every month. On the fifteenth, we get a phone call. You can set your watch by Jack Foster."

Mrs. Brandt clearly didn't consider Foster corrupt. In her book, he wasn't just a good guy but a great one. And judging from his dedication and devotion to Jarrod's family, Sara waffled on her own opinion. Maybe Foster *was* a good guy. These certainly weren't the actions of a man seeking only a star for his shoulder.

"Colonel Foster tried to help Miranda, too. She had a hard time with Jarrod's death. Even with Royce there to help her, she struggled." Mrs. Brandt sobered. "That there is no security is a hard lesson to learn, Dr. West."

"Yes, it is. Harder for some than others." In her practice, Sara had seen refusing to accept that truth destroy many lives.

Mrs. Brandt digressed, talking wistfully about Jarrod as a child, a teen. Sara listened, thinking that remembering was good for the mother in the woman, and feeling guilty as hell about that mother mourning a son who was not dead.

Solemn, her thoughts riveted back to Foster. He was held in high regard here, but Sara's signals on him and his character remained mixed. She couldn't slot him with any degree of certainty. Foster habitually did whatever he deemed necessary to accomplish his job, and yet his treatment of the Brandts and even Miranda proved he also had a compassionate side. At least, he did when being compassionate didn't interfere with his job.

Had he kept in touch with the other families, too?

Probably not. Unless the patients were all Shadow Watchers, and that was extremely unlikely. Yet, he had kept tabs on Sara, Lisa, and Brenda—and even on their brother, Steve.

Could all of her patients have been Shadow Watchers?

*   *   *

Sara drove back toward Braxton, passing the store with the broken phone and the old-fashioned Coke machine. Her tires kicked up a trail of dust behind her.

She had left Mrs. Brandt's house and had gone to a motel, where she had phoned each of the other PTSD patients' families, with the exception of Brenda. All of them lived too far away to visit personally.

Then she had spread out all the information gathered on the bed and had compared each file to all of the others. Some damaged men had not been in intel jobs. Lou was an arms expert. Ray, a medic. Michael, a contract negotiator. David and Jarrod were Shadow Watchers. ADR-40 was a scientist whose primary duty dealt with a project developing laser technology.

Aside from all of them being transferred to Braxton from IWPT, the only common bond noted was that most of the patients, including Jarrod, had been in relationships with faithless spouses or significant others. From her research, Sara knew that bond was significant. Time after time in the research documents, infidelity had been cited as the number one vulnerability of soldiers in the application of psychological warfare.

Sara also felt certain that Jarrod no longer had as many memory blanks as he claimed. His survival instincts had kicked in, and he had incorporated a protective device to insulate himself from betrayal. She couldn't be angry with Jarrod about that. Not knowing how he felt about her and about his relationship with Miranda. But knowing that he was insulating himself and that he wasn't as diminished as he had led her to believe, did alleviate some guilt about Sara taking advantage of him.

She braked at a stop sign, waited for a blue Jeep to pass, and then drove on down the pothole-filled road leading to the gate. Maybe falling in love with a patient was wrong. But it was easier to bear than falling in love with a patient who was mentally diminished.

A flash from the ditch snagged Sara's gaze. Someone

jumped out onto the dirt road. She slammed on the brakes and skidded to a stop. Reaston?

He walked around the hood of the car. Shaking hard, having no idea what this meant but damn certain it couldn't be good, Sara rolled down the window. "Reaston, what are you doing out here?"

The sergeant stepped up to the window. "Saving your ass, ma'am." He opened the driver's door. "Scoot over."

Sara slid over the gearshift and into the passenger seat, dumbfounded.

Reaston got behind the wheel, shut the door, and then slapped the gearshift into Drive. "This car is a rental. You phoned U.S.A. Rentals to pick it up outside the gate yesterday afternoon. An agent for the company did so. You have not been outside the facility at any time since yesterday morning. Understand?"

Sara nodded, afraid to say anything for fear of saying the wrong thing.

Reaston stomped the gas, drove down the dirt road toward the gate. About two hundred yards out, he slowed down and aimed right for the ditch.

Sara grabbed the dash, bracing herself. "What the hell are you doing?"

The car rolled though the ditch and into the woods beyond it. Reaston cut the engine. "The car will be here. You'll need it shortly. Keep the keys in a safe, accessible place." He passed them to her. "Go in through the gate. Koloski will let you in. I have the flu. When you get inside the facility, skip the security points. People have been briefed. Just avoid Mick Bush or your ass is grass. Once you're inside, get lost. Somewhere obscure, where you don't usually go. Whatever you do, stay the hell away from the lab. William's there."

"Okay." Sara couldn't get over this. The Braxton underground had galvanized to help her. But why? "I don't get it, Reaston. People won't even talk to me. Why are they doing this? Why are you?"

"Look, Major. You didn't get it. You still don't. We didn't know you, and you didn't have a clue we were all lifers—

hell, you didn't know *you* were a lifer. The gate at Braxton swings one way. In. To get out—unless they want you out temporarily—you leave one way. Toes up. Who wants to pass on news like that?"

They hadn't been afraid of being tagged security risks by associating with her. They hadn't wanted to be the ones to shatter her illusions with the truth about her leaving Braxton.

She let that sink in. It felt right. Especially in light of all those helping her now. "Does anyone know I've been gone?"

"Not for fact." Reaston fingered the door handle, clearly eager to get out of here before they got caught. "Fontaine is suspicious and Mick Bush is certain, but he can't prove you left the facility. I don't know what the hell you did to tick him off, but he's out for blood."

"I don't know, either. But if Fontaine's had him looking for me, and he's riding Bush as hard as he's ridden me, that's more than reason enough right there."

"Fontaine is on his back. He's on everyone's back. Pulling personal inspections throughout the facility."

Great. Just great. A raging bull. Exactly what she needed.

Jarrod heard the buzzer.

He looked toward the door, hoping to see Sara. Instead, he saw Fontaine, wearing a brown suit, a bright purple tie—obviously Mrs. Fontaine hadn't returned yet—and a frown too big for his face.

"Where is Dr. West?" he asked. "I was told she was in with you." Fontaine let his gaze slide down Jarrod, shoulders to toes. "And where did you get street clothes?"

"They're part of my therapy." Jarrod slid a hand into his pocket. "You didn't pass Dr. West in the hallway?"

"No, I did not."

"Hmm. Well, I can't imagine why not. She just left here." Fontaine pursed his lips. "Did she say where she was going?"

"To check on her other patients."

"I see." Fontaine stepped closer. "I understand you're making significant progress."

"So she says." Jarrod shrugged. "Personally, I don't see it."

Fontaine stepped close to Jarrod, turned his back to the camera, and dropped his voice to a faint drone. "Joe, what is Operation Red Haze?"

A memory rammed through Jarrod with the force of a lightning bolt. He struggled to suppress any outward reaction, and lied. "I don't know." Affecting a vacant look, he reached for his crayons. "Am I supposed to know?"

Fontaine studied Joe hard, looking for any crack in his demeanor, any sign of deception or deceit. "No. No, you aren't."

Joe fingered the flap of the crayon box. "I like color. Blue and green and orange and . . ."

Fontaine left the Isolation room, his black loafers squeaking on the floorpads.

From under his lashes, Jarrod covertly watched Fontaine go, futility and frustration making mincemeat of his stomach. Sara was in danger. He loved her, wanted to help, and to protect her. Stuck in here, he could do so little, and every instinct in his body warned him that she needed so much.

Warned him that she was in lethal danger.

That she was a part of Operation Red Haze.

eighteen

☆

Beth was in the med room, but the call couldn't wait. Shank spoke softly into the phone. "Sara's on her way back in, sir."

"Good. Thank you, Captain." Foster cleared his throat. "Has she fallen in love with him yet?"

Foster, talking about emotions? To her? Despite his lecture on trusting leaders, Shank didn't trust this behavior, or him. Would a *yes* or a *no* get Sara killed? "I'm not sure," Shank said. "Maybe."

"Unacceptable, Captain. Yes, or no."

"I'd say no, but I think yes." Why did he always push for definitive answers when typically there weren't ones? Did he suspect Shank hadn't been honest? "Joe's definitely got it bad for her."

"She's fighting her conscience," Foster speculated.

"In a huge way," Shank agreed. "Trying to keep things ethical."

"Excellent." Foster let out a satisfied sigh. "Excellent."

So Sara had acted exactly as he'd expected her to—again. "Have you gotten clearance to get her into IWPT, sir? That's going to be the first thing she asks me."

"No, but don't worry. The plan is unfolding exactly as anticipated."

Skepticism rippled through Shank. How could things be unfolding as anticipated? There were more uncertainties in this operation than holes in a chunk of Swiss cheese. Foster had to be blowing smoke. "I suggest you somehow let Dr. Fontaine know that. He's been nipping at her heels like a rabid dog."

"He has been handled, Captain."

"May I ask how, sir?"

Foster's voice chilled. "This afternoon, the director received a memo, reminding him that all military personnel must receive psychological-warfare training. The situation is under control."

An icy shiver crept up Shank's spine. Now why would Foster expose himself to remind Fontaine about psych-warfare training?

Only one reason came to mind, and it terrified Shank. Foster was working *with* Fontaine. But he couldn't be, could he?

All he wants is that star. That's all he wants. And if Braxton and IWPT go down—without him being associated—he'll get it.

Oh, God. Foster had double-crossed them all.

Sara ran into Shank in the hallway outside ADR-40's room.

"Thank God you're back." Shank stuffed the keys to the med room into her pocket. "Fontaine has been personally searching the facility for you, and Mick Bush has been hanging on to friendlies as tight as a damn leech."

"Does Fontaine or Bush know I've been gone?"

"They're suspicious, but I don't think they can prove it. If they could, they'd have assembled a Security team to find you and bring you back. The friendlies have been stonewalling. William hasn't helped." Shank twisted her lips in a respectable frown. "He's been spouting off how pissed he is at Fontaine about the demotion and fine, but I'm not buying it. He might be ticked enough not to report you AWOL with Fontaine, but I wouldn't bank on it. William can't be trusted. Flat out."

AWOL—absent without leave. Another acronym. "What about Bush?" Sara asked, licking at her dry lips. "Reaston said he was out for blood."

"He is." Shank stepped into an alcove near the end of the hall. "Bush is a fanatic. That's what makes him so good at what he does in Security. It also makes duping him darned difficult because he takes any irregularity personally. He noticed that your car was missing from the parking lot."

"I gathered that when I got back."

Shank paled. "You didn't drive it back in here."

"No, Reaston hid it."

"Good. Joe arranged that." Shank swiped at her thighs. "We covered it, but you can bet your ass Bush reported it to Fontaine."

"So do I go to Fontaine and tell him I know he's been looking for me, or do I wait for him to find me?"

"Go to him," Shank said. "That should throw him for a loop. But see Joe first. He's been worried sick about you, and really feeling the pinch because he's stuck in here while you're out there alone."

He'd definitely recovered. Definitely. And he wanted to protect her. Warmed by that, Sara nodded. "Did you get Foster?"

"Yeah. He says you getting to IWPT is handled." Shank's expression darkened from gloomy to glum. "I don't trust him anymore, Sara. All of this, and he says everything's going according to plan."

"Sounds impossible. But with Foster, who knows? Could be possible, feasible, and logical."

"Could be," Shank agreed. "But if it is, then why do I have this gaping hole in my gut that's burning acid?"

"I don't know. If it helps, I've got the same symptoms." Unsure if that was reason to rejoice or mourn, Sara headed toward Isolation.

Koloski buzzed her through, and Sara entered Joe's room.

Relief flooded his face, and Joe rushed to the door. He clasped her hands in his. "Sara, are you okay?"

She nodded. "I'm safe."

"We need to talk." He blinked deliberately. "I remember. I think, all of it."

Sara whispered back, knowing the equipment wouldn't be able to pick it up. "All of what?"

"Operation Red Haze."

"We'll have to wait." She darted a glance at the Plexiglas window. Empty. "Fontaine's on a witch hunt for me."

"I know. He was here." Joe avoided the camera. "You should be covered."

"I've got to go placate him, and then I'll come back and we'll go outside. You can tell me about Red Haze there."

"Okay." Joe blinked, and his voice went soft. "I'm glad you came back."

A rush of pure warmth spread through her chest. For Joe, those were difficult words to speak. She blinked back and smiled. "I'll always come back to you, Joe."

"Careful, Doc." He didn't smile, but his eyes lit up from the bottoms. "I might hold you to that."

"I'm counting on it." Sara squeezed his hands, then stepped to the door. "I'll be back as soon as I can."

The door closed behind her and Sara walked past the Isolation nurses' station. The Plexiglas distorted Koloski's reflection. William stood beside him.

"Major West," William shouted out. "Dr. Fontaine is looking for you."

"Joe just told me. I'm on my way down there right now."

Sara stepped into the elevator. Beth was in it. Sara nodded, but Beth ignored her, and the sickly-sweet smell of her perfume made Sara's stomach flip. It was sucking up all the air. Queasy, she looked out at the station and, before the doors slid closed, she saw William lift the phone. Pissed or not, he hadn't changed.

The elevator descended to the first floor, and the door opened. Mick Bush stood front and center just outside it, waiting for her.

Expecting him, after William's call, Sara smiled. "Hi, Sergeant Bush."

"Dr. West," he said stiffly. "Dr. Fontaine wants to see you in his office immediately."

"Joe mentioned he was looking for me. I'm on my way. I just need to stop by X ray—"

"No, ma'am. Dr. Fontaine wants to see you now." Mick stepped aside so she could exit the elevator. "I'll escort you."

"Fine." With Mick Bush at her side, radiating cold fury, Sara walked toward Fontaine's office, her stomach in more knots than a hangman's noose.

*　　*　　*

Sara stood at attention in Fontaine's office, staring straight ahead.

He paced back and forth between his credenza and desk, delivering her a dressing-down that would have given her mother—an undisputed lecturing pro—a run for her money for the best-of-the-best award.

He was furious, and made no effort to hide it. He actually wagged a finger at her. "We both know you accessed confidential, classified files. We both know you violated the privacy of patients and security procedures in this facility. Procedures put into place to protect both the patients and the facility. You were briefed, Major. You knew Braxton was a high-risk facility and the patients in this facility were high risk. What possible reason could you have to justify circumventing the measures put into place to protect both?"

Sara had to lie. Admitting the truth could jeopardize Koloski and Joe. Both had covered for her.

"And don't you dare cite your rights under your agreement with the DoD. In fact, to hell with your agreement. You do *not* have a blank license to do whatever you want to do here."

"No, sir. I don't." She paused, effected a guileless stance. "I'm confused. Sergeant Bush verified I was with Joe when someone used my code to access the computer. We were in a monitored room, and I heard Koloski inform the sergeant of that myself. As for my DoD agreement, it does give me full authority over my patients and their therapies," she said, attempting to bury her temper. There was a time for anger and one for contrition. This definitely rated as a time for contrition—and a minor concession. "From what you're saying, there are records on my patients that I haven't seen. I was promised full access to all pertinent information and I'm sworn to laws governing confidentiality, so if there are other records, I'd like immediate access to them."

"Denied." Fontaine glared at her.

"Why?" Sara gave him her best innocent look. "My purpose here is to effectively treat my patients. How can I do that if pertinent information on them is withheld—"

"Damn it, Major," Fontaine shouted. "Your request is denied."

Sara stilled and stared at him. She'd made her point. If she pushed any further, she would only destroy the doubt she had created—and weaken his fear that she would demand access to those files and get it. Definitely time to back off. "If I stepped on toes, I apologize. I'm relatively new to the military and not yet well-versed on its protocol."

Fontaine stopped pacing and stared at her. His expression made it obvious that he didn't trust this apology any more than he trusted her. "Why have you been difficult to locate for the last twenty-four hours?"

"Difficult to locate, sir?" She slid him a perplexed look.

"Yes, damn it, difficult to locate."

"I don't know, sir." She retained her stiff-spined stance. "I've been performing my duties on pretty much the same schedule since I've been at Braxton."

"Fine." An expression she swore could grow no more grim did. He plopped down at his desk. "I can see you won't admit the truth, but we both know it, Dr. West." He looked up at her from under his lashes. "Stay out of my computer system, and get the hell out of my office."

"Yes, sir." She saluted, toed a turn, as she had seen Reaston do, and left.

Martha sat at her desk in the outer office, but her hand was nowhere near the intercom button. With Fontaine shouting, there had no need to eavesdrop. Martha had heard every word just fine.

Sara walked out into the hall and headed straight for the elevator. She needed that secure line. She needed to talk to Foster.

"You didn't lie," Sara told Foster, speaking into the secure-line phone at the second-floor nurse's station. Thankfully, it was a "new shipment" day at the facility's exchange, so Beth had taken a long lunch hour to shop. "I found David. I still haven't found out exactly what happened to him, but I will soon."

"Do you intend to tell Brenda?"

Foster's deceptively light tone didn't fool Sara. Her answer probably ranked as one of the most important ones of her life. "If I told her, I'd be committing treason."

"Yes, you would," Foster agreed. "You'd also be putting her and Lisa in jeopardy. And everyone at Braxton."

Sara propped her elbow on the desk, dropped her chin into her hand, and rubbed at her throbbing temple. "Don't you think I realize that?"

"I take it then you've decided against telling your sister."

"For now. It would only make matters worse for everyone." Sara blew a sigh through the receiver that she meant for Foster to hear. "Do you realize the enormity of what you've done here, Foster? My sister has married four other men—and is about to marry a fifth—and her husband isn't even dead."

"Legally, he is. But you already know that, don't you, Sara?"

Why lie? Obviously he too knew about her accessing the records in the computer. He had probably meant for her to do it, or he'd never have mentioned the permanent admission records to her, or blocked her access to David's file. Foster *never* gave anything away without a specific reason. "Yes, I know David is legally dead."

"No curiosity about how I learned that bit of trivia?" Foster asked.

"I expect the OSI received a report from Colonel Fontaine, complaining that in his humble opinion I had violated security and therefore the terms of my agreement with the DoD."

"Excellent deduction."

"The OSI picked up a special coding on my file and forwarded the report to the AID who, of course, forwarded the report to you." Sara repeated the trail Foster had given her about Joe.

"Again correct." Foster sounded pleased. "You're learning quickly, Sara."

"And resenting every damn minute of it." Especially her innate belief that Foster hadn't been apprised by the OSI or the AID at all. That he'd heard directly from Fontaine. Why she felt certain of that, she wasn't sure, but something had sent her instincts barreling off in that direction. And just the possibility of it being true scared her right out of her socks. "Why did you isolate David from me for so long?"

"I had to know how you would react. It was a matter of national security."

Plausible. Possible. True. "He's a vegetable, Jack." Emotion put a tremble in her voice, and she doubted he'd miss her using his first name.

"I know." Empathy and regret laced his tone.

It sounded genuine, sincere, and, God, but did she hope it was. She thumbed the edges of the desk blotter's pages. "What happened to him?"

"I don't know, Sara." Foster's swallow sounded through the phone. "On my word of honor, I don't know."

The truth hit Sara between the eyes. "That's why I'm here. To find out."

"Certainly no one could be more persistent than you at pursuing the truth."

So many emotions attacked her at once—relief, certainty, regret, doubt, fear, anger—she couldn't compartmentalize them, and they flowed over into her speech. "Oh, I wish I knew if I could trust you. I wish I knew if you were a good guy or corrupt."

"I'd take offense, but in my type of work, sometimes the lines look blurred."

Sara dropped her voice. "Will you tell me the truth? Are you corrupt, Jack?"

He hesitated, as if torn, then finally answered. "I kept my word, Sara. You've gotten answers about David."

"And raised more questions about what happened to him," she added. "I'm really angry with you. You brought me to Braxton without telling me everyone inside it is stuck here for life."

"I told you they were all volunteers. I also told you that you wouldn't be canceled unless you became a threat."

"But you refused to tell me what constitutes me becoming

a threat. Have you forgotten? When I asked for your word that I'd walk out of here, you hung up on me."

"I haven't forgotten."

"Good. Because I damn sure haven't. I'm going to give you another chance, and ask you again. Am I going to die of old age here because I know Braxton exists?"

"I hope not," he said. "But that choice really is up to you."

"In that case, I choose to live."

"I'm glad to hear it," Foster said. "I'll do all I can to help make it happen."

She narrowed her eyes, frowned at the receiver. "What do you mean?"

"You wanted answers about David."

"I want the truth."

"Well, you're going to get it." Foster paused. When he went on, his voice turned stiff. "If you can live with it, then you'll also know a life after Braxton. As I said, it's up to you."

Sara got the strangest feeling. The hairs on her neck lifted and gooseflesh rose on her arms. He knew more than he was telling her. Typical for Foster, and in this case, dangerous for her.

Lethally dangerous.

nineteen

☆

Sara left Isolation with Jarrod.

Koloski stopped them at the station. He circled around the Plexiglas and lowered his voice. "Are you going out on the grounds?"

"No. A therapeutic outing," Sara said.

Koloski shifted his gaze to Jarrod. "Mick Bush is on duty at the gate. Better take an alternate route out."

Jarrod nodded.

An alternate route? Sara knew of no alternate route, but held her silence. Obviously this was something the Braxton underground had under control.

She led Jarrod through the security checkpoints. No one attempted to detain them. When they stepped outside onto the stone path, Jarrod veered south, across the lawns, moving island to island toward the woods.

"Where are we going?"

"To your car." He clasped her hand and tugged lightly. "Move quickly, Sara. We're exposed."

Out in the open, crossing a grassy expanse, they were exposed. They took cover in a clump of trees, then walked a path that from the bent grass had been walked many times before, closing in on the woods. "There's an electric fence," she reminded him.

"I know." They entered the woods, followed a trail through the fragrant pines and palmettos. Birds twittered and some small animal scurried in the undergrowth out of sight.

They came to the fence. Foliage half buried it. Jarrod stepped into a dense tangle of vines, shoved them aside, and exposed a small gate. He stooped to the ground and swiped at the dirt, revealing a black electrical switch, then flipped it.

The gate swung open.

Jarrod and Sara stepped through. He grabbed a twig and toggled the switch. When the gate closed, he brushed dirt back over the switch. Straightening up, he dropped the twig, and swiped loose dirt from his hands. "Your car is this way."

Numb all over, Sara followed him. "Just how many times have you been out of Braxton this way?"

"Since you arrived, only once."

Staring at the back of his head, Sara stopped dead in her tracks. "And before then?"

Jarrod turned back to her on the path. He looked down into her eyes, and felt her confidence in him plummet. "I wasn't capable of leaving before you arrived."

"But—"

"Sara, please. Can we get to the car and get the hell out of here? Then I'll tell you everything you want to know."

"Fine." Sara felt used. Used and betrayed, and damned angry. "Lead on, Jarrod."

They walked to the car in silence, and Jarrod opened the driver's door. "Do you want me to drive?"

Sara cocked a brow in his direction. "Are you capable?"

"Probably."

She stepped around him and slid onto the driver's seat. "I'll do it."

Jarrod closed her door and then got in on the passenger's side. Explaining all of this was going to be more difficult than he imagined. Far more difficult . . .

Cranking the engine, Sara glanced over at him. Jarrod was pale and a sheen of sweat glistened on his skin. "What's wrong?"

"There's no air in here."

"I'm the one with claustrophobia," she reminded him, gripping the wheel. "You need to buckle up."

"No." Sweat beaded on his forehead. "No straps." He swiped at his face with his forearm. "Roll down the windows, okay?"

Remnants of the sensory-deprivation torture, she realized. The box he had symbolized as a coffin. Sara hit the buttons and rolled all four windows down. She didn't nag him on the seat-belt issue, though she had strong, strong feelings on the wisdom of wearing them. "Remember your breathing exercises," she said, backing out of the woods and onto the dirt road.

The sun dipped behind the clouds, casting a dreary, dim pallor on the woods lining the road. "Where should we go?"

"Pass the store and take a right. There's a lake out there with a picnic area. We can talk there."

Sara drove to the spot and turned off the ignition. A single picnic table sat under a sprawling, moss-laden oak. The lake was actually a wide spot in a creek with a sandy beach. Tranquil. She glanced at Jarrod, who was not. "You okay?"

"Yeah." Jarrod opened the door and stepped outside. "I'm still fighting residual responses, like the seat belt and windows, but time will take care of them."

Sara sat down on the bench and leaned against the wooden table, not sure she was ready to jump into his explanations with both feet. "I talked to your mother, Jarrod."

Hunger filled his eyes. "How is she?"

"Graceful, composed, genteel, and still mourning you."

He lifted his chin, looked out over the water. "It couldn't be avoided."

Sara looked up at him. "Why?"

"The mission required it."

Sara's temper flared. She tamped it. "Look, it's really hard to identify allies and enemies around here. I told you I needed your trust, and I needed to know you trust me. Do you trust me, Jarrod?"

He slid his hands inside the pockets of his slacks. "If I didn't, you wouldn't be here. You would have been caught accessing the computer and leaving Braxton."

She believed him. "I trust you, too."

"I'm glad to hear it."

"So I want to know why you've pretended to be more seriously diminished than you obviously have been."

"I wasn't pretending." He leaned a hip against the table near her, his thigh brushing against her shoulder. "I started improving when we painted the isolation room. I made drastic improvements when we started going outside. I'm not a hundred percent yet, but I'm almost there. I can't explain this, Sara, but it felt as if the infusion of color negated whatever they had done to me."

"It makes perfect sense. Sensory deprivation, combined with other therapies that fall into the psychological-warfare arena, produce *exactly* those results. As long as you remained sensory deprived—which you did in isolation until we painted—then you were psychologically controlled."

Understanding flashed through his eyes. "But break the deprivation cycle, and you break the control."

"Exactly." Ants crawled in the dirt at her feet. Sara scooted up to sit on the table. "How big is the underground at Braxton?"

"Small. But effective. It hasn't occurred to some of the employees that they'll never leave."

Sara filled Jarrod in on her deductions about IWPT, about the commonalities between him and the other patients, ending with, "Something out of line is happening at IWPT."

Watching him sort through the information, she draped her hands over her bent knees. "I believe Colonel Foster pulled you from a lower-priority mission and sent you to IWPT undercover to investigate. I also think someone there realized you were a Shadow Watcher and sacrificed you. You were deliberately damaged." Sara rubbed at her temple. "What I don't understand is why you weren't damaged more severely. Obviously they have the capability to destroy a human mind. Lou, David, and ADR-40 prove that. So why weren't you destroyed? Why were you only impaired?"

"I don't know," Jarrod admitted. "I was sent in undercover as a trainee. Dr. Owlsley, IWPT's director, profiled me. I remember that vividly. It was a lengthy interrogation. Very intense. The training began, and was going fine. Typical survival-school-type stuff. Sleep deprivation, hours and hours of interrogation—nothing I haven't experienced a thousand times before in training." He pursed his lips. "I remember being put in a box. I think I spent a couple of days in it. It was cramped—too small to sit or stand and too short to stretch out. And there was this low-level percussion. It didn't bother me at first. I imagined it as a heart beating. But the longer it went on, the more irritating it became. By the time I got out of there, it had me half-crazy."

Too agitated to sit, he stood up and stepped away from the table. "When they let me out of the box, the light was blinding white. It hurt my eyes. I was disoriented and confused, but I remember being injected with something. I don't know what." Jarrod's voice quivered. "The next thing I remember is waking up in the middle of a nightmare. I was being strapped into an electric chair." He shook as if sloughing off the memories. "That's all I remember about it. Except for—"

"What?" Sara asked.

He stared down at her. "A red pinpoint of light."

Sara rested a hand on his thigh, grounding him there with her. "Where did the light come from?"

"I don't want to think about this, Sara," he said stiffly. "I can't push. The rage will come."

"No it won't. Not anymore." She gave his thigh a reassuring squeeze. "You're stronger now and it's weaker because you know what it is. That gives you the power to fight it. Your will, Jarrod. That's your defense. Haven't you stopped the rage from coming?"

"Yes."

"How did you stop it?"

"Focusing elsewhere. On the Celtic music. On you."

Sara smiled. "See? Your will proved stronger because you knew what you were facing and how to defend against it."

"Okay." Jarrod swiped a hand at the hair at his temples. Weak sunlight streaked through the clouds, cast his shadow on the ground. "But if I start to lose it, get in the car and lock the doors."

"I will."

He closed his eyes, and thought back. "I was in a dark room. Like a warehouse. Strapped to the chair. There were armed guards, and Dr. Owlsley. Some other man in uniform was there."

"Did you know him?"

"He seemed familiar, but it was too dark. I couldn't see him clearly."

"So they strapped you to the chair."

"Yes." Jarrod let out a shuddery breath. "I sensed something was wrong, but ignored it. Then, I saw this machine. I didn't know what it was, which is odd because I'm briefed on all our latest technology. When I noted structural deficiencies, I started worrying."

"Structural deficiencies?"

"The building had exposed wires—it wasn't an approved military structure. The Air Force only permits working in areas that are safety hazards in critical situations, and there was nothing to suggest Alert Condition Alpha much less Delta."

"So this machine is where the red light originated."

No answer.

"Jarrod?"

His chest heaved. He opened his eyes, stared down at Sara, fear and finality riddling his gaze. "It was a noninvasive laser, Sara. It triggered memories."

Sara's heart beat hard and fast. She'd read about this! "They stimulated memories that caused intense reactions. Aggressive reactions."

"Yes." Jarrod sat beside her, clasped their hands. "They hammered on memories of Miranda and her affair with Royce. Over and over, I relived walking in on the two of them."

Sara chewed at her lower lip, getting a firm fix on this. "Jarrod, if you hadn't already made peace with Miranda's infidelity and her and Royce betraying you, how do you think that hammering and reliving the event would have affected you?"

Jarrod stiffened and stared straight into her eyes. "It would have driven me insane."

"Like Lou and David?" Sara speculated. "Like ADR-40?"

"Maybe." Jarrod dragged a hand through his hair, thumbed a slat on the tabletop with his nail. "Maybe not."

"Except for David, they all had unfaithful spouses or significant others. They all had been betrayed."

He stared out into the woods surrounding the little clearing. "This laser can trigger thoughts and manipulate them, Sara." Jarrod grunted. "It sounds almost implausible."

"It's not only plausible, it's happening. There are contracts between technological firms and the DoD right now, studying this exact technology. I read a recent report on noninvasive microwave laser technology, Jarrod. Scientists were effectively using the technology to manipulate attacks and counterattacks in exercises. The conditions were controlled, but the experiments were working."

"So if they're working, then why push people over the edge?"

"Probably attempting to perfect the technology. Testing its parameters. The experiment I read about had the exercise participants divided into two groups. Red and blue. Red was the enemy."

Jarrod jerked. "I remember that. Red is the enemy. I heard it in the dark room."

"Mobile field units of the blue team utilized the noninvasive laser technology on the red team. The goal wasn't to kill them, of course, but to render them incapable of fighting. The stimulation planted thoughts of severe stomach cramps. The men fell to the ground on the field, writhing in pain."

"So it worked."

"Short-term. It could inflict the desired response, but it couldn't sustain it."

"Who headed that experiment?"

Sara swallowed hard. "Dr. Owlsley."

"He's pushing the parameters, Sara," Jarrod said. "That, or something else is going on at IWPT. Something not covered by the DoD contract." Agitated, Jarrod moved away from the table. "We have to find out what they're doing."

"I know." Sara shuddered. "That's why, as soon as it can be arranged, I'm going to IWPT."

"Are you insane?" Jarrod strode over to her, grasped her shoulders and squeezed hard. "Sara, you can't go there."

She lifted her hands to cover his on her shoulders. "I'm not insane, I'm scared stiff. But we can't stop them from out here. I have to go."

He stared hard at her. "The soldier in me understands. The man in me doesn't want you in danger. Sara, this is serious. You won't come out the same as you go in. That's a proven fact. Fontaine *is* involved and he's going to do his damnedest to make sure you leave IWPT in worse condition than ADR-40."

Just the thought terrified her. "I know the risks. Really, I do." Trembling, she pressed her face against Jarrod's chest. "But if I don't get in there, then I can't prove they're doing anything wrong. They won't stop, Jarrod. You know they won't stop. Look at the timing on this. Gaps of months between David and Michael being damaged and sent to Braxton. More gaps between Michael and Ray. But now the pattern has changed and the gaps have closed. It's almost as if time has become urgent to them. Instead of months between transferees, it's become weeks."

"You're right. I know you're right." Jarrod swallowed hard, his Adam's apple bobbing in his throat. He let his hand drift down her face and cup her chin. "But I don't like it. I don't want you at risk."

"Jarrod," she said just above a whisper. "We're all at risk."

His hands cupping her face shook. And because no words would convey all he was feeling, he kissed her hard, letting his emotions flow to her through touch.

And Sara kissed him back, burying the guilt, shoving it aside, wanting just this once to be totally free to love him.

"Sara." He lifted his lips from hers and looked into her eyes. "You're fired."

Her arms circling his sides stilled. "What?"

"You're fired." He stared at her mouth, let his gaze drift to her eyes. "Let go of the guilt about breaching your professional ethics and make love with me, Sara. You're not my doctor anymore."

She wanted nothing more. "You can't fire me. You need me, Jarrod."

"Yes, honey." He tightened his hold on her, brought her closer. "As much as I resent it, I do."

He could replace her professionally but not personally. Sara's heart melted. "I need you, too."

They undressed and made love atop the picnic table, eagerly, urgently, and Sara swore she would never regret it.

Still hazy in the afterglow, she snuggled to his side and mentally drifted. He was definitely the one.

They talked quietly for a long time, then strolled along the sandy beach, hands linked, hearts and minds attuned. On the way back to the table, Sara sat down in the sand near the water's edge. She felt content. Amazing, with all of the uncertainty ahead that she could feel that way, but for the moment, she did.

Jarrod sat down beside her and looked out over the water. He laced their fingers and braced their hands on his thigh. "I admire you for going to IWPT."

His rough denim jeans didn't feel nearly so good as his skin. "Don't. I'm not driven by ideals, I'm driven by fear. Mind control in any form gives me the creeps, but this . . ." Her voice trailed off and she forced herself to reveal her deepest fear. "I'm afraid of what I'll be like . . . afterward."

"You should be afraid." He briefed her on details, leaving nothing he recalled out, fearful that anything he omitted would be exactly what Sara needed to survive. He talked and talked, randomly, generally, and then specifically. "Before you go in, it's imperative that you deal with any outstanding emotional issues. Owlsley's profile is thorough. He'll find your Achilles' heel and then exploit it with the laser. You'll already be weakened, confused, and disoriented from the percussion therapy and sensory deprivation. You won't be able to avoid it, Sara. You *will* come out of this scrambled. The difference is degree."

He looked from the water to her. "I've thought about this, and I'm convinced you're right. The degree of damage depends on the depth of emotion engaged. The more intense the emotion he taps into, the more power he has over you, and the greater amount of damage you sustain."

She leaned her head against his shoulder. "Family is my Achilles' heel. It always has been. I've wanted my own family for so long, but with what happened to Brenda, well, I couldn't have one."

"Honey, I see where you're going with this, but I don't think Brenda would want or expect you to deny yourself a family because hers was torn apart."

"I know." Sara rocked her cheek against his shoulder. "But I felt that it wasn't right for me to have what she had lost. It sounds crazy, but that's how I've looked at this for a long time. Anyway, I called Brenda this morning. I'm meeting her and Lisa tonight, to hash through it."

"So you've decided to tell her about David."

"Knowing I might not come out of IWPT able to tell her, I have no choice."

"You always have a choice, Sara."

"Then, my choice is to tell her. She's his wife. She has a right to know. If it were you, I'd move heaven and earth to find out the truth. If I did anything less, I couldn't live with myself. She loves him."

"And you love her."

"Of course. She's my sister." Sara stared at the rippling water. "I trust her, too. She'll handle this discreetly because she'll know indiscretion could harm David and Lisa. Brenda wouldn't do that."

"And what about you? Who's going to protect you?"

"At the moment, I'm more concerned about being locked in a box than protection."

"Claustrophobic. I've been thinking of that, too." He pivoted toward her. "When you're in there, think ice. Imagine yourself sitting on a free-floating iceberg. That'll help. It's feeling closed in and like there's not enough air that gets to you. Develop a tool to combat it."

"This sounds like a survival-school technique."

"It is." Jarrod smiled. "And it works."

"Okay." Sara drew in a deep, cleansing breath. "I'll think ice."

He pecked a kiss to her temple. "You can think of me, too."

Her heart skipped a little beat. She picked up a small stone and tossed it into the water. "What should I think about you?"

"That no matter what happens, I'll be there for you, doing everything I can to help you."

"Really?"

He nodded.

Sara gave him a liquid smile. "I'll think of you a lot, Jarrod."

He didn't want to risk asking—the grooves alongside his mouth proved it—but he did. "Only while you're in the box?"

Reassurance. He needed it as badly as she did. She gave him a negative nod. "Always." She let her promise shine in her eyes.

He kissed her softly, gently, and left her as dizzy and breathless as when they'd made love. Hugging him tightly, she buried her chin at the curve of his neck. "I don't like leaving you at Braxton."

"I'll be fine. Shank, Koloski, and Reaston are there." He swept her back with tiny, possessive circles. "It's you I'm worried about."

"I'm leaving my car keys with you. Then, if you want to get out, you can."

"How are you going to get to IWPT?"

"A rental. I'll order one to be delivered to the gate." Sara had surprised him; she saw it in his eyes. "I can't take this car. The rental company picked it up, remember?"

"Right." He smiled and brushed a light kiss to her lips. "You're getting good at this."

"Don't tell me that." She looped her arms around his sides. "I don't want to be good at this."

Jarrod pulled back. "Until it's over, you had better want to be great at it. I want you back here alive and healthy. You matter to me."

"You matter to me, too." God, but it felt good to admit at least that much out loud. "There's something else you need to know." She had debated on telling him this, but there was no room for lies between them. "I've gotten proof to the outside that Braxton exists and staff and patients are on the premises. If I shouldn't come back okay, use it to get yourself and the underground out of here. Call Lisa. She'll know what to do."

"Your niece?" He sounded surprised.

Sara nodded. "I know. I hated to involve her, and she is young, but she's more stable than her mother right now, and I trust her."

"What kind of proof?"

"Fontaine's handwritten notes."

Jarrod nodded, then stood up and extended a hand to her. When she grasped it, he tugged her to her feet. "Just remember to deal with your emotions. Don't try to bank them. You can't do it, honey, and trying only gives Owlsley more power."

"Jarrod?" Sara tilted her head and looked up at him. "I'm really glad you fired me."

He gave her a soft smile, let his fingertips trail down her cheek to her chin. "Me, too."

She let her hands slide around his ribs and stepped closer. "Before we go back, would you please fire me again?"

He let out a masculine groan. "Gladly."

Smiling, their teeth touched. They embraced, and Sara enjoyed the pleasure free from guilt, but not free from fear.

As soon as Foster provided the means, she was going to IWPT. She would leave scrambled. The question was, to what degree?

twenty

☆

At sixteen hundred that afternoon, Sara received an interfacility memo from Dr. Fontaine.

To: Dr. Sara West, Major, USAF, staff physician
From: Dr. F. Fontaine, Colonel, USAF, facility director
Subject: Intelligence Warfare Psychological Training

Major West, be advised of the following:

1. Upon review of your personal records, we have determined you are deficient in the aforementioned subject training, which is required for all military personnel. This deficiency must be rectified immediately.

2. You are to report to the Intelligence Warfare Psychological Training Center in Alabane, Alabama, at 0800 tomorrow morning. Transportation is your responsibility. This training will last for five days, at the end of which you are to return to your duties at this facility.

3. Official orders will be cut and available for pick-up at the director's office within one hour.
Regards,

Franklin Fontaine
Colonel, USAF
Commander, Facility Director

Sara read the memo and began to shake. She'd wanted to get into IWPT, but not as a trainee and not without a little preparation time and notice. What about her patients? What about—

No. No, what Shank had said was true. Sara's answers to what had happened to David, Joe—all of her patients and ADR-40—were at IWPT. Going there as a trainee gave her the best odds of finding out the truth and getting the evidence she needed to end whatever they were doing there and to get her patients reunited with their families—including David with Brenda and Lisa, and Joe with Mrs. Brandt. If Sara was lucky, maybe she and Joe could be a part of each others' lives. That was her best, and worst, hope.

She flicked at the edge of the memo with her thumb. It proved one thing. Foster had been honest with Shank. He'd said that he had Sara's going to IWPT under control. Evidently, he'd been right.

The niggle that he and Fontaine were working together with IWPT grew stronger, coiling in her stomach, warning her that she might encounter more at IWPT than expected. Maybe more than she could handle. . . .

Sara turned into the store's parking lot at ten minutes before six and cut the engine.

Three cars were parked in the lot. The second one to her left was Brenda's Honda Accord. Sara didn't see Brenda, but Lisa sat in the front seat. She spotted Sara and got out of the car.

Sara left her car. The humidity was high, so was the heat. Feeling as if she'd been smacked in the face with a wet washcloth, she fell into step beside Lisa and walked past the old-fashioned Coke machine to the side of the building, away from any structures. If Foster had sent her here, she could bet her backside the place was bugged to the rafters.

Lisa hugged her, and Sara squeezed her hard. "Oh, I've missed you."

"Me, too." Leaning back, Lisa smiled up at Sara. The fading sunlight caught on her hair, slivering it with streaks of spun gold. "Mom's inside getting a drink."

"So how was the dance?"

"Cruddy." Lisa frowned. "Taylor Baker was a phony. He pretended to care about me, but only because he thought I was like Mom."

"What do you mean?"

Lisa shuffled her feet. Dust clouded around her ankles and splotched her white sneakers. "Easy."

Sara's chest went tight. "I'm sorry."

"Me, too." Lisa shrugged. "But the world's full of jerks."

"It's full of good people, too."

"Yeah, but you have to look for them. The jerks find you."

She had a point. "So what's new at home?"

"Mom and H. G. or G. H. Williamson set the wedding date. Three weeks." Lisa crossed her chest with her arms, blocking the writing on her T-shirt.

Sara knew what it said. She'd given it to Lisa. "Peer Pressure? I am the peer. I follow me."

"Now would be a good time for that miracle, Aunt Sara." Lisa watched the door. Brenda stepped outside, carrying two canned soft drinks. "I promised I'd warn you, so I am. She marries him, and I'm gone."

Sara wrapped a protective arm around Lisa's shoulders. "It won't come to that. I promise."

"How are you going to stop it?"

"You'll see." Watching Brenda walk toward them, her navy slacks sweeping against her ankles, her silk blouse clinging to her breasts, Sara felt a twinge of envy. Brenda always had appeared to be the willowy, self-assured, graceful one of them. The confident and capable one. Sara had wished many times for a little of her sister's façade, but never more so than now.

"Hi, Sis." Brenda brushed a kiss near Sara's cheek. "You okay?"

"I'm okay." Now that the time had come, Sara wasn't sure how to go about doing this. How did one tell an engaged-for-the-fifth-time woman that her first husband was still alive?

"Good." Brenda smiled. "So tell me why we're baking out

here when we could be sitting in a cool restaurant celebrating my engagement." She wiggled her hand in front of Sara. An engagement ring with a diamond the size of a small rock glistened on her finger.

"Nice," Sara said.

"Thanks." Brenda smiled. "So? Why *are* we standing out in the dirt by a rundown store out in the middle of nowhere?"

"I needed to talk to both of you privately. I'm going to be out of pocket for a while. Doing some . . . training."

"More head stuff?" Lisa asked.

"Sort of." Sara took in a deep breath. "I've gotten some information on David." She let her gaze slide to Brenda. "I'm going to check it out."

Brenda's entire demeanor changed. Serious and still, she tucked a strand of hair back behind her ear. "What kind of information?"

Recognizing the nervous gesture and not yet ready to address that question, Sara ignored it. "This training is dangerous. It causes mental confusion. You're not to worry, I'll be fine. But it will take some time for me to get over it."

"What the hell kind of training is this, Sara?" Brenda held her arms akimbo.

"The kind that's going to tell me what they did to David."

"They—who?" Lisa asked. "Daddy committed suicide."

"No, honey." Sara softened her voice. "He didn't."

"He *is* still alive." Brenda gasped, panted, and clutched at her chest. "Oh, God. Oh, God."

Sara nodded. "I'm sorry, but there's no easy way to say this. He's a vegetable, Brenda. The damage is permanent."

Tears welled in her eyes and she crossed her chest with her arms to hold in all the pain. "Where is he?"

Sara braced for the fallout. "I can't tell you that."

"What do you mean, you can't tell me? Damn it, Sara, he's my husband."

Sara lifted her chin. "Look, if you charge in there—with or without the authorities—David and a lot of other people will be killed. So will you, Lisa, and me. We've got to do this my way."

"Which is what?" Brenda challenged. "For you to do some training that's going to screw up your mind?"

"Temporarily confuse, Brenda. There's a difference." Sara dug in her heels. "You're going to have to trust me on this."

"But what if something goes wrong?" Lisa asked.

It could. And from her taut expression, even Lisa realized it. "It's the only way I can find out what exactly happened to David and get the proof I need to shut this operation down."

Lisa persisted. "So what if something goes wrong?"

Sara gazed at her niece. "Then you know what to do."

"Dr. Kale?"

Sara nodded. "Have you heard back from him?"

Brenda interrupted. "Who's Dr. Kale?"

"A friend of mine," Sara said.

"The testing is done." Lisa claimed Sara's attention. "All of the notes were written the same day by the same person, except one. Same person, different time."

The sample of Fontaine's writing Sara had swiped. "Good."

Lisa continued. "There was also stuff strongly indicating they weren't authentic accountings."

"What are you two talking about?" Brenda demanded.

"You don't need to know. At least, not yet." Sara turned to Lisa. "Don't tell her."

"Sara!" Brenda protested. "Don't instruct my daughter to lie to me."

"She's not," Lisa said flatly, her gaze boring into Sara's. "She's trying to save your life."

"Hang on to what you've got, Lisa." Sara pulled an envelope from her purse. One containing a full accounting of her findings and her suspicions. "Do *not* open this. It's my protection, and yours and your mom's."

Lisa tucked the envelope into the waistband of her pants, then dropped the tail of her T-shirt over it. "Should I take it to Dr. Kale?"

"No. Just keep it someplace safe for now. If I don't contact you within the next two weeks, then take all of it to the press. Not the local press."

"Wolf Blitzer at CNN?" Lisa suggested, her eyes sparkling.

"Wolf or Bernard Shaw," Sara said. "Either one of them will do what's right and safest for you."

Brenda stared at Sara in sheer disbelief. "You're sending my daughter to CNN without telling me a damn thing?"

"If necessary, yes, I am," Sara said. "Because I love you, Brenda."

She popped the top on the canned drink. The soda fizzed and dripped over her fingers. They weren't shaking. In fact, her entire reaction to David being alive seemed almost anti-climactic. Brenda didn't seem stunned, shocked, or even surprised. *Why?*

As if a light bulb had gone on in her mind, Lisa stared openmouthed at her mother. "You knew. You've been looking for Daddy."

Brenda lifted her face to the breeze, but her voice went whisper-soft. "I didn't know he was alive, Lisa."

Even Sara heard the duplicity in that remark. She glared at her sister. "The last thing I want to hear right now is more half-truths or lies, Brenda. Spill it."

"She's been looking for Daddy," Lisa interceded. "That's why she's marrying every guy who asks her. Then, as soon she finds out they're not Daddy, she divorces them."

It made sense. Sara turned a questioning gaze on Brenda. Her face went red, but she didn't deny it. "Well?" Sara urged her. "Is that true?"

"I knew David's coffin was empty." Brenda looked down at the dirt. "I wasn't supposed to know it, but I did. I wasn't sure if he'd died on a mission, or if his cover had been blown on a covert operation and he'd elected to legally die and take on a new identity so he could keep his job. He'd never settle for a non-Intel assignment. I couldn't make myself believe he had willingly forfeited me and Lisa, but it was the not knowing that chewed me up and spat me out."

"And so," Sara speculated, "you looked for him in the eyes of every man who showed interest in you."

Brenda nodded, her eyes filling with tears she wouldn't cry. "Sometimes covert operatives who are exposed receive plastic surgery and new identities. I knew David loved us and if that had happened to him, he'd find a way back to us."

Finally, Sara understood. Brenda *had* been searching for something. But not for peace or acceptance or even for a new love. She'd been searching for David, seeing sparks of him in other men. "I understand now."

"I'm sorry." Brenda looked at Sara, then at her daughter, and removed the engagement ring from her finger.

As if it were worthless, she dropped Williamson's rock into her purse. To her, it was worthless. He wasn't David.

"I couldn't tell either of you the truth," Brenda said. "If one of the men turned out to be.David, I would be risking his life."

That made a twisted kind of sense. All of Brenda's husbands had been new to the area and all had had David's brown eyes. "Risking lives brings up another point I need to discuss with you," Sara said. All of this discussion had been hard, and what was coming wouldn't be any easier. "This training I'm going to go through uses your emotions against you. So, to minimize damage, I have to resolve my outstanding issues so they can't use them against me."

"What issues, Aunt Sara? You don't have any—do you?"

"Oh, yes, Lisa. I do." Sara's mouth went dry. She licked at her lips. "I've worked hard to become a PTSD expert and to find out what happened to David for the two of you— because you're my family and I love you—but I've done it for me, too. I want a family like you guys had more than anything in the world. Yet I couldn't have one because I couldn't have all you had lost. It seemed . . . selfish." Sara shrugged. "So I had to fix things for you two first. Then, getting what I want wouldn't flaunt all your broken dreams in your face." Sara shook her head. "Oh, hell. This isn't coming out right."

"Sure it is, Aunt Sara. You would have felt guilty. I get it."

"It sounds ridiculous, really. Totally illogical and absurd for a shrink, but it's the truth. The point is, I'm not some perfect paragon. I've got as much emotional baggage as everyone else."

"What your aunt is saying, Lisa," Brenda chimed in, "is she has realized she's just a mere mortal like the rest of us, and she's going to do something really dangerous to help us find out more about your dad." Brenda cut her gaze to Sara. "Isn't that what you're saying?"

Sara nodded.

"I can't let you do it, Sis." Brenda sighed. "All my life, you've bailed me out. It's time for me to take care of me. I'll go."

"You can't just step in," Sara insisted, lifting a hand. "And what about Lisa? I *will* come out of this confused, Brenda. It'll take weeks for me to get normal again." Provided all went well, it would. "Lisa needs you normal."

"She's done fine for the past five years." Brenda set her jaw in stubborn mode. "I've hardly been normal, Sara."

"That's true," Sara admitted. "But it's also different—and it's been damn hard on your daughter."

"Mom, there's something you're not getting." Worry laced Lisa's tone. "Isn't there, Aunt Sara?"

Sara didn't answer. Lisa was far more intuitive and insightful than her mother. Even if the news about David hadn't stunned Brenda, she had been delivered a whale of shock that rocked her world. It dulled her thinking.

Brenda shoved her purse strap up on her shoulder. "What do you mean?"

"Aunt Sara is afraid she could be more than confused. She's afraid she could end up like Dad, or maybe even die."

"What?" Brenda spun toward Sara. "Is that possible?"

"It's not probable."

"It's possible *and* probable, Mom." Lisa stood before Sara. "Stop protecting us. I talked with Dr. Kale. He doesn't want you to go, either."

"How does he know I'm going?"

"We hacked into the computer and figured it out."

"You what?"

"It's okay," Lisa assured Sara. "He's got clearance. Anyway, we think it's too dangerous for you to go."

"If I don't, they'll do to other men what they did to your

father. I can't turn my back on them, Lisa. Please, don't ask
me to do that. I've seen these men and how they suffer. I've
watched one man fight the demons from hell in his mind until
he was so exhausted he couldn't lift his head off the floor. He
whimpered like a wounded child. I can't just take the safe way
out and protect me, knowing I'm condemning other men to
that. I can't, and I won't."

"Forget it, Lisa." Brenda put an arm around her daughter's
shoulder. "It's her noble side. You can't break it."

"I don't want to break it. I think she's right." Lisa turned
a troubled gaze on Sara. "I just don't want to lose you."

"I don't want to be lost, either." Sara swallowed hard. "A
friend has been helping me. We've found a way to minimize
the damage."

"Major Jarrod Brandt," Lisa said.

Surprised, Sara frowned at her. "How did you—"

"Dr. Kale. I told you, we've been working together. He
says Jarrod's a good man, and don't worry. We'll watch over
him."

A lump formed in Sara's throat. "Thank you, Lisa."

Lisa sent her a speculative look. "He's the one, huh?"

Sara nodded. "Yeah, he's the one."

"Damn," Brenda groused. "You're in love, and I didn't
even know it. Why doesn't anyone tell me anything around
here?"

Lisa rolled her gaze heavenward. "You don't tell people
high-risk stuff when you think they've lost it, Mom. That'd
be a stupid move, you know?"

"I guess, but still . . ." Brenda looked at Sara, pain filling
her eyes. "David will be all right? I mean, he's being cared
for and treated well?"

"He's got one of the finest nurses I've met in my life,
Brenda. I swear it."

Her eyes glossy, her jaw trembling, she nodded. "Okay, but
get us to him soon, Sara. He belongs with us."

"I will." She hugged her sister. "Just as soon as I can." Her
throat thick, she cleared it and backed away. "I've got to get
back."

Sara gave them her promise to be careful, hugged them good-bye, and then drove back to Braxton. Lisa had watched through the rear window until Sara had driven out of sight. She hadn't missed her niece's tears. They tore her heart right out of her chest.

Sara was really proud of Lisa. She seemed far better at covert operations than Sara. At least she would be there to help her mother deal with this, and she would be more content now that the wedding to the judge—H. G. or G. H. or whatever-his-name-was Williamson—was off. David was alive. Brenda now knew it and she had taken off the engagement ring. She'd never remarry.

Would Sara ever marry?

Maybe. If Jarrod could work past his fear of betrayal. It had a firm grip on him, and what had happened to him at IWPT had made it stronger. Even if he could work past it, it would take a while. But that was okay. He was worth the wait.

One thing was clear. Sara had been wrong in deciding what she was worthy of having or not having in her life based on what Brenda and Lisa had in theirs. Hearing herself verbalize her feelings and seeing their reactions had been a revelation. Somewhere along the line, she'd become obsessive and skewed about this family business. It wasn't right.

Thank God. Because she was tired of being wrong, and alone. Especially now that she had found Jarrod and he had fired her.

She pulled the car back across the ditch and into the woods. Pocketing the keys, she headed for the fence, mentally reviewing the things she still had to do before leaving for IWPT. Three items remained on her list.

Talk to Foster.

Prepare Shank.

Say good-bye to Jarrod, and pray it wasn't forever.

Shank kept an eye out while Sara used the secure line to call Foster. He didn't answer. Twenty minutes later, he still wasn't answering. And at twenty-one hundred—their agreed-upon contact time of nine P.M.—he still didn't answer.

Sara gave up.

"No luck?" Shank walked back to the desk.

"No." What did she do now?

"Let's go outside."

They went down the stairs, and then out to the pond. It was eerie out there at night. Dark and shadowy, a moonless night. Chills lifted on Sara's arms and she rubbed at them.

Shank shifted on her feet, obviously uncomfortable. "Sara, there's something about Foster you need to know. He's going up for promotion to general. He's wanted that rank since God was a baby, and he'll do anything to anyone to get it—including to you. That star has always been Foster's passion and his obsession."

"In other words, you think he's corrupt."

"It makes me sick to think it, much less to say it, but things point in that direction. Flat out."

"My feelings are mixed. I know it looks bad for Foster, but something is niggling at me, Shank. Something's telling me to be careful about condemning the man without knowing all the facts."

"Honey, with Foster you'll *never* get all the facts."

Of course I've got a hidden agenda. I'm AID, for Christ's sake. "I know that, too," Sara said, recalling Foster's own comment. "We have a long history, and it hasn't been a pleasant one."

"Then why did he bring you in on this?"

"I have no idea." Sara grunted, slapped at a mosquito on her sleeve. "I've spent a ridiculous amount of time trying to figure that out, but I still haven't."

"Well, there's got to be a reason. Foster only leaves to chance what he can't avoid. He didn't just pull you out of a phone book."

"We've been going toe-to-toe for over five years, and I've given Foster more static about his military red tape than any one man should have to hear. I can't imagine why he chose me. He knew from the start I'd push the limits and break the rules to get to the truth."

"Maybe he wanted them pushed and broken."

"I considered that," Sara said. "I've also considered that he could be working with Fontaine and the head honcho at IWPT, and now that he's up for promotion, Foster wants his star *and* respectability."

"Burying the skeletons." Shank inched closer to the pond's edge. Water lapped at the bank. "It's possible."

"I'm hoping I'll get a handle on him at IWPT."

"That's possible, too." Shank glanced back over her shoulder. "I heard back from my friend. IWPT's director is Dr. Carl Owlsley. He's doing research on noninvasive microwave laser technology under a high-dollar contract with DoD."

"Did you say *Carl* Owlsley?" Sara had heard that name before. In Fontaine's office. When she'd first reported to Braxton, Fontaine had been on the phone with Carl, demanding money.

"One and the same." Shank dropped her voice. "There's more, Sara. My source says Fontaine and Owlsley are working this together, and Foster is right in there with them."

There was their sought-after, direct link between Fontaine and Owlsley. But Foster? "How does your source know that? Is there hard evidence?"

"Of the first order, unfortunately," Shank said. "When I called to give Foster your twenty-four-hour ultimatum, I got really suspicious of him, so I reported the Fontaine/Owlsley, IWPT/Braxton connection to the IG—the Inspector General's office. They referred me to the AID, who eventually referred me around to Foster. He put me in Braxton. You, too. And unless I miss my guess, Joe is one of Foster's men and he put him in here, too. No matter how you cut it, Foster knows what's going on at IWPT."

"But is he perpetuating it, or trying to stop it?"

"That I don't know. But I've got a bad feeling about you going there as a trainee. Flat out." Shank clasped Sara's arm, squeezed, and her voice trembled. "Don't do it, Sara. Please."

First Jarrod, then Brenda and Lisa, and now Shank. Sara wasn't ready to fight this battle a third time, but it appeared she would have to do it. "I have no choice. Look at ADR-40, and Lou and Fred. Do you want more men destroyed?"

"Of course not."

"If we don't find out what they're doing, then how do we stop them?"

"We don't." Grim resignation settled over Shank. "But you've got to know that they have no plans of ever letting you leave Braxton alive."

"A possibility, but I'm bound by confidentiality laws not to disclose anything, and Fontaine's wife was allowed to leave."

"Fontaine's wife isn't on any European vacation." Shank snorted. "She's supposedly at a facility undergoing intensive therapy. The confinement got to her."

"Supposedly?" Sara picked up on the uncertainty in Shank's voice. "What do you think happened to her?"

"Nothing. I think she's acting as a go-between for Fontaine and Owlsley. Some things you don't want discussed even on secure lines."

Tension knotted her neck muscles. Sara rubbed at them. "Makes sense."

"Scary sense." Shank turned and started walking back inside. "You'd better stop by and see Joe. He's worried, Sara. The man's in love with you."

"He cares, but it's not love. Men who have been betrayed—"

"Are as vulnerable as everyone else to falling in love again, and he did. I knew it the morning he ate breakfast so you wouldn't worry about him."

"You watch over him for me, okay?" A lump lodged in Sara's throat.

"I will." Shank sighed. "I take it you love him, too."

"Oh, boy. I know all the rules about ethics—"

"Honey, forget them. Patients are plentiful, but a good man is hard to find."

"He fired me." Remembering their lovemaking, Sara warmed.

"Good. No guilt or being torn on ethics issues." Shank sidestepped a palmetto, then skirted a bed of fragrant flowers. "You gonna tell him you love him?"

"I thought about it but, no, I can't."

"He'd like to know, Sara."

She shuffled down the stone path, her footsteps heavy. "Not if I don't come out of IWPT okay. He'll feel pity, bound. I don't want that for him. I want him—"

"Loved." Shank sighed again. Deeper. "I know. You don't want him dragged through that with you."

"No, I don't. He's been dragged through enough already."

Sara talked with Joe for a few minutes inside Isolation. Mindful of the camera and listening devices, she caught him up on her meeting with Brenda and Lisa, and with Shank.

He stepped into the corner, a blind spot for the camera. "So you've resolved your issues, then?"

"As much as possible."

"Good." He hugged her hard, then squeezed her shoulders. "Be careful, Sara. Think ice." His gaze seared, committing to memory her every nuance. "And come back to me."

The urge to tell him she loved him slammed through her. She fought it hard. It wouldn't be fair to him. She kissed him instead, and then left him without looking back, afraid if she did, she wouldn't have the courage to go through with this.

Midway down the hall, she stopped. She might not get back. She might not come out of IWPT as well off as ADR-40. And if she didn't, then Joe would wonder forever. He would be as tormented as Brenda had been because he wouldn't know for fact that he had been the one.

Sara turned and ran back to Joe's room. He was watching her through the little Plexiglas window, his hand pressed against the pane.

She lifted her hand and touched it to the glass, matching their fingertips, and then mouthed the words, "I love you, Jarrod."

"I know." He smiled, his eyes glistening. "I love you too, Sara."

She smiled back, taking his words down deep inside. No matter what came, she had them to hold on to. No matter what came . . .

twenty-one

☆

IWPT looked exactly as Jarrod had described it.

The typical gate, guard, tall fencing, and a long and deserted asphalt road between the gate and the actual compound. Sara drove past an obstacle course, complete with tires, low-strung barbed wire intended for belly-crawling, and what she had called monkey bars in grade school, where the kids crossed an expanse, hand over hand, bar to bar, from one end to the other.

Two large white buildings faced each other on the main street. A third building, smaller than the others, was tagged as the administrative building. According to a sign, quarters were located one street over, though she couldn't see anything of them through the thick trees. Between the two large buildings—the core of the training center—stood rows of small boxes. The coffins.

Sara suppressed a shudder. Short of breath, she quickly looked away. Off in the far distance, nearly obscured by a wooded thicket and disconnected from the rest of the compound, sat a huge metal building. No sign or directive identified what was in it and—she double-checked—the building didn't appear on the map given to her by the gate guard. *The warehouse Jarrod had mentioned.*

Sara parked and then entered the administration building, where a professional, but totally dispassionate, Sergeant Emerson signed her in.

"You need to execute this release." Doe-eyed, in her late twenties, the sergeant shoved the paper across her desk to Sara.

It was an inventory listing of her personal effects and a

notice that they would be confiscated until her training had been completed. Passing over her purse and car keys had her stomach in knots. Poising the pen over the form had her nauseous.

She quickly scrawled her name and then pushed the paper away.

Emerson retrieved it. "Report to Dr. Owlsley to be profiled at fourteen hundred. Building One."

Sara nodded. "Is that all?"

"That's all."

Summarily dismissed, Sara went to her quarters and located her assigned cot. It was a dormitory-type setting with two rows of twelve beds separated by tall metal lockers. Considering they'd taken everything but the clothes off her back, the lockers seemed wasted. She lifted the handle and checked. Empty.

At the end of the room was a community bath with four stalls, three showers, and a sign on the wall that read "Latrine." The place seemed innocuous, impersonal, and—except for her—unoccupied.

The military had perfected that impersonal façade to an art form. She checked her watch—one forty-five—and headed over for her appointment with Dr. Owlsley.

During the three-block walk, Sara did breathing exercises, reminding herself of all that it was imperative for her to remember—and to forget. She would forget Jarrod. Not mention him at all during the profile. Owlsley would use him against her, and Jarrod was her ace in the hole. Her refuge and, hopefully, her saving grace. She would remember his advice and warnings. And, she reinforced to her subconscious, she would remember that her outstanding emotional issues had been resolved. Admitting that she was terrified was paramount to admitting defeat before even starting, so she denied it. Firmly and with conviction. And she prayed her will proved strong enough to carry her through this.

After a ten-minute wait in a sterile reception area devoid of magazines, the typical television tuned in to CNN, or piped-in elevator music, Sara was ushered into an office she deemed plush by military standards.

A deep-cushioned, forest-green sofa faced a mahogany executive desk that gleamed. Behind it, sunlight streamed in through two large windows. Outside them, a white-lattice partition covered with winter-dormant roses blocked the view. Dr. Owlsley sat behind his desk in a tall leather chair that swiveled. Currently, his head was dipped and he sat slumped over a file. Her file.

He looked up. "Major West."

"Good afternoon, Doctor." Sara forced a smile. Looking at him, it was hard to imagine him deliberately hurting anyone. Somewhere in his mid-fifties, sharp-featured, and damn near blind. The thick lenses in his glasses distorted his eyes so much she couldn't determine their color and he had that pseudovacant look common to scientists preoccupied by their current projects. He couldn't be military. His skin had a yellowish cast that starkly contrasted with his white lab coat, and he was a good thirty pounds overweight—a transgression that could get a military member hauled before a board and demoted—and even more telling, he slumped.

His coloring concerned the physician in her, and knowing just how intensely researchers tended to focus and to block out anything unrelated to their work, she elected to mention it. "Dr. Owlsley, I don't mean to intrude, but have you had liver function studies done lately?"

"I'm fine, Major." His jaw snapped shut. "You are our current concern."

"I'm sorry. I didn't mean to offend you. It's just that your coloring—"

"Have a seat." He cut her off, motioning to the sofa.

He was aware, after all. Sara sat down, and allowed herself to be interviewed. The warm glow of the room and homey, comfortable atmosphere had been cleverly designed to put trainees at ease. They made Sara more wary.

Jarrod had warned her that the profile would be extensive and intensive. And it was. Omitting anything about him, she was as truthful as possible—until Dr. Owlsley questioned her about claustrophobia.

"Any symptoms of it?" he asked, his pen poised above her file folder.

The question surprised her. Her claustrophobia had never been documented. Anywhere. But remembering the coffins, she supposed she should have anticipated him asking. If trainees were claustrophobic, and they were going to be detained in the boxes she had seen, then Dr. Owlsley and his staff needed to be prepared for possible claustrophobic reactions. He didn't know she actually suffered from it, thank God. Yet she had to give him some weakness or he'd keep digging. So she would give him one—but not an existing, real one he could use against her. She looked him straight in the eye and lied. "No, no claustrophobia, though I did once have a phobia of snakes." She let out a small laugh to create doubt she was truly over that fear. "A former patient cured me."

Owlsley smiled and rocked back in his chair. "In our work, that's often the way of it, isn't it?"

"On occasion, yes."

"How did this cure come about?"

"During a PTSD flashback, he locked me in a closet with his pet boa constrictor."

"Amazing response."

"Not really." Sara shrugged, crossed her legs, and let the upper one move in a relaxed swing. "If you spend three hours with a huge, hungry snake and it doesn't harm you, you realize your fear is misplaced."

"And no claustrophobia while locked in the closet?"

"None whatsoever," she said lightly, praying to God the man believed her.

Owlsley didn't push, but went on with his questioning, focusing largely, she realized, on subtly getting her to reveal her fears, her deepest secrets and desires—anything and everything that could be used to stimulate intense emotions in her.

Oh, yes. He was digging deeply and, though it wasn't mentioned in the outline she'd been given of what to expect here, he had every intention of putting her through the noninvasive microwave laser technology segment of this training.

That opened the door to a lot of questions in her mind. She

stared past Owlsley's shoulder, through the window. A blue jay perched on the white-lattice partition. Fontaine and Owlsley had decided to damage her. Judging from the probing nature of the questions, extensively. Foster had gotten her here. Had he been included in making that decision? If so, from what perspective? As Fontaine and Owlsley's ally, or as the bent-on-bringing-them-down commander of the Shadow Watchers?

Dr. Owlsley concluded his questioning, and closed her file. "While this training is an across-the-board military-member requirement, in your occupation it's highly unlikely you would ever be positioned where what we provide would be necessary to your survival." He nodded to a single sheet of paper. "For that reason, you've been given an outline of what you can expect. Your personal training will naturally deviate in small ways."

"Why?" Every instinct in her body warned Sara to brace. She forcefully continued to swing her leg, to appear relaxed and at ease.

"To dovetail with your personal profile." Dr. Owlsley wrinkled his nose, inching his glasses up on its bridge. "Our goal is to maximize the effectiveness of our training to your personal benefit. Obviously, we can't formulate the best means of doing so until after your personal profile is factored into the equation."

"I see." Boy, did she. Maximize terror. Maximize fear. Maximize doubt. Study the habits of the prey, and then exploit them.

The comfortable, cozy room suddenly seemed too small with too little air. "Will that be all, Doctor?"

"Yes, Major." He spared her a glance. "You may return to your quarters until you're summoned."

Sara forced herself to smile at Owlsley, stood up, and then left his office. Deviations? She could bet on them. But how bad would they be? And was she strong enough to withstand them? Those were the questions worrying her.

As she stepped outside, the sun disappeared behind roiling black clouds, dark and swirling, mirroring her inner turmoil, and the air felt sultry, thick and humid and oxygen-free. She rushed down the sidewalk, hurrying to get back to her quarters before the rain started.

Two armed guards approached her on the sidewalk. An eerie feeling slithered up Sara's spine. Her intuition warned her to hide. She looked for a place, but there was nowhere to go, nothing to duck behind. No cars were parked on the street. No buildings or trees stood nearby. And no one else was on the sidewalk in front of her.

A man approached her from behind. "Major West?"

Startled, she stopped and turned. "Yes?"

"Lieutenant Gordon Kane." He passed her a blue armband. "You've been assigned to the blue team. Wear this around your left upper arm."

The lieutenant didn't look her in the eye. He looked past her shoulder at the two men approaching. "Are you finding everything all right?"

"Yes." She took the band, tied it over her sleeve, instinctively picking up on the danger the two men posed. "Is there anything else, Lieutenant?"

"Yes, ma'am." He offered her a smile tempered in steel. "Stay put."

The men walked by, so close Sara could smell their skin. Both wore red bands, and both made a point of pretending not to notice her while watching her intently. The senior of the two, a beefy lieutenant, glanced back at her. A dispassionate distance burned in his eyes.

Sara focused on Lieutenant Kane. He blinked hard and fast. "You already know you're in danger here. Do *not* go back to your quarters. Your portion of this mission has been canceled, Doctor. Colonel Foster deemed the risks too high. He's ordered you out."

"Out where? *How?*" Sara whispered urgently. "They've got my personal belongings, including my car keys. I can't just walk out of here."

"No, ma'am, you can't. You'd be detained and brought back." Kane nodded that they should walk. "Backup plans are being initiated, but there are . . . complications." Worry flickered through Kane's eyes. "You've got to hide, Major."

"Where?"

Kane nodded toward the woods, beyond the large metal building. "Out there." He glanced back at Sara. "A Shadow Watcher will find and extricate you as soon as possible. Until then, stay out of sight."

Shadow Watcher. Kane had to be one of Foster's men or he wouldn't know about Shadow Watchers. "Won't people from IWPT be looking for me?"

"Yes." Kane's expression turned grim. "Don't let them find you. We can't protect you."

Sara's heart beat hard and fast, and the sultry air suddenly seemed as thick as mud. "How can I tell the difference between IWPT's men and Foster's?"

"Foster's will wear blue bands."

"Okay." Sara swept a hand through her hair, looked down at her skirted uniform and black military pumps. "Can I at least go change clothes?"

"Only if you want to be caught and tortured."

Sara broke into a cold sweat. "I'll, um, manage as I am."

"Wise decision." Kane led her down the sidewalk. "I'll walk with you as far as I can. Once you enter the woods, you're on your own. Trust no one unless you hear them use the code word."

Her heels grated against the concrete sidewalk. "What is the code word?"

Lieutenant Kane slid her a level look. "Red Haze."

Rain spit down on Sara.

It tapped loudly against the leaves on the trees, splattered in the wet dirt and dead leaves littering the ground, and stung her exposed skin. The heels of her pumps sank into the soft mud for the thousandth time in the past hour. Cold and soaked to the bone, she swiped at the water dripping down her face and trudged deeper and deeper into the woods.

Wandering aimlessly was crazy. She needed a plan. She had no idea whom to trust. No way to identify the good guys from the bad ones, except for a blue band anyone could get and a code word anyone could know. To get out of this, she needed to forget thinking like a woman or a doctor and to think like a Shadow Watcher. Like Jarrod.

Exactly. Exactly. Spotting an oak with a huge trunk, she paused, leaned against its rough bark, and removed her shoes. She slammed the pumps against the tree trunk until the heels cracked off, then put the flats back on her feet. A good distance away, she buried the heels, and then walked on, leaving false trails, backtracking, and taking off in different directions to confuse anyone pursuing her.

What else would Jarrod do?

He'd have a clue which direction was south. The main highway, leading to IWPT, lay south. But Sara was navigationally challenged. The downpour blocked the sun and without it she was screwed. Even at home she had to hang a painting of fish on the south wall so she could keep her directions straight.

Wait. Wait. She studied the trees. There'd been a hurricane in northwest Florida—actually two of them—a few years ago. The winds had come from the south, from the gulf. She studied the bent trees, the direction those that had snapped and cracked had fallen on the ground. South became evident.

She headed in that direction. Leaves crackled behind her. Someone had found her.

Sara stumbled into a gully, half-running, half-sliding, rolling and then crawling on her belly through the mud, deep into a clump of palmettos.

I'd be getting rid of those palmettos, Dr. West. The durn things ain't good for nothing but rat nests.

Hearing her yard man's voice in her head, Sara shuddered, and recalled that Jarrod had been placed in an actual rat trap and had suffered multiple bites. If he could stand that, then, by God, she could stand this.

The footsteps came closer. More than one person. Two. At least two. Smearing more mud on her forearms and her face, she peeked out from between the thick leaves. The beefy lieutenant and sergeant she had seen on the sidewalk were tracking her. She hadn't had time to cover the evidence of her descent down the wall of the gully. From their angle above it, could they see her tracks?

Scarcely daring to draw breath, Sara watched them, not daring to so much as blink.

The beefy lieutenant looked down at an instrument attached to his watch. "She can't be far. Head north."

The men walked on.

Had the gully given them a false reading? Something must have. But how had they found her so quickly? How were they tracking her? From watching Jarrod, she had learned to camouflage her movements.

Her gaze slid down to the blue band Lieutenant Kane had given her. She took it off, examined its deep folds, and found a device the size of a button. Lieutenant Kane, the son of a bitch, was a red team member. An enemy.

But how had he known about Shadow Watchers and Operation Red Haze?

Only one answer seemed possible. Foster.

Sara crawled on her belly through the mud and out from under the bushes, grateful that the rats had taken refuge from the storm elsewhere. Thunder rumbled through the trees and a deep sense of betrayal rumbled through Sara. She'd been crossed. And double-crossed.

The door to Jarrod's Isolation room buzzed.

Knowing the news couldn't be good, Jarrod watched Shank barrel into his room. She didn't look merely worried. The imperturbable woman looked frantic.

"Something's gone wrong," she said. "I can't get Foster. I called Donald O'Shea and he has no idea where Foster is."

If Foster's assistant didn't know where to find him, no one did. That worried Jarrod. "When was his last official sighting?"

"On his way to recruit Sara. Captain Grant and Lieutenant Kane met his flight when he arrived at Eglin from the Pentagon. That's been verified. O'Shea says Foster called in once after that and said he would be concluding Operation Red Haze shortly."

"What did Operations say about that?"

"They had initiated a full-scale plan with Colonel Foster prior to his leaving the Pentagon. Lieutenant Kane and a team of Shadow Watchers were to infiltrate IWPT, and at the first sign of deviation from the standard training session, they were to intercept Sara, shut down the operation, and handle the arrests."

Jarrod rubbed at his nape. "Is the team in place?"

"Communications are down. O'Shea says they're operating from the perspective that Sara's on her own."

Jarrod's heart stuck somewhere between his backbone and throat. "I've got to get out of here."

Relief flooded Shank's face. "You're covered until tomorrow at midnight. Koloski's on duty. William will be back then, which means you damn well better be, too."

"Fine."

"What about transportation? You're welcome to take my plane."

Jarrod smiled and pulled the keys to Sara's car out of the hole he had made in the wallpad where the cave had once been painted. "Covered."

"Joe, be careful. I'm worried about her. I'm worried about you, too. Are you up to this?"

"I'm up to it." To help Sara, he'd force himself to be up to anything.

Shank moved toward the door. "Reaston's down on the first floor, running interference."

Jarrod rushed down the hall, when a detail body-slammed him. "Shank, where the hell is IWPT?"

"Reaston's got maps and intel for you."

Shank left him at the elevator. As the door slid closed, she called out, her voice cracking, "Don't you let them kill her, Joe."

"I won't," Jarrod promised, praying it was a promise he could keep.

Sara's teeth chattered.

She was exhausted, freezing, and the rain showed no signs

of letting up. Mud dripped down her face and stung her eyes. She swiped a fingertip across her lid and blinked hard, trying to clear her vision.

A large clearing stood straight ahead. Avoiding it, she bore right, hugging a grove of oaks. She twisted between their gnarled trunks, sidestepping exposed roots that stuck up from the ground like crooked fingers.

Someone grabbed her by the throat.

Sara came to an abrupt halt, darted her gaze to her assailant. The beefy lieutenant. *Oh, damn. Bloody damn.*

"I've got her," he shouted out.

Two other sets of footsteps crunched over the leaves and came closer. The sergeant and Lieutenant Kane.

Sara's heart sank, and then rocketed against her ribs. She had to act—now. She kicked the lieutenant in the groin then followed up with an uppercut to his jaw.

He rocked back from the force of the blow, his knees gave out, and he crumpled to the ground. "You . . . bitch."

Sara ran. Blindly. Full out. A stitch caught in her side. She pressed a muddy hand over it and kept running, knowing she was maybe five yards ahead of the sergeant and Kane.

"Sara!" A man called her name. It sounded like Jarrod. Her mind playing tricks on her. Had to be. He was locked up at Braxton. Yet, she instinctively looked back. The beefy lieutenant turned his back to her, raised his gun, and fired.

Jarrod? The man he shot looked like Jarrod. But that was impossible. *It had to be impossible!*

Kane and the sergeant grabbed her, one at each arm, and dragged her back to the lieutenant. They stopped before him, and his face contorted in anger. Sara let her gaze drift from him to the man on the ground. He was breathing. With his back to her, she couldn't be sure he was Jarrod, but—*oh God*—she felt certain he was, and he was breathing.

The lieutenant slapped her. Her head jerked, her face stung. Before she could recover, she felt the burn of a needle entering her arm. "Is that man going to die?" she asked Kane.

"From a stun gun?" Kane frowned at her. "Where the hell did you get weapons-qualified, Major?"

Sara heard his question, but it sounded as if he were talking from the far end of a long tunnel. Her vision blurred. Her head felt heavy, her legs like lead. She struggled to stay upright but felt herself slumping, consciousness fading, enveloping her in darkness with the ease of clicking off a light.

twenty-two

☆

Sara awakened in the dark.

Something gritty grated at her face. Hazy and thick-tongued, she curled her knees to her chest and lifted a hand to her face. Dirt. It was dirt. Dried mud. She had to have been here for some time.

Her calf muscles cramped. She tried to straighten her legs but couldn't; the box was too short. With gliding fingertips, she felt the rough edges of the box. Wood. Rough and unfinished. Too small to sit or stand, too short to lie stretched out. Dirt floor. *Oh, God. Oh, God. It was the coffin!*

Don't panic, Sara. She heard Jarrod's voice. *You can't afford to panic. Think ice.*

Ice. Yes. Ice. She took in a cleansing breath. Her head throbbed—definitely a drug hangover. Rohypnol?

Maybe the date-rape drug, but it could be any of dozens that produced short-term amnesia.

They shot Jarrod.

No, they hadn't. It was impossible. It couldn't have been him in the woods. Jarrod was at Braxton. She shut out any other possibility. He was at Braxton.

The walls shrank in on her. Shivering, in a cold sweat, she fought the symptoms, forced her breathing to steady, warning herself not to hyperventilate. Frustration and futility swarmed through her chest. She couldn't combat claustrophobic feelings, too. Not now. She just . . . couldn't.

Her uniform was gone. She ran her hand down the length of her body, felt a one-piece jumpsuit of some kind. She didn't want to think about who had put it on her, or what they might have done to her while she was unconscious. Instead, she would be grateful she was dry and still alive, if more thirsty than she'd ever been in her life.

A low thud sounded. Then again. Soon, the beat was rhythmic, steady, constant. Feeling herself growing irritated, she recalled Jarrod describing this. A heartbeat. Yes. A heartbeat.

One that eventually had driven him beyond reason.

No. Don't think that. Don't let it happen. You choose. Let it comfort you.

The walls closed in, sucking out all of the oxygen. She couldn't get enough air.

Think ice, Sara.

Ice. Yes. Free-floating on a large iceberg. The sun shining down on clear, blue water. Jarrod smiling at her. *I know. I love you, too, Sara . . .*

The low-level percussion grew louder, stronger, thumping inside her head. Her heart rate mimicked it.

Deal with the emotions, Sara. Don't bank them. You can't bank them.

She twisted onto her back; the top of the coffin was less than a foot from the tip of her nose. The damp wood smelled strong. Cedar. God, but she hated the smell of cedar. Almost as much as pine.

Deal with the ice, Sara.

No. No, not with the ice. Deal with the . . . something. She couldn't remember. *She couldn't remember!*

Panic shot through her stomach, tightened her chest. She curled up, warned herself to calm down, to stay calm. She could deal with this. She really could. But, God, she had to have air to do it.

She sucked in deep lungsful. There was no air on this iceberg.

Or any water.

Her chapped lips burned and her mouth was so dry that her inner lips and cheeks stuck to her teeth. Already, she was beginning to dehydrate. She could feel it. Vivid images danced before her eyes, tormenting her. Tall glasses of iced tea, gallons of water sliding down her throat. Parched and achy, hot, she called out. "Water." Her voice croaked, thready and weak. "Water," she tried again.

Minutes passed, then something splashed against the outside of the box. A thundering sound drowned out the percussion. Someone was squirting the top of the box with a water hose. The splattering water trickled down between the top slats of the box, near her feet. Sara stretched and scooted, strained to reach and catch the drips in a cupped hand.

As she got her hand positioned, the splashing stopped.

The dripping ceased.

The percussion returned.

Her chest constricted and, near tears, she pressed the precious droplets dampening her palm to her cracked lips, swearing that next time she would be ready—and praying it wouldn't be too long until the guard again picked up the hose.

The persistent thumping returned with a deafening vengeance.

No, no. She grabbed her head and squeezed, cursing it. Low-level percussion, Jarrod had said. It didn't feel low-level. It felt like bass drums pounding inside her skull. She had to get out of here. To get water. Now.

But which way was out? Dirt beneath her. She could dig her way out. Yes. She scraped at the lower edge of the box, shoving aside the loose, sandy dirt. Something sharp cut her fingers. They stung and burned, and warm blood dripped down her fingertips.

A metal strip. Jagged edges. She couldn't dig herself out.

It's okay, Sara. You can deal with this.

Jarrod's voice in her mind. Helping her. She could deal with this. Oh, please, God, help her to deal with this.

Minutes turned to hours. How many, she couldn't tell. Each second seemed lifetimes long. And the steady thump grated at her, deeper and deeper.

She ground her teeth, searching for something to combat it. Rage was the worst possible thing she could allow. She'd end up more scrambled than Jarrod had been. Suffer more incidents of episodic rage.

Episodic rage.

The music had stopped the incidents.

No water. No air. Oh, God, no air.

Think ice.

It wasn't working. She couldn't hold the images in her mind. She was too fuzzy. Frantic, she searched for alternatives. Meditate. *Meditate.*

Squeezing her eyes shut, she slowed her breathing and chose her word. *Jarrod. Jarrod. Jarrod.*

And in the distance she heard faint strains of music.

Celtic music.

Thump. Thump. Thump.

Sara awakened, unsure if it was day or night, the percussion thundering inside her head.

"You ain't sleeping in there, are you?" a man shouted from outside and kicked the box.

Tormenting her. Again. How many times now had they awakened her? Four? Five? She forced herself to remember. Seven. Seven times. She had to have been in here for days. Her mouth felt stone-dry, her tongue thick and swollen. Caked with dried mud, her skin itched, and she needed a rest room so badly her stomach cramped continuously and her eyes burned.

How long had she been here? Where was here?

Deal with the ice, Sara.

She shook her head. Sandy dirt sprayed from her hair, stung her face. No, *Deal with the ice* wasn't right. But what was right?

The infernal thumping droned on and on and on. If only it would stop, then she could think. *Why wouldn't it stop?*

Hopelessness flooded her. Tears welled in her eyes, tumbled down her cheeks. *Jarrod, I can't fight this anymore. I can't feel the ice. I can't breathe. I can't hear anything but that damned hammering. I'm going to die in this box. It's going to be my coffin.*

For the first time in hours, maybe days, she heard Jarrod clearly. *No, Sara. Deal with the emotions. Deal with the emotions.*

I've tried and tried. But I'm too weak. Her stomach burned and ached from hunger. Her tongue stuck to the roof of her mouth—*so dry*—and her lips were split and cracked; the corners of her mouth, raw. *I'm too weak. Too tired and too weak.*

This was her coffin. She would die here. *I just need to go to sleep and it'll all be over.*

You'll never wake up, Sara.

It'll be over. The rhythmic thumping seduced her, mesmerized her, and Sara let her eyes drift closed.

Where are you, Sara? Her voice, not Jarrod's. *What about the others? They'll die, too. Will you let them die, too?*

She shoved the voice away. Why wouldn't it leave her alone? No one would leave her alone.

Sara, damn it, tell me where you are. Tell me what will happen to the others.

Where she was? What would happen to them? She snapped her eyes open, fear shredding her insides. *I don't know.* She began to cry. *Oh, God. I . . . don't . . . know!*

Salty tears slid over her cracked lips, setting them on fire. She prayed for water, swore that right now, she would kill for water. She slammed a fist against the top slats. Tried to call out, and failed. Her throat was too dry. No sounds would come.

But someone must have understood; the splashing noise—the sweetest sound Sara ever had heard—pattered against the box. This time, the water didn't come in just at her feet. It covered her head to foot, gushing into the box. She lay in bliss, jaw stretched wide, mouth filling and swallowing the cool water down. Elated and overjoyed, she drank until she couldn't drink anymore—and still the water came.

It puddled under her, turning the dirt to mud. Soon, the water began rising inside the box, higher and higher. When Sara's nose bumped against the underside of the top slats, she began to panic. "Turn it off!" she yelled. "Turn the damn water off. You're going to drown me!"

The water kept coming, kept rising. The gap between it and the top of the box dwindled, becoming more and more narrow. Sara's fear rose with the water. She dragged her fingertips over

the rough-hewn slats, measuring. Eight inches . . . Five inches
. . . Two inches . . . *Oh, God, two inches!*

"Hey! Hey, I'm going to drown in here! I'm—" Water
splashed up over her face, flooding her mouth and nose. She
sputtered, swallowed and coughed it up, then craned her neck,
seeking precious air. One inch. *One inch—and narrowing.*

They *were* going to drown her!

Urgently, she felt the bumpy boxtop, found a knothole at
the edge of a slat. She braced her arms, curling her fingers in
the mud for leverage, and thrust her nose up into the knothole.
Water covered her ears, lapped at her eyes. She closed them
and prayed the knothole too didn't fill up.

The gushing water buried everything except the tip of her
nose. She inhaled short, rapid breaths, fearing that with each
of them, she'd inhale water instead of air. Why hadn't Jarrod
warned her about this? Had he not remembered it? Good God,
how could he not remember it?

Her muscles cramped and twitched, protesting the strain of
holding her up. Clenching her teeth, she forced herself not to
relax her arms. If she did, she would die, and she knew it.

By the time the gushing water stopped, she ached from the
small of her back to the base of her neck. Her arms were
numb. Her fingers and wrists as stiff as if rigor mortis had set
in. Still, she sobbed in relief. The water had stopped coming
in, stopped flowing out through the top slats.

Little by little, the dirt absorbed the water and the level
began to recede. When it finally drained low enough, Sara let
her elbows bend. Her arms collapsed in spasm and her head
thudded against the muddy floor. Still, triumph flooded her.
The bastards had done their best to kill her, and they had
failed.

This time.

twenty-three

☆

The box lid opened.

Light flooded the darkness, and Sara shrank back from the blinding brightness.

"She's pissed herself," a man said.

"They always do. You got a bladder that'll hold for three days?"

The voice sounded familiar, but Sara's eyes hadn't yet focused. Foster? Was it him? No. No, it was the beefy lieutenant.

"Get her out of there and hose her down."

Two men grabbed her by the arms. A woman stood back, watching them. Why was she watching?

They pulled Sara out of the box. Her leg muscles stiff and cramping, her knees too weak to hold her upright, she tripped over its ledge. Confused and disoriented. Dizzy. Depth perception off. Bones fluid, lacking substance. The constant thumping still inside her head. Light-headed and nauseous, she leaned heavily on one of the guards, stumbled to keep up with them, and inhaled deep breaths of crisp autumn air. Air that wasn't stale and used and urine-tainted.

They rounded a five-foot cinder-block wall, a topless cubicle. She could see over it, thank God. Thank God. No more claustrophobia. Metal bands attached a pipe to the wall. Midway floor-to-top was a crank handle and, at the top, a showerhead. Water. Sweet, blessed water.

The woman was wearing fatigues, a red band on her upper arm, and a grim expression. Outside of the cubicle, she climbed onto some kind of step. "Major," she shouted. "You are a prisoner of war. Strip to your skin and leave your clothes on the floor."

The concrete scraped at Sara's bare feet. She leaned against the wall for support, unzipped the jumpsuit, and then shrugged out of it. IWPT. She was at IWPT, and this was part of the psychological warfare training. So far, aside from being drugged and maybe nearly drowning, everything she had gone through had just been part of the program. The near-drowning might have been intentional.

The woman turned the crank.

Water hissed in the pipe and sprayed over Sara's naked body. Cold water. Frigid water. Chill bumps raised on her skin. Her teeth began chattering. Folding her arms, she covered her chest and rubbed, elbows to armpits, shivering hard.

She tipped her head back, drank in huge gulps of fresh water. Never in her life had anything tasted so good. After the near-drowning, which seemed to have happened lifetimes ago, she hadn't been given anything more to drink. Even as she cursed the cold, cursed her years of taking warm showers for granted, she reveled in the feel of the caked mud sliding off her body, of feeling clean again.

The water hit her stomach and rushed back up her throat.

"Wet your head," the woman ordered, as if not noticing Sara was vomiting. "It's as filthy as the rest of you."

Sara wet her head, rinsed her mouth, and took small sips of water. This time, it stayed down.

She wanted soap. She didn't ask for it; that would only open her up to censure. POWs make no demands, not without suffering. But in her mind, she visualized it. Lavender soap. She smelled it, felt it lather on her skin.

"That's enough." The woman turned the crank, shut off the water.

Inside, Sara rebelled.

The woman tossed her a towel. "Dry off."

As good as the sips of water had tasted, they burned Sara's throat, her stomach, and again she fought the urge to heave. She rubbed dry with the scratchy towel. Her skin was chafed and irritated from the mud and wet clothes that had dried stiff and crusty on her body. Wincing, she slung the dripping water from her hair, and then passed the soggy towel back across the wall to the woman and waited, hoping for clean clothes. And shoes. Oh, how she hoped for shoes. Her feet felt like chunks of ice and shoes would be warm. She craved warmth. Warmth and comfort. She craved Jarrod.

"Put this on," the woman ordered. "Hurry. Transport is waiting."

Sara moved to the dry end of the cubicle, leaned against its rough surface, pulled on the blue jumpsuit, and then zipped it up. Still dizzy, she hugged the wall, letting her hand glide over its ragged surface to the opening, struggling to orient herself.

The woman shouted an order to the two guards and they again clasped Sara by the arms. She would object, but she lacked the strength to walk alone. She needed their physical support.

They stopped in front of the woman. The beefy lieutenant shoved up Sara's sleeve. The woman inserted a needle into Sara's arm. She drew back, fighting the sting. "No, not again."

She blacked out before the needle left her arm.

Sara awakened in a small room, sitting in a metal folding chair, her head resting against a wobbly metal table. A low-slung light dangled from a cord above her head and emitted a blinding yellow light that reflected off the empty chair across the table from her. The rest of the room fell into deep shadows, but on the west wall, she saw a three-by-four-feet reflective surface—a two-way mirror. No windows. One door, to her left. An armed guard standing beside it, wearing a red armband and glaring at her.

He rapped his knuckles against the door. "She's awake."

Two men came in. The beefy lieutenant and Dr. Owlsley. The lieutenant looked impatient; the doctor, ill but maddeningly calm.

He sat down across the table from her. "I'm disappointed in you, Sara."

The beefy lieutenant stood directly beside her, off her left shoulder. Sara sat up straighter, looked at Owlsley, and said nothing.

"I had hoped you'd be totally honest with me in our initial discussion. Instead, I learn you've withheld important information." He paused, but still Sara said nothing. When it became apparent she wasn't going to answer, he went on. "Tell me about Joe."

Oh, God. "He's a PTSD patient."

"And?" Owlsley prodded.

Her face reflected in his glasses. The thick lens distorted her features, made her look ghoulish. "And he's not recovering—yet."

The beefy lieutenant slapped her. A thunderous sound cracked through the room. Certain he'd broken her jaw, Sara felt her heart catapult to her throat. But her face didn't sting. He'd hit the table, she realized. Not her.

Owlsley didn't seem ruffled at all. Evidently he was used to the lieutenant pulling punches. "Tell me the nature of your relationship with Joe."

"I did," Sara insisted. "He's a patient suffering PTSD."

Owlsley removed his glasses, glared at her. "And do you have a personal relationship with him?"

He was searching for an Achilles' heel. "That wouldn't be ethical."

"Answer the question."

"No, I do not."

Owlsley nodded, pursed his lips. "I see." He feigned a sigh. "So you hug and kiss all of your patients, then?"

Fontaine had briefed him. Or Bush or William. Maybe all of them. Sara swallowed her fear. She couldn't let him get to her. She wouldn't be the only one to suffer the consequences. "No. Only those who need it to help them attach."

Owlsley stared hard into her eyes, looking for any emotion to latch onto. Sara refused to give him one.

"Well, then. You should find this interesting." He nodded to the guard, who opened the door and then wheeled in a television and a VCR. "Your patient obviously feels an attachment to you that goes beyond the bounds of a professional relationship, Sara. He followed you here." Owlsley laced his hands against the tabletop. "Unfortunately, he was misidentified as a terrorist and shot. But he did have some enlightening things to say to you." Owlsley's expression turned grave. "Considering the circumstances, we accommodated him." He nodded, and the guard started the tape.

Her heart stuck somewhere between her breastbone and throat, Sara watched the screen. Jarrod appeared. Lying in the woods on the ground, just as she'd seen him. Blood covered his chest. It hadn't been a stun gun.

Two men she hadn't seen squatted down beside him. "Get the medics out here," one yelled. "He's still alive."

Her heart slammed against her ribs. He was alive. It had been him. And he was alive. *Thank you, God. Thank you.*

A cut in the film and she saw Jarrod in a hospital emergency room, lying on a gurney. Half-conscious, he called out her name.

A woman who looked like Sara—exactly like Sara—stood at his bedside, clasping his hand. "It's okay, Joe. I'm right here."

"Sara." He looked up at her. "I'm going to die."

"Don't say that." The woman's voice dropped, anguish flooded it. *"Please."*

"Shh, don't." He pressed her hand to his lips. "Promise me you'll have the family you want with someone else."

Tears slipped down the woman's face. Terror slid through Sara. How had they cloned such an accurate disguise of her? When had they done it? When they'd given her the first blackout shot? But how did they know about her wanting a family? Aside from Jarrod, no one at Braxton knew it. He damn sure wouldn't have told them.

"Promise me," Jarrod grated out.

"I promise." The woman's voice cracked.

"I loved you, Sara." Jarrod lowered their hands to his side, gasped, and died.

Sara's heart shattered. She blinked hard, fighting tears. Swallowed a knot of them down from her throat, knowing she couldn't let any emotion show. Not now. *Oh, God. Jarrod was dead.*

Dead. And she couldn't react, couldn't mourn him.

Owlsley studied her. She struggled under grief and loss, sucked it down deep inside, and buried it. Jarrod would expect it. No, he would demand it. How could these bastards justify this?

"As you can see, Sara, we know the truth. You and Jarrod had planned a family together. That's hardly the type of thing that would happen in a professional relationship. Now, I want you to be honest with me."

She forced a strength she didn't feel into her voice. "I have been honest with you." Jarrod. Dead. *Dead.* "Your informant for that charade was wrong."

"Let's discuss your DoD contract. How did that come about?"

She was a POW. It was time she started acting like one. She reeled off her name, rank, and serial number.

"This is no time for you to get patriotic or flip, Sara," Owlsley warned her, removing his glasses. "I want the truth, and one way or another, I'm going to get it. You can make it easy on yourself, or as difficult as you like. It doesn't matter to me." He replaced his glasses on his nose. "Now, who arranged for that contract and sent you to Braxton? What was your mission there?"

Fontaine had prepped Owlsley well. "Sara West. Major, United States Air Force. Serial number four-three-five, seven-two, sixteen-ten."

"What diagnoses have you made on your patients, Sara?" Owlsley persisted.

She repeated her name, rank, and serial number.

The beefy lieutenant clutched at her shoulder, let his fingertips dig in. Pain streaked up her neck, down her arm, but Sara didn't flinch. Physical pain, no matter how intense, couldn't compare with the pain of losing Jarrod.

"Let me teach her a little respect, sir," the lieutenant told Dr. Owlsley.

"No." Owlsley spared the lieutenant a glance. "Sara doesn't defend herself. She defends her family."

The lieutenant nodded, a dark gleam lighting in his eye. "Brenda?"

"No," Owlsley said. "Lisa."

Sara's heart raced. Brenda. Lisa. What were these people going to do?

The overhead light snuffed out. The lieutenant shoved at her chair, turning it to face the two-way mirror. "Watch, Dr. West. You'll enjoy this."

Lisa sat huddled on the floor in what was obviously a cell. Her hands were bound with duct tape. She was blindfolded. Even from this distance, Sara could feel her fear. Two men were in her room. Sara bit her tongue until she tasted blood, forcing herself not to ask what the men intended to do to Lisa—if it was Lisa. Her being here would explain how Owlsley knew about Sara wanting a family—and about her wanting that family with Jarrod. But the girl in that room could be the woman who had masqueraded as Sara with Jarrod on the tape.

Dispelling that notion, Sara's clone walked into the room. She rushed over to Lisa and jerked off the blindfold. "Are you okay? Did they hurt you?"

"Aunt Sara." Lisa began crying hysterically. "Why are you doing this? I thought you loved me."

"I do love you," Sara's clone insisted, soothing Lisa's tangled hair with a gentle hand. "I'm a prisoner here, too, honey, and you're refusing to cooperate with them." The clone sat down beside Lisa on the floor, cradled her shoulder with a protective arm. "I warned you that I'd be confused. I can't tell them anything, and you won't. How can you do this to me?"

Lisa calmed and sniffed. "I wasn't sure it was really you."

"It's me," the clone assured her. "Lisa, this is very important. Those men are going to rape you unless you answer their questions. I can't stop them. Do you understand? I can't stop them."

Sara's flesh crawled, her heart skipped a beat then raced out of control, and a fear so deep she couldn't say where it started or stopped suffused her. Rape Lisa? No. Oh, God, no.

Lisa went rigid. "They can't do that. It's against the law."

The clone stroked Lisa's hair. "They're going to do it anyway, honey. You have to tell them what they want to know. Please. I don't want you hurt."

"But there's nothing to tell them. I already told you. You didn't tell me anything about any of this."

The men advanced. Sara's terror tripled. She stood up, shouted at Owlsley. "Stop them!"

"Certainly," Owlsley said, his voice cool and detached. "Just as soon as you answer me honestly."

"This is a training exercise, for God's sake. She's an innocent child. How can you justify letting those idiots rape her?"

"I don't have to justify anything, Sara. But if you let this happen, you're going to have a lot to justify. Mainly, to Lisa."

The clone's voice caught Sara's ear. "Catch me up on things at home. Did you tell your mom anything about IWPT?"

"She's so hyped-up about marrying Williamson, she doesn't have time to talk about anything else. She doesn't even think about anything else."

"You're lying to me, Lisa. Now, they're going to hurt both of us." The clone feigned deep disappointment, stood up, nodded to the men, and then left the room.

The men advanced on Lisa.

Sara's blood ran cold. She broke out in a cold sweat. "Owlsley, you're a doctor, for God's sake. You took an oath to heal. You *can't* let this happen!"

"I'm not letting anything happen. The choice is yours, Sara."

The men ripped at Lisa's blouse. Her scream filled both rooms. "Damn it," Sara shouted. "Stop them!"

Owlsley rubbed at the bridge of his nose. "I demand honesty."

Sara inwardly crumbled, her defenses breached and destroyed. She'd tell him anything, do anything, to prevent this.

"If those men touch Lisa, I'll die before telling you anything.
I swear it."

"You are not in a position to negotiate."

Lisa screamed. "All she talks about is marrying Williamson. That's all she thinks about—and that's the truth."

Lisa's words reverberated in Sara's head. She went statue-still, dropped back down into her chair. *Williamson*? Not *H. G. or G. H. Williamson*? And—Sara thought back—not once had Lisa uttered the word *stuff*. It had ended up in every conversation they'd had since she'd turned ten. Why not now? A memory flashed through Sara's mind. A memory of Sara and Brenda and Lisa standing in the dirt at the store, talking. Brenda wasn't marrying Williamson. She knew David was alive. She'd taken off the engagement ring.

Sara looked back into the mirror. The girl wasn't Lisa.

She couldn't be Lisa any more than the woman talking with Jarrod had been Sara. Had the man who'd died been Jarrod?

"Well, it's decision time, Sara." Owlsley propped his hands on the tabletop. "Do you sit by and let those men rape your niece?"

She stared at the girl through the mirror. She was someone's daughter, but she wasn't Brenda and David's, and she was acting of her own will. That much was clear. She wasn't Lisa.

God, please don't let me be wrong about this. If I'm wrong, I'll never forgive myself. Sara turned, leveled Owlsley with an uncompromising gaze. "If you have that girl raped, then it's on your conscience, not mine."

Irritated at not achieving his desired response, he frowned at her. "So it's true, then. You will allow your own niece to suffer the worst indignity possible for a woman to suffer just to save yourself."

"She's not my niece." Sara looked him right in the eye. "She looks like Lisa, moves like Lisa, even sounds like Lisa. But your Lisa-clone doesn't think like Lisa any more than your Sara-clone thinks like me."

Owlsley's face mottled red and the veins in his neck bulged. "Well, then. I'd say it's time we see how Sara West does think." He snapped a sharp nod to the lieutenant. "Take her to the lab."

Two armed guards escorted Sara to the electric chair.

The blindfold had just been removed. Inside the building, the lighting was dim and her eyes hadn't yet adjusted. She stumbled and looked down to see why she'd tripped. During transport, someone with a bad attitude and a warped sense of humor had tied her shoestrings together.

The beefy lieutenant clasped her shoulder and shoved her down onto the chair. She landed with a thump that jarred her teeth. Jarrod had drawn the chair, had told her about it. But Owlsley hadn't yet found out what he needed to know from her. He couldn't damage her yet. This had to be an intimidation tactic.

The soldiers worked quickly, efficiently. One at each side, they strapped her forearms to the chair arms and cinched down the straps, stemming the blood flow to her fingertips. They whitened and began to throb. She tried to flex them, but failed. The damn bands were too tight.

With utility knives, the soldiers split open the legs of her prisoner's jumpsuit, and then shackled her ankles to a wooden base bolted to the floor. The heavy metal gouged into her chafed skin and pain streaked up to her knees. "Is all of this really necessary?" She refused to flinch, remembered Jarrod's words, and repeated them. "I'm a POW. I get the message, okay?"

Hearing his words aloud infused her with strength. She *could* get through this. She had the tools. Jarrod had given them to her.

The lieutenant backhanded Sara across the mouth.

The sound echoed in the cavernous metal building, inside her head. Her lip split. Tasting blood, feeling the sting of the man's hand on her face, Sara refused to react outwardly, just buried her outrage within. Her time would come.

"You're supposed to pull back," the second guard whispered to the beefy lieutenant. "She's bleeding."

"What's the difference?" The lieutenant sent him a knowing glance. "In here, a split lip is nothing."

"But she's a major."

"You mean she *was* a major."

Was? Sara's stomach flipped over. She ordered herself to calm down. They couldn't be going to damage her now. Not without breaking her. Owlsley and Fontaine had to know what she'd unearthed and who she'd told about it. They had to know the extent of the breach in their operation.

The beefy lieutenant spared her a feral smile. "You ought to feel privileged, Doc. You're the first woman to get this training."

Sara swallowed her fear and a sharp retort. She didn't need another slap. Her ears were still ringing from the last one.

They circled her chest, neck, and forehead with thick leather bands, jerked them tight, and then attached them to the back of the chair. Her chest and throat didn't have room to expand. Trussed up, she had to fight for every breath.

She worked with it, drew in shallow puffs to combat the restrictions, but her oxygen intake still rapidly diminished. Spots formed before her eyes. Sweat beaded on her brow, trickled down between her breasts.

Don't panic. You survived the boa constrictor, the jammed elevator, the box and nearly drowning, and the god-awful torture with Jarrod and Lisa. You know how to fight this.

Following her instincts, she dove into antistress techniques and focused outward, disassociating and reminding herself that every indignity was inflicted for one reason: to inspire fear. That, she couldn't give them. Not without forfeiting her mission to save the patients, Lisa, and Jarrod. *He couldn't be dead. He was at Braxton. At Braxton with Shank and Reaston and Koloski and the rest of the friendlies.* Jarrod was a Shadow Watcher, and Shadow Watchers didn't forfeit missions, or anything else. Instead, they died. They knew the drill—*duty first*—and the Shadow Watcher creed: "Accomplish the mission. Whatever, wherever, whenever." And living by it, they routinely survived seemingly insurmountable odds. If the methods worked for them, then they would work for her—

provided she had the courage to employ them.

She thought of Foster. God, but he was going to get an earful when this was over. And not wanting to miss any details she could heap on his head, she scanned the structure. Four men, all wearing fatigues and all armed, were positioned inside the building; one at each of two entrances and two beside her. The building was about eighty by ninety feet. Metal walls, painted white. Concrete flooring, unpainted. The metal ceiling, about sixteen feet high, followed the pitch of the roof. Electrical cables ran through PVC pipes positioned alongside the exposed beams overhead and wide gaps between the pipes left electrical wires exposed. Definitely a safety hazard and it had to be a breach of at least one of the million military regulations.

A stark white light flickered on and shone directly into her face. Seated on the structure's south end, she squinted and scanned north. Two men she hadn't seen earlier stood in the shadows, talking softly. Unfortunately, too softly. Their voices echoed like dull droning bees, but their words were lost.

The man on the left shifted into the light. He wore an Air Force uniform. The glare made seeing his face impossible, but there was something familiar about him. Sara dipped her chin against the glare but still couldn't peg what struck her as familiar. She couldn't make out the man's rank, either. That baffled her. How could the blinding light reflect?

Ah, the metal ceiling. The rank had to be metal. Most officers now wore cloth rank on their uniform shirt's epaulets but this man evidently preferred the metal rank tacked to his collar. Another hard-core diehard resisting change?

The second man was Dr. Owlsley. Anger surged through her, had her blood hot and threatening to boil in her veins.

Clearly in charge, Owlsley shuffled around a machine small enough to be used by mobile field units. About three feet high and eighteen inches wide, it was dull black with a cone-shaped nose that pointed right at Sara's chair. It had to be the laser.

A sinking feeling pitted a hole in her stomach. Doubt filled it. She hadn't told them, but had they discovered her real purpose for being here on their own?

*If so, then you're a dead woman. You know Foster didn't
recruit you for the obvious, and he didn't arrange to bring
you here to find the obvious, either. He never operates that
way. Think about it, Sara. Foster wanted you to find something
here . . . or to keep you from finding something. Which is it?*

Not knowing, her worry deepened, and she shifted on the
seat. The bands gouged into her ribs, cut into her throat. Choking, she gagged. The bands dug deeper and pain shot through
her neck.

This was damned ridiculous. Strapped and banded from
head to foot and yet the chair seat was padded. That seemed
strange, out of place. Panic swelled in her throat. Her breathing
grew rapid, shallow, even more difficult.

She had to get a grip. They couldn't have their answers—
she was still alive and undamaged, wasn't she? Maybe they
weren't going to use the laser on her yet and they were trying
to scare her into believing they were to get their answers.

Only one thing was certain. This wasn't part of the normal
psych-warfare training program. If it were, then this environment would fall under strict controls and regulations. Her gaze
drifted up, back to those exposed wires. She licked at her split
lip, tasted blood, and her heart rate kicked up a notch. Definitely outside the normal program. That, or regulations weren't
followed here. Possible, but not likely. This place and these
people were too sadistic, smelled too desperate. Especially
Owlsley. He oozed desperation.

But was that by design? To strengthen the impact of the
training? Or was it another simulation designed to optimize
maximum effectiveness, like the sensory-deprivation tactics
simulation she'd already undergone in the box?

Wrong. Her instincts flashed a warning. *You're wrong,
Sara. This has nothing to do with effectiveness and it's not
part of any program. Listen to me. Listen. Forget the damn
program. It's the laser. They're going to torture you into telling them what you know about their operation, then they're
going to kill you.*

Sara had learned early to trust her instincts, to rely on them
to survive. Here, like at Braxton, attacks were plentiful. From

the enemy, and from allies. And right now, through her confusion, her instincts were screaming a warning.

She curved her spine to lessen the tension on the bands so she could breathe deeper, clear her mind. She hadn't fully recovered from her stint in the box, from the medication she'd been given, or from the Jarrod and Lisa charades—*God, please. They had to have been charades.*

They were. Of course they were. Intentional intimidation tactics. Just as intentional as Owlsley putting her through this now, hitting her while her defenses were down and she was weakest, physically and emotionally.

"Dr. Owlsley," the beefy lieutenant said. "We're ready, sir."

"Very well." Owlsley's shoes scraped across the bare concrete. He signaled the familiar man, who then nodded to a guard near the wall. He reached over to a switch and the bright lights snuffed out.

The stark white walls went black.

Sweat poured down Sara's face. Her heart thudded and fear gripped her hard. She would be scrambled. Mentally destroyed. A vegetable like David.

No, Sara. You have the tools. You know how to fight this. No rage. Feel no rage. No intense emotion.

Dr. Owlsley stood behind the machine, and another man in uniform stood at his side in the shadows. He wasn't Fontaine. But he was familiar.

A quiet whir sounded. Out of the darkness, a pinpoint of red light streaked from the cone-nose machine directly at her head. Her skin prickled, her senses went on high alert, and Sara braced for pain . . . but felt none. She felt nothing.

A long moment passed, then the point of red light swept across her skull. Memories flashed through her mind. Incidents long since forgotten. Insignificant events. Simple, happy times.

Then her thoughts twisted to memories of Steve's wife committing him for mental evaluation—the injustice done to her brother that had led Sara to become a psychiatrist. Memories of Brenda and David and Lisa. Memories of being huddled in a corner of the Laundromat on prom night, wrapped in a stolen towel, washing her dress, waiting for it to dry.

Memories of being locked in the closet with Rudy, the ten-foot boa constrictor, and stuck between floors in the broken elevator at the bank. Then came dark memories that held desolation and despair. Memories she had buried in the deepest recesses of her mind and had forgotten, until now. Christmas nights spent by herself. Lonely nights, and dinners for one. Standing before the mirror, her eyes filled with tears, pleading with her reflection to tell her why someone couldn't love her.

The point stopped moving, probed. Roused vivid images of her watching Brenda and David and Lisa together, hungering for a family of her own. Images of her aching for a husband and children to love, and them loving her.

Owlsley had found her Achilles' heel.

And as Jarrod had promised Owlsley would, he hammered on it. Probing again and again until Sara couldn't think rationally any more, couldn't avoid the grueling emotional pain ripping through her chest, clawing at her stomach, torturing her mind. She tried to shut down, to force her thoughts away from the agony and anguish to the tranquil and peaceful, but she had no control. Regardless of what technique she used, the laser overrode it. She sat helpless. Helpless . . . and hurting.

The deluge of unwanted memories rushed on unrestrained. Relentless. Merciless. Battering her, digging deeper and deeper into her past, arousing more and more gut-wrenching memories. Arousing more and more rage. And for the first time, she truly understood "the rage" Jarrod had described. Understood his hatred of it; his hatred, and his fear.

Physically and emotionally spent, she mentally retreated, shutting out all of the ugliness and pain. Time and space ceased to exist. The low-level thump grew louder and louder inside her head. There was no escape from the tormenting thoughts being stimulated. Even prepared by Jarrod, Sara hadn't expected this to be so bad, so inevitable. Dear God, nothing this bad could be endurable.

Sanity was slipping away.

Sara felt it. Felt it, and fought it. And failed.

No, Sara. Don't give in. Don't give up. You can beat this.

You have to beat this for you and me—for all of us. Deal with the emotions. Deal with the emotions!

She focused on that, on dealing with her emotions, and the deep sense of loss and anger and aggression lessened. Lessened, and then faded to mild confusion.

Think ice, Sara. Free-floating ice. Clear, blue water. Think of me, Sara.

Jarrod. She had to fight. For herself, for her patients and family. For Jarrod.

Jarrod returned to Braxton defeated.

Reaston greeted him at the back entrance. "Christ, man. You're three days late. The friendlies have covered, but it's been a challenge."

"Who's on duty?"

"William."

At Reaston's side, Jarrod strode to the stairwell. "What did you tell him?"

"Shank faked orders from Dr. West to take you to a camera room on the fourth floor. You moved back to Isolation today. I've taken you outside."

"Good." Jarrod shoved open the stairwell door. Never in his life had he felt like such a failure. Not even when he'd walked in on Miranda and Royce. He loved Sara, and he'd had to leave her. She was being tortured.

"Did you find Dr. West?" Reaston asked.

Jarrod nodded. "But I couldn't stop it." His emotional upheaval slid into his voice. "I needed a weapon and I didn't have one. They popped me with a stun gun and got her, Reaston."

"Oh, damn." Reaston slammed a fist against the stairwell wall, denting the Sheetrock above the metal banister.

Jarrod didn't have to explain why he couldn't pull Sara out of IWPT once she had been taken hostage. Reaston understood the ramifications. The technology—thousands, maybe millions, of lives—could be forfeited. Jarrod had had to choose between costing the country the technology and leaving Sara, so he had done what she would have done: the right thing.

And he had prayed ever since that she could withstand what Owlsley would do to her. She had a chance—provided they had been right in deducing that dealing with emotional issues minimized the damage. But what if they were wrong?

His stomach curdled, lodged somewhere between his ribs and throat. Living with this decision was going to be a bitch. He had done what he'd had to do, but he hated it. God, how he hated it.

Nursing red knuckles, Reaston caught up with Jarrod on the stairs. "What do you expect?"

Jarrod opened the second-floor door, hating the words he was about to say, and fearing them even more. "The worst. They know Foster put her here." Lieutenant Kane being at IWPT proved that. He was supposed to be heading the Shadow Watcher task force to extricate Sara. Instead, he was an enemy red-band at IWPT—and it damn sure wasn't a cover. The bastard had violated ethics and the creed. Jarrod would make the call and get Kane bounced from the program, but the damage was done. Sara wouldn't be extricated. She was on her own.

"They'll kill her," Reaston speculated.

"No. That, they won't do." Jarrod turned into the hallway leading to Isolation. "It'll be worse."

Reaston fell into step beside Jarrod. "How can anything be worse than death?"

"They'll do their damnedest to damage her more than they did ADR-40."

The blood drained from Reaston's face. "Oh, God."

Just the idea of Sara facing that devastated Jarrod. Knowing she had taken this on herself for him and others like him only made the feelings worse. Their deductions had to be right. Had to be. Then she'd be okay.

But what if they weren't right? What if dealing with the emotions didn't protect Sara?

Jarrod clenched his jaw. "I'm going to kill Fontaine and Owlsley with my bare hands.'

"I'll back you up."

Jarrod looked over, saw his disgust mirrored in Reaston's eyes, and nodded.

Sara lay on a gurney in a room absent of anything that wasn't white. She had regained consciousness a short time ago, but she kept her eyes closed. Her thoughts were scrambled, though not nearly to the extent Jarrod had suffered. She owed him for that. He had gone into this blind, and because he had, he'd given her the ammunition to fight them. She wasn't a hundred percent, but she was going to be okay. She had suffered their worst and survived.

And now she knew what was being done and who was doing it, though not why. Using a combination of psychological-warfare tactics, sensory-deprivation therapies, and noninvasive microwave laser technology capable of stimulating specific thoughts, Dr. Owlsley was pushing the boundaries. His strategy was simple and effective. Strip a person of dignity, defenses, and any sense of control, and then, via laser, see what parts of their brains are active and what triggers a desired emotional response.

Her mind drifted. Sara didn't fight it. The gurney was moving, rolling out of the building. The sun felt warm on her face.

A helicopter's props whipped in the distance. The sound moved closer and closer. The gurney tilted. They were putting her inside, taking her back to Braxton.

Jarrod was at Braxton. Alive and waiting for her. She knew it deep down, with every beat of her heart. If he were dead, she would sense it, know it, and she didn't. She knew he was alive . . . and worried. He would help her until she was normal again. He was safe. Safe. She could rest.

Sara awakened.

Her mind was clearer. Not right. Not totally coherent. But better than it had been earlier. The medications were wearing off. Whatever they had been, they were short-term. Now, she had to worry about triggers. Jarrod's had been colors and keywords. What were hers? Did she have any?

She tried to orient to her surroundings without opening her

eyes. Vibrating. The sounds of the whirring props. Smells of fuel and aircraft. Still on the helicopter.

"She doing okay?"

Sara recognized the woman's voice. She had watched Sara shower.

"Fine," a man answered. "Just sleeping off the medication. We like to keep them quiet during transport. Dealing with episodic rage at fifteen thousand feet isn't our idea of a good time."

"She's no threat," the woman assured him. "She's a vegetable."

Good, Sara thought. They were convinced. Episodic rage at any altitude sucked, but especially when it was suffered as the result of abused noninvasive microwave laser technology. Sara had read the preliminary hopes for the technology, and it had brimmed with the promise of saving thousands of lives in battle by arousing fear or the desire to surrender in the enemy, making it paramount to survival. But used improperly, pushing patients beyond their limits of endurance, the technology permanently impaired, inflicted severe and irreversible mental dysfunction. It reduced a vibrant, vital human being to a vegetative state. Fathers and husbands and sons. Men like David. Like Lou, and ADR-40.

David had been a victim early on in the research. Then the men had started getting better—coming out of the therapy less severely damaged. But once again, the pattern shifted, and each man suffered more than the last, left IWPT more damaged than the one before him. *Why?*

Sara again drifted. Heard the drone of the propellers turning, the voice of the pilot talking into a radio to ground control. Ground control's static-ridden response.

It was almost as if Owlsley had to hurry. She remembered the yellow cast to his skin and asking him if he'd had liver-function studies done lately. He was ill; that much was obvious. But was his illness the reason for rushing his research, or was his contract about to expire? Or was it corruption? Maybe he intended to sell the technology and he had an impatient buyer. Men had done worse for greed.

Greed.

Money. Fontaine. Research money. Facility money.

Sara thought back to the conversation she had overheard on first standing in Fontaine's office. He had been on the phone, raging at Carl Owlsley about a lack of money and demanding more of it.

Owlsley *could* be pushing the bounds, attempting to gain more research funds. But to gain any real money, he would have to sell the technology.

Dear God, he was going to black-market the technology. Maybe that's why Foster hadn't shut the operation down.

If anyone with the technology needed an assassin, by using the laser to trigger aggressive behavior, they'd have one. Effecting assassinations didn't fit the profiles of what she had read about Owlsley, or with her observations of the award-winning egomaniac Fontaine. Yet, she could see either of them selling this new technology on the black-market. To secure their personal agendas, they would deny—even to themselves—what would be done with the technology once it had been sold.

It fit. God help them all, this black-market sale made sense. She let out an inadvertent groan.

"Was that her—the noise?"

"No. She's a vegetable, I told you."

Someone listened to her heart with a stethoscope, and she felt yet another needle sting in her arm.

Within minutes, the mild confusion returned and, exhausted, Sara took advantage of the time to rest. Soon, she would have to feign severe impairment. For now, she would take solace in knowing Jarrod had endured worse and he had survived. She would survive, too.

Sara came around slowly.

The gurney was rolling down a bumpy path. They were outside. She smelled the god-awful pines. Cranking open an eyelid, she saw Shank pushing the gurney.

"I told you," Fontaine said from behind Sara. "She never arrived at IWPT for training, Shank. Local authorities found her in her car about twelve miles from there. They contacted IWPT because she was in uniform and it was the nearest facility. No one saw anything and no one knows what happened to her. The AID—a Lieutenant Kane—is investigating."

Lieutenant Kane? The enemy. Was he one of Foster's men? Either way, Foster was investigating. Foster. Should she rejoice, or mourn?

Lieutenant Kane had known about Shadow Watchers and Red Haze. That *had* to have come from Foster. She should mourn.

Sadly, but definitely, she should mourn.

twenty-four

☆

Shank got a sleeping Sara settled into a room on the second floor.

As soon as the falsely concerned Fontaine left for his quarters and she had verified it, Shank left Reaston watching over Sara and made a beeline for Joe.

Koloski was on duty in Isolation. For that, Shank felt grateful. She'd just as soon shoot William as to deal with him or his antics right now. "Buzz me through, Koloski," she said, not slowing her hurried steps.

She passed the heavy metal doors and rushed down the hallway to Joe's room. As soon as the alarm sounded, she shoved the door open. "Sara's back. Fontaine's saying she never got to IWPT."

"What?" Jarrod jumped to his feet.

"It's bull." Shank motioned for him to come with her. "Sara's drugged to the gills."

Reaching into the torn-out cave between the wall pad and Sheetrock, he asked the question he feared being answered. "Is she okay, otherwise?" He pulled out a pair of sneakers and jerked them on, heading toward the door.

"Mildly confused," Shank said, following him out of the door. "I think it's more medication than damage, thank God. At least, it looks that way. Orders say she's a vegetable, but she's not. She's slurring her words and her thoughts are pretty random. She was resting when I left."

"You left her alone?" Jarrod doubled his stride.

"Of course not. Reaston's guarding her. Fontaine's in his

quarters, but Mick Bush is patrolling, so I didn't want to take any chances."

Jarrod passed the metal doors. "We need to get her outside."

"Now?" Shank sounded stunned.

Jarrod figured she was stunned. "Now, or sooner." Passing the Plexiglas barrier, he nodded to Koloski, who lifted his hands, questioning. Jarrod gave him a thumbs-up, his hollow heart now full. Sara had survived.

Jarrod pushed Sara out through the exit door in a wheelchair. When he neared the pond on the stone path, he stopped. She slumped to her side, and Shank pulled the lap belt across Sara's thighs. Sara whimpered.

"No. No straps." Jarrod shoved the belt aside. "They strapped her in the chair."

"Torture?" Shank's eyes clouded.

Jarrod nodded, and then squatted down in front of the chair. "Sara?" He softened his voice. "Honey, look at me."

No response.

He kept talking, working at it to keep his worry from his voice, using soothing tones and gentle words, explaining all that had happened.

The more he talked, the less glaze covered Sara's eyes, and the more horror filled Shank's. He talked on, until both cleared completely, and Sara was lucid.

"Jarrod." She reached for him. Hugged him tightly. "You're not dead."

A knot swelled in his throat. When he could, he swallowed it down. "I'm fine," he said, hugging her back, warning himself not to hold her too tight, not to crush her to him. "Are you all right?"

"A little confused," she said against his neck. "We were right. Dealing with the emotions was the key."

"Are you sure?" He cupped her face in his hands, saw Shank step away and turn her back, giving them a moment of privacy. "When I got hit with that stun gun, I saw them take you. I couldn't stop them." His hands trembled. "Oh, God, Sara. I'm sorry. I couldn't stop them."

Sara gave him a weak smile, touched his beloved face with her fingertips. "It was you."

Too emotional to speak, he nodded.

"Shank?" Sara glanced toward her. "Come here."

Shank rejoined them. "You seem okay. Are you really?"

"I think so. They gave me these injections. I'm not sure what they were, but they caused temporary amnesia. Some were strictly sedatives. At least that's what they felt like— drug hangover and all."

"Was it worth it, Sara?" Shank asked. "Going through all of that there?"

"I think so." Sara looked up at Shank. "I know what they're doing and who they are. Definitely Owlsley and Fontaine. Maybe Foster. Lieutenant Kane is working for him *and* Owlsley. Kane knew about Shadow Watchers and Red Haze."

"Foster set you up." Jarrod frowned, furious. "The son of a—"

Sara interrupted. "I'm ninety percent sure they're intending a black-market sale of the technology. What I don't know is to whom, or when." A thought occurred to Sara. "But Foster might know."

Jarrod blinked hard, then blinked again. A suppressed memory flashed into his mind, filling in a blank. "Foster *will* know. This *is* Operation Red Haze, Sara. It's why he sent me to IWPT."

A cold chill shimmied up Sara's spine. Of course Foster knew. Of course he did. He spied on spies, for God's sake. He had always known. Since David, he had known. So why hadn't he stopped them?

Shank worried at her lip. "Intel says in two days Fontaine and Owlsley are going to D.C. for a briefing. I'm doubtful. There's no reason for the two of them to attend any one briefing. Braxton stands alone."

"The sale." Sara looked from Shank to Jarrod. "They're arranging the sale."

"It's possible," Jarrod said. "If the AID suspected Fontaine and Owlsley of wrongdoing and corrupting the program—it's extremely sensitive, Sara—calling in Foster would be a logical step."

Sara gripped the arm of her wheelchair, looked down at the IV line taped to the back of her hand, rehydrating her. "Sorry, but that doesn't sit right with me." She looked back at Jarrod. "If the AID knew about this corruption, then there would be no reason for Foster to bring me into it. He'd use AID resources, not an outsider. The only reasonable explanation is, that Foster is involved and the AID is unaware."

Jarrod stood up, his knees cracking. He mulled that over, stuffing a hand into his slacks pocket. "Are you suggesting Foster is working with Fontaine and Owlsley?"

Sara responded to the incredulity in Jarrod's voice with dead calm. "That's exactly what I'm suggesting."

"Sara, no." Jarrod's expression turned grim. "I know this man. I've trudged through hell with him hundreds of times. Duty and honor mean something to him. He would never do anything like this for money."

"Not for money," Shank interceded. "But he might do it for respectability."

Jarrod turned to Shank. "What the hell are you talking about?"

"This research has been going on for over five years. We know that because of Fred. What if Foster was working with Fontaine and Owlsley, but now he's up for that star? He wants to make general more than anything else in the world. He always has, and anyone who knows him is aware of it. What if he wants to disassociate from this project and come out of this lily-white? Wouldn't he send in another Shadow Watcher and claim his involvement was a covert operation all along?"

Jarrod looked poleaxed. In physical pain. Sara understood that. Shattered illusions cut close to the bone. "I considered that, Shank," Sara said. "And for a while, I believed it might be true. But I don't anymore." Sara swept her hair back from her eyes, struggling to stay awake. She was so tired. "When I was at IWPT—in the metal building where they do the laser experiments—I saw a man in uniform with Dr. Owlsley. He seemed familiar. Remember, Joe, you mentioned that, too—about the second man seeming familiar?"

"I remember." Feet spread, Jarrod crossed his chest with his arms. "His metal rank reflected off the ceiling." A strange look rippled across Jarrod's face. Dread and regret chased it. "It was Foster."

"Yes, it was." Sara clasped Jarrod's hand, knowing he was hurting.

Shank let out a sigh laced with resignation. "That proves it, then."

"What it proves," Sara interjected, "is that Foster is aware and involved. No more, and no less."

Jarrod stilled, stiffened. "He's under deep cover."

"Could be." Sara nodded, not at all surprised Jarrod had followed her line of thought. "Under deep cover and playing out his own hidden agenda."

Jarrod looked down at her, enlightenment shining in his eyes. "Which is why he wanted you involved. To insure his cover."

Shank caught the drift of the conversation. "The AID doesn't know he's involved Sara in this?"

Sara gave Shank a negative nod. "His missions worldwide would be in jeopardy. The security risks would render them worthless. Would he chance that?"

Jarrod paced a short path, strode back and forth, three steps in each direction. "No, this isn't right. He'd never put his men in additional jeopardy. We're off-base here." On the fourth turn, Jarrod stopped. "You're his out-of-the-system witness, Sara. You're Foster's alibi."

Sara weighed the possibility. It fit. She could be Foster's protection and proof, just as her copies of Fontaine's forged peacock-blue notes were her protection and proof that Braxton existed.

Shank toed the grass. "This would make sense if one of the early patients were one of Foster's men. Otherwise, how would he have become aware of this?"

Sara looked at Jarrod and saw his almost imperceptible nod.

"That's exactly how Foster found out. My brother-in-law, David, is Fred. He worked for Foster."

"Then why not call in the IG?" Shank asked. "Why not follow the normal procedure of guilty until proven innocent?"

"Because Dr. Owlsley isn't military," Jarrod said. "He's a civilian. Without hard evidence, Foster couldn't touch him."

Shank digested that. "So Foster's either working with them and now weaseling out so he doesn't jeopardize his star, or he's attempting to get hard evidence to take Owlsley and Fontaine down."

"I vote he's gathering evidence." Jarrod cocked his head. "That's the only sensible reason I can see for Foster involving Sara in this. Foster's under deep cover, and he's involved. But not in selling the technology. He's planning on buying it. That's the only way he can be certain of keeping the technology safe."

Sara had doubts about that deduction. "Where would he get the money to do that?"

"He inherited a fortune when his father died, and his wife, Rebecca, is independently wealthy. Stock market." Shank darted her gaze from Sara to Jarrod. "So he's under deep cover, and he's afraid he's so deep he can't get out? Is that what you're thinking?"

"Exactly," Jarrod said with a nod. "He needed someone he could count on to help him."

"Help him?" Sara guffawed. "I despise the man and he knows it. He wouldn't look to me to help him, Joe." Sara shifted on the wheelchair's seat. "Well, I did despise him," she amended. "Now, I'm not sure what to think of him."

"Regardless, you stayed on his back, Sara." Jarrod stepped closer to her chair. "For five years, you gave the man hell, demanding information on David. You never let him intimidate you, you never let up on him, and you never quit."

"I never succeeded in getting that information, either."

"Didn't you?" Jarrod smiled. "Sara, you do now know exactly what happened to David."

She did. Sara frowned. "Okay." She wasn't sure she believed this, but a strong case could be built. "So I'm his protection and proof that he's on the right side of this."

"Or his patsy." Shank shoved her hands in her pockets. "You could be no more than a front he put into place to cover his ass if he got squeezed."

"That's possible, too," Sara conceded. It didn't feel quite right, but then she wasn't feeling quite right. Now wasn't a great time to make decisions or deductions based on instinct and intuition. "There is one person who will know. We need to get to her to find out the truth."

"Her?" Shank sounded baffled.

"Who?" Jarrod asked, sounding no more clear on Sara's thinking than Shank.

"Rebecca." Sara looked from one to the other of them. "Who would better know the man's motives than his wife?"

Jarrod stared at Sara. "We've got to get out of Braxton—without Fontaine knowing it, or he and Owlsley will call off the buy and bury the evidence so deep an archaeologist couldn't find it. And we need to get to the AID for help. This has gone too far and, as much as it kills me to say it, we don't *know* Foster's position in this. Even with whatever Rebecca tells us, we can't be sure. Alone, we're leaving too many people in jeopardy. We need help."

"We could contact Foster." Even to Sara that suggestion sounded hollow and foolish. "Ask him straight out what his role in this is."

"We can't," Jarrod countered. "He's acted outside AID perimeters. He'll sacrifice himself and his star and reschedule the buy to save the country. He reschedules and we risk Owlsley and Fontaine finding another buyer."

"Reasonable," Shank says. "So who in AID do we trust? Anyone we go to is going to consider Foster guilty as hell."

"I'm not sure I don't believe he's guilty as hell." Sara rubbed at her temples. A dull throb ached behind her eyes.

"First, we'll call Donald O'Shea." Jarrod gripped the handles on Sara's wheelchair, and began rolling it back toward the building.

"Who's he?" Sara asked.

Shank answered. "Foster's aide at the Pentagon."

"Is that a wise move?" Sara saw serious flaws. "What if this O'Shea contacts Foster? What if O'Shea's been to IWPT? Owlsley profiles everyone. Who's safe and who can be turned into an assassin with a keyword or a trigger?"

"I've considered this, Sara." Jarrod began pushing the chair back toward the building. "O'Shea is our only choice."

Sara supposed O'Shea was their only choice. He would likely be loyal to Foster. Hopefully, that would encourage him to keep his mouth shut.

And if he didn't?

Everyone at Braxton would be canceled.

Shank got Beth out of the way, and Sara ran interference, giving Jarrod the all-clear sign.

He left her office and went to the nurse's station. Using the secure line, he phoned O'Shea. "Donald, I need help at the local level. Security Condition Delta."

Sara swallowed hard. Delta. Level four. Highest priority in security circles, reserved for the most severe threats.

"No," Jarrod said into the phone. "No one in the group, but someone in the loop on Red Haze."

Jarrod listened, glanced at Sara. She checked the hallways, then nodded that everything was fine.

"Eglin. Pensacola NAS is closer, but I highly recommend keeping it in-house."

He meant, "within the Air Force," Sara thought.

"Captain Marshall Grant. Yeah, I know him. Eglin. Thanks." Jarrod paused, then added, "Cancel Lieutenant Kane's security clearance and get an arrest warrant on him. He's compromised. Hold off serving him for forty-eight hours." Jarrod listened, then added, "Oh, really?"

Sara's antennae perked up, and she lifted a questioning brow in Jarrod's direction.

He raised the mouthpiece and whispered, "Grant got Kane booted out of the AID program. Deficient ratings. He's got an axe to grind."

And Kane was grinding that axe by getting himself assigned to IWPT where he could get involved on the opposite side of Operation Red Haze. "Does Kane have a problem with Foster?" Sara asked in a whisper. "Or did Foster recruit him?"

Uncertainty clouded Jarrod's eyes. "We'd better prepare for either possibility," Jarrod said, then talked into the phone. "Code Nine, Donald."

That, Sara couldn't decipher.

"I'm sure," Jarrod said. "He could be sacrificed."

Foster, Sara deduced. Don't tell him, or he could be sacrificed. Jarrod didn't mention that Foster could sacrifice himself, Sara noted. Was that intentional? Or was Jarrod's faith in his boss wavering?

In a way, it bothered her that Jarrod's faith could waver. By his own admission, Jarrod had trudged through hell with Foster hundreds of times, and no doubt he had trudged through it hundreds more times under Foster's orders. But then she too had doubts. How could she hold Jarrod to a standard she couldn't meet herself?

She couldn't. They didn't know the truth about Foster. That was the bottom line. Jarrod not questioning Foster would be the most dishonorable act of all. It would mean he had put the man before the good of the country. That would be easier on Jarrod as a human being, but he would hate himself for it. It would cost him his self-respect. And, she confessed, it would cost him her respect.

No one man, no matter how important and respected and valued, could rate more important or valued than the country. That would be the ultimate act of betrayal to its ideals and values, and to all that had been sacrificed over the centuries to provide and protect them by men like David and Lou.

Jarrod hung up the phone, rounded the edge of the desk, and joined Sara. "Ready?"

"We're leaving now?" She'd only gotten rid of the IV an hour ago.

"We've got a lot to do between now and the meeting in D.C., Sara. We can't do it here. Are you up to traveling?"

Picking up on his worry and his skepticism, she nodded. "I'm a hundred percent."

Clearly relieved, he motioned toward the stairwell. "Let's go."

"Joe, they're not going to just let us walk out of here."

He clasped her hand. "I know that, honey. While you were recouping and sleeping off the effects of the drugs, Shank and I developed a plan . . ."

twenty-five

☆

Awaiting Koloski's nod, Shank peeked around the corner.

He stood talking with William, outside the Plexiglas barrier at the Isolation nurses' station.

"Something's wrong," Koloski told William. "Joe's pulse is weak and thready, his skin is clammy, and he's not verbally responsive. The man's in real trouble, and I have no idea what's wrong with him."

William reached behind the barrier, hit the buzzer to open both doors, then headed toward the heavy metal ones. Koloski nodded at Shank, and then followed William.

Jarrod lay waiting. When the door opened, he prepared. William rushed across the pads, and Jarrod attacked, slamming a fist into William's stomach. Koloski grabbed William from behind, Jarrod from the front, and Shank hurried in, syringe poised and ready.

"Let go of me," William shouted. "What are you idiots doing?"

"You've got Reaston's flu." Jarrod immobilized William's arm, exposed his inner elbow, then squeezed his upper arm. The vein bulged, and Jarrod nodded at Shank. She inserted the needle, then emptied the syringe.

William's knees folded, and Koloski and Jarrod let him slide to the floor. Shank and Koloski began stripping off his clothes. Jarrod shrugged out of his pajamas and put on a pair of jeans and a blue shirt, while Shank and Koloski put the pajamas on William.

Shank buttoned the last shirt button. "Position his back to the camera so his face isn't visible."

Koloski shifted William on the floor pad. "How long will he be out?"

"About four hours," Shank said.

"That's not long enough." Jarrod tucked the tail of his shirt into his jeans. "The meeting isn't until tomorrow."

"We can handle that," Shank said. "Koloski, put him on a four-hour injection schedule, but give the first two every three and a half hours, just to be safe."

"Yes, ma'am." Koloski stared down at William. "There's going to be hell to pay when he comes out of this."

"Won't matter," Shank said. "By then it'll all be over."

Koloski looked worried. "Will this hurt him?"

"No," Shank said. "He'll have a good sleep and a helluva hangover, but that's about it." She turned to Jarrod. "Sara's keying in the orders for the medication at the nurse's station." Shank glanced up at the camera. "You got the timing down? Every four hours?"

The door alarm buzzed as verification.

"Good." Shank turned to Jarrod. "Reaston's waiting at the elevator on the first floor. He'll get you past Security. Keep an eye out for Fontaine. Martha told Beth he left the office for parts unknown about ten minutes ago."

Jarrod reached into the hole where the cave had been, pulled out the gun Reaston had provided him with after his return from IWPT, and then tucked it into his waistband. He wouldn't be caught unarmed again.

Sara waited for him, keeping a watch on the halls. "I jammed the elevator." Sara fell into step beside Jarrod, her heart pumping hard. "It's waiting."

They entered the elevator and rode down. Uneasy, she glanced up at Jarrod.

"It's not the box, honey. You're all right." His eyes were clear, cold, filled with purpose.

Reassured by that, she clasped his hand.

The bell chimed, and the door slid open.

Reaston stood waiting. "We've got a problem."

"Fontaine?" Sara asked.

"No. He's in his quarters having a reunion with his wife.

She returned a little while ago. I had to bring the car into the compound. Heavy rain last night. It would have bogged in."

Jarrod passed the gun to Reaston. "Who's on duty at the gate?"

"Mick Bush." Reaston grimaced. "He's the problem."

"I'll take care of it," Jarrod said. "Just get us out of the building."

Reaston walked them through the security checkpoints. It'd taken him hours, but he had members of the Braxton underground on duty. The only variable was Bush. Otherwise, Jarrod and Sara's leaving Braxton would be a clean exit.

The three of them walked out through the main entrance. Reaston gave the Glock back to Jarrod. "The car is parked next to Shank's plane. Keys are in it."

Jarrod nodded. "Give us twenty minutes, then get down to the gate."

"Yes, sir." Reaston didn't so much as blink. "Will I need a clean-up crew?"

"Hopefully not. I'd rather not cancel him. He's just doing his job. If he survives, sequester him for forty-eight hours. If not, notify O'Shea. Tell him to put a forty-eight-hour hold on disclosure."

"Yes, sir." Reaston saluted Jarrod. "Good luck, sir. Ma'am."

Sara nodded, saw Jarrod salute back. He was a hundred percent. No doubt about it. And he had a plan. But at a hundred percent, Jarrod Brandt kept everything close to the chest. She understood the value in that, respected it, even if she didn't like it. How *would* he get them past Mick Bush?

"You drive." Jarrod rounded the hood and got into the passenger's seat, and then closed the door.

Sara slid in behind the wheel. "Jarrod, I'm scared. I'll do what I have to do, but I think when you're afraid, if you admit it outright, then you drain the strength from the fear, so I just wanted you to know that I'm scared."

He brushed a kiss to her lips. "I'd be worried about you if you weren't." He looked at the seat belt and shoved it aside. "Reasonable fear is healthy, Sara. It keeps you sharp and attuned. You lose it, you lose your edge. You lose your edge, and you end up dead."

"Then I should live a long time." She stared at the seat belt. Visions of the straps, the chair, flashed through her mind. She swallowed hard, forced herself to face it, and grabbed the safety belt. Jarrod couldn't do it yet, but then, he had suffered more. Because he'd blazed the trail, the impact on her had been far less traumatic. Still, pulling that strap across her chest and lap proved difficult. Dread dragged at her. She clenched her jaw, determined that Owlsley and Fontaine would not win. Not against her. Not on this. Too many had suffered too much to let it be for nothing. She grabbed the seat belt, inserted the metal, and shoved it into the clasp.

It clicked into place.

Though her hands still shook, a sense of victory urged her on, and she cranked the engine. Gripping the gearshift, she shifted into Drive and hit the gas. "How are we going to get out of here?"

"Stop at the last curve before the gate. I'll meet you on the other side."

So she would face Mick Bush alone. "Jarrod, I'm not on the man's list of favorite people. He caught me coming back into Braxton one night. I lied to him and he knows it. He's been out for blood and watching me like a hawk ever since. No way is he going to just let me drive through that gate."

"I know." He patted her hand. "Just trust me, okay?"

Her emotions churned and mixed. She wanted to trust him. Needed to trust him. Would love to trust him. But her survival instincts had kicked in, and they weren't so accommodating.

She braked to a stop at the last curve.

A hand on the door handle, Jarrod paused and looked over at her. "I don't want to kill him, Sara. But if I have to, I will. If we don't, that technology could end up in the wrong hands. Thousands, if not millions, could die." A frown creased Jarrod's brow. "You understand that, don't you?"

He was seeking absolution, and Sara gave it to him. More than ever before, she understood the dilemmas that military members, working high-risk missions on a daily basis, faced.

And more than ever before, she grasped the full weight of what those dilemmas cost them personally. "I understand."

He got out of the car, leaned down, and then looked back in. "Give me five minutes, then go."

Sara nodded, gripped the wheel so hard her knuckles turned white, praying she wasn't seeing him for the last time. Jarrod was not the only person involved in this who had a gun. And she'd bet her name badge Mick Bush was a crack shot.

She checked her watch. The second hand seemed to move in slow motion. Aside from when she'd nearly drowned, five minutes never had seemed so long. She thought of David, Brenda, and Lisa. Of her mother and her hard-line attitude, which Sara had cursed most of her life. Maybe she'd been wrong about that. If her mother had been different, then wouldn't Sara and Brenda? Would either of them have had the fortitude to endure what life had forced them to endure?

Probably not. And that flash of insight startled Sara. Years and years of anger and resentment peeled away like layers from an onion, and what was left was fortitude, a willingness to go to the wall for something she believed in. She owed her mother a debt of gratitude for that, and if Sara survived this, she would get it.

She again checked her watch. Three minutes down. Two to go. Where was Jarrod now? He had left the road at the side of the car, moved into the woods and underbrush, and disappeared. God, but she hoped Mick Bush was like Koloski and buried his head in a book at every opportunity. But even as she thought it, she knew Mick wasn't. He would never read while on watch. He'd never do anything *except* keep watch. Mick Bush was a good man. He played straight and by the book, and he took his job seriously. She admired that about him, even if he opposed her and made her life miserable. The problem was, he didn't see the big picture. But then, how could he? He'd been kept in the dark as much as if he had been physically blindfolded.

God, but she hoped he didn't kill Jarrod.

And she hoped Jarrod didn't kill him. Mick was doing his job for her. For everyone.

Finally, the time was up. Sara shifted into Drive and drove toward the guard shack, doing her damnedest to calm down and breathe normally. She had to work at it. What would she find at the gate?

No one was in sight. The gate was closed.

She braked to a stop.

Mick Bush came out of the guard shack, saw her behind the wheel, and frowned. "Patients are not allowed to leave the premises, Dr. West."

"I'm no. longer a patient." She lifted her arm. "See? No wristband." Jarrod approached behind Mick. She had to do something to cover any sounds. She coughed and flicked at her name badge, rustling it. "They've given me back my badge."

"I'm sorry, Major. You're still listed as a patient. I can't let—"

Jarrod delivered a powerful chopping cut to Mick's neck and followed with a clutch to the soft hollow near his collarbone. Sara couldn't see what else Jarrod did, but Mick slumped to the ground.

Jarrod checked Mick's pulse, took the keys from him, and opened the gate. His feet soundless on the pavement, he ran back, locked the guard shack, and pocketed the keys. He dragged Mick around to the side of the shack. The building blocked Sara's view. She stared at the white clapboard, wondering if she really wanted to ask Jarrod what he had done to Mick, and knowing she couldn't not ask.

He rushed back to the car, swung open the door. "Go. Go!"

Sara stomped on the gas pedal. The dirt road was slick and still wet from the heavy rain. Potholes were now the size of small ditches, and muddy water splashed up on the windshield. She hit the wipers, her tires spinning and slinging mud.

When she passed the store and saw the old Coke machine, her heart stopped threatening to burst and settled down to a gallop. "Is he alive?" She didn't have to explain. Jarrod would know she meant Mick Bush.

"Yes." Jarrod forked a hand through his hair. "He'll be all right, Sara. Reaston will take him to Shank and Koloski.

They'll keep him in an Isolation room for a few days, and he'll be fine."

"Good." She made the turn onto the concrete road, grateful not to be slipping and sliding in the dirt anymore. The ditches lining the road were filled to the brim. Water rushed through them. "Where exactly is AID?"

Jarrod hesitated before answering. "We're not going to AID."

Sara glanced over at him, perplexed. "Why not?"

"Because they'll consider Foster guilty until he proves himself innocent. They'll arrest him first and then ask questions. I can't do that to him, Sara. Not without knowing for a fact he's guilty of a crime and it won't screw up his operation."

"Why would they do that?" She glanced down at the speedometer. Forty-five in a thirty-five. Chiding herself, she eased off the gas.

"It's the military way. You're dealing with national security. You can't afford the risks of being wrong, so you plug potential holes and then find out if they were leaking."

Okay. Okay, so it didn't sit right—and it was the direct opposite of how things worked in the private sector—but she did see why the military had to function this way. This wasn't about one crime that affected one person, or one small group of people. This was about a crime that could impact a nation, perhaps the world. "So where to, then?"

"Eglin." Jarrod reached for his safety belt, clasped it. "O'Shea recommended a guy at Eglin to help us. He's local and in the Operation Red Haze loop. Captain Grant."

Jarrod had worked past the straps. Silently thrilled, Sara bit a smile from her lips. "Does a captain have the kind of clout we need on this?"

"No, he doesn't."

She frowned. "Then why go to him?"

"Because he has the ear of General Scott, who does have the clout we need on this. But there is a small problem."

Sara glanced over at Jarrod and waited for an explanation.

"The general is pissed off at Foster."

Great. Just great. "Will he be fair?"

Jarrod shrugged. "It's political. Foster snubbed the general when he came through to recruit you. Scott took it personally. But O'Shea faxed me a dossier on Scott and, from everything in it, he's no slouch. I'm betting he'll do the right thing."

"I could pulverize Foster for getting me into this. He did it because he hates me. I know you don't agree, but that has to be why, out of all the PTSD psychiatrists on the planet, he chose me."

"He didn't choose you because you're a PTSD expert, Sara." Jarrod eyed her levelly. "He chose you for the same reason he chose me. He trusted us not to let go of this until it was resolved."

"Foster trusted me?" Sara guffawed and took the ramp onto I-10, heading east. "Sorry, darling, but you're dead wrong on this. The man hates my guts."

"The man respects you and your tenacity. And you respect him."

"I sure do," she agreed, merging into light traffic. "About like you respect a rattlesnake."

"He admires the hell out of you. I told you this, out by the pond, remember? You never stopped pushing him about David. No matter how much he stonewalled, you kept pushing." Jarrod laced her fingers with his, gently squeezed. "You know, I think I half fell in love with you, hearing about you from him."

"Did you?" Her heart raced.

"Yeah, I did."

"Foster talked about me a lot to you?" She checked the rearview mirror. All clear. So far, so good.

"Yes, he did. And once—when you went to the Pentagon and pulled a check on him—he told me if he ever got his ass in a jam he hoped you'd be on his side, pulling him out."

She passed a truck with a shotgun in a rack behind the driver's head. A bumper sticker above his license plate read "Wife Wanted with Boat. Send Picture of Boat." "At one time, you thought he had sent me to betray you."

"I wasn't totally recovered then, Sara. When I attacked you and you came back, I knew Foster had brought you in to pull me out." Jarrod's voice went soft. "Now, I'm thinking he brought you into Red Haze to pull us both out."

Sara wished she could be sure, but she wasn't, and she refused to lie. "I know you think he's under deep cover and he was afraid he wouldn't be able to get out—that I'm his alibi. But I have reasonable doubts, Jarrod. Maybe Foster is trying to protect the interests of the country by keeping this technology out of the wrong hands. Maybe he did commit a self-sacrificing, honorable act by going under such deep cover that it could be misconstrued and get him convicted of treason. But maybe he isn't protecting anything but his own backside and his star, and maybe he has committed treason. I'm not sure. And until I am, I won't trust him. I can't. All I have to do is look at David and Lou and the rest of them, and I know I'm right not to trust him. Not as long as I have doubts."

Jarrod stared straight out of the windshield, and said nothing.

Sara felt defeated. Defeated and angry. "Look me straight in the eye, Jarrod Brandt, and tell me you have no doubt whatsoever on this? Can you do that?"

Jarrod dipped his head to his chest. He stilled for a long moment and then looked at her, pain flooding his eyes. "No, Sara. I can't. I wish to God I could because being uncertain makes me feel disloyal to him." Jarrod looked away. "But I can't."

Jarrod and Sara strode into Grant's office.

Sitting at his desk in a green leather chair, Grant glanced up. Surprise flitted through his eyes and his voice. "Brandt? Hell, I thought you were dead."

Jarrod extended a hand across the desk. "The reports were a little exaggerated."

"I should have known." Grant clasped his hand and smiled. "You've been dead—what, three? No, four times now."

"Who's counting?" Jarrod released his hand and stepped back. "This is Dr. Sara West."

They shook hands. "Nice to meet you," Sara said.

"Thank you, ma'am."

"Is this area secure?"

"No. Let's move to the situation room." Grant stood up, then led them down the hallway to a large room in the center of the building that smelled of old leather and lemon oil. "Please have a seat."

A large conference table filled the room. Twelve chairs surrounded it. Sara chose the closest one, and sat down. Jarrod sat beside her, Grant across from them.

"O'Shea called and told me someone would be coming." Grant laced his hands across the table. "Any casualties getting out?"

"No." Jarrod met Grant's gaze easily. "Is Foster on the right or wrong side of this?"

Grant sobered and uncertainty clouded his eyes. "We've had concerns."

"Then why hasn't he been pulled in?" Beneath the edge of the table, Sara rubbed a bit of her black slacks between her forefinger and thumb. The grating feel of the fabric helped her calm down.

Grant tapped the conference table. "He hasn't been pulled in because turning traitor doesn't fit his profile." Grant's voice went soft. "And because I haven't reported my concerns."

Grant didn't want to be responsible for wrecking Foster's career. Sara grasped that. Even if proven innocent, the slime of not being above reproach with all possibility of corruption being sheer lunacy would stick to Foster forever.

"This technology effectively manipulates the mind." Grant rubbed at his thumbs. "It can direct thoughts."

"When combined with other therapies," Sara corrected Grant.

"Actually, no," Grant corrected. "It can't effect deep-seated change in a patient without the combination of therapies, but it can trigger and effect purely physical reactions."

"I don't understand." Sara frowned at him. "I've experienced the effects of this technology. So has Jarrod, and—"

"Neither of you have experienced the full military applications of this technology, Dr. West." Grant's expression went from sober to grim. "I watched a field study three months ago.

Dr. Owlsley was attempting to get more research funding. There were fifty men divided into two teams involved in a battle engagement. Red and blue teams. Red was the enemy. Blue team effectively stopped the red team without lifting a finger, much less a stun gun."

"With the laser?" Jarrod asked.

"I read the report on this," Sara said, her stomach knotting.

Grant nodded. "What you didn't read, because it wasn't disclosed, is that blue team stayed in its bunkers. The laser was directed at individual red team members. The stimulation was to produce severe stomach cramps, and it did. They fell where they stood and stayed down long enough for the blue team to capture them. Not a shot was fired." Grant rocked back in his chair. "Red team was totally incapacitated, Jarrod. Totally. And the effects were sustained. That's what wasn't disclosed in the report. Do you realize the implications of this?"

"Unfortunately, I do," Jarrod said, worry furrowing his brow.

Sara's mind whirled. Finally, she reasoned through it. "It stimulated a thought that was purely physical. One that engaged no emotions. So it worked. But if the red team had expected it, and had built an emotional defense against it, then the experiment would have failed."

Grant looked at her as if she'd lost her mind. "There's no evidence of that, Dr. West."

Jarrod tapped her thigh with his under the table. Sara got the message, loud and clear, and shrugged. "Just a theory."

"I appreciate it, but right now, we need facts." Grant shoved his chair back. "We want to work outside normal AID channels, considering the doubt about Foster, but that leaves us with only one choice. General Scott, the Eglin base commander. Convincing him might take a little work."

Jarrod frowned. "I know he's ticked off at Foster. How political is it?"

"The general invited Foster to dinner and Foster was a rude ass about it. The general felt slighted. You know how these things can get."

"My goal is to protect the technology, and to do it, I need some clout," Jarrod said. "I've worked for Foster a long time, Grant. I trust him. It'll take hard evidence to prove to me the man's corrupt."

"Which is exactly why I haven't reported him."

Jarrod nodded, a shared understanding lighting his eyes. "We need Scott's clout to keep Foster out of Leavenworth—provided he shouldn't be there—and to put Fontaine and Owlsley in it. Are we going to get his support?"

"Scott is sharp and hard, but fair. He'll do the right thing," Grant said. "The key is, what is Scott going to consider the right thing?"

Sara didn't like the shaky sound of this. "Captain Grant, do you think Foster brought Jarrod or me into Operation Red Haze to assure his promotion?"

"No, I don't," Grant said. "In fact, I'm sure he didn't. When he came here to recruit you, I was his liaison. Word was out then he would be selected for general. It was already a done deal."

Sara mulled that over. Foster looked guilty of treason, but if the promotion was his passion and obsession and he was already getting it, then why commit treason? It wasn't logical. It had to be as Jarrod thought. Foster was undercover. So deep he was afraid he would be sacrificed. And he wanted Jarrod and Sara to pull him out. Or if pulling him out wasn't possible, to protect the technology.

That, Sara thought, or he had suckered them.

Damn it, it still could be either way.

Grant stood up. "I'll make the appointment with General Scott."

"He's going to want to talk with Rebecca Foster," Sara said. "Actually, he's going to demand it."

Grant nodded, and left to make the calls.

General Scott was an imposing-looking man. Graying, tall and lean, with broad shoulders that looked capable of carrying a lot of weight. He was about fifty-five, serious-expressioned, with inquisitive green eyes that Sara instinctively knew missed nothing, and he sported two stars on each of his shoulders.

She sat at a conference table with him, Grant, and Jarrod, and largely listened to them brief him. The general clearly was familiar with Operation Red Haze, but he had been on the fringes, not a main team member. He absorbed the information like a sponge—and without expression. Was that good or bad?

Unsure, Sara let her gaze drift to the walls, to photographs of aircraft and presidents, then to the polished-brass holders, anchoring Old Glory and the Air Force flag.

A light tap sounded at the door. A moment later, a woman in uniform opened it and looked inside. "General, Mrs. Foster has arrived, sir."

"Please show her in, Captain." Scott glanced around the table.

"Yes, sir."

Rebecca Foster came into the briefing room carrying a triangular box clutched to her chest. Red hair, blue eyes, and soft features, but her spine was ramrod-straight. She didn't look afraid, she looked defiant. Maybe even outraged. She knew why she was here.

"Please, Mrs. Foster, have a seat." Scott motioned to a chair near Sara.

Her black skirt swishing against her calves, she stepped up to the table. In front of General Scott, she set down the triangular box: a gleaming oak-trimmed glass case that held a United States flag.

"I understand there's some question about Jack's motivation on a mission." She moved to the empty chair beside Sara, but Rebecca didn't sit down. "I wasn't told what mission, but then, I never am, and that's as it should be."

She looked at each of them, then back to the general. "That flag was draped over my father-in-law's coffin. They buried him at Arlington with full military honors when Jack was six. At the funeral, Jack watched the planes fly the missing-man formation and heard the twenty-one-gun salute, and by the time the last note of taps faded, he had decided he wanted to be a general." A smile touched her lips. "At the end of the service, his mother let Jack accept the flag for the family."

Rebecca swallowed hard, her voice became stronger. "From that moment on, nothing could deter him. Not his mother's fear that he'd be killed in the line of duty like his father, nor his grandparents—whom he loved deeply and feared more— begging him to pursue a safer career. His mother even stooped to soliciting Marcus Wetherwood, Jack's best friend, to help change Jack's mind. But even Marcus couldn't sway Jack. One day he *would* be a general."

Behind their chairs, Rebecca moved slowly around the table. "For twenty-three weeks, he saved his allowance. When he had enough money, he commissioned a local artist to build that case for the flag." She let her fingertips drift over the beveled-glass triangle, over the gleaming oak. "He's kept it with him ever since. Through school. Through the obligatory stint at the Air Force Academy. And through twenty-eight years of assignments to military bases in fourteen countries around the world."

She pulled her hand away, stepped back from the table. "It's always held a prominent place in our home. On the mantel, in homes that had one. Across from his desk in his study on a special stand I call 'the shrine,' in those that didn't." She tilted her head and her voice softened, as if she were thinking back rather than speaking to them. "Seeing that flag always kept Jack focused. Disciplined and determined to give his best. He's worked hard and long to do that."

Rebecca glanced up at the general. "I don't need to tell you what missions he's accomplished, not that I could. But I have lived with the effects of those missions on him. Some have been . . . challenging. He's served his country well. That much I do know. And I know the man." She stopped near the general and stared down at him. "A boy six years old doesn't save every penny of his allowance for twenty-three weeks, or commission an artist to build a case for a flag, unless that flag and all it symbolizes means an awful lot to him."

General Scott listened patiently, without interrupting, which elevated Sara's esteem for the man. She studied his body language; not condescending, he was genuinely listening.

"I can't tell you exactly what my husband does to serve this country. I can tell you he serves it in any way it asks. He embraces all the ideals and values that flag symbolizes—as must the rest of you, or you wouldn't be here." Rebecca looked from the flag back to the general. "When you're judging him, remember all of this—and remember one more thing."

General Scott nodded. "What's that, Mrs. Foster?"

Her eyes brimmed with unwavering confidence. "If forced to choose between death and betraying the convictions of that flag, Jack Foster would die."

A silent moment passed. Sara conceded that Rebecca Foster painted a compelling, vivid picture, but was it the whole picture? That Sara didn't know.

Jarrod cleared his throat. "I agree, General. Everything I know of Jack Foster tells me he is exactly as Mrs. Foster portrays him."

The general looked to Grant. "My vote goes with Jarrod's."

All gazes shifted to Sara. "My experiences with Colonel Foster have been different, but then I've been on the opposite side of the fence, attempting to get information from him that he wasn't free to give me. I understand that. I have observed him being evasive, stonewalling, and at times, making my life a living hell. I've also observed him using covert tactics—some acceptable, some not—in recruiting me, and in disclosing the true nature of his rationale for that recruitment, which he also might not have been free to tell me. So while I accept all you're telling us, Mrs. Foster, I also must acknowledge that Colonel Foster's respect for this flag could be attached to the fact that it was draped over his father's coffin. A father who was killed in the line of duty. Your husband *could* resent that flag. To him, it could symbolize the life with a father that this country stole from him. And his feelings could be so strong that he would do anything for retribution."

Scott stared at Sara—hard. But he had listened and heard her. "Thank you, Mrs. Foster. We appreciate your insight on this matter. I'm going to have to ask you to stay with us for a time. We'll attempt to offer you every comfort."

"That's very kind of you, General Scott."

Here, Sara thought, was the quintessential military wife. One who under the most adverse circumstances retained her dignity, her faith in her husband, and grace, never faltering outwardly while inside, everyone in the room knew, she was burning with outrage that the motives of her beloved would dare to be questioned.

Sara admired Rebecca Foster a lot. And if Rebecca Foster admired and respected Jack Foster as much as she obviously did, then there had to be an enormous amount of good in the man.

Yet even an enormous amount of good in him didn't make him innocent. Especially not in the eyes of the guilty-until-proven-innocent military.

Rebecca was escorted from the room. When the door closed, General Scott noticed the flag still on the table. "She forgot it."

"No," Sara disagreed. "She didn't forget it. It's a visual reminder of all she said."

Scott nodded, then turned the subject. "I've received intel that this meeting between Fontaine and Owlsley won't be at the Pentagon." The general's eyes dimmed then turned the color of steel. "They're meeting at IWPT."

Jarrod frowned. "Did this intel come down through normal channels, sir?"

"No, actually it didn't, Major." General Scott looked pleased. "It came from an inside source. Mrs. Fontaine."

What did that mean? Sara looked at Jarrod.

"She's working with the AID," Jarrod speculated.

The general nodded, and sighed. "It's a sad thing when the interests of the country come between a man and his wife, but in this case, I'm damned happy to report that Mrs. Fontaine is more of a patriot than her husband. She's been working with the OSI for nearly a month, and when the nature of this operation became apparent, the OSI contacted the AID, who brought in Colonel Foster."

Sara stiffened. And because Foster hadn't reported the incident with David, the AID considered him suspicious, as well,

but it lacked any evidence of actual wrongdoing. Yet if they
had pulled him in, then they would have lost Owlsley and
maybe the technology. The puzzle pieces were falling into
place.

"I'm tagging this Security Condition Delta," General Scott
said. "And I'm assigning a Special Operations team to intercede."

"Sir," Sara interjected, "I want to warn you about this technology. I've studied it both in theory and, as we disclosed
earlier, I've experienced its practical applications."

"I know it's capable of taking out an entire team short-
term, Doctor."

"Sir, it's capable of taking out an entire battalion short-
term. It's imperative that the Special Operations team be emotionally prepared for this mission or they *will* be rendered
incapacitated."

"She's right, General," Jarrod added, giving weight to her
claim. "I was."

"I sincerely appreciate your concern, and your opinion, Dr.
West." Scott looked from Jarrod to Sara. "But there's no
proven data on that and this is a military mission. I cannot,
and will not, put a military mission in the hands of a civilian psychiatrist who lacks military conditioning. Our Special
Operations teams have received the most extensive
psychological-warfare training in the world. They can handle
this mission."

Hard, yes. Yet anything but fair. "With all due respect,
you're wrong, sir."

He glared at her. "If so, I'll accept full responsibility."

Furious, Sara had to bite her tongue to keep her mouth shut.
The man's mind was made up and that was that. She could
waste time beating a dead horse or drafting an alternate plan.
She opted for the alternate plan.

Glancing Jarrod's way from under her lashes, she wasn't
surprised to find him watching her. When he was certain he
had her attention, he blinked.

Sara blinked back. The message had been sent and received. An alternate plan was necessary and unavoidable. They would just have to pray that implementing it spared the loss of lives.

Their own, and those of Scott's Special Operations team.

twenty-six

☆

Sara looked across the front seat of the car at Jarrod. "Can we talk here?"

"Yes." He glanced her way. "It's been swept. No bugs."

Sara licked at her dry lips, uncomfortable at being dressed in fatigues. "I know General Scott ordered me to stay out of this, but his team is going to fail, Jarrod."

"Yes, it is." Jarrod frowned at the monotonous scenery of tall, twisted pines lining I-10. "Which is why we're going back to IWPT anyway. They need our help."

Just hearing the name of the place had her skin crawling. They had to go. Of course they had to go. But she didn't have to like it, and from Jarrod's grim expression, neither did he. "How are we going to stop them?"

"Any way we can." Jarrod cast her a look of sheer determination. "Sara, can you kill a man?"

A lump the size of Dallas lodged in her throat and every nerve ending in her body rebelled. "If I have to, I will. But I'd rather not."

"We'd all rather not, honey."

"I know." She did know. And she remembered a comment Foster once had made to her. If he had to sacrifice her, he would. *Her or many, many others. Which would she choose?* She'd hated it then, and she hated it now.

Jarrod turned onto the road leading to IWPT. It was deserted. He pulled into a Jitney Jungle store's parking lot. At the far end of the lot stood a weatherworn blue building. A faded sign above it read "Bob's Bar and Grill."

"We can't go in through the gate," Jarrod explained, parking in the middle of a group of cars.

"No, we can't." The engine shut off. "How much time do we have before the Special Ops team moves in?"

"About twenty-five minutes."

"Is that enough?"

Jarrod opened his car door. Its hinges squeaked. "It's going to have to be."

They walked just inside the stand of trees that acted as a barrier between the road and the training center grounds. Two hundred yards out, Jarrod cut deeper into the woods. Sara followed, praying no wildlife decided to descend upon them. She wasn't crazy about woods in general, and the last time she had been in these woods, she had ended up in the box. Give her concrete jungles with plush carpet and microwaves. Keep the campfires and tents.

Jarrod stepped over a charred, fallen pine. "We can get in here."

There was a break in the fence. Not a gated break, like at Braxton, but a section of ten feet or so that had been stomped down. Evidently, previous trainees who were not undergoing the noninvasive microwave-laser technology had found a way to get to Bob's Bar and Grill on foot.

Ten minutes later, she stood beside Jarrod. Both squatted low to the ground beside the big metal building, using leafy evergreens as cover.

"They're coming." Jarrod nodded toward the administration building.

Fontaine, Foster, and Owlsley walked toward the huge metal building. They were surrounded by armed guards. Sara's stomach fell. "Jarrod, how can we do this? There are so many of them."

"Shh, calm down, Sara. I have a plan . . ."

Jarrod recognized the beefy lieutenant.

So did Sara, and anger churned in her stomach. The man had been brutal and cruel to her here.

Jarrod gave her the nod, and Sara stepped out onto the

sidewalk. "Lieutenant, excuse me. May I ask—" Sara got no further.

Jarrod felled the man even more quickly than he had felled Mick Bush, then dragged the lieutenant around to the back of the building.

The leashed fury in Jarrod's body language worried her, and Sara followed him, rounding the corner to the sound of a slap. The lieutenant was holding his face. His lip was bleeding. "Jarrod, don't!" Sara called out.

Jarrod looked up at her. "He got a hell of a lot less than he gave." Jarrod took aim with the man's gun and fired.

Sara nearly fell to her knees. "*What* are you doing?"

"It's a stun gun." He passed the gun to Sara, and then ripped the rank off the man's shoulders.

The gun wasn't heavy, but what it represented weighed a ton. She'd better get a grip on her feelings. She couldn't afford this. Not now. Shank, Koloski, Jarrod—all of them had had time to get used to things like shooting people. Well, as used to it as anyone human can get, and instinctively she knew they didn't like it any better than she did. She had to focus on the purpose. On *why* they were shooting. To protect and serve.

Which is why Jarrod's ripping the military rank from the man's uniform filled her not with disdain, but with a sense of rightness. The lieutenant had dishonored it, the military, and the American people. Everything the country stood for. He wasn't fit to wear the rank, and he insulted all who did. Still, the compassionate side of Sara was glad the man was out cold and oblivious to the experience of being stripped of it.

Jarrod handcuffed the lieutenant to the trunk of a tree, then joined Sara. He glanced at his watch. "We need another stun gun."

He didn't want to kill any of the guards, either. Sara understood why. They were following orders. No more, and no less. "The administration building. There's always a guard posted outside."

"Too obvious. He'll be missed."

. They scouted and located a guard en route to the metal

building. Using the tactic they'd used before, Sara distracted the man and Jarrod attacked.

When they had the second gun, they headed back toward the metal building, walking quickly and passing no one.

Fifty yards out, Sara heard the first screams.

Two entrances.

Sara and Jarrod took the back one into the metal hangar. Chaos reigned. Owlsley stood behind the laser, sweeping it across the open expanse, hitting whoever happened to be in the red beam's path. Men dressed in black for a surgical strike lay writhing on the floor, gripping their stomachs. Totally incapacitated. Once-armed guards lay among them. So did their weapons. None were capable of retrieving them.

In the confusion, Sara spotted Fontaine and Foster. Both stood beside Owlsley, and neither attempted to stop him or to gain control of the laser. Sara stooped behind a metal drum, aimed, and hit Owlsley. He fell to the concrete floor, bumping the back of the laser. The beam streaked up to the metal roof, then deflected back down on the men.

"Oh, God." Sara watched in horror.

Jarrod slid along the back wall, aimed, and took down Fontaine. Foster didn't turn off the machine. *Why didn't he turn off the machine?*

Because he was one of them. He had to be one of them.

As if sensing her there, he turned and looked at her, then skirted the red reflections of the beam and walked toward her, toward the exit. He was going to just walk out of here? Just walk out and leave?

"Stop." Sara held up the gun with both hands, aimed it right at his chest.

Foster smiled and kept coming.

"I said stop." Her voice shook as much as her hands. She'd wanted to believe. And maybe him leaving was normal behavior for a Shadow Watcher. Maybe he *couldn't* be here when the military police and agents from the OSI arrived. Maybe—"Damn it, Foster, I said stop."

He was getting closer; not ten feet away. The red haze went out. Jarrod had turned off the laser.

Foster kept coming. "We both know you aren't going to shoot me, Sara."

"I will." She licked at her dry lips. "I swear it."

"You won't. Now put that damn thing down before you hurt yourself."

"Stop!" she screamed. "I don't *know* for sure. Not for *sure*."

Still, he kept coming.

Sara fired.

A stunned look crossed Foster's face, then it went lax, and his knees folded. "Sara . . ."

twenty-seven

☆

Sara paced in the hallway outside the briefing room. Inside, General Scott was interrogating Foster.

"Sara," Jarrod said from a metal chair against the wall. "Sit down, honey. You're pacing a hole in the carpet."

"How can you be so calm?" She lifted a hand and slapped at her thigh. "What if Foster wasn't working with them? I shot the man, Jarrod."

"With a stun gun." He grabbed her hand and tugged her onto a seat beside him. "Look, I know this rattles you. But you had to shoot him, honey. You couldn't take the risk. If Foster's clean, we'll soon know it. If not, well, we'll know that, too."

"He was going to leave, Jarrod. To just walk out."

"I know." He looked away, toward the window, then back at her. "No one likes being put in this position, okay? You deal with it as best you can. Sometimes you're right, sometimes you're not, but you're all right as long as you act in what you consider to be the nation's best interest. You did that, and that's all you can expect from yourself."

"I just don't want to malign the man."

"I understand." He clasped her hands and let her see the truth in his eyes. "I really do understand."

He did; she could see it in his eyes, and never had she loved him more.

The briefing room door opened, and General Scott walked out.

Jarrod stood up. So did Sara.

The general faced them. "We've concluded the interrogations," he said, his stern expression drawing down the lines on his face. "It appears that I owe you an apology, Dr. West." He looked her right in the eye. "You tried to warn me about this technology, but I didn't listen. I accept responsibility for it." His eyes filled with self-loathing. "Now, I have to live with it."

"I'm sorry." She was, for all of them. But General Scott had faced this apology with dignity. She admired that.

"At least it was a successful mission and none of the team were seriously injured." Jarrod offered the general solace. "We got them, the technology is safe, and we lost no lives."

"But we did lose lives, Major." Regret filled the general's voice. "Those of the damaged men at Braxton."

Sara couldn't stand the wait another second. "Is Colonel Foster innocent or guilty?"

"Why don't you ask him yourself?" Compassion burned in the general's eyes. "He wants to talk with the two of you, and I agree that he owes you personal explanations." The general nodded toward the briefing-room door. "Take all the time you need."

"Thank you." Sara moved toward it.

"Dr. West?" The general's voice stopped her.

She looked back at him over the slope of her shoulder. "Yes, sir?"

"Your country owes you a debt of gratitude," he said, his voice thick with emotion. "So do I."

Sara's heart softened. Scott was hard but fair, and an admirable man. "Consider it a token repayment for military services rendered all my life."

Admiration shone in his eyes. "You're welcome, Dr. West."

Sara walked into the briefing room. Jarrod followed behind her.

Sitting at the head of the table, Foster rubbed at his chest. "I can't believe you shot me, Sara."

"Be grateful it was just a stun gun." Unsure whether or not she should feel guilty, she twisted her lips. "I did warn you I wasn't sure, but being a hardass, you wouldn't stop."

"I wanted to see what you would do," he said easily.

"Well, now you know." Jarrod held out a chair, and she sat down in it, then looked back at Foster. "Were you in with them, or under deep cover?"

Foster cocked a brow. "What do you think?"

"I think I'm sick of games." Her voice rose to match her temper. "I think for you to do what you do, you have to be innocent. I know I want to hear it from you."

Jarrod's eyes glittered. "If he were guilty, General Scott would never have left him alone in this room, Sara."

She lifted her chin. "I want to hear him say it."

Foster leaned back in his chair, and said nothing.

Jarrod leaned forward, laced his hands on the tabletop. "Owlsley was frustrated by research restrictions. Fontaine by the lack of research funds. So the two teamed up. Fontaine would hide Owlsley's mistakes at Braxton if Owlsley would share research funds to give Fontaine some fiscal relief. So why did the damage go from heavy to light and then back to heavy?"

"Because Owlsley had to push the envelope." Foster leaned back in his chair. "He was running out of time."

Jarrod grunted his opinion on that remark. "Couldn't he get an extension on his contract?"

"It wasn't the contract he was fighting," Foster said. "It was death."

"Owlsley is dying?" Jarrod's brows shot up on his forehead.

Foster nodded. "He has cancer. This technology is his family, his legacy to the world. He wanted to complete it before dying. To him, leaving it behind proved his life had mattered. He had mattered."

Sara's chest went tight. She tried to find compassion. To understand the powerful forces driving a man facing death with no one to mourn him. But he had left devastation and destroyed lives. David, Brenda, and Lisa had been irrevocably changed. Lou, the rest of the men at Braxton, and their families had been irrevocably changed.

Compassion swelled in her, but not for Owlsley. For his victims. He had the rare opportunity to reverse tragedy and stop pain, yet he chose to cause more. "He could have slain the dragon," Sara said, a tremble in her voice. Her eyes burned and she blinked hard. "Instead, he slew innocents."

Jarrod cleared his throat. "What about Fontaine? Tell me he didn't do all of this just for money."

"No," Foster said, straightening in his chair. "Fontaine believed in Owlsley's research. Truly, its potential is remarkable. Fontaine believed that, long-term, implementing this technology in the field would save lives. But aside from the money and the technology's potential, Fontaine owed Owlsley. They had been together in the Desert Storm conflict. Fontaine took a direct hit. Everyone thought he was a dead man, but Owlsley came up with an experimental procedure that saved Fontaine's life. Fontaine won a Purple Heart with a cluster in that campaign and Owlsley won enough respect to get the contract for his research."

Jarrod dragged his teeth over his lower lip. "An ally for life."

"Understandable," Sara said. "So what happens to them now?"

"Fontaine will be court-martialed, and Dr. Owlsley tried in a civilian court, though we expect he'll die before we complete the investigation and release him to civilians for trial."

In other words, they'd never release Owlsley and jeopardize the technology. Like his victims, he would be sequestered for the duration of his life. "And Mrs. Fontaine?"

"Very astute, Sara." Foster smiled. "She's been working with us."

So he could tell the truth when he chose to do it. Sara looked down at the table, and then lifted her gaze to Foster. "Why didn't you stop this sooner?"

"Civilian law requires hard evidence. It took time to gather it."

Jarrod sighed. "And more time to make sure you had total control of the technology."

"That, too."

General Scott came back into the briefing room, and took a seat. "Are we up to speed?"

Foster and Jarrod sat back down.

"Yes, sir," Jarrod said.

Foster's eyes glinted. "I think Sara's still debating on whether I'm guilty or innocent."

General Scott hiked his brows. "I've learned to value Dr. West's opinion." He swiveled his gaze to Sara. "What do you think?"

Sara stared into Foster's eyes and spoke softly. "I think that until all of this happened I never understood how many sacrifices a man or a woman in uniform has to be willing to make. I understand now. Jack Foster wasn't just willing, he made those sacrifices. This wasn't about him getting a promotion." That had been in progress before he'd recruited Sara. "This was a selfless act. A sacrifice he willingly made for you and me, to make sure the technology never fell into the wrong hands. Because Dr. Owlsley wasn't in the system, the colonel had to use extraordinary measures. Ones that cost him a few good men, which, I suspect, troubles him deeply and always will. Those measures endangered him and cast doubt on his integrity." Sara looked from the general to Jarrod, then on to Foster. "I think his was an act of honor, General Scott. And if necessary, I'll devote my life to proving it."

Foster's expression didn't change, but the gleam in his eyes warmed.

"That won't be necessary, Dr. West." General Scott claimed her gaze. "Colonel Foster has been cleared of any wrongdoing." He stood up. "Jack, it's my privilege to inform you that not only will you be getting your star, you'll also be getting a commendation for your handling of Operation Red Haze." Scott extended a hand to the colonel. "Congratulations."

"Thank you, sir." Foster stood up.

General Scott left the room, and Foster turned to Sara. "And thank you, too."

"You're welcome. But if you need my help in the future, you'd better play straight with me. We could all have been spared a lot of needless agony."

"I was trying to keep you out of the line of fire."

Sara grunted. "You were trying to keep me in the dark."

"To protect you."

"To protect Shadow Watchers."

"Them, too."

Sara sighed. "So what happens to my patients?"

"They'll be cared for by Shank."

"Not good enough." Sara gave Foster a negative nod. "I want their families notified and given access to them. It'll be good for the families, and for the patients. And I want Shank and the rest of the staff given the freedom to leave Braxton whenever they choose."

"I'll agree to your request on the staff, though I'm not sure how we'll secure it, but I can't give outsiders access to Braxton, Sara. It's dangerous for them and for the patients."

"There's an alternative," Jarrod interceded. "Transfer the patients. They're all low-risk and none of them will be able to return to active duty."

Foster rubbed at his chin. "I can do that." He looked at Sara. "Give me two days. I'll have them transferred to facilities near their families."

"How will you explain this to the families?" Sara asked.

"Mistaken identity," Foster said. "But there won't be a reason given for their conditions. Those will officially and forever be listed 'cause unknown.' We will provide counseling to help everyone adjust."

Sara didn't like it, but this was as good as it was going to get. Announcing to the world that the U.S. had this technology would be a huge security risk. And in this case, tight security was warranted. "Will I be canceled?"

"I'd be a fool to order that." Foster didn't hesitate or flinch. "Never know when I might get into trouble again and need you to pull me out."

Jarrod chuckled. Sara shot him a glare, then sniffed. "I'll want hazardous-duty pay. Lots of it."

"That can be arranged." Foster headed toward the door. "Jarrod, why don't you take a couple of weeks' leave? I think you could use the time off."

"Thank you, sir."

"I'm grateful to both of you." Foster walked out, then closed the door behind him.

"That man is a real piece of work." Sara turned to Jarrod and hugged him hard.

"Forget Foster," Jarrod said, hugging her back. He kissed her until she slumped against him, then let out a satisfied sigh. "Do you have affairs, Sara West?"

She looked up at him. With his history, marriage and commitment were akin to curses, but he'd come around. Eventually. He was the one, and she'd bet her name badge that they ended up married with a house in the suburbs, and two or three kids. Better yet, she'd bet her heart. But that commitment was going to take a little time and a lot of trust. "Not usually." She slid her hands up his chest and circled his neck. "But in your case, I'll make an exception."